The

ACES

Anthology

Tales from Northern Nevada

2024

The ACES Anthology

Cover design by Stephen H. Provost
Front cover photos: American Flat (foreground) and Virginia City
looking east by Stephen H. Provost/public domain graphics
Back cover photo: On the road to Jarbidge by Stephen H. Provost

Interior images are in the public domain with the exception of the
map by Ken Sutherland accompanying "Hardship, Nevada."

Published by Dragon Crown Books 2024
All rights reserved.

ISBN: 978-1-949971-56-9

Contents

"It takes a heap of sense to write good nonsense."

— Mark Twain

Editor's Introduction

This is the second edition of the ACES Anthology, following the first release in 2023. As with that volume, the present collection spans a variety of genres, from historical fiction to fantasy, from humor to the paranormal. Once again, the purpose is to introduce readers to some of Northern Nevada's best writers; the pages ahead are devoted exclusively to authors from this unique corner of the American West.

The northern half of the state, from Elko and Ely west to Lake Tahoe, provides fertile ground for storytellers—and it always has. The authors included here are heirs to a rich heritage dating back to Mark Twain, Dan De Quille, Alf Doten, and others who forged careers and became legends during the Comstock boom.

Nevada is a state of sagebrush, cowboys, saloons, gambling, nuclear testing, ghost towns, and abandoned mines whose character is reflected in many of these stories. Not all are set in the Silver State, but Northern Nevada has imbued each of these writers with something of itself, be it a thirst of history, a draw to the paranormal, the romantic allure of the West, or a love of the open road.

The ACES Anthology

Fourteen of the authors whose works appear here also submitted stories for last year's anthology, while the remaining nine entries are from newcomers to this project. Returning authors include Ken Sutherland, whose first published work appeared in the 2023 edition and subsequently was named a finalist for the John Steinbeck Award. Michael K. Falciani, whose story "The Shadow's Edge" was (narrowly) named by a panel of judges as the best in last year's edition, returns as well.

One of last year's judges, Bill Brown, submitted a story for this anthology as well.

Most of the stories here are appearing for the first time in print. Others have appeared elsewhere in the past or will appear in forthcoming releases, so the reader can get a taste of what's available from some of the authors' catalogs, some of which have grown substantially in just the past year.

Indeed, many of the authors featured have been busy working on new projects and introducing them to the public. Andrea Smutz released four novels in her *Hopefield Chronicles* series, while Janice Oberding released a pair of titles in her *Virginia City Mystery* series this summer.

Jay Crowley published a new murder mystery titled *A Touch of Murder* that touches on the history of Carson City and with a touch of the paranormal. And, speaking of Carson City, capital-based author Sandie La Nae worked with Arline Laferry to produce a book on the famed *Territorial Enterprise* newspaper in Nevada.

Bill Brown released a trio of novels: *The Child*, *Beneath*, and *The Gift*, bringing his overall catalog to 17 titles and counting. Ken Sutherland, likewise, produced three novels: *Balance*, *Heartbreaker*, and *The Hollywood Diamond Murders* (*the latter two part of a new mystery series*).

The ACES Anthology

The editors of this anthology, Stephen H. Provost and Sharon Marie Provost, released a collaboration of horror short stories titled *All Hallows' Nightmare's Eve* this summer. On his own, Stephen published four books of historical non-fiction: *Bonanza Highway*, *Virginia City Then & Now*, *The Comstock Chronicles*, and *Chinese Camp*. Sharon, meanwhile, made her solo debut with the *Shadow's Gate* collection of short horror short stories and is hard at work on her debut novel, *Dark Arts*, due for release on Black Friday 2024.

Jade Griffin also has a new work being released this fall, *Mr. Smith Who Works at the Front Desk*.

The purpose of this work is to introduce readers to the creative works of some very talented writers. It is an outgrowth of an online project known as ACES, which was established with that same game. ACES stands for the Authors' Collective e-Shop, an online sales hub at acesofnorthernnevada.com (see the QR code below). For the purposes of this work, it might also stand for Authors' Collection of Exceptional Stories.

As outstanding as last year's collection was, I feel that this year's group of submissions is as strong or even stronger. I'm grateful to each of the authors whose stories appear here for taking part in this project. My thanks also to Sharon Marie Provost for her partnership in coordinating this project and for her assistance with the editing. I'm proud to present this superior collection of stories for your enjoyment.

Stephen H. Provost
October 6, 2024

Richard Arbib

One Wish

Jack Dennings was looking down the bar, just having started his fourth drink, when the door swung open, and an enormous man waddled in. It wasn't the fact that the man must have weighed over 300 pounds that caught Jack's attention. It was the strange manner in which he was dressed. His clothes were made of silk; he wore long, baggy pants and a shirt that were both bright purple, and a shiny gold sash with tassels was tied around his incredible waist. His beard was short and curled up into a point, just as his pink slippers did. It was the kind of appearance that might have prompted one of the drunks in the bar to laugh or even make a disparaging remark had it not been for the sheer brute size of the man and the long, curved sword he wore at his side.

"Oh, no," the bartender muttered. "This guy looks like trouble," he whispered to Jack and the two other men at the small bar.

"I don't think so," Jack answered. "I'll bet he's a Shriner or a Mason. They dress like that for conventions."

"There ain't no Shriner convention in town," the bartender

said. "He looks like a nut to me. I just hope he don't start waving his sword around, that's all."

Instead of walking up to the bar, the stranger took a seat at one of the small tables. The chair creaked under his massive weight. Before the bartender could say a word, Jack eased himself off the barstool and ambled over to the table.

"Hi. I'm Jack Dennings," he said, holding out his hand to greet the stranger. The man shook his hand. "Can I buy you a drink?" Jack asked.

"You are very kind. Thank you very much." The man had a strange accent. Jack was sure it was Middle Eastern. He now wondered whether the guy was a Shriner or a rich oil sheik with eccentric taste in clothing. In either case, the man had aroused Jack's curiosity, and now it had to be satisfied.

"May I sit down?"

"Please, sit down and accept my humble company."

"You're one of the Shriners, right?" Jack asked, eagerly waiting for the answer to prove him right.

"I am so sorry, but I am afraid I do not understand all the words in your language. What is a Shriner?"

"Oh, so you're not a Shriner. You must be from the Middle East, right?"

"Yes, I was from the Middle East. But that was so very long ago," he said, with a sad look in his eyes.

"What would you like to drink? Jack asked.

"I will drink whatever you are having."

Jack ordered him a drink. The bartender eyed him warily, then went back behind the counter and resumed watching a baseball game.

Jack noticed the sorrowful look in the stranger's eyes again. "Is there something wrong?" he asked.

"Yes, my new friend. There are many wrong things for me. I

have been away from home for too many years and can never go back. I have seen every friend I knew die and turn to dust long ago. I am in a strange country where everyone dresses oddly, yet they stare at me as if I am the odd one. No one knows or appreciates the things I can do. But what of you, my friend? I can see that behind your smile is a heart with a heavy burden. What troubles you?"

The question took Jack by surprise. He had sat down next to this peculiar fellow out of curiosity and now felt somewhat uneasy that the stranger should be interested in him. Yet, the sincerity in the big man's voice compelled Jack to confide in him.

"What's troubling me?" he asked, taking another gulp of his drink. "My wife—she was killed in a car accident. It was about two months ago." Jack's eyes began to get misty and water. Wet with grief and red with too much to drink recently, they told the story of his present condition.

"I am very sorry," said the stranger. There was compassion in his voice that surpassed that of Jack's closest friends. "Tell me, how did it happen?"

"We had been married for two years. It was the happiest marriage that anyone ever had. Then one night, a policeman came to my door and told me that she had been in a car accident. She ran into a tree. It had been raining that night, and the road was slippery, and...." His voice trailed off as he made no attempt to hide his emotions. The tears flowed down his cheeks. The men at the bar shook their heads in sympathy. They had heard this story many times, just as they had seen Jack change from a sober, happily married man into a grieving alcoholic in only two months.

"I am so very sorry," repeated the stranger.

Jack wiped his tears away. "Well, there's nothing you can do about it. You don't have to be sorry. My best friend, Bill, says he's sorry too, but it doesn't help."

"Alas. I am always sorry to hear of people's troubles, and so I try to be of service whenever I can."

"What are you talking about? What can you do for me?"

"I can do anything," said the stranger. "Anything at all. You see, I am—oh, how do you say it in your language? A genie? Is that not the proper word?"

"What is this? Some kind of joke? Cause if it is, I don't like it," Jack said as his sorrow turned to anger.

"No, my friend. It is not a joke. I am being truthful with you."

"Yeah? OK, then prove it. Show me something to prove you're a genie."

"But of course. I can do anything you like. Anything."

"You can, huh? OK, let's see you make this glass disappear," Jack said as he pointed at the glass that had held his fourth drink but was now empty.

"If you do not wish to see the glass on the table anymore, I am certain the bartender would take it away for you."

"Aha! I knew it! You're trying to get out of it already. But then, I guess it's just as well. If you made it disappear, I'd have to get another glass to hold my drink."

"Surely you would not waste your only wish on a cheap parlor trick such as making a glass disappear."

"What do you mean, my only wish?"

"I can give you one wish. It can be anything you want, but I can give you only one. I cannot change it or give you a second wish."

Jack's mood began to change as he eagerly leaned across the small, round table toward the man. "You can grant me any wish? Anything?"

"Yes, but only one wish. For your own sake, be absolutely specific. I cannot change a wish once it has been granted."

"Well, you know what my wish would be. I want my wife back."

"My friend, you must phrase your wish precisely. You said your wife was killed in a car accident two months ago. If I bring her back right now, I doubt you will be at all pleased."

A horrible vision of a rotted and mangled corpse appeared for a second in Jack's blurred consciousness, and he shuddered.

"No! That's not what I meant! Wait. Let me rephrase it. You can change the past and future then?"

"Oh, yes. The future is really many different paths, all leading to different places. A person traveling along the journey of life just picks the path of his choice and hopes that it leads where he wishes to go. But there are many, many paths in the journey of life. If you took the wrong path, it is possible to go back and pick a different one—provided that you have the assistance of a genie, of course."

"All right, I have to be specific." Jack mulled over the instructions again, but those damn drinks made it so hard to concentrate properly. "OK, I have it," he said, after a minimum of deliberation.

"Your wish?"

"Yes. I wish," he began, then paused to be sure the words were just right. "I wish that everything would be as if my wife had not been killed in the car accident!"

No sooner had the words been uttered than Jack found himself back in his living room. There was thunder rumbling outside, and a patter of rain on the roof jarred his senses. He stood up and stared at the calendar. August! The month his wife had been so tragically taken from him.

"Diane! Diane!" he yelled as he ran from one room to another. The house was empty. He looked at the clock. It was 10:55 p.m. He remembered the night the policeman came to the door to tell him of the accident. It had been 11 p.m., the worst time of the worst day of his life. He looked at his watch to reconfirm the time and ran to the window to see a police car pulling into the driveway. The glare of the headlights made him squint. A policeman got out of the car. What was this? Some horrible reliving of the one event Jack wanted to forget? Why did everything seem to repeat itself? These thoughts flashed through his mind when he saw the policeman go to the passenger side of the car and open the door. Diane was getting out of the car and walking with the policeman up to the house! Jack flung the door open and hugged her tightly as the tears ran down his cheeks.

"You're back! Oh, thank God, you're back!"

"Your wife must be the luckiest person in the world," said the policeman. "She just survived one of the worst car accidents I've ever seen. The car was totally crushed, like an accordion. I don't know how she was able to get out without even a scratch. It's a miracle, I tell you. A miracle."

"The important thing is you're back," said Jack.

Diane said nothing. She appeared numbed from the experience.

The policeman interrupted the silence. "Well, I've got some papers in the car for you and your wife to sign. It's just routine, you understand. I'll be back in just a minute."

"Diane, what happened? How did you have the accident?"

She stepped back from Jack to look at him. Her eyes were red. She had been crying and looked as though she was about to start again.

"Jack, I'm so sorry. I don't know how to say this, but I can't hide it any longer."

"Hide what? We don't have any secrets from each other. Just tell me what's wrong. Whatever it is, we'll work it out."

"I went to the doctor today. He said I'm pregnant."

"Why honey, that's great. After two years of trying, it finally worked. And I had thought we couldn't have kids. Well, we sure showed that doctor, didn't we?"

Diane stared at the floor. Her voice dropped so low that Jack could barely hear her answer. "It's not your baby, Jack. It was someone else—Bill, your best friend."

He slapped her before he knew what he had done. A powerful swipe of his hand had knocked her to the floor. He was shocked at his reaction. It had come automatically.

"I'm sorry," he said, astonished that he had actually struck her. He forgot completely about the baby and thought only of his reaction to her and how he should have controlled himself. "I didn't mean to do that. I'm sorry."

She said nothing, just lay there where he had knocked her down. She stared at him blankly.

"I'm sorry," he repeated as he bent down to pick her up. He cradled his hand behind her head to lift it, but it slipped off, and her head rolled to the side. Jack's hand was covered with blood, and it ran into the cracks of the bricks in front of the fireplace.

"Diane?" his voice mouthed weakly. "I didn't mean to slap you. I'm sorry."

Her lifeless eyes stared back at him as the blood flowed onto her hair.

"No! This isn't the way it was supposed to be! It was supposed to be...." He stopped and remembered the words: I wish that everything would be as if my wife had not been killed in the car accident.

"Come back!" he yelled to the genie. "You've got to fix this. You can't leave me like this."

He listened for the genie's return, but there was a horrible silence, broken only by his own heartbeat and the sound of the policeman knocking at the front door.

The ACES Anthology

B.B. Arbogast

Zeetageia Finds Her Voice

He stole my heart! I thought he loved me, that he wanted to be together forever. Last time I trust a pirate! I'm not the first siren to have been taken in by a smooth talker, but that scallywag will pay for his plundering ways, one way or another. Once we find him.

We were the last three of the Siren species. Our voices had lured ships of evil-hearted humans into our clutches for thousands of years. Songbirds, with womanly figures and features, we also had plumed wings that carried us on fragrant winds like colorful clouds dancing above the waves. Razor-sharp talons at the ends of our bird feet and wings punished those whom we deemed unseaworthy.

I'm Zeetageia, the youngest of the Geia sisters. I also carried the title of most gullible. My oldest sister Ranigeia was called for her purpose: to plunder. Plouigeia, my middle sister, was named after her ability to inhabit the bodies of her victims while they listened to her song.

"Zeet! Quick! Get over here!" called Ranigeia.

What does my sister want with me now?! Frustrated that I couldn't reply to her, I followed her echo. Almost hidden amongst the dark weeping stones, she tapped her bird-foot. Her sleek silhouette was outlined by the light shining through the rear mouth of our cave.

On the horizon bounced the reflection of the gigantic merchant vessel. The waves lapped at the boat's well-worn hull as it approached our little inlet. It grew larger, louder, closer to us. The coral-pink glow of the sun spread across the horizon.

Like an unsuspecting fly, the craft would succumb to our spiderweb of song. Soon, the ship would be within my sisters' grasp. The fate of its no-good sailors was already determined by the magnetic pull that was our life's mission.

Ranigeia broke into a ballad in her powerful, compelling sound. My middle sister, Ploui, joined her, with orange eyes in sharp contrast to the bright blue of her plumes. Her talons gripped the slick, rocky edges of the path as she made her way to us. They sang in perfect harmony.

I pruned newly grown rectrices within my reach and prepared to exhibit my glorious display of long, colorful tail plumage. *May not have my voice anymore, but I can still lure sailors in with my beautiful rainbow butt.*

As the daylight moved to mid-morning, the craft continued to sail in our direction. *It's getting close—almost—time!* I sprang from my perch in our cove and soared toward the ship. The mariners screamed their surprise. A short, fat one pulled out his sword, but not in time.

Opening the talons of both feet, I grabbed the stout seaman, forcing him to drop his weapon with one claw. I swept another nameless, stinky sailor up with my other foot. Without stopping, I swirled up and out over the open water. Circling sharks waited to greet the doomed seafarers. I let go. Men splashed into the depths of the sea, fodder for their hunters.

Eager for more, I swiftly returned to the boat. A few of the crew shrieked. Most were silent, transfixed by my sisters' song.

From the deck, I plucked the screaming sailors and soared to a different place above the Mediterranean. I spotted a couple of giant squids, called by my sisters' song to their next meal, and plopped the ill-doers for my tentacled friends. The squids burst forth and wrapped around their thrashing prey.

Ploui launched from our rocks and joined me, grabbing the remaining crew members who struggled against Rani's voice. Her cerulean, blue plumes soared past me in a blur. She harvested another sailor and hoisted him high in the air. His screams were silenced as her wing talon pierced his heart. She set him on the edge of a cliff. Shaking her upper knives, my sister dislodged his lifeless body, and his corpse plummeted into the sea below. Left behind, his discarded shirt flapped on our mountaintop.

I flew back to our cave. Over my shoulder, I watched my middle sister dive to the sea vessel and land, voice strong, singing a mournful tune. The captain shuffled in her direction like a sleepwalker. She walked into him. Leading with her arm, the rest of her body was absorbed by his. Ploui walked through him, leaving the husk of the captain on the bow of the ship like a snake shedding its skin.

I hid my head, not wanting to witness his shell fall to the floor. Plouigeia continued to sing lyrical instructions for several sailors to mop the deck of gore. *Just like her, hating to leave a mess behind.*

Ranigeia sang her sweet melody and captured the remainder of the crew. With her melancholy song, she instructed some to jump overboard. The Captain's First Mate dropped anchor in our harbor. I landed on the vessel again in time to catch a glimpse of

overlooking Corsica.

"I hate that you cannot talk with us!" Ploui shouted over the crashing waves 30 feet below. "Can't read your feathers while you're flying."

Rani swooped in. "Any sign of Captain Icy?"

A single tear slipped from my eye. Frustrated, I wiped it away. *He's not going to get the better of me. He WON'T win!*

Ploui sat in a fluff of blue down that drifted from her wings. "I'd be happy to go out and search for him with you tomorrow."

"Count me in!" Ranigeia shouted.

I hopped up and tried to sing. *Oops. Forgot. Pathetic.* Instead, I danced, tapping my tail to show my agreement to my sisters.

"We're going to get it back." Plouigeia crossed her heart with her fingers. Then she crossed it again with her front talons. "I swear we'll get your voice back, Zeet!"

Discouraged but not defeated, we flew home, examining waves crashing on rocks and surging swells in cave-strewn inlets as we went.

"What a gorgeous voice and what lovely lilac eyes you have," my lover crooned to me, playing with my necklace. He gifted me a lock of his jet-black hair to be placed inside the gold and silver concentric circled pendant as a token of his love.

From the crook of his arm, I stared up at him. His chiseled chin had a shadow of a stubble. I brushed a curl from his face to gaze into the ice-blue pool of his eyes. "Thank you."

"We make a marvelous couple, you know," he continued, his tone soft and husky in the morning dew.

Snuggling closer to him, I agreed. "Umm."

With unusual gentleness, he stroked my onyx-black hair away from my face. "With your song, I wouldn't have to sail the seas. I could stay with you and bring riches to me—us. We could stay in this cave forever, lost in love."

I played with the necklace he wore that matched mine. His twin locket held a tiny purple feather from my wing. Lazily, I traced the indentations of his well-sculpted abdomen with my upper talon.

His countenance changed from tender to harsh in an instant. "Pffft! Get your wing out of my face. Pffft!" The moment was lost.

"Zeetageia, pffft! Get your wing out of my face!" Rani poked me with her upper talon. "The sun's rising. We should find Captain Icy," my sister referred to my former lover, "and his murderous ship."

Plouigeia washed her face in a puddle beside our nest. "Let her sleep, dear sister. She has tail-feather growing to do." My mid-sis chuckled and half-flew, half-hopped closer to our side of the branches we neatly assembled.

"Look what I found yesterday in Alalia before our flight back home from Corsica." Plouigeia pulled out a scrap of parchment that was stuffed between her feathers.

Beware of pirates with a captive siren.

My big sis cleared her throat. "Sounds like the warning from yesterday's victims about a pirate ship with a siren hostage. Merchant ships came to them." She raised an eyebrow and cleaned beneath one talon with another talon from her other side, engrossed in nail care. "Sound like anyone we know?"

I sat up. *Sounds like my memory dream... well, sort of.* Morus, my former lover, suggested he and I stay together and lure ships to us.

Blowing the dust off her dark knives, Ranigeia wiped them on her ample chest. "We need to teach Icy a lesson for stealing Zeet's voice." She held out her talons for inspection.

19

My mid-sis put a bright black and blue wing across our eldest sister's shoulders. "We all agree. But if *Siren's Scythe* wasn't between here and Corsica, where is it?"

"I'm not sure. But the ship before last had an area circled on..." Ranigeia stretched her lean body and, with her human hands, pulled out a well-worn map from a hidey-nook beside our nest. "This map." She smoothed it out, careful not to rip it. "The captain of that ship was clear. 'Avoid the circle' were his last words—didn't say why."

"Why didn't you show this to us earlier?!" my blue-clad sister swatted at her. "We should be flying above that circle."

"I didn't think it had anything to do with Zeet! Giant stingrays live there! But after yesterday's fruitless hunt and two rumors of warning, I think we need a plan," my green-eyed sister pulled away and spat back. "What if Icy trapped *our* voices?"

I gasped. Usually, Plouigeia was the cautious one. But Rani was right. With no idea how Morus stole my voice, we required extra precautions. He dare not steal *their* songs, too!

Ploui's clementine eyes widened, then squinted, squinching her face. She pursed her lips and opened her mouth to speak. I could almost see the wheels in her mind turn.

Even if I tried to come up with a plan— it didn't matter. My protective sisters had taken over. I had no choice but to let them. Besides, if I thought of a plan, I'd need to communicate with pantomiming, wing pointing, and long-feather tapping.

My middle sister licked her lips and bit the lower one. "First, we need to find *Siren's Scythe*."

"Fantastic plan!" My oldest sister stood, ready for take-off.

"Wait! I'm not done." Ploui peered at the circle on the map. Words tumbled from her lips. "The Sea of Marmara. That's so far from here! Do you think many vessels are able to navigate those waters? Could *Siren's Scythe*? And how will we stay warm?"

The Sea of Marmara! Morus... Captain Icy-Eyes, himself was heading for the Pontus Euxinus. Locals call it the Black Sea! And we were going to head him off.

"We could disguise ourselves," Rani volunteered as she yawned and stretched her bright green wings in a graceful display.

That's an amazing idea! I tapped, clapped my human hands and my wings together, and nodded in agreement.

"Zeetageia agrees," chuckled my blue-plumed sister. "Okay. What kind of costumes do you want to use? Our feet and wings are hard to hide."

"Capes. Let's find capes from the next pirate galleon, merchant ship, or war vessel. No doubt even evil seafaring men get cold."

My sisters assembled a plan. Ranigeia devised a pack for our prized map from part of a boot and strapped it around her waist. It stuck to her back above her little pink fuzz.

Ploui also fashioned a pouch for herself from the bloodied shirt left behind by the tortured sailor from yesterday's hunt. It had a hole where her talons pierced it, but she was able to make it usable.

I didn't have a pouch. My colossal floofy tail had too much volume to strap down with a pouch. We planned to put purloined capes in their bags for safekeeping while we flew.

Finally, the time had come. Together with my sisters, we left our home south of Sicily and flew east and north. Three sirens in search of an island with cliffs in which we could roost.

Fate was unkind, for soon, we found ourselves engulfed by a storm. The Etesian winds picked up speed. Black clouds rode swiftly on the wind, darkening the sky in an instant. Ozone in the air warned of lightning.

Flash!

I dodged to my left, Ranigeia to her right. Thunder shook the air.

Flash!

I weaved, narrowly escaping the strike.

"Ahh!" Ploui plunged toward the dark, storm-swelled seas. Her right wing smoked as she careened.

Ranigeia descended after her. "Ploui! Ploui!" Our sister splashed into the dark tide below.

Following both sisters, I dove and pulled up before I was swallowed in the waves. Hovering where Ploui went under, I scanned the horizon. *A ship!* I motioned to Rani.

She sang, drawing the vessel toward us.

My oldest sister landed on the approaching barque, which displayed a tell-tale flag. *Oh no! More pirates!* The black flag with a white skull and crossbones blew in the breeze.

I drifted onto the deck. So much different from our last pirate ship attack. *We need help from these men.* Rani cleared her throat and sang a gentle tune.

"Pfft!" Plouigeia's head popped up, coughing and sputtering water. Her blood darkened the surrounding water.

That was close. But she's hurt!

With the help of Rani's song, two charmed crewmen volunteered to pull my sodden middle sister out of the sea. Her beautiful black, royal blue-and-aqua plumes, now stained purple, were charred. The smell of barbecued flesh wafted from her right side. A bloody gash flapped open along her ribcage. Her wing bent in an unnatural position. In a panic, my eyes met hers, and she passed out. She resembled a bloody, singed, bluish-purple angel asleep on the bow.

Rani and I tended to her. With the entranced pirates' help, we bandaged her wing and let her rest in the captain's quarters. "We can't fly to the Black Sea now." There was a sharp edge in

Ranigeia's tone. "We need to stay put until Ploui's healed."

Ugh! I turned away from my sister and hid my tears as they flowed over their lids. My heart was stolen, my voice pilfered. I couldn't take another loss.

Rani sang a hypnotic lullaby to our hosts. In her song, she included whistling low undertones—subliminal messaging—telling the proprietors of the ship to keep our presence a secret. She sang tales of tarring the deck and trimming the sails with the wind. She even had the pirates singing along with her song while they performed their chores.

With the pirates convinced not to reveal our presence and to continue their normal activities, Rani and I were free to care for our sister.

"I'm going to check on Ploui," said Rani and walked away humming.

The scallywags she left behind offered to share provisions with us and lend us a berth.

Thoughtfully, I peered out into the Aegean. If *Looty Booty* hadn't shown up when it did, my sweet, beautiful sister would be a goner. Not knowing how long we'd have to be here, I went to our designated berth and lay down to sleep. I wanted to look after Ploui when my big sis required rest.

Ranigeia shook me awake. "Ploui's awake, but something's wrong. Come with me." I followed her, along with a strange, revolting odor, to the captain's cabin. Rani stopped but motioned for me to keep going. When I glanced in, my mid-sis was gone!

Where'd she go? What the heck?!

"Ha! Ha! Ha!"

The laughter caught me by surprise. I checked behind me, but it wasn't my sister at all. A good-natured gold-toothed pirate chuckled.

"Had you going, didn't I?" He wiped spittle from his chin.

"You thought I be yer sister!" He slapped his thigh and laughed even louder than before. "Captain Looty's the name. Don't think we was properly introduced."

He stuck out his hand. I shook it and bent forward. "Buster Looty." He returned my bow.

Puzzled, I peered around his large frame and peeked into the captain's cabin again. There sat both of my sisters. Rani was upright in a chair; Plouigeia was propped high on the bed with pillows. My sisters held hands. Big sis cooed a sweet, healing song.

In awe, I watched as my middle sister's quills began to grow back. Beneath sodden bandages, her blackened flesh was exchanged with supple pink skin, and spiked burnt feathers from the lightning strike were gradually outnumbered by the downy aqua-blue feathers that replaced them. The smell of burnt flesh was switched to that of new-baby skin-scent.

Holy Styx! I had been conned! Didn't know anyone could bewitch a Siren!

The giddy sailor beamed at me. He looked pleased with himself—but stunk like rum and stale pee. "Bet you wondering what I did, ain't you?" He placed his hand on my elbow and guided me aside.

I nodded.

"Uh-huh. Challenging with no voice. That's the first part to mimic." With his thumb beneath his chin, he tapped his temple as he thought. His mouth gaped open. He winked. "Ah ha! Them tail feathers and lilac eyes of yours."

I'm sure my raised eyebrows and puzzled expression made him want to clarify because his eyes lit up as if a flame ignited in his brain.

"You can use them to glam' a guy." He pulled me over to a bench and table farther away from the captain's cabin. I could still see the shadows of my sisters in the distance, but Ranigeia's lovely tone was barely an undercurrent within the volume of the sea's churn.

"We be no ordinary pirates," Looty confided with his hand in front of his mouth as he revealed his secret. The gold tooth glimmered like sunshine trying to burn through the clouds. "We be magic-like."

I thought I heard my sisters calling. Nearly tripping on my long rainbow tail, I rose to join them. He grabbed my arm. Firm, but not rough. He glanced toward his cabin. "They be fine. Sit down, and I'll tell you what kind of magic we be."

This should be interesting. I listened while the charming captain with a golden grin shared his fascinating story of how *Looty Booty* came to be filled with marauders who could do spells. These bandits were able to convince folks into giving money over to the crew without bloodshed.

"My mates and me don't rape, pillage, or plunder. We lives by a code. A special code," he said, nodding his head as he spoke. "We likes our rum and these open seas," he continued. "Don't wanna hurt nobody. Don't want to bring on your Sirens' wrath. What I did to you just now—that there was a glam' spell. We use it to gets people to give us drink, food, money, or what we need."

Whomever they focused on was mesmerized by them, seeing only what the pirates projected into their minds.

"That's how I came to you as yer sis. And how you didn't see nothing the first look in my captain's cabby."

"I can teach you, and yer sissies how to glam." He rose from the bench, satisfied with what he shared.

With the ability to glam, we wouldn't need cloaks and could walk onto Siren's Scythe *and steal my voice back with hardly a stir. But... what's the catch?*

Our days aboard the *Looty Booty* turned to weeks. Each day, we grew more tired of the pitching and yawing. Meanwhile, our friendships strengthened, and my sister healed.

One starry night, Buster and his mates left us on their ship while they went off to "bargain" with a nearby village. When they returned, Buster stormed into his quarters, out of breath. "I picked up this here locket." He held it high. "It be different."

Gold and silver concentric circles shimmered in the moonlight as the pendant swung from a delicate silver chain. He opened its inner circle. A curl of jet-black hair escaped and floated to the floor. Buster slid the locket closed.

My breath caught in my throat. I think my heart stopped beating.

"I reckon we be on to something. Glammed the gal who wore it. She claimed 'twas a gift from Captain Morus before that scoundrel dismembered her parents while she be forced to watch."

I squinted and clenched my teeth, trying to contain the hurt and anger as it grew inside my chest. *How kind.*

"Icy... gave *her* a locket?! ... Like Zeet's... that cheating..." Rani burst out of the room.

I paced back and forth like a tiger in a cage. My plumage, a heavy, drooping curtain of colors, dragged behind me.

Buster handed my other sister a petite piece of folded parchment, which had been folded to fit inside the locket, and left the room.

"We can't be too far from him." Ploui reached over and touched my arm, stilling me. She unfolded the tiny parchment and read. "Set gold in silver in a ring of pearls. Open. Open.

Breathe."

"Hmm." She raised an eyebrow. Her forehead crinkled with concern, but her eyes glimmered with hope. "I'm getting stronger."

How could he?!

I removed my sister's hand from my arm and sprinted from the cabin. Launching off into the night sky, my tears fell like rain. *Not fair! Ploui was not fully healed. Set gold in silver? Ring of pearls? Is this* how I was supposed to get my voice back?

My sisters found me at the top of a cliff near our pirate ship. Plouigeia put the locket around my neck and half-smiled. "It's a start."

It was also motivation. *Change of plans.*

Over the next few weeks, we took short trips from the barque to practice our skills. The pirates taught us more of their glamour skills. Using *Looty Booty* as a base, we went after simple poachers, gradually moving to larger prey. Rani and I attacked while Plouigeia soared overhead, singing her hypnotic tune. One after another, Ranigeia plunged her front talons into the men on poaching sloops—and then merchant ships. I flew by and pierced them with my feet, shaking them off into the cold waters below. Afterward, we combed the empty vessels for rings of pearls or new clues about my beloved.

Ex-beloved.

At long last, my sisters and I were ready to roost on rocky cliffs and punish more crooks who sailed the seas. On my mind was the biggest thief of all. I WOULD get my voice back.

We arrived at the mouth of a larger sea and bid farewell to our gracious hosts—those strange pirates who befriended us.

Ploui embraced the good captain, putting her feather into his cap. "Thank you for your hospitality and friendship," she whispered into his ear. "You have our bond."

"And you ours." Captain Looty said, "We will never glam you," upon receiving my tail feather with a little bow. I returned the bow with a wink and a smile.

"And we will never mesmerize you," my oldest sister assured him, shaking his hand and placing her tail feather into it.

In the end, my suspicions were unfounded. The only catch: our vow to never Siren them.

My sisters soared above me to the cliffs surrounding the sea's entrance. They found a roost in the crag of a bay on the Black Sea. They were talking about our latest kill when I joined them. In my mind, I repeated the short prose: *Set gold in silver in a ring of pearls. Open. Open. Breathe.*

As the sun rose, we heard the song from *Siren's Scythe*.

MY SONG!

I was furious. Upon hearing my voice coming from Morus's ship on the sea, my sisters flew in a flurry of feathery circles.

"How DARE he?" screeched Ploui.

Rani cried, "We'll stop him!"

Morus's mates attacked a small, hapless vessel. No doubt, there were few to no riches to be found. From afar, we watched as bodies from the smaller craft's tiny crew splashed overboard.

After their conquest, my melody was not silenced. *Siren's Scythe* was still on the prowl. Slowly trolling the edge of the bay, she waded her way beneath us. Her song—MY song—was a pleasant lullaby in the lazy afternoon sun. The sweet tune beckoned a pirate barque to her.

Looty Booty!

Captain Icy-Eyes was not going to go easy on fun-loving, glamour-spelling pirates. Our friends were in peril. Because our timing was too late to hide their ship, I focused on a smaller, people-based glamour spell. I had to obscure our friends from our enemy.

Swooping onto the deck of *Siren's Scythe*, I landed in all my rainbow glory. My tail spread out in a luxurious fan of multi-colored plumage while my wings created a breeze that fluffed my tail and puffed the plumes along my legs.

Plouigeia did not yet have the strength to walk through Morus's men. She sang from a safe distance, high up on the mast of their galleon. To the pirates who listened to her voice, she invited death.

Like a colorful vulture, my eldest sister circled her prey and hummed their funeral march.

Some sailors from *Looty Booty* hid in fog on their ship, which Morus's men tethered to *Siren's Scythe*. In the surprising afternoon mist, I watched most of our friends as they staggered onto Icy's terrible ship, summoned by my stolen voice. Silently, I tapped my glamour spell with my tail feathers. Crossing my fingers, I hoped the image I was sending to the enemy pirate minds would be effective.

Phew!

My friends proved to be protected and unseen by my new glamour spell.

My formless singing stopped. Time stood still. Waves lapped at the hull of the ship.

Smiling, Morus sauntered out of his cabin. He stopped— stood still on *Siren's Scythe*'s deck opposite me. *Ye Gods, he's attractive!* His smile faltered. *And wearing my twin pendant.* My face contorted as I struggled with concentration to protect our friends. *Left his cabin door open!*

With a glance, my mid-sis saw me and changed notes. Despite the agreement we made with them, she sang to enchant our friends. She pushed them back onto *Looty Booty* in single file.

Rani didn't miss a beat. She dove deckward with a paralyzing screech that froze the captain and crew of *Siren's*

Scythe.

I leaped passed Icy through the cabin doorway. In the dark corner of the captain's quarters, the tail of a mermaid glistened. As I gazed around, there were more disgusting displays of his prowess.

A tusk from a walrus. Jaws of a great white shark. Over his bed hung a stuffed blue marlin. On his bedside table below the mermaid's tail sat a locked jewelry box, onyx and amethyst stones inlaid in its polished silver.

Shaking, I removed his locket from my neck. The smell of mildew and decay from my lover's trophies hung in the air of the dimly lit cabin like smoke.

Having memorized the clue, I repeated it. *Set gold in silver in a ring of pearls. Open. Open. Breathe.* Placing the gold circle into the pearl-lined indentation, like a key, I tried the lock. Didn't work. *Shoot!* I turned the locket to face outward. Opened the pendant. The latch clicked. Opened the box. Bent my head down and breathed out. With an enormous inhale, I sucked my voice back deep into my throat.

Its soft melody soothed my pain. As I purred sweet revenge on the murderous pirates from *Siren's Scythe...* they cried for mercy.

My song's sound grew stronger, nourished by the air of my lungs. I didn't take pity. For Captain Icy-Eyes, no peace. Terror. Blood.

With the bejeweled box hidden close to my body, I glided out of his cabin into bright new daylight. Screams of agony echoed. Dark liquid oozed and dripped along the planks of the ship's deck. The smell of burning flesh, fresh meat roasting on a fire. I relished in the anguish of my tormentors' pain.

My sharp talons gleamed in the sunshine.

Morus shuffled toward me, entranced. He shook his head

briefly, clearing it from the charm of my song. He pulled out his sword. Slash.

I stopped singing and ducked away from the point of his weapon.

He swung his sword again.

Recovered, I sang.

Swipe. I tore at his arm. The limb tumbled to the deck, still holding its sword. Humming, I gritted my teeth and kicked him to the ground.

He struggled to stand. I stood on his torso with one leg, pinning him beneath me. With my other leg, my talons tore open his chest. Reaching into the gaping cavity with my hand, I plucked his heart from its home. He lay on the floor, engulfed in the fluids of his demise. The flame behind his icy-blue eyes went out.

I placed my prize, his heart, into the silver box. Slammed its lid with a click. Removing the locket from its chain, I placed it into the ring of pearls on Icy's bejeweled case. My hands still dripped with bits of my lover as I refastened the chain around my neck. Tucking the small silver chest for treasure under my arm, I strode to my waiting sisters.

"Let's fly!" I sang.

"Zeetageia Finds Her Voice" is ©2024 by B.B. Arbogast. It appears here for the first time. Since her youth, B. B. Arbogast has had an interest in myth, the occult, and the macabre and releases that part of her imagination in poetry, short stories, and flash fiction. She wrote her first two picture books in German while learning the language when she worked briefly as an Au Pair in Germany. She is in the process of writing novels for a variety of audiences ranging from early middle-grade to adult in multiple genres, including magical realism and horror.

A retired software and database developer, she is making her second career as an author. In her free time, she enjoys hiking, skiing, and walking her dogs with her husband in Reno, Nevada. You can find her online at http://bbarbogast.com.

Rene Averett

Nightshade

With a clang and a shudder, the bus lumbered to a stop, barely off the road. Iris Holder's head tipped up in surprise. After a long shift at the Speedi-Mart, she'd dozed off. She gazed around, noting only she and the driver remained.

"End of the ride," the driver called out when she didn't move.

"I'm at the Flint Street stop," she answered.

"Bus won't make it. I'm calling dispatch to send assistance. Sorry, miss, you'll have to get off here."

Here? But it's still far from my stop. She cast an alarmed look out the window and tried to pinpoint where they were. This wasn't even one of the bus stops. She gathered her shopping bag and purse and made her way to the exit door. As she stepped out, the light touch of moisture in the night air dampened her cheeks, and she detected a sweet scent in the breeze.

She shuddered. *Nightshade. From the cemetery. Oh, sweet Jesus, the graveyard is just ahead. Of all places for the bus to break down.* Iris spun toward the driver, but he faced the other way, on the phone. She stepped back to the door and cleared her throat.

"Excuse me. Will there be another bus?"

"Sorry. No more tonight. Can I call a cab for you?"

She shook her head. She didn't have money for a taxi. Resigned, she turned and walked toward the next block. One more would take her to Old Faith Cemetery, the oldest burial site in Silvervein. Cutting through it diagonally would shorten the distance, but she'd never done it at night.

"Don't you go into the cemetery after dark," Grandma Mari had said many times as Iris was growing up. "And especially don't go near it on All Hallows' Eve. There are ghosts and demons about in the night." The trick-or-treaters were gone, but the night remained.

Her feet dragged as she crossed the street and drew closer to it. Just a few yards ahead, the entrance jutted out to the sidewalk. As she came to it, she saw the partially open gate. *Odd for this late.* She stopped to peer through the vertical bars. Little firefly lights darted through the grounds, dipping into the plants, resting on the nightshade, and making it seem like a fairyland. *Was Grandma right? It seems calm enough, nothing scary moving around.*

She glanced at her watch: 11:38. After a moment, she decided to risk the shortcut to get home before midnight. Gathering her courage, she pushed the gate open farther and marched onto the cobbled path, determined to get across as quickly as possible.

Iris barely stepped three feet on the stones when a chilling draft slapped her face, and a chorus of crickets chanted her name, "Iris, Iris, Iris," over and over. *Just my imagination,* she thought as a tremble snaked down her spine, urging her to move forward quickly. She picked up the pace to carry her a few yards down the tree-lined path, even darker without any moonlight. Behind her, she heard a squeak, and she turned in time to see the gate slam shut with a bell-like clang.

Her legs felt like lead as she scrambled back to the gate, where she pulled, trying to open it. Then she shoved, yet the portal remained immobile. Fearful, Iris stepped back to gaze at the walls surrounding the cemetery. Made from heavy stones held together with cement, they didn't give enough purchase for anyone to climb them, let alone a 5-foot-2 young woman wearing platform pumps. The metal gate appeared to be equally unscalable, with no places to gain enough purchase to climb it.

Dismayed, she stepped back, turned to face the path, and resumed walking, her footsteps less resolute than before. Would she be able to open the gate on the opposite side, or was it as impenetrable as this one?

As less light came through the trees and the path lights winked out one by one, Iris grew more uncomfortable. She pulled out her cell phone to call for help, but it registered no bars. She switched it to flashlight mode and continued, shining the comforting, albeit small, ray of light ahead. After a short time, the darkness enveloped her so much that she only saw the path in front of her. She couldn't determine if she walked in the right direction.

Without warning, her phone light went out, plunging her into complete blackness. No street lamps in the area. No moonlight or even stars penetrating the cloudy sky and thick canopy of trees. Iris punched her phone, trying to get the light back. In her frantic efforts, the phone slipped from her grasp, landing with a thud along the path. She reached down, her fingers seeking the oblong object until they landed on several fuzzy and wiggling things. She shrieked, yanked her hand back, and jumped aside. She choked out a panicked sob, facing the worst of her situation. Alone on All Hallows' Eve, she stood locked inside an old cemetery and uncertain of which way to go.

Her shoulders drooped as Iris stumbled—tripping over a tombstone—back to the path. Uncertain if she faced the correct way, she shambled along the path, keeping her free arm out to the side to determine if she passed too close to any headstones. "Why did I do this? What was I thinking? To save fifteen minutes? Ha!" she mumbled, grateful for the sound of her voice in the still night.

Since Iris had cut through the cemetery in daylight a few times, she knew several paths branched off from the diagonal passage and that it branched at a midpoint. She could accidentally take the wrong branch. It already seemed like she'd been on this path for a long time, but without her phone to provide light, she experienced sensory disorientation.

In a blink, a light appeared about fifteen yards ahead of her. As the illumination moved away, it flickered and bobbed like a lantern being carried. Iris swallowed her fear and called out, "Hello? You, with the light, can you help me?"

No one answered, and the light kept moving, flickering and beckoning her to follow. At least, that's what Iris chose to believe. She picked up her pace and set her sights on catching up to whoever held the lamp. Although it seemed strange for anyone to have an actual flame for light, she didn't care so long as they could lead her out.

She gained about 15 feet on the light when a ghostly figure cut across the path in front of her. Eyes popping, Iris yelped and stumbled backward. Attired in top hat and tails, the spirit used a cane as he trod across. A foul odor of decay emanated from the direction where he'd emerged, leading her to glance that way. Another apparition appeared, a woman clad in a prairie dress, shawl over her shoulder, and a bonnet. Lips trembling, Iris stepped more paces back as another, then another, followed the previous two specters, moving at the same funereal pace as the leader.

Her eyes followed the procession as it marched, without any hint of seeing her, into the darkness on the opposite side. A milky-white halo surrounding them illuminated the area as they ventured deeper into the tombstones until the glow faded away. Iris's shopping bag rustled, drawing her attention to her shaking hand. She gulped, pulling air into her lungs, and peered ahead, seeking the lantern's light.

There it was! She hadn't fallen too far behind, so she pushed her shaky legs to catch up with it. When she came closer, she tried to see the person holding the lamp but couldn't make out anyone in the soft glow cast by the flame. She called to the light-bearer again, "Please wait up. I need your help. Can you take me to the gate?" Her voice faded as a twisted flare shot out, and the illumination turned to the right.

Iris hesitated, knowing the turn was a side path, not the way she needed to go. Yet the flame beckoned her on, teasing her with the swaying of the moving lantern. Mesmerized, she followed, her eyes locked on the glow. Step by step, she caught up to the lantern until she was about three feet from it. Shock skittled through her spine when she realized no one held the floating lantern. She could see every detail, but no hand clutched the ornate brass lamp containing a golden flame, shining through the clear sides. Symbols raced down the sides of each panel, moving like a stream cascading over rocks.

Iris couldn't believe her eyes. What magic was this? Wonder turned to fear, then back to amazement. She wet her lips and, in a hoarse whisper, asked, "Why did you lead me here?"

The symbols on the sides paused, reformed, and spelled out a message.

"Follow me," she squeaked. "Where?" The symbols resumed flowing, but no more words formed, and the lantern moved past the headstone, leading through the grave markers and tombstones.

Iris followed the lantern as it weaved through the

dilapidated and unkept graves, taking them deeper into the cemetery. Her fear of being trapped in the dark kept her moving, not wanting to let the light leave her sight. The scent of wet earth, rotting leaves, and more of the tomato-like nightshade assaulted her. While she hadn't seen any of the deadly plants, she knew vines grew along the walls and older tombstones.

After what felt like many minutes of weaving and tripping, the lamp halted at an open grave. Iris stopped two steps later and stared at the opening in the damp earth. A few earthworms wiggled through the dirt, and she could just see the shape of a coffin. Why had the lantern stopped her? She lifted her eyes to the light, seeing it dip and rise like it wanted her to approach the grave.

Nerves tensed, she minced closer to the edge, leaning toward it to see down. The lantern swooped lower, illuminating the casket's surface and revealing a greeting-card-sized leather-bound book. Although the lamp maintained its height, she watched it dip toward the book, rise, and dip again. It repeated these actions two more times as Iris puzzled over what it wanted her to do.

"Do you want me to get the book?" she asked, feeling dumb talking to a lantern.

It bounced again. Apparently, it did, Iris concluded, and peered into the grave again. With the casket, it wasn't a far drop, but could she climb out?

What am I doing? I just want to get out of this place. I should turn around and try to find the path. Her inner voice cautioned her, but a melodic whispering encouraged her to do as the lantern asked. The urge to comply overrode her senses, so she set her shopping bag on the ground, knelt and dropped a leg into the opening, then slid the other over, landing with a resounding thud on the wooden coffin.

An echo from inside the box triggered a jolt of fear, making her jump back. She hit the back wall of dirt, and several clumps thudded onto the wood and into the grave. Iris gasped, ending it with a fearful wail. The lantern tilted down again to cast light on the book. Her hand shaking, Iris picked it up, noting the volume was slim enough to tuck into the front of her jeans.

Satisfied, the lamp rose again to cast the light on the ground above the grave. Iris knew she couldn't jump out, but she was tall enough to reach her arms over the top. She ran her hands over the ground, seeking purchase to pull herself up. Her fingers found a vine's edge, and she withdrew them. For a horrible moment, she feared she'd found the nightshade. She pulled in a deep breath, trying to calm her nerves.

A cool breeze slipped across her face, and that whispery voice said, "More to your right."

Iris obeyed, aware she had no choice. When she reached out this time, her fingers brushed against the thick root of an elder tree. She tugged it to ensure it would hold her weight, then grasped it with her other hand and pulled herself upward. Three grunts later, she'd gotten her right leg up enough to swing it over the top and used it to leverage her hips onto the ground. While she sprawled in the dirt, she reflected that she couldn't look less graceful and was glad the only observer was the lantern.

She sat up, brushed dirt off her clothes, and pulled the book from her jeans to get a better look. What was it, and why had the lamp directed her to it? A twisted symbol on the front appeared to be carved into the leather. Carefully, she ran her fingers over it, tracing the smoothness of the edges. The cover appeared well-worn, suggesting it might be quite old. Carefully, she opened it to the first page. Spidery handwriting displayed words and symbols she didn't know. Not English or anything that resembled any language she'd ever seen. Maybe it was Greek or

Latin or...

The light on the pages dimmed and moved away. Iris looked up to see the lantern drifting through the tombstones again. Jumping to her feet, she shoved the book into her shopping bag and set off after the recalcitrant light source. Where was it leading her?

The air grew cooler, and Iris shivered, wishing she'd worn a sweater instead of her hoodie. As she walked, the air seemed to resist her advance, but that made no sense. Maybe she had touched the nightshade, and she was experiencing a reaction to its poison. But the lantern continued forward, so she kept putting one foot after the other, determined not to lose the light. Still, a weight pressed against her, and the steps became harder. She stumbled, falling to her knees, and gasped for air. She knew she was suffocating. *Oh, God, I'm going to die here*, she thought. Before her eyes closed, she glimpsed a vision of a woman holding the lantern, her other arm outstretched, motioning for her to continue. Iris struggled to reach a hand toward her, and then she passed out.

II

Iris's head ached like she'd partied too hard the night before. Only she didn't recall going drinking with anyone. She opened an eye, seeing only darkness and blinked it shut again. She rubbed a hand across her eyes, then opened them both to see mostly black night, but with a few oblong shapes within it. Shapes like... Tombstones! She was in the graveyard!

"Finally, you're waking up," a woman's voice said, coming from somewhere near her right shoulder.

Iris pushed up and peered toward the sound. Gradually, her vision zeroed in on a beautiful young woman wearing a sarong around her hips and a breast cover-up the size of a bikini top.

Chestnut-colored hair wound in a braid with flowers and twigs sticking out around her head. Most notably, a faint silver glow illuminated her presence. "Who are you?" Iris asked, wondering about the skimpily-clad woman on a chilly October night. She pushed herself to a seated position, legs sticking out in front of her.

"You may call me Briar," the woman responded. Her words were proper but hesitant as if she didn't speak English much. And you are?"

"Iris. What happened?"

The woman waved toward the area just in front of Iris. "Apparently, you can't cross through the veil. Most humans can, but for some reason, you cannot, little flower. I wonder why that is?"

Iris swallowed hard. "The veil? You mean to... uh... to?" It seemed ludicrous to ask, but she was staring at a woman who literally glowed.

"The fae world?" Briar replied. "Yes, of course. Didn't you know the veil is thin tonight?"

Alarm shot through Iris as she clambered to her feet. She'd heard the stories. Grams had told them to her since she was a little girl. She'd warned her about the cemetery on this night of all nights. "And you're a fae? Right?" Her voice sounded harsh.

"I am a dryad," the woman replied. "And this place borders on the edge of my forest."

"I... was following a lantern... when I... Was it trying to lure me through to your world?" Her voice ascended an octave, and a touch of panic set it. She was facing a creature of myth. *I must be dreaming*, she tried to rationalize.

An uneasy feeling spread through Iris as she recalled some of the folk tales in Silvervein. Tales about the town touching on the fae world and people disappearing in the mists and fogs that sometimes blanketed certain places. She recalled Grandma Mari telling her to be aware of the "other world" and, if she found herself in it, not to—

"Would you like a drink? You look thirsty," Briar asked.

Iris blinked. She could use some water, but she didn't trust the dryad. Instead, she looked for her shopping bag, spotting it a few feet from her. "I have water in my bag."

She grabbed her bag, opened it, her fingers touching the book inside, and pulled out a bottle of orange vitamin water. Twisting the top, she swallowed a gulp. "That's better. Now, why did you lead me here?"

Briar's lips dropped into a frown. "I need your help, human girl." She picked up the lantern from behind her and started walking back into the cemetery. "Come along, and I'll tell you a true story."

Reluctant but curious, Iris followed. Besides, Briar had the only light in the area, and she still needed to find her way out.

"Many moon turns ago, a powerful elf wizard crossed the veil to your world. He sought ways to grow his power. He made a spell to entrap human souls in a dead place where he could feed off them."

"That's ghastly! Is that why the cemetery is haunted? Why so many wandering souls gathered near us?"

"One reason, yes. But there is more. The wizard—he was called Nyxaran—made a faulty spell. It came back on him, drained his power, and he died in this graveyard." Briar motioned around her as she related her story. "The magic book you found was his."

A chill caressed her spine and made her shudder as Iris turned back to her bag to gingerly pull out the leather book. "This book? You're saying this book belonged to a wizard? The one responsible for all the ghosts in the cemetery?"

Briar dipped her head once.

"You want the book? Take it." Iris held the volume out for the fae woman to take.

But the dryad shook her head. "I can't touch it. You need to open it."

"Oh, frog farts," Iris muttered. She didn't want any part of this. "Why did you pick—?"

"Frog farts?" Briar interrupted. "I once knew a human who said that often. You know her?"

Iris's mouth dropped open in surprise. "My grandmother... she said it." *Beware of the fae.* Iris could hear Grams' voice whisper in her mind. Well, double frog farts! She was in trouble here. "What happens if I open the book?"

"Nothing. Stuff only happens when it's read out loud."

"So, it's a spell book?"

Briar nodded, her golden eyes flashing with green flecks and a big smile.

"How did you know my grandmother?" she asked, ignoring the book.

The fae's eyes rested on her for several heartbeats before she spoke. "Long ago, she crossed the veil with an elven friend. We tried to find the book but couldn't."

"Why not? You led me to it."

"We didn't know then it could only be found on All Hallows' Eve. When I learned it, Mari refused to enter the graveyard on that day."

"So, Grams knew about all this and knew to stay away on this night. But now it's after midnight, so why could I still find it?"

"In our lore, the entire night is All Hallows' Eve."

"Until daybreak," Iris whispered. "Now, you need me to open the book because you can't. Why?"

"I am forbidden. If I could do it, I would not need you."

Iris traced her fingers over the carved images on the front. A grimoire, Grams had called it. If one is a magic user, they can initiate spells from it. But she didn't use magic. "Look, I'll open the book, but..." She flipped to the first page, which appeared to be an index; however, she couldn't read any of the words. The handwriting was neat, listing about twenty lines on the page, each with a page marker, but the words looked like gibberish to her. "You'll have to read, Briar."

"I can't read."

"Neither can I." She flipped a few more pages. All the same unreadable scribbles. "None of it."

"You can," Briar insisted. "You are a magic user."

"No, I'm not. I am simply a human trying to get home."

Briar shook her head again. "You are a magic user. Otherwise, you would not see me or the lamp."

Did that make sense? "The lantern held a flame. Of course, I saw it. But not you. Not until I woke up back at the veil."

Briar pursed her lips and tilted her head to one side. "You can't see the light, not even flame, unless you have fae blood."

"That's crazy! I don't have fae blood." *Or do I?* She questioned her belief. *What if Grams...? No, it couldn't be. Then again, all those stories about the Fae world...*

Without warning, Briar's fingers touched her face, pressing something moist and smelling like honey mixed with carnations onto her cheeks. "You try again."

Iris pulled back and wrinkled her nose. "What did you put on my face? It feels sticky."

"No harm. It helps stimulate your blood so you can read elf writing,"

Although doubtful, Iris opened the grimoire again. At first, it looked like the same gobbledygook as before, but then the words became clearer and more familiar. "Wait! I can read it! It sounds like a spell's name."

Excited, Briar clapped her hands. "I knew you were the one! Look for the undo spell."

"Undo? Is that the name? Is it a general spell to reverse any magic?" Iris thought a basic spell wouldn't be practical. What if it undid every enchantment the wizard had cast?

The dryad shrugged, her shoulders rising awkwardly and knocking two twigs from her hair. "I don't know how it works. I only heard the wizard say there is an undo spell for the cemetery enchantment."

Iris's eyes narrowed. "Were you with him when he cast the spell?" How involved in this was the dryad?

"I was nearby, watching him."

"Watching? Or helping?" Iris slammed the book shut. "I won't do it."

"I... I didn't help him do it. I have tried to undo it for almost two hundred years."

"Two hundred? The souls in this cemetery have been trapped here that long?"

Briar's mouth turned down in a sad look. "I need your help to free them."

Well, shite. My great-grandparents and grandpapa are buried here, Iris realized. *They're stuck in this awful spell.*

Muttering under her breath, she opened the book, ran her finger down the page, and read each spell's name, looking for one that suggested a reversal. Almost to the end of the page, she spotted the Suck Souls spell and turned to it, reading the words silently. The instructions said to speak the words under a full moon and trace a hex on the ground with dragon's tears. *The incantation seems simple enough, but where did he get dragon tears?*

With a sense of foreboding, she turned to the next page,

anticipating it being the spell to reverse this awful curse. Sure enough, the words at the top of the page indicated it was an Unravel. She read aloud, "The narrative says it will untangle the strands of any spell by reversing the actions and incantation, but the exact opposite of the conditions must be met, save for any magical potions used, which must be the same.

"Oh, double frog farts! According to this, you need a new moon night, need to trace the hex in reverse, and use dragon tears! It can't be reversed, Briar." She held the open book out to her as if she might understand it better.

Briar blinked at her. "It is a new moon now, right? Trace the hex backward. I know where dragon tears are."

"Where?" Iris's stomach churned with trepidation, and she hoped the dryad didn't say they'd have to find a dragon and make it cry.

"In vault. Nyxaran left it there after he cast the spell."

After a few moments, Iris said, "Look, Briar, take me back to wherever the tears are. I'll help you get them, but then I want to leave the cemetery."

Briar considered her offer as she sipped something out of a flower cup. Where did she get that? Iris wondered. "Deal. You help me; I help you."

III

Briar stepped onto a path, leading as she added, "Vault is this way."

Iris followed, not wanting to lose sight of the only light in the place. In fact, she couldn't detect any light beyond the cemetery either. "Why did the lights go out? And my phone?"

"Wizard said light is blocked out by fae magic. Maybe his or mine, but I don't know." She turned to the right, taking them deeper into the old section.

From her eye's corner, Iris spotted a man's ethereal presence, lingering by a tombstone, watching them pass. It moved out and drifted along behind them. A few minutes later, a second apparition joined him, then another. "We're being followed."

"True. Spirits sense the book's power—and yours."

"Not mine," Iris said. "You're the magical one."

Briar chuckled. "We'll see."

She led them to a narrow path with five big urns set along it on the right side, where she stopped and pointed. "One of these holds the key to the crypt."

"Which one?" Iris asked, gazing at the line of big pots.

"Don't know. You need to check each one."

Iris glared at the dryad, then stepped forward, motioning with her free hand. "Bring the lantern." At the first one, she looked for any clues that it might hold the key, but it was a simple clay urn with no markings of any sort. She pointed to the jar's mouth. "Shine the light over it."

Briar lifted the lantern so they could see the inside, where a blackened, crooked object stuck out of the dirt.

"Maybe this is it." Iris reached for it and yanked, feeling some resistance, and tugged harder. It came out with several more attachments. She dropped it and stepped back, muttering, "Cripes! It's bones!"

"Just bones," Briar said. "Look for the key."

Creeped out, Iris rubbed her arms. Then she got an idea. Signaling Briar to bring the light, she went to the nearby trees. Searching the ground, she found a broken branch about the thickness of her little finger and twenty inches long. She snatched it up and strode back to the urn. With the stick, she dug into the pot, turning the soil over and feeling for anything that could be a key. It caught onto something, and she pulled it up, revealing the rest of a hand. She turned a sour face to Briar, who shrugged it off.

After she ran the stick through the loosened dirt a few more times, Iris stepped back and moved to the next pot. A quick check showed it was also unmarked, but this one had a vine growing in it. She sniffed to detect a honeyed scent like sweet peas, then used the stick to dig, trying not to disturb the vine too much. After several minutes, she determined the key wasn't in this one either.

They went to the third urn, finding it in worse shape than the others. A crack jogged down the side to the base, and the pot appeared only half-filled with dirt. Iris jabbed the stick in again, and it stuck on something inside. Excited, she thought it might be the key and tried to yank it up, but the crack broke open, tipping the whole pottery over to shatter on the ground.

With a wail, a spirit shot out of the crumbled clay and darted straight toward Iris. She jumped back, shrieked, and ran toward the crossroads, thinking the ghost was after her.

"Wait!" she heard Briar's voice calling, so she glanced back over her shoulder. No spirit pursued her. Briar pointed to the left, and Iris looked, catching a glimpse of the fleeing ghost joining the other host of spirits that seemed to be accumulating along the sideroad. When had they all started coming? Stopping, Iris took a minute to catch her breath and calm her wildly beating heart. *Just find the key, get to the crypt, and we'll be done with this,* she told herself. She stomped back, glaring at Briar for bringing her into this fiasco. If it weren't for those poor imprisoned souls...

"Key's not here," Briar informed her. The dryad was still checking through the debris, but it looked like she was correct. No key.

Without a word, Iris moved to the fourth urn, hoping this one held the key. Like the second one, this pot held greenery in the shape of a small fern. She detected a grassy fragrance and dug her stick into the soil. Several bugs scurried out, including a three-inch-long scorpion who ambled up her digging stick. With a healthy respect for poisonous bugs, Iris dropped the stick and screamed, "Scorpion!" As she scrambled back, the scorpion leaped forward, catching her sleeve and started up her arm. "Do something, Briar!" She waved her arm away, hoping to dislodge the ugly bug.

Briar rolled her eyes and scampered to her, snatched up the scorpion, and broke it in half. Elated, the dryad ate the bug and licked her fingers like she'd just finished a sticky bun. As her stomach revolted, Iris vowed never to dine with Briar.

"Now, we find the key." Briar spun around, going back to the urn. Iris followed her, picking up a bigger stick along the way. Together, they shoved the same pot over where it broke, spilling dirt along the path. Iris stood back as dozens of bugs scurried from the tree roots, and Briar routed out another scorpion. She tossed this one a few yards away instead of dining on it.

Iris dragged the stick through the dirt, spreading it out. Before moving to the last urn, she shoved it into the root cluster in a last attempt and knocked a metal object out. "What's this?" She picked it up, turning it over in her hand. She motioned to bring the lantern closer. Rough flakes of rust pricked her thumb as she ran it over the artifact.

"It could be the key!" Briar said with an excited bounce. "It looks like it could open the vault."

Iris's lips tightened, and her eyebrows lowered, doubt showing in her eyes. "It doesn't seem like one to me." A twisted knot symbol was etched into the middle. "What does this mean?" she asked, pointing to it.

"It's a magic symbol. Maybe the key matches a door with it?"

Given it could be an elven or fae key, Iris yielded. "Okay, let's go see if this opens the vault."

With a clap of her hands, Briar danced along the pathway, with Iris speed-walking behind, followed by a slower-moving cluster of spirits. Iris glanced back, observing the lost-souls gallery had increased. Did they know what she and Briar were trying to do?

Ahead of them, a rectangular building made of marble stones came into sight. It looked worn, with a few cracks around the front corners. Nightshade grew alongside, seeping into the mortar splits. Iris's nose itched from the scent, causing her to move to the path's center. Briar reached the locked door and turned, waiting for her.

With only a peek at the keyhole, Iris faced the dryad. "At a glance, I can tell you this key—" She held up the oblong object. "—doesn't fit that door."

Briar frowned. "Must be another key. Perhaps it fits another lock that hides the one to the vault."

Iris huffed out a breath. "I thought you knew about it."

"I only saw Nyxaran hide dragon tears in the vault. I didn't know where he put the key, but he dropped something in urns."

Iris's eyes widened. "Were you helping him?"

"I only watched. No matter. Look for something that key fits. It must be close." Briar stepped past Iris to search.

With the light moving away, she fell into step close to the dryad. Briar had evaded answering her question, but she suspected the wood fae knew more than she was revealing. The light flashed on one headstone after another, lingering only a few moments before the dryad moved on. But at one mid-sized tombstone, Iris glimpsed something. "Wait. Look at this, Briar."

The dryad brought the light back and raised it to where Iris pointed. The old, worn tombstone had a recessed arch-shaped area where two jailer-type keys dangled against the stone. A small iron box with a unique-looking lock protected whatever the keys hung on.

Iris turned the rectangular object she'd found to the narrower end and held it against the irregular hole in the iron. "This is it," she whispered, feeling like Lara Croft opening an ancient treasure as she inserted the key and turned it. Rust and grime prevented it from going far, but Iris took a deep breath and applied all her strength. The metal creaked but finally yielded with a snap. The small door on the box opened, revealing the stone knob holding the keyring.

"Most wonderful!" Briar set the lantern down and reached to take the keys.

"Hold it! Are you sure they aren't hexed or something?" Iris picked up the lantern and held it closer.

"They're not spelled. Take them."

Iris touched each key and detected nothing odd, so she lifted them up. "Why two?" she asked.

Briar shrugged. "Maybe something else in the tomb is locked?"

"Whatever, let's go try them."

Nerves tingling, Iris inserted a key into the vault's lock, prepared to exert her strength to move it, but it turned with ease, and the door creaked open. "This is it." She turned to Briar. "Go get the dragon tears."

Briar stepped back. "No, you must go. I cannot enter."

"What?! You expect me to get the vial?"

Briar nodded.

"I am not going in there alone."

"You must."

Iris's jaw locked in grim defiance. "No. This is your Geis, not mine."

Briar stood firm. "I am forbidden. You must do it, Iris Holder."

51

"Na... na..." She tried to form a negative response, but she felt something pushing her, compelling her to enter the vault. Although she attempted to fight it, Iris moved, snatching the lantern from Briar's hand as she entered. *Why can't I fight this? How can the dryad force me?* Then, she recalled Grams' words—names have power. Briar knew Iris's family name.

Iris moved deeper into the vault, surprised at how big it was. And rundown. Dirt smudged the stones, and fat spiders scurried from the light. She spotted cracks in the walls where the insects could come and go as they chose. She shuddered. What other creepy crawlies might invade the building?

She cast the light along the walls on each side while darting her eyes around, looking for a cache that might hold the vial. Ahead, a well of darkness lay beyond the light's edge. "How deep is this vault?" she mumbled and moved forward another step.

"Is someone there?" a male voice called out.

Iris froze, her heart pounding against her ribs. Holy shit! Someone was in here. Who?

"Hello?" the voice spoke again. "Please help me. I can't escape."

With her stomach fluttering, Iris walked forward, holding the lantern in front of her. Fifteen paces farther, the light revealed a wooden door with a two-foot-square opening with four iron bars in it. She swallowed hard and stepped up to peer inside. Gasping, she covered her mouth with her free hand while her eyes widened.

Inside, a pathetic-looking ghost, skinny with his clothes falling off him, stared at her with pleading eyes. Through him, she saw a skeleton dressed in the old and fraying brown jacket with a wide collar and breeches he'd once worn, draping around the bones as he'd starved.

"Who put you here?" Iris asked, her voice hoarse. Was this

more of the wizard's work?

"An evil creature," he replied in a broken voice. "She bound me to this place, never to go free." His voice broke as long-held emotions emerged.

Iris's stomach jumped when she caught sight of the pitiful expression on his ghostly face and eyes that no longer held life. *Is this what all the trapped spirits in the graveyard are like?* Appalled, yet she didn't know how to help him... except by breaking the spell. As she thought, she frowned. The spirit said, "she." Did someone else hex the souls? Did the wizard have a female accomplice? Aloud, she asked, "Tell me, was your captor a woman?"

"That she was. A beautiful and wicked woman. Can you help me?" His voice held both sorrow and wonder as he spoke.

"Can you describe the woman?" *Could it have been Briar?*

"Blonde hair, blue-fire eyes, and lips like ripe cherries. She was enchanting, and I fell into her trap."

Not Briar. "I don't know," she said. "But if I can find the vial of dragon tears, there's a chance.

The spirit's arm rose, and he pointed to a recess in the wall a few feet to her left. A niche Iris hadn't noticed as she'd approached the locked cell. She hurried to it and held the light up. A petite wooden door with a familiar-looking keyhole covered the niche. She pulled the oblong key from her jeans and used it, opening the compartment with ease. Inside, a small bottle half-full of a clear, shimmery liquid glistened in the flickering light. Dragon tears... magical ones. Turning, she called out to the spirit. "Thank you. If my companion can break the spell on the cemetery, it might release the one on you also. I hope it does."

"So doth I. God speed, mistress," the spirit responded, a touch of hope in his voice.

Triumphant, Iris hurried back to Briar; the vial lifted high for her to view. "I got it!"

Delighted, Briar danced in a circle three times, then took the lantern and urged Iris to follow her to the crossroads. "We go to where the slanted road crosses three other paths."

When Iris fell into step, she noticed the ghostly host had doubled while she was in the vault. Now the spirits followed them like an adoring mob.

Once they arrived, Iris opened the grimoire and found the reversal spell for Briar. When she held it out, the dryad said, "You must read it."

Exasperated, she opened the book. "I can't actually read it either. I mean, I see the words, but I don't know what they mean or how to pronounce them."

"You say the word, and I'll tell you if it is spoken right," Briar replied as if it were a simple thing.

Her head shaking, Iris read the first line.

"You're close." Briar corrected, and Iris repeated to get the words down. Then she read the next line, and they repeated the process until all the words were read.

Iris crossed her eyes and spat out, "Did you memorize them, Briar?"

The dryad nodded.

"Good. You can do the spell."

"It's not for me to do. You must."

"Listen to these instructions. 'Draw the hex symbol in the middle of the spelling circle in reverse of the original. Sprinkle dragon tears on the symbol, then walk the circle in contra direction three times, repeating the spell.' I can't do that. You're the fae. You do it!" Iris almost shouted. Around them, the spirits shifted positions, and she thought they felt threatened by their arguing.

"I cannot."

"Why not?"

"I am constrained. Forbidden."

Iris's mouth opened, no words coming out as she realized what Briar said. With a gulp, she said, "The wizard hexed you, didn't he? He used a spell to stop you from doing anything to help these souls yourself."

Tears forming in her eyes, Briar looked down. "Yes. He tricked me. I hunted many years for someone to break the spell."

"But I'm not that person." Iris's shoulders dropped as the tension flowed from them.

Briar lifted her eyes and said, "Look what you've done so far. Located the book, found the key, opened the vault, and recovered the tears. You have a fae gift. Trust me."

Iris looked at the book, staring at the knotted-looking symbol that must be drawn in reverse. How could she do that? "I... I can't."

Like whispers on a breeze, the stories Grams told her about the fae realm and how people of Silvervein disappeared in the mist, never to be seen again, came to mind. *Wise humans never give their real name to the fae. Likewise, the denizens of faery don't reveal theirs either.* She realized that while Briar didn't have her entire name, she had enough of it to compel her to do her bidding.

But she wanted to free these souls. "I'll try, but you must help me figure out this hex symbol."

The dryad nodded and started by using a glowing stick to draw a six-foot circle in the middle of the intersection. "Not fae dust, but this works."

They paced to the center, and Iris set the book down so they could both see the image they had to draw. Briar stared for a full minute, then pointed to a connection on the right. "This starts the image. You must trace it from here to left to unwind."

With a silent prayer to whatever saints might be listening,

Iris took the stick to trace the image in the dirt, surprised it continued to glow. She tried to keep it small enough that it wouldn't take all the dragon's tears to activate yet big enough that she could follow the twists in it. Twice, she had to stop, erase a section, and redraw it until she finally completed it. With a sigh of relief that appeared to include the watching spirits, she straightened and gently poured drops of dragon tears into the etched path. They didn't sink into the dirt but shimmered like diamond dust on top.

Now for the incantation, she thought. She moved the book to a headstone and motioned for Briar to bring the lantern. With a half-turn to the hex symbol, she began chanting the elvish words and marching counterclockwise in the circle. "*Vinthar thrice ciran ael, dor thanelen ruath yre fanath. Enelûn vóras eledan thar, silaran e'mael caerath.*" Her mind translated them as she spoke the foreign language. "Contra three times around I go, to undo what was done to enslave the souls. Release them now to flee beyond, ending thus my frozen spirit bond."

At first, she didn't detect any reaction to the words, and the cemetery remained eerily silent. She repeated the chant a second time, then several gusts of air brushed against her cheek and swirled around the open circle, picking up leaves along the way. Iris's eyes grew wider, and hope rushed through her veins. Speaking louder, she started the third pass, moving to walk around the outer edge of the circle, where the spirits gathered closer.

Nerves stretching, Iris grew fearful. *Will the spell work, or will it backfire, and I'll end up like the wizard or the man behind the door in the vault?* Licking her dry lips, she chanted the final phrase. With each word, the breezes grew stronger and the air colder, like a storm brewing.

"It is working!" Briar shouted.

She glanced at the dryad, who urged her on with arm gestures and an expressive eye-roll. On the final word, a cracking sound like thunder split the air, and breezes erupted, blowing leaves and dust all around the circle. The surrounding spirits shrieked in joy and began dispersing, disappearing into the ether as a silver light illuminated the graveyard. They were freed. The grimoire snapped shut like an invisible hand closed it.

Iris grabbed it and pulled it to her chest as she faced Briar. Over the dryad's shoulder, she spied a familiar ghost coming out of the vault and smiled. Apparently, the undo spell reversed that one as well. "Are we done?" she asked. As she turned away, she spotted oily-looking spirit blobs coming toward them. "What are those?" She pointed at the oozing apparitions.

Briar turned and squeaked. "Bad spirits. Evil. Run!" She spun around and sprinted toward the veil, lantern bouncing in her hand.

"I'm going home," Iris yelled and ran in the opposite direction, taking the broad path she hoped would lead to an exit gate.

Briar turned and chased after her. "No, come with me. It's our only escape." But Iris ignored her and picked up her pace.

Behind her, she heard the dryad scream, "Iris Holder, you *must* bring the book and *come* with me now."

For a moment, Iris froze as she felt the strength in the words summoning her, then a small smile touched her lips, and she resumed running.

With Briar and the pack of dark spirits in pursuit, Iris glanced back to see one surge ahead, knocking Briar aside. As it closed in and reached out to touch her, Iris heard two words in her mind, words Grams had repeated many times.

Emboldened, she whirled around to face the spirit, the incantation on her tongue, when the dark creature shoved an appendage into her. Dodging, Iris evaded the thrust to her heart, feeling icy cold penetrating her chest and seeping into her lungs as she fell to the ground. As the thing loomed over her, ready to strike again, she mustered her strength and screamed, "*Malum excidere*," while holding the grimoire and thrusting her other hand into the oily slime. Like a rubber band, it snapped and vanished. Aching, she pulled to her knees to see the other dark entities drifting like they'd lost their direction before they popped like balloons and vanished.

In their wake, Briar emerged, racing toward her. She scrambled to her feet and stumbled to the gate as dawn's first light glimmered.

Briar yelled, "Iris Holder, I command you to stop and return to me. I demand you give the book to me. You cannot resist." Tattered and breathless, the dryad stomped toward Iris.

For several moments, Iris felt the command's tug, but she conquered it. There is power in names, Grams said. Luckily, she used a nickname, but she recalled a name her grandmother told her belonged to a fae she knew. "You can't stop me," she shouted back, "and I possess the grimoire now. Brystara Willowbark, I command you to return to your world."

Shocked, Briar gaped but submissively turned and marched back toward the veil.

Relieved, Lirisabelle Wildes Holder, a newly baptized Wildes witch, resumed walking to her home, clutching her prize grimoire. "Thank you, Grams. Guess I did inherit magic," she whispered, ready to learn more from the old woman.

is a multi-genre author who has published twenty-two books, ranging from low-carb cookbooks to children's books, suspense romance, sci-fi fantasy, and paranormal tales. She also writes under Lillian I. Wolfe and Riona Kelly.

Teresa Breeden

Bailey Makes a Plan

B efore entering the bowling alley, I make a list: smile at six people, say Hi to anyone whose name I know, and talk to at least one person. It's harder than it sounds. Despite spending my whole fifteen years of life in Blundage, I haven't really made any friends. Helping on Grandpa's ranch doesn't give me much time to hang out with people.

To steady myself, I take a deep breath, then instantly regret it. It smells like old sweat and mildew in the alcove of the doorway. But the stench helps me get moving. I push open the door and prep a smile.

As expected, Chastity is working tonight. She works most nights. Like me she helps support her family. And my smile is suddenly real at the sight of her. I hate my name. Bailey: the outer wall of a castle. It's rough and uncultured like me. It fits my personality. And that's why I hate it. But for obvious reasons, Chasity's name is even worse. I have trouble not smiling every time I hear it. Which suits me fine tonight as smiling is on the list.

"Hi, Chastity," I say with a grin.

"Hi, Bailey" she says without smiling back. Her voice is as

thin and reedy as her arms, and with the effort of those two words, she sounds as worn as the old flannel I'm wearing. She gives me a discount on the shoe rental, though, which makes me smile even wider.

I go to my lane and type "Bailey" into the score machine. I hate it, but it is my name. I'm not so wishy-washy as to change it and pretend to be someone I'm not. Not like my sister, who had a perfectly fine name, Jesse, and goes by Cassandra because "it's more elegant." Like anyone in Blundage could be elegant. It's just not that kind of town.

Speaking of Cassandra, there she is, on the last lane with her best friend. They dress similarly, almost falling out of their low-cut tops despite the fact that it's winter. You might think it's a good thing that my sister's here—that I'd have someone to bowl with now—but Cassandra and I don't exactly see eye to eye on, well, anything.

But saying *Hi* is on the list, so I wander over and smile and say "Hi, Delilah. Hi, Cassandra."

I think I'm being nice using her new name, but she scowls at me anyhow. Coming close, she leans into me. "You need to learn to smile with your mouth closed," Cassandra hisses in my ear. She's referring to my crooked teeth. Hers are the same, and she's taught herself this awkward fake-smile where her lip covers most of her bottom teeth. Me, I never practice smiling. I figure if I'm happy, I'll smile, dammit. But now I am most certainly not happy. And I have three people left to smile at.

I return to my lane and begin to bowl. I bowl slowly. I'm terrible at it, but that's not why it takes so long. I got here early to secure a lane before things get busy and now I need to bide my time. I can't afford to pay for another whole game.

Sure enough, the alley fills up, and soon I'm surrounded by laughing, chatting people. I'm fine being alone in my lane, with a long stretch of seat next to me as I sit to rest. Fine not chatting and laughing with anyone. I'm used to being alone.

At exactly 6:07, the girls from my school show up. They are seven minutes later than they said they'd be when I overheard their plans in class. They are shiny, these girls, with smooth, freckle-free skin and brightly colored jackets. Their cheeks are rosy from the cold outside, and they brought their own shoes.

I busy myself with my bowling ball. I can't throw it—the game is almost over—so I pace with it in my hand, take a couple practice swings. And it happens, then, just like I pictured it. "Hi, Bailey!" Carley's voice is as bright as her pink windbreaker.

"Hi, Carley!" Only two more smiles to go. Though I'm not sure this one counts since my lips are pressed together tight as a cinch strap on a recalcitrant ranch horse.

"Hey, the lanes are all full, would you mind if we used this one?" Carley asks, her smile faltering a little at the edges.

"Well, I was about to start a new game," I hedge, "but if you buy the next game, I'll let you join me." Carley pauses and glances around. Her friends are silent. No one is smiling except me now, and mine is as brittle as day-old bread. Some kind of secret signal must get passed because suddenly they are all nodding. "Of course!" Carley gushes. "What fun!"

I wonder how many times she's practiced *that* smile in a mirror.

With all the girls watching, I throw my final ball and, of course, it swerves into the gutter. The time it takes to roll into the darkness at the end of the lane feels like forever. I wait it out, my arm still thrust out like a plea. I reel it back in and set it by my side. Even standing feels awkward with an audience. A light sheen of sweat beads my brow despite the cool air. I'd like to be that ball right now, about to disappear. But no, I'm here to do the opposite. To be seen. To practice smiling and talking to people.

To maybe make a friend.

My classmates gather around the console, a flock of brightly feathered parrots, chatting away. They laugh at each special nickname Carley punches in. When she gets to the end she pauses and glances my way, her gaze settling on my mouth. I jerk my lips together and then force another half-smile.

"What do you want your name to say?" Carley asks. It's a simple question, but I freeze, my lips locked into a smile, my lower lip pressed inward against my lower teeth to cover them. *Popular. Funny. Interesting.* That's what I want my name to say. I don't think *Pretty* though. Some things just aren't possible.

"Bailey. Just Bailey." I choke out. For a moment I hate myself even more than my name. Wanting to change it, wanting to change me, feels like someone's tied me to a chair. I can't move. It's hard to breathe. And it's made worse by the fact that I'm the one doing the tying.

Just be yourself. That's always the advice. But I've been myself for 15 years, my freckled crooked-toothed quiet self, and it's left me with no friends and the nickname ghost. Not that anyone talks to me to use it.

I'd rather, even if it's just for one night, try being someone else.

We begin to bowl, and I'm smiling so wide I know my lower teeth must be showing. I'm at a lane with the girls from my class. For tonight, at least, I won't feel lonely.

Each girl poses before she bowls, and the others laugh and tease. I'm not sure how to pose. I've never tried it. But it seems like left hand on a thrust-out hip and a kissy face is the most common, so that's what I go with. It's harder than it looks. The bowling ball is heavy in my right hand, and I'm not sure where to hold it. Shoving my hip sideways puts me so off balance I almost fall over. And I'm not sure exactly how to pucker my lips. I mean to be cute, but I feel more like an off-kilter Halloween ghoul.

And it must show. Because instead of laughing, they get quiet. Scanning their faces, I see nervous smiles. Not the ones they've practiced in the mirror but frozen I'm-uncomfortable-so-I'll smile it off looks.

I'm used to the quiet. The ranch is several miles out of town, and it's just Grandpa and me in the main house now that Jesse found an apartment in town. Well, Grandpa, me and Adlai, the drifter I found collapsed on the road in front of the ranch a month ago. But, just like Gramps, he mostly keeps to himself.

But this quiet is different. It's heavy like Lady, our mare, pinning me against the corral fence. And just like that, I have trouble catching my breath. All the air's whooshed out of me, sucked away by their pained smiles and the weight of the silence.

I turn to bowl, their gazes sticking to me like molasses. It's harder than stacking hay bales, bowling in front of them. Sure enough, my ball gutters before the halfway mark. Cheeks blazing, I keep my eyes on the ball return, not risking their expressions. On my second try, I knock down a single pin. Shuffling to the empty seat on the end, I drop into it. I try to make it casual, but I'm so busy not looking at anyone or anything that I miss the seat and almost fall off the edge.

The closest girl, Jenna, keeps her back to me as she leans toward the rest of the conversations. They gossip about school and dating and the upcoming winter festival dance.

I thought nothing was worse than being alone. I was wrong.

When it's my turn, I go through the motions woodenly, waiting for the game to end so I can get the hell out of here. When I finish, the girls are huddled together like a sports team about to yell out their name. I picture it in my head, all their hands in the center, then popping up like the spokes of an umbrella as they yell, "Go, Popular!" I snicker a little at the image. I can actually see them doing it, celebrating themselves like they're in a competition. I dislike competition. It feels too much like conflict. And I'm learning I dislike being ignored even more than being alone. I can't quit midgame; that would be weird, but as soon as the game ends I'm outta here.

But for now, curiosity is eating at me. What could be so top secret important that they are practically standing on top of one another to discuss it? I move closer. I still can't hear much, but watching their heads pop up one by one like a pack of gophers to look across the bowling alley, I figure it out. Adlai has entered the bowling alley. And the girls in my class have definitely noticed. I lean in further.

"But who is he?" Jenna asks.

"It looks like he knows Jesse," Carley says, gesturing toward where Adlai and my sister stand talking.

"His name is Adlai." I say it a little too loudly, but it works. The huddle opens like a flower blossoming as all the girls turn toward me. "And she goes by Cassandra now," I say to Carley. I don't know why I'm defending my sister. She wouldn't return the favor.

"Wait, you know him?" Carley sounds incredulous.

I straighten my shoulders. "Course I do. He's living with us." The girls cluster around me, bees after nectar. For at least this moment, I'm the center of attention, and it's hard not to smile with my teeth showing.

"Where's he from?"

"How long is he staying?"

"How old is he?"

The questions come too fast to actually answer, but no one seems to care. The huddle has reformed around me, and shoulders press in on mine from either side. It feels like a giant hug.

"Can you introduce us?" Darla asks, and the other girls go quiet.

When I first met him, Adlai reminded me of a stray dog, feral but hurting. He'd likely bite you as thank you when you tried to help him. But after a month at the ranch he's calmed way down, and we get along well enough. But Cassandra would tear my head off if I descended on her lane with a posse of excited girls. I don't want to get chewed out in front of them.

Plus, I can see her flirting with him from here. Her head tilt and fluttery eyes are dead giveaways.

But I don't know how to say no, either.

Luckily the questions aren't over.

"So what does he do all day? What is he interested in?" That from Sloane, who is the smartest of the girls.

I shrug. "He mostly just helps out on the ranch."

"You actually live on a ranch then?" Carley asks.

I nod.

"With, like, horses and cows, and pigs and stuff?" Carley's tone sets me on edge.

"Yeah." I say, straightening fast enough that the girls on either side of me fall off balance. "Well, not pigs. But horses and cows. And chickens."

"Chickens! I've always wanted to pet a chicken," Carley squeals. A ranch that had her wouldn't need pigs.

"Maybe we could come over to meet them?" She shines the full beam of her smile on me then, all hopeful and glossy.

"Sure." I say, uncertainly, squinting in the light of her enthusiasm.

"Tomorrow?" She presses.

"Sure." I say again.

Satisfied, Carley's gaze returns to Adlai. I can see why; he's as good looking as they come, more movie star than anyone in

Blundage could dream of meeting. And I know she's probably not really coming over to pet a chicken, but I don't care. I'm finally having friends over.

When the game ends, Carley calls for a group selfie. The girls pile in together, like they do this at every event. "Come on, Bailey," Carley says, "get in the picture." Grinning, I squeeze in, and Carley takes a few shots. Then she hands me her phone. It's on the contacts screen and Bailey is at the top. "Put your info in," Carley instructs me. My hands are shaking so hard it's difficult to type, but I manage to finish and hand the phone back. I'm one of Carley Winebuckle's contacts!

I'm still giddy when I get home. The first thing I do is open our old laptop to check Instagram. And there it is. The picture of us from the bowling alley. The other girls are making kissy faces and have their heads all tilted to one side or another. My face is straight on, looking at the camera, freckled and pale and crooked teeth on full display. But I don't mind. I feel as happy as I look in the picture. "Girls night out" it's called, and I am one of the girls.

I scroll through the rest of her posts, and my smile falls away. Under a picture of an arm and torso wearing the bowling alley work polo are the words "Skeleton sighted at Greco's. Isn't it a little early for Halloween?" There are more. Pictures of parts of Chastity. A knobby elbow titled "deadly weapon," the back of her frizzy ponytail titled "hope it's shearing season soon." And there's a photo of my sister leaning over to pick up her ball, her boobs on full display. "Who will Jesse Spears spear next?" It's a stupid caption. They all are. But I want to unscroll. To go back to the moment I had only seen the group picture. Is this really who I want to be friends with? Will I have to make fun of people like others have done to me my whole life?

I think of the ranch. The peeling paint on the old farmhouse and the smell of shit permeating the air around the chicken coop and the horse stalls. The constant buzzing of flies and the gravel drive. I can't imagine them here, or worse, I can imagine them here, their pale hands batting away flies and their pert noses squinching up in distaste. And I can imagine, too, what they'd say about it afterwards.

I'm still awake, staring stupidly at the screen, when Adlai finally gets home.

"Something in your eye?" he asks, and I wipe at my face.

"Just dust."

"Yeah," he says. "That happens on a ranch."

He looks over my shoulder. The group picture is back on the screen, my face grinning away like I just won the lottery.

"Happy tears?" he asks.

I shake my head.

"The one in pink looks a little like a pig. Her skin's almost as pink as her coat. And check out her nose." Carley's face is tilted up just a little, and her kissy face caused her nostrils to flare out. I remember her squealing "Chickens!" and snicker. Adlai pats me on the back and heads upstairs.

At lunch the next day, Carley and her friends make a beeline for me, all smiles and Hi's. I start to smile back until I remember Carley's posts about Chasity and Cassandra.

Carley links her arm with mine. "We still on for today?" she asks.

"Ah. About that. We have to fix a fence today. So maybe some other time." The fences are all fine of course. But I looked at the posts again this morning, and I'm feeling right now like I'd rather knock a fence down myself than have them come over.

"Tomorrow then?" She's persistent. "And will Adlai be around?"

I see an out. "Adlai is working in the far field all month, so you won't be able to see him if you come over."

"Oh." Her arm falls from mine, and I sigh in relief. Who links arms like we're gonna do-se-do together?

"Actually, he said," I start. I mean to tell her about the pig comment, but I just can't do it.

"What? What did he say?" There's that squeal again. "He said... petting chickens is lame."

Carley's face falls. "Yeah. It is."

Ah. There it is. She finally sounds like she's saying something true. "So are you coming over tomorrow?" My smile is as wide as the interstate out by Wattsville.

"Ah. I forgot. I have something tomorrow," She peels away and the rest of the girls follow.

I see Chastity sitting alone on a step, eating a bag lunch and remember my list from the bowling alley. Smile. Say Hi. Have a conversation. It's just as nerve-wracking as in the bowling alley, but I made myself do it then. I can do it again.

"Hi, Chastity," I say, smiling without worrying about lips or teeth. Looking up in surprise, she mumbles a hello, one hand over her mouth to cover her chewing. "You ever wanted to pet a chicken?" I ask, and immediately feel like an idiot. Could I have said anything dumber than that?

Chastity swallows and shakes her head. "They're really soft." I add, feeling awkward. "I mean, you could come over today after school if you wanted to. To pet a chicken, I mean."

"I have work today," she says.

"Right. Of course," I say, backing away.

I'm turning to flee, when she says "But I have Thursdays off." It hangs in the air between us for a moment. I've forgotten to breathe. I inhale slowly and say "You want to come over Thursday?" I turn back toward her, half expecting her to laugh in my face. "Yeah." She says, looking down at the floor. But she's smiling, and I realize it's the first time I've ever seen Chastity smile. She has a dimple on her right cheek and her face looks flushed. From the heat in my cheeks, mine is too.

"OK." I turn and really do flee this time, grinning, crooked teeth and all, all the way to my next class.

"Bailey Makes a Plan" is ©2024 by Teresa Breeden. It appears here for the first time. The author lives in the high desert at the base of the Sierra Nevada Mountains where she finds inspiration in both the serenity and the chaos of the spaces around her. Teresa has one novel, "Falling by Tori Briar" (available on Amazon), has published over 60 poems in various journals and anthologies, and is a recipient of the NV Arts Council Fellowship for Literature. Her writing revolves around relationships: with people, the environment, and even inanimate objects.

The ACES Anthology

Bill Brown

Lady in the Lights

Sometimes being a Good Samaritan can take you to places and uncover feelings you never thought possible…

Henry Wadsworth Wilson, or Hank to his friends, had been on the road for 10 straight hours with only short stops for gas and once at a food stand for some burritos and tacos that, unfortunately, gave him insufferable gas. He was glad at this point he was driving alone.

It was close to midnight, and to keep himself awake, he pondered his name yet again. His parents had christened him after their favorite author and their favorite president. The last choice he didn't agree with, but, so be it.

Done with that, and knowing he was close to his destination, he struggled to keep his eyes open. It had been such a long day loading video gear and computers with all his notes for the pitch he would be giving in the small Northern California coastal town of Juniper.

Juniper is located north of Fort Bragg just as you headed into the redwoods—but no one had ever heard of it. In fact, he couldn't even find it on a map. But they had a town council and a population of just under 2,000 with a weekly newspaper that tended to run super conservative. That wasn't his favorite thing, but they needed some PR and video with a next-to-nothing budget.

They had, however, promised a few hundred dollars and an old beat-up farm on a cliff overlooking the Pacific with jagged rocks below and a crashing surf you could hear for miles. At least that's what they *promised*. Realizing he was most likely the only person who took the job, and also thinking about that farm and the chance to build a retreat for his other work, he had accepted.

He had seen pictures of the "village"—he couldn't really call Juniper a town. It had a gas station, a small grocery store, a couple of shops, but the "village" was hoping to be so much more. A recent land exchange with the Forest Service had freed up a great deal of property along the shoreline to help save the surrounding forests. Hank was pretty sure they really didn't want to offer him that spot of land, but they needed help; good solid help.

He popped open another caffeine-enriched soda though he wasn't sure that would help at this point. He could pull off the road and nap, but could he then make the 10 am meeting? Plus, he had his reservation at the village's one and only inn. The inn that didn't look like much from the photos he saw, but he was told they had been sprucing the place up for his stay.

No, he had to keep going. He had sent a text saying he would be in shortly after midnight and they had replied that was fine and to just ring the bell. Ring the bell? Someone had to ring *his* bell right now. As much as he wanted to continue, he was a hazard now to others on the road and he knew it. Sighing, he knew he had to find a spot to pull off. He could sleep in the inn's parking lot if he arrived later than anticipated since he wouldn't want to wake them. But for now, he was running out of time.

There had to be a spot just to pull off and not be a hazard—but wait, what was that? Up the road in the car's high beams—and his Land Rover had *high* beams—he could see what looked like the figure of a woman walking along the shoulder of the road. Well, now he was sure he had to be hallucinating. She was dressed in white, walking slowly towards town, and her long white hair was flowing in the ocean breeze—or maybe it was the high beams that made her hair look white? He had both hands on the wheel so he couldn't pinch himself but he could kick himself with his left leg, after he took his foot off the accelerator.

"Ouch!" Yeah, he was awake. He slowed down as he got closer to this figure. He could just drive by, or he could stop and ask her if she needed help—and it was his nature to always help. Besides, he seemed to be wide awake, for the moment. Slowing down next to her, he buzzed the window down.

"Ma'am, are you okay? Do you need help? It seems to be very late to be walking on this highway. What can I do to help?"

The woman didn't slow her gait, nor did she break her gaze which was straight ahead, never blinking.

"Ma'am, please. Let me call for help if you don't trust me. Let's get someone you do trust. Please. I think you need help. I mean it."

Still there was no response, and for a moment he shrugged his shoulders and thought about rolling on; he really needed to get to bed. Accelerating slowly, he pulled away heading for what sleep he could get. *Wait, no, that was not your way,* he said to himself. All his life, and in his professional career, he had been told he would be a lot richer if he spent more time worrying about money and less time worrying about others. He had tried to break that mold, but some things a person is just born with.

He pulled off to the side a little farther ahead, so the lights were not blinding her. As he looked back at her, it was odd...

there seemed to be light all around her. Getting out of his truck, he carefully stood to the side so he wouldn't block her way.

"Ma'am, hello. I'll get back in the truck and go away as soon as you say you are okay. Otherwise, may I help you?"

The woman stopped. Breaking her forward gaze she locked eyes with Hank.

"Will you give me a ride up to my home?"

Hank relaxed at her response. "Yes, of course. Is it in town?"

"It is just up the road a ways, but not in town. Not anymore."

Noting the woman still hadn't blinked and knowing how tired he was, Hank still had to ask, "Ma'am, you look awfully pale, and your hair is so white. Should I be taking you to a doctor?"

"No. Not anymore."

Hank wasn't comfortable with that answer, but his energy was really beginning to fade—he just wanted to get to someplace to sleep. Opening the door, he started to help her in, but an owl with a loud call or hoot seemed to be very close by. He turned to see it as he offered his hand to her. Feeling only a wave of cold air next to him, he turned back and saw she was already in the passenger seat, staring straight ahead again.

Still, Hank didn't feel ill at ease—just concern for her and wanting to help. Starting up the Land Rover he pulled back onto the road.

"So, how far are we going, ma'am?"

Still looking forward, she answered in a soft voice, "Not far. It will be on the right. You're not like them."

Hank slowed a little as he pondered what that meant. Thinking it might be better to just say "thank you" and leave it alone, he couldn't help himself; he was too curious.

"Not like *who*, ma'am?"

They continued down the road, her gaze never straying from the front window.

"The ones who did it. The bad ones."

Hank knew now was the time to stop talking and get this woman some help. But before he could speak, she looked over at him, smiling, and gestured to the right.

"This is where I must leave you now."

Hank didn't see a house or any buildings in his headlights. What he did see was a cemetery.

"Ma'am, this is a cemetery. No one lives in a cemetery. Now I can take you to town and we can get some help..."

"I live here, Henry Wadsworth Wilson. This is my home." Seeing the shocked look on her driver's face, she continued. "I looked inside of you, Henry. I saw that you are a very good man." Her voice was measured and soothing. "You are a very good and decent man—an honest man. Fare thee well, Henry Wadsworth Wilson. Fare thee well..." Turning, she walked toward the cemetery gates.

Not sure of what was happening or what to say, all Hank could do was shout, "You know my name! I don't know yours!"

The woman stopped near the gates and turned, looking as though she was trying to remember.

"My name... my name is..." She struggled with the answer but then smiled. "My name is Jenny. Yes, Jenny. Thank you for asking, Henry."

As she reached the gate, Hank saw her disappear. It was impossible, but he saw it. He wondered about this whole night. Had he been asleep along the roadside somewhere and dreamed all this? This time he *could* pinch himself. "Ouch!" No, he was wide awake. But what had just happened?

Still wide awake, Hank drove into town and quickly found the inn. It wasn't hard to find, as it was close to the highway and there only so many buildings in the downtown area of the village. He hesitated to ring the outside bell and thought about just sleeping in his car. As he pulled his finger back from the bell, the door opened.

"Mr. Wilson! We have been waiting for you." Hank thought the woman, somewhat in silhouette from the lights of the lobby, appeared to be middle-aged with her hair drawn back in a bun and wearing an apron that showed she was in the middle of cooking.

"Uh, hello." Hank wasn't sure of anything anymore. "I didn't want to wake you."

"Nonsense, Mr. Wilson. Actually, I am still up baking for the meeting tomorrow. We are very excited to have you here!"

"Well, thank you." Hank pulled his bag out of the car. "Will my camera gear and things be safe out there tonight? No offense intended."

"They will be fine. This little town loves you already without even knowing you, and we know that eventually you will love us, too; and love living here. Just come in, sign in and we'll get you settled."

Hank, being a PR/Videographer, was used to judging people at the first glance. At last he was comforted by someone who didn't disappear. At the front desk, which was a really small desk, he bent over to fill out the register, noticing the page was empty.

"I guess business hasn't been that good? Well, we'll change that." He started to pull out his driver's license and credit card.

"Oh, that won't be necessary, Mr. Wilson. This is all covered for you." She smiled as she turned the register around. "We do get people, Mr. Wilson, but not as many as are going to come. I thought you should be the first guest for the new inn."

"Oh, well, that is very kind. Thank you." Hank picked up his bags. "I would have been here even earlier, but there was this woman walking along the road on the way in. She was out there all alone and I know it sounds weird, but she was all in white. I mean *all* in white. Do you know anything about..." Hank saw the lady's face turn just about as white and then she calmed down.

"We have given you the room that is the closest we have to a suite. It's lovely and it overlooks the entire downtown. I hope you will be happy."

Hank had to wonder but still asked, "I'm sorry, did I hit a nerve?"

"This is a beautiful town, Mr. Wilson. And you are going to make it even more beautiful and help the people here. We desperately need your help."

"But—"

"Some things are better left unsaid."

After that putdown, Hank picked up his bags and trusted his gear would be safe outside in the Land Rover. It had been a wildly unpredictable night and he needed sleep.

The woman smiled and added, "I took the liberty of letting the council know that you were getting in very late, so it might be better for the meeting to be at 1 p.m. I hope that is all right?"

"Oh my, you are an angel. Thank you so much." Hank felt the wave of exhaustion sweep over him as he entered his room. It was spacious for an old Victorian, but he would have taken anything at this point.

"Breakfast is normally from 7 to 9, but you being special and all we'll make do. Bacon and eggs with potatoes and some sausage on the side. Will that be fine? I do the cooking myself."

"Ma'am, that sounds wonderful. Thank you for your kindness and for waiting up and everything."

On the way out the door the woman turned. "You're more than welcome. You are going to do great things for us and our town, no matter how long it takes." Turning, she walked to the door but paused and turned back again. "Mr. Wilson, I didn't mean to be abrupt. It's just... well... a lot of folks see things around here. This is that kind of area—lots of stories and things. This is a little-known area on the coast. Up here, you can't always trust your eyes. 'Night, Mr. Wilson." Smiling and nodding she left, closing the door behind her.

Despite being so tired, Hank was feeling uneasy. That last message about "not trusting your eyes" was unsettling... Regardless, he needed sleep, and there was a pitch to be delivered tomorrow. A pitch that could bring him the little spot in the universe he had always wanted.

After fitful sleep, the morning came all too quickly. Hank knew what he had seen, the woman he had talked to, and that it wasn't just a vision of a man too tired to drive. It was real. But, now was the time to put all of that aside. The old broken-down farm on the ocean cliff beckoned. What he could do there! He could get out of the San Francisco environment and, with the proper satellite coverage or even the broadband, he was going to be able to bring in, it was going to be good.

It was about 10 a.m. when he finally climbed out of bed—later than normal, but last night was not normal either. Regardless, he began to enjoy the relaxed small-town atmosphere. Looking out the window, he saw people going about their morning lives in small town America, relishing how everyone seemed to know everyone else and would take the time to stop and chat. Yes, this would be a good place to set up shop.

The bacon was thick and perfectly cooked. The eggs, sunny side up, were exactly the way he liked them. He loved to break the yokes and spread them on the ample serving of country-fried potatoes. The sausage was a treat. Everything was locally sourced. This was America as it should be, except for that nagging thought at the back of his mind. Who was that woman, and why can't I forget her?

Savoring his last bite, Hank smiled. "Ma'am, that was the best. I don't remember the last time I had a home-cooked breakfast like that."

"Oh, come now, Mr. Wilson. I am sure your girlfriend makes you something just like it."

"No, she, uh, she passed not too long ago. She never was much of a cook, but I loved her anyway." Hank tried to smile but couldn't seem to find one.

"I am so sorry, Mr. Wilson." She put the dishes into the sink to be hand washed. Hank made a mental note to get her a dishwasher if this whole deal worked out. "I saw you signed in as Hank. May I call you that?"

"Yes, of course."

"Hank, this is a beautiful place to raise a family. There are some lovely ladies up here, too."

This time Hank did find a smile. "And your name?"

"Martha."

He sipped the last of his coffee as she waited to pour more. "Well, Martha, I am taking a break. My wife was one of a kind."

"I understand, Hank. I tend to get a little motherly at times."

"Thank you, Martha. And thank you for being motherly— I've needed that. But there is one thing. Something I can't shake. Who was that girl last night and why wouldn't you talk about her?"

Martha poured herself a cup of coffee and, pulling a flask from the shelf, gave it a little extra morning fortification. Offering it to Hank, who poured just a little in his cup, she answered. "Hank, it is not my place to talk about her. And I don't know anyone who will. Instead, let me tell you about the other side of this beautiful village, and I shouldn't even be telling you this much." Martha took a long slow sip, savoring the coffee and its fortification.

"A man by the name of Louis Chapman owns most of the land around here. He even owns the farm you're going to get. You saw the people in town this morning, I'd guess? Well, they weren't always this happy. They see prosperity coming because of you. They see people coming in who will help them get out from under Chapman's thumb. Some of the folks here have small farms and homes, but he pulls the strings—him and that bastard son of his." She paused, wondering if she had gone too far.

"Not a word of this leaves this room, Martha."

Martha continued. "Oh, they are all right about loaning money to everyone, but if a payment is late, Chapman gets the land. No one knows where he came from. He just showed up one day with a bag full of cash, and we've never been the same. But still, it was okay until that night—the one night that changed everything."

"*That* night?"

That's all I can say, Hank. And I've said too much already, but you promised nothing was going beyond this room."

"And nothing will. Thank you, Martha."

The drive to the town hall for the presentation wasn't far. He could have walked there except for the equipment he wanted to show them. As he pulled into the parking area, a portly man opened his door just as Hank was setting his parking brake.

"Mr. Wilson! Mr. Wilson, we've been waiting a long time to meet you. I am Mayor Courtney. I was the one who put out the post to find you."

While the mayor was still furiously pumping his hand, Hank apologized. "I am sorry for the delay. I got in so late and Martha over at the inn was kind enough to call…"

"Oh, I'm not talking about that, sir. I am talking about what you can do for Juniper! Look. The town council is here along with others who want to hear how you're going to help. We really need you."

"Well, let me get my gear for the demo."

"Mr. Wilson, you won't need that. We just want to hear how you plan to proceed. We're all behind you."

Hank thought this was going to be the easiest presentation for a client he had ever made. But still, he dropped a little 4k camera into his pocket as a small demonstration. Walking into the town hall chambers, he was greeted with smiles and even applause. It appeared this contract was a done deal regardless of what he was about to say. Shaking hands as he made his way to the council table where the mayor would do his introduction, he noticed the conference call button blinking on a speaker phone at the center of the table. Pointing to it and looking at Courtney, he tilted his head.

"Oh, that is Mr. Chapman. He couldn't be here, so he's listening in. He's very busy."

Hank saw what looked like sweat beginning to form on Courtney's forehead. He didn't know anything about Chapman except for what Martha had told him, but that was enough to dislike him.

Without hesitation Hank spoke loudly enough for all to hear. "Mr. Chapman, thank you for joining us. I understand you are very prominent in this community, and I am sorry to take you away from your other business."

Hank thought you could hear a pin drop in the room as they waited for a response. Chapman answered—Hank thought the voice sounded distant and cold.

"I am happy to be with you, Mr. Wilson, and the others. I have seen your work, your website. I believe you are the man for the job."

Hank wasn't sure, but he thought he sensed a wave of relief sweeping over the room.

"Thank you, Mr. Chapman. Your support will be vital to remaking the village of Juniper into a destination where people will want to come, to live and enjoy." Again, Hank wasn't sure, but he thought he saw looks of joy in the audience.

"Please continue, Mr. Wilson." Chapman's voice had not warmed a bit.

"Ladies and gentlemen, thank you for having me here today and for the warm reception. In a nutshell, you are sitting on a gold mine, and now you are going to dig..."

Hank launched into his pitch knowing it was not really necessary, but he wanted to wow them anyway. He told them about the ad campaigns, the social media presence, and even the video he would be shooting while he was there. For a few minutes he forgot about the lady in the lights as he reveled in his environment and profession. When he finished, there was another round of applause, louder than the first, and he noticed the button on the speaker phone was no longer lit.

Mayor Courtney guided Hank through all the handshakes and congratulations. "Mr. Wilson, I'm sure you want to see your new home. We've got a ride for you waiting outside to show you the way."

A dusty older Ford F-150 idled on the street.

"This is Maggie. She will run you out there and let you look around. Then when you are ready, we have the deed prepared for you to sign."

"That's awfully generous considering what that real estate will be worth."

"Oh, old man Chapman, I mean *Mr.* Chapman, can afford it. Actually, he thought it was the right price to get you here. Mind you, it will take some work, but it's livable." Courtney opened the truck door.

"Hop in, Mr. Wilson." Hank saw a smiling face on a pretty, petite brunette with short hair behind the wheel. "I am your taxi."

Settling in, Hank was happy with what he thought was the first legitimate smile he had seen.

"I am..."

"You are Hank," Maggie interjected. "Martha said it was okay to call you that. She and I talk nearly every day. She also said you're a nice guy, so that's out of the way, too." Maggie hit the accelerator as Hank was trying to get his seatbelt on. "Please fasten your seatbelts and place your tray tables in the upright, locked position."

"And you are Maggie. Very nice to meet you. Thanks for the ride."

"Oh, you really could have found it yourself—it's tough to get lost around here. But they want to make sure you are happy."

Hank thought about that for a moment. "Oh, I'm happy. Maybe too happy. People are over the top here. What do you do?"

Right about then, they hit a dirt road and the truck began to bounce through the ruts. "I own the antique shop in town. Old stuff, just like everything else around here." The truck took a big bounce as she slowed down. "Sorry about that, Hank. I tend to get a little excited."

"There's no worry. I have been through far worse in my job. There is something else, though—something Martha wouldn't talk about. Since you talk with her almost every day, who was that woman I saw last night? She rode in my truck and then just disappeared at the gates to the cemetery."

"There's your house, over there on the right." Maggie smiled. "Let's look at that and then I'll take you to someone who can answer your questions."

For the first time Hank saw just how beautiful this woman was. Her smile was infectious, and it made him smile, too. Answers could wait.

From the outside, Hank saw a beautiful farmhouse. Two stories. Probably lots of bedrooms, a big main room and a kitchen. As he went inside with Maggie, he wasn't disappointed. Checking the lights to make sure they worked, he heard Maggie giggle. "They did turn on the power and cleaned the septic, but beyond that, cowboy, you're on your own."

Hank chuckled. He liked this woman more and more. One of the reasons? She didn't appear to take any crap from anybody. The hardwood floors needed refinishing, there was dust and cobwebs everywhere, but his attention was drawn to the sliding glass door in the back. That was something he didn't expect in an older farmhouse.

"What's with this?"

Still smiling, she answered, "Just look around, Hank. Just look." And look he did. Not far beyond his backyard was the cliff that led into the ocean. He had an unobstructed view of the horizon and the glistening waves with the sunlight dancing on the water. *This*, he thought, *was heaven, and it was worth a fortune. Why would a man like Chapman give this up?*

"Why, Maggie? Why? These few acres and this view—this property is worth a fortune."

"I don't know." She walked up next to him to enjoy the view, and he welcomed her standing this close to him. It had been a long time since he had felt... sociable. "I wanted to buy it from him a long time ago, but he wouldn't part with it. He told me it was part of the new development. I couldn't afford it anyway, but that was before all the land-swap deals began. It's a beautiful home and land. It just needs some care."

"Tell me about him."

Maggie didn't break her gaze from the ocean. "He's a bastard, a prick, and I don't want to swear any more than that. But I can tell you his son is even worse. When the old man dies, who knows what's going to happen here."

Hank did turn away from the view for a moment and looked at his newfound friend. "Well, now I am not so sure about helping out here."

"Shush there, big man. The town needs you. We all need you. And who knows? With you here, maybe we can attract enough big-time people to turn things around." She turned away from the view and, with a voice that sounded wistful, she said, "Now check the toilets and the plumbing, and let's go get you some answers."

Hank was quiet on the bumpy road back to town. Every now and then, they would hit a rut or dip that which made him glad that he had buckled up. A couple of times he glanced over at Maggie, appreciating her more each time. If this deal worked and he stayed here, she might be one of the big reasons.

"Maggie, I am sure you have more to do than ferry me around. Your boyfriend must be wondering where you are by now."

Maggie didn't even blush, but she did smile. "For a big city boy, you don't fish well."

That made Hank blush, though, as he realized he wasn't being subtle enough. But it had been awhile, and something about her straightforward talk was new and welcomed.

"You're right, Maggie. It's been awhile and I'm out of practice. So... do you?"

Maggie was still smiling. "Not right now. Not much to choose from around here. But I'm doing okay."

Properly put in his place, Hank tried to relax back in his seat as much as this road would allow. His thoughts turned back to the other matter—who was going to answer his questions? The answer came as they arrived back in town. Parking outside the office of the *Juniper Gazette*, the town's weekly paper, Maggie pointed to the front door.

"The editor, publisher, and sole reporter's name is John Walden. Go on in. He knows you're here. I am going to park around back so not too many people see. I'll join you in a minute."

Hank thought, *This just keeps getting better and better. A town on the brink of exploding, but people still have to hide what they're doing. It doesn't make sense, at least not yet.*

Inside, Hank saw a small office with an older man sitting behind an even older computer, and apparently he wasn't happy.

"Damn thing! Damn thing! Do what I want you to do!"

"Mr. Walden?"

"Yeah? Oh, it's you." Walden pounded the desk one more time while he was writing. Then he appeared to relax a little. "I am supposed to tell you *we're* so happy to have you here, but *I* am personally happy to have you here. Maybe you can do something for this town."

"What's the problem with the computer?"

"Oh, it's a new system, and it's not the software. I am having a problem making the switch to Apple. The software is 'High

Sierra' or 'Mojave' or whatever the hell you want to call it. I am a PC man. I hate this shit." Walden pounded the desk again.

"You know, you can run PC software on this. Here, let me show you."

Walden gestured with both hands toward the keyboard and backed away in frustration. Sitting down in the chair, Hank noticed it was warmer than he would have thought. He realized the older man had been sitting here struggling for a while.

"I am not an Apple fan either, but I have to use them. Now, let's see. Oh, there is your problem. Let's reload this program here. Now this is the PC version, and it will run. It will be slower, but it will be what you are used to."

"Thanks, Hank. Oh, and I do know your name. There's not much that isn't known in a town this size. I hear you're a nice man with good intentions. We need good intentions."

"I guess not. Where did you hear that?"

"Well, there's Martha, and, of course, Maggie. She thinks you might be able to help us. She likes you, you know."

The front door opened behind them, and Maggie walked in.

"Why are my ears burning?"

Hank could only grin as he turned back to Walden, but something was stirring inside of him—something he hadn't felt for a long time.

"You know, Mr. Walden—"

"John. Call me John."

"Whoa, you *must* be special, Hank. John here insists on 'Mr. Walden' from most folks." Maggie joined the conversation, still near the door as if to stop anyone from coming in.

"Maggie tells me I can get answers from you, John. And that you are a journalist. I was one, too. I know the brotherhood of the truth."

"I don't know much..."

"John, you tell him now. He needs to know." Maggie's voice was emphatic.

"Damn. I love that woman and I don't love her at the same time. You ever been there, son?" Walden scratched his head and moved back to his computer

"I was there once." Hank looked to Maggie, who returned his glance, but with a smile and a nod. "Let me start. There was this woman walking along the road as I came into town last night. She was all in white. Everything was white, even her hair, and I could... well, I could see right *through* her. Then she just disappeared into the cemetery. Now I would like to know..."

"You met Jenny. Poor, sweet Jenny. And you lived. That's not too bad."

A wave of relief swept over Hank as he grabbed the nearest chair, and realized in that moment that he wasn't crazy.

"Yes, that is what she said her name was. So I wasn't hallucinating?"

"No. Far from it. You both better grab a chair. I am not supposed to talk about any of this, you know. Old man Chapman funds this paper and, well, I am too old and I need the money, so I stay."

The three of them sat down, and Hank noticed that Maggie moved her chair close to him, a gesture that didn't bother him at all. Walden continued. "Jenny is real, Hank. She is real, and you are the only person who has had close contact with her who has lived. Chapman has a son, Richard, who is a bastard, and a total waste of flesh. He is using up the air the rest of us need. But the old man only has his son left; he drove everyone else away, including his wife. She died broke and alone but probably happy since she didn't have to be around those two."

As Walden spoke, his voice was hypnotic. It was as though Hank could see the events in his mind as Walden described them. He barely realized that Maggie reached out to hold his hand, but he did notice.

"Jenny was a beautiful young woman just barely out of high school. Every young man wanted her. But she didn't want to stay here. I remember talking to her in happier times about her dreams and where she wanted her life to go—college and then maybe med school. She studied so hard, she didn't have time for high school romances and, well... hijinks."

Hank thought he had an idea of what was coming, but he wanted to know the end of the story... if there was an end.

"She seemed very gentle, very innocent."

"Did she actually speak to you?" Walden was amazed.

"Yes. She said I was not like them. That I was a good man. No, wait... she didn't actually say that 'good man' thing, but I heard her voice in my mind. Maybe I imagined that."

"No, you didn't." Walden thought for a moment before saying something that might just scare the great hope of the town away. At one time, he had been a journalist—and a good one—so the truth still mattered. "You know you'll be living in her house, don't you?"

Still holding Maggie's hand, Hank leaned back into his chair and looked up at the ceiling.

"No, I didn't know." Hank shot a questioning look at Maggie.

"It wasn't my place, Hank. It wasn't my place to tell you."

"No, it wasn't, Hank," Walden interjected. "Maggie could have been in big trouble if word got out she had given you the story. You see, Chapman needs *me* to spread *his* views. Plus no one else will take the job. He doesn't need anyone else here, and he's been plain about that. I am betting he already knows why you are here, but he won't do a thing about it."

Hank squeezed Maggie's hand, not wanting to let go, but he wasn't through yet with Walden. "So what happened?"

"One night, five drunk teenagers went roaring through town, knowing if they got stopped they would only get a wrist slap and be sent home. They were driving down the road, and Richard, Chapman's son, saw Jenny walking along the road towards home. Richard, also known as Dick—which is an appropriate name for that bastard—was angry at her because she had turned him down for dates, and he was used to always getting what he wanted. According to the others, he stopped the truck, got out and argued with her until she began to cry. But the others clearly heard her say, 'No'! Richard hit her hard, knocking her down. He got back in the tuck, and that should have been the end of it. Instead, he drove down the road a bit, spun around, gunned his truck and ran straight into her. His truck, a gift from daddy, had one of those big push bar grilles on the front, so there was hardly any damage—at least nothing the sheriff deputies could find after it had been cleaned up."

Maggie could see Hank getting angry but tugged on his hand, tilting her head toward Walden. It was only her touch that kept him from exploding in anger.

"The autopsy report, thank God, indicated she was killed instantly. The story goes that Dick and his friends picked her up, took her to the highway and dumped her body in a ditch near the cemetery. With what you said, plus the services and all, that's home now."

Hank couldn't wait any longer. "But what about the rest of the kids in the truck? Didn't they want to talk?"

"Oh, yes, they did, but he threatened them all on the way home. They didn't mind being the friend of the 'big man in town' who could get them anything. At least two of them tried to tell the sheriff's deputy later about what had happened. An investigation was opened, and then... well, it just went away. I hope I didn't scare you away. The town needs you, Hank. We need you."

For moment, Hank wasn't sure what he wanted to do, but he turned to Maggie and saw her watching him intently, waiting for his response. Still holding her hand, he answered, "No. There are a few reasons I want to stay here." This time, Maggie did blush, but she didn't let go of his hand. "And when the big money comes in here, I mean more money than Chapman ever dreamed of, he'll get his share, but he will move to the bottom of the food chain. They won't put up with his shit, and if they have to invest in an election to get a fair and honest sheriff, then that sorry prick will never know what hit him."

"I am glad of that." Walden pulled out an old-fashioned handkerchief and wiped his brow. "That was a close one. You've got guts, son. I am here to help."

"Tell me, John. I know that jerk son of Chapman's is still running around but what about the other kids?"

"This is where the story gets weird, Hank—if it can get any more weird. Two of those kids split off from Dick Chapman. Two didn't. The two who did tried to tell the truth and are still alive. But the other two... well, one of them was found along the highway near the cemetery in bits and pieces. That is still unsolved, but written off as a horrible traffic accident. The other one was found in his bedroom in rigor mortis, with his hands up like he was trying to defend himself. I talked to one of the investigators on that. He told me the reason they did a closed casket was they couldn't get the look of terror off the boy's face."

"Jenny?"

"Maybe..."

It wasn't far to drive Hank back to his car at the town hall, but he rode in silence. Maggie kept looking at him as she drove and finally couldn't wait. "Hank, are you okay with all this? It's real. No one will blame you if you just say you're outta here. Not even me."

"Umm, actually I was thinking about Jenny. How terrible to have your life, your dreams ripped away from you by a spoiled, misbegotten, freak of nature."

"That's a big word there, Hank. I can tell you're trying not to swear, but it's okay around me."

"Okay, an asshole. A piece of shit that is fouling the air we breathe." Hank grinned and reached out for Maggie's free hand. "I think we should sit down with Martha and let her know that it's all good, and then go get some dinner. Is there a good restaurant around here?"

"Yeah," Maggie smiled, too. "My house."

"Why, thank you, ma'am. I was hoping that I, I mean that *kitchen*, was on the menu."

Back at the inn, they talked with Martha, who obviously felt relieved that Hank had heard the full story and still decided to stay.

"Can I fix you two some dinner? I've got a nice roast in the oven, and it looks like the fog will come in early tonight. Nothing like a little comfort food."

"Actually, Martha, I don't get to cook for someone very often, so I thought I would try that tonight." Maggie sipped her fortified coffee with a smug look.

"Oh, I see. I'm being thrown over because a younger, more beautiful woman is in the picture." Martha winked.

"Well, it depends on how late you're up, Martha. I'm sure I'll be back for a chat." Hank wasn't getting uncomfortable, but he also wasn't sure what he was feeling. He did, however, know what he was hoping for.

"Don't count on it, cowboy. And like I said before, for a very smart man, you don't fish well." Maggie stood up. "I need the ladies' room."

Once Maggie had left the kitchen, Martha looked Hank in the eye. "I love that girl. She is like a daughter to me, and I don't know when I've seen her so happy, so confident. She's got her swagger back, Hank."

"It's been a long time, Martha. A very long time. I never thought I could get over the death of my wife and maybe I never will, but Maggie has something... something special."

"Hank, don't you believe your wife would want you to be happy?"

"Yes, but..." Hank hesitated. "I can't shake the feeling that somehow I'm cheating on her. It's been eight years, but..."

"When you got here and had gone to your room for a moment, Maggie told me that she thought you were the most honest and kindest man she had ever met. She had a husband, too, and he died in a car accident. Since then she hasn't even looked at another man. Don't you think that maybe up there in heaven they are working this out to see if you two like each other?"

"Martha, you are a joy." Hank stood and kissed the woman on the forehead.

"Oh my!" Martha flushed red. "Don't tell my husband. He's very jealous, you know!"

"He's got a great woman. He knows that."

Maggie came back to the kitchen. "Martha, you're right. That fog bank is out there. It's going to be chilly tonight. But I've got that hot tub all warmed up..." Martha giggled at Maggie's comment and flushed red again.

"I didn't bring a swimsuit, so..." Hank was getting flustered realizing that he shouldn't have said that, or maybe he should. Heck, it's been so long since he felt this way, he just didn't know.

"You know what, Hank? Not only do you not fish well, but you talk too much. Time to go."

Hank watched Maggie walk out of the room realizing what he was feeling wasn't only desire for her, but something much more. He knew now he had to make this work. Turning back, he said, "I didn't lock my uh, my uh..." as he gestured up the stairs with his thumb.

Martha giggled again. "She hasn't called anyone cowboy since her husband died. Don't worry, I got the room."

"Uh, yeah. Um, okay. Thanks, Martha. Wish me luck."

"You don't need it, son. You don't need it."

Across town and up on a hillside, Randy Cummings was sipping a beer and vaping a little pot on his parents' back porch. He knew the man who could help save the town was here. He knew that he would learn what happened, and he knew if that man left town, he would be one of the reasons.

Randy loved his parents and the town. He had stayed as far away from Dick Chapman as he possibly could. He even went out of his way to avoid him at events. But on the rare occasions when he did see him, Randy could always feel Chapman's eyes boring through him—seething with hatred because he had tried to tell the truth.

As much as he didn't want to do it, Randy had decided to apply to a university up in Oregon and transfer his credits. When he was at school here, he worried about the guilt that he felt. And when he was at home, the sense of foreboding was overwhelming. With the beer and the pot, he had a chance to relax.

The sun was getting ready to set, and from his porch he could see the ocean reflecting the orange glow as the sun began to drift down behind the clouds. The scene was so beautiful, but he had to go. He had to put this chapter of his life behind him. For a few moments since making this decision, his conscience was clear. He would be on the road tomorrow. With the pot taking hold, he closed his eyes and rested his head on the chair cushion. He didn't see the trees moving, and why should he? There was no wind, just a cool summer evening. He was so relaxed he didn't hear the voice—the first time.

"R-a-n-d-y-y..." He moved a little. But the next time he did hear it, as if drifting into his consciousness. "R-a-n d-y-y..." the voice was a like the breeze in the trees, but as he opened his eyes, he saw there was no wind; no breeze of any kind. In fact, the air was deathly still.

Suddenly, the pot and the beer held no comfort. He realized who it was. Panic hit him harder than any comfort drug could. She was here!

"NO....NO!..." He bolted for the sliding glass door on the porch. Forgetting that the screen was closed, he tumbled back onto the deck. Hearing her lilting laughter drawing closer, he tried to clear his vision. Getting up, he forced the bent screen door open and staggered inside, locking the heavy sliding glass behind him and drawing the drapes. The thought that he was dealing with a ghost who could move through anything at any point in time didn't occur to him. He panicked, and all he felt was pure terror.

Stumbling over furniture, knocking over chairs, half crawling then running, he made it to his room and locked the heavy oak door. He had shutters on his windows, the decorative kind but they could block out the outside, and he slammed them shut and locked them. For a brief moment he wished he had a gun—something he had never wanted before. But he knew he could never shoot anything. He hadn't even wanted to be there that night—that awful night.

Covered in sweat even though the evening was cool, he cowered in a corner of the room... waiting. The minutes ticked away with nothing happening. That was the strongest pot he had vaped yet; maybe that was what had caused this. Maybe it was probing the deepest recesses of his mind, finding the guilt he kept trying to hide from.

Ever so carefully, he looked all around his room, and then searched his bathroom. Nothing. It had to be the pot and the beer. He vowed not to mix them again as he thought they preyed on his mind. As quietly as possible, he unbolted his door and peered into the living room. No one was there, and all he saw was the overturned furniture. He would have to get that straightened up fast before his parents came home. Even though they knew he was leaving tomorrow, they had gone out to dinner. That might seem harsh to some, but that is the way this family worked. Sometimes they were supportive, and sometimes not. Maybe he'd see them at breakfast.

With the living room back in order and the drapes open again, but keeping the slider door locked as it was getting dark anyway, he retreated to his room. His bags were packed and already in his car. The only reason he was still here was to have breakfast with his folks as they had promised—a brief concession on their part.

Feeling very tired with the beer and the pot taking hold again, he bolted his bedroom door as he had done every night since the first two guys had, well... died. Briefly sitting down on the corner of his bed, he could see the last fading rays of sunlight over the ocean through his window. The ocean and the sunset were the things he would miss the most. His on-again off-again parents? Yes, they could be loving when they wanted to be, but not so much since that night. That awful night.

Confident this episode had passed, Randy went to the bathroom wanting to splash cool water on his face before he tried to sleep. It was way too early, but the effects of pot and the beer were way too powerful.

The cold water felt good. As he grabbed a towel and looked in the mirror, it wasn't his reflection he saw but a ghostly white face with hair that seemed to be flowing where there was no wind.

She was here.

"Hello, Randy. I have come for you."

In sheer panic, he tried to back out of the bathroom, but the door slammed shut behind him.

"A mirror is like a door for us into your world, Randy. I have come for you."

"Jenny! Please, no! I am sorry. I didn't even get out of the truck that night. I hated what was happening. I didn't help the others. I haven't been able to live with this!"

Jenny began to emerge from the mirror... but only so far.

"Did you try to stop them?"

"I was too scared. I couldn't even speak!"

"Did you try to stop them?"

"No! No! I was a coward!" Randy began sobbing uncontrollably. "I was a coward. Jenny, and ever since in my prayers I have asked for your forgiveness. But I can't live with this anymore. So, just do whatever..."

Jenny's voice was calm, ethereal, unearthly.

"I forgive you, Randy."

"What?" Randy used his hand to wipe his nose and the tears streaming down his face.

Jenny had taken on full form now and was standing before the cowering human.

"I forgive you, but you must go to Henry, the man who has come here to Juniper. You must confess all you saw to him and to Maggie. You didn't always tell the truth, Randy. You lied sometimes because you were afraid. Tell them everything, and my forgiveness of you will be complete. If you do not, you will join me in my home, near the highway."

For the first time Randy felt a sense of redemption. He had a chance to make this right. "Thank you... thank you. How will I find them?"

"They are at Maggie's home. Tell them, Randy... tell them everything and agree to cooperate later. If you do this, I will not visit you again. I see much, Randy. I see that you can have a wonderful life with a family and children. Do you want that?"

Randy's panic was gone. His tears stopped, he felt strangely at peace.

"Yes, very much."

"Then you must go now. Someday you will be able to return, even live here, but not now."

Randy wasn't sure, but he thought he saw a small smile.

"Jenny. Jenny. I wish I had been braver. I wish I could have stopped all of this. I am so very sorry. Thank you for your forgiveness."

"Make it complete now, Randy. You must go now. Do as I have asked and live without guilt."

Randy didn't even panic as Jenny reached out to touch him. As she stroked the side of his face, he felt a great sense of warmth, of happiness—and then she was gone. This time he knew what he saw was real. His guilt was almost gone, but he had a job to do, and he knew the way to Maggie's.

Maggie's cabin wasn't actually a cabin. She had built onto it over the years. There was a large great room with a high-pitched log ceiling. A grand, stone fireplace dominated one side of the room, and that soon held a roaring fire as the cold from the fog moved in. Like Hank's potential new home, Maggie's, too, was situated on a bluff with views of the ocean and a pathway to the beach down below.

To Hank, this was perfection. But then, so was Maggie.

Hank saw the pictures on the expansive mantle of a man and Maggie, and suddenly felt like he was intruding. He knew his biggest problem was he was always feeling too much. But he couldn't turn that off. He didn't want to turn that off.

"I am guessing these are of your husband?"

"Yeah. He was a good guy and did all he could. But honestly, although I loved him very much, he wasn't that bright. But he was a good husband."

"But you are very intelligent. I can tell. And you are still here?"

"I wish I had some smart cliché about 'you can take the girl out of the forest, but you can't take the forest...' bullshit, but I don't." Maggie popped a couple beers, handing one to Hank. "The truth is this town needs me cuz I am not afraid to stand up to old man Chapman. It's also true that I need this town more. Cheers."

As they clinked cans, Hank began wondering if he had found a new way, a new path. He knew he would be able to help Maggie and the town and he wanted to get to work.

"So look, Maggie, I will need to rely on you, Martha and the others. I have ideas to turn this town around, but—"

"Not tonight, cowboy," she smiled. "Tomorrow is soon enough."

One thing Hank knew was when to shut up. So, with a seemingly endless supply of light beer, and hitting the couch in front of a crackling fire after being chased out of the kitchen when he tried to help, he began to feel a sense happiness he hadn't known for years.

Somehow Maggie managed to whip up an epicurean dinner of steak with salad and potatoes while he just watched the flames, wondering if he had found heaven.

"Maggie, that was incredible. Your 'restaurant' is great."

"And now to the hot tub—and we will switch to wine." Hank noticed there was a certain seductive quality to her voice. "If it makes you uncomfortable, Hank, I'll wear a suit."

Hank marveled at the fact she could say that with a straight face. This was quite a woman. But she was in charge. And if he was right, she was doing the seducing... not him.

"If I don't get one, you don't get one."

After they slipped into the hot water, Hank was again impressed that she didn't appear to check out his 'attributes.' This woman was honestly interested in him, not necessarily just a part of him. And she was not shy about her own body, which Hank thought was beautiful. At first she stayed on the other side of the tub pointing out the brilliant nighttime sky with millions of stars that they could easily see because there was no ambient light. But eventually, apparently realizing she had to make the first move, she slowly drifted to sit next to Hank—a move that was not lost on him. While he was reaching for his glass of wine, he pulled the old high school move of 'reaching and encircling.'

His arm was around her, pulling her closer. She didn't seem to mind.

"So, cowboy. You like us? You going to hang around?"

"Yes, Maggie, I am going to hang around, and it's not just because of the town or Chapman—although I would do that, too. The truth is, Maggie, I want to be near you. That's really it. I think that's the right thing to do. If not—"

"Like I said, Hank, you talk too much."

Since it had been a few years, Hank wasn't sure he was doing this right, but Maggie met him halfway for the kiss. He didn't grab or pull or feel. He just savored the moment of kissing someone he knew he was falling in love with, and it was wonderful. Maybe Martha was right. Maybe this came with a blessing.

"Umm. Excuse me. Maggie?"

The kiss abruptly ended with the two naked people staring at a teenager standing next to the hot tub. Immediately, Maggie covered herself as best she could trying to decide if one hand could cover her breasts and the other should drop down.

"Alexa! Turn on the bubbles!"

As the tub began to gurgle and bubble, Maggie felt a little better protected—but not much. Looking up, she saw Randy Cummings, looking terrified.

"Randy? What are you doing here?"

Hank reached back for the towels to help her, but she gestured for him to hold off, as the bubbling water seemed to be doing the job. Even if that wasn't the reason, he could see Maggie sensed something he didn't.

"I am very sorry to be here, but I have to tell you something. Actually, I was *told* to tell you something."

Hank thought he knew what was coming and he was right.

"Who told you to come here, Randy?"

"As crazy as this sounds, I just had a talk with Jenny. She came right into my room. I couldn't keep her out. I tried." Randy started to cry. "I asked her to forgive me. And she did!" Still crying but with a smile of happiness, he continued. "She did... She actually did." Randy turned away realizing he was crying. Hank and Maggie took the opportunity to wrap themselves in towels as they climbed out of the tub.

Maggie had already laid out a couple bathrobes, and they slipped into them.

"Why are you here, Randy? It's okay. It's okay to cry. But try to tell us why you're here?"

"I never touched her, you know... that night. I didn't help them, but I didn't try to stop them, either." Randy was still crying. "I didn't. But she knows."

Ever the journalist and video producer, Hank spoke softly. "You're safe now, Randy. You're here. I have seen Jenny, too. And I've talked to her. So why did you have to come here, now?"

"You're the guy." Randy began to slowly recover. "You're the guy I am supposed to find. I was told that I have to tell you and Maggie what happened, and maybe you can do something."

For the next few minutes, Randy talked about that awful night. He didn't leave out any details because he had promised Jenny to tell the truth.

"That is it, Mr. Wilson, Maggie. I am also willing to testify, to do whatever it takes to see that this is made right. I tried to do that before, but no one would listen."

"All right, Randy. I am sure you can get a good night's sleep now. Let us know how to stay in touch." Hank cinched up his robe, although he wished he was still in the water.

"Mr. Wilson? Do you think you can help Jenny? She was always so sweet, and tonight she was again."

"Randy, you have to keep this a secret, and if you don't, she'll know."

The young man nodded.

"Yes. I think we can. A lot of times it's not what you know, but who you know, and I know some people. We might just turn this county upside down, for the better."

Nodding, he blew his nose and replied, "Thank you." Then he left, promising to text them his contact information.

Maggie, standing next to Hank, wasn't shy as she put her arm around his waist. "So, do you really know *some* people?"

"I know two guys with the Attorney General's Office, and they both owe me favors. Yeah, I think we can get this rolling." Hank looked back to the hot tub. "I guess we have to go back in now, huh?"

"Why would you say that, cowboy?"

Hank had heard 'cowboy' enough to think it should be a good night, and it was. After telling Maggie he hadn't done this for a long time, she had responded, "Neither have I." The next morning they woke up late—well, 9 a.m. *was* late for the both of them, but they needed their rest.

As Maggie finished scrambling eggs and flipping some bacon she asked, "What now Hank? What can we do?"

"Today I begin making calls and calling in favors. But I don't think it will take much convincing. This *is* California after all, and this is a town that needs help. They should jump on this."

After breakfast, he went onto the deck overlooking the ocean and began dialing. There were a lot of messages left, and he explained to Maggie that this is the way government works. But as the afternoon wore on, the calls began to be returned.

"Hank! Hank, how the hell are you? My god, it's been a long time."

"I'm up north in Juniper, getting ready to move here and build the studio and my business. There is, however, a problem with the sheriff and a local big wig. I think a murder has been covered up, and no one in this county will look into it. It's money."

"We've heard a lot about that up there. What's his name... Chapman? But we've got nothing to go on. What have you got?"

"I've got witnesses."

"All right, let's talk..."

The conversation went on for about an hour, with the names of those who had died, the one who was willing to testify, and the one still left besides Chapman and his son. Maggie had come out to sit next to Hank and brought two cups of coffee. Hank smiled and blew her a kiss, but he'd had enough coffee this morning"—and then he tasted it. Briefly coughing, he put the cup down, flashing a big thumbs up. It was clearly Martha's morning, afternoon, and evening recipe.

"Yes, I'll be here." He glanced over at Maggie. She was wearing sunglasses, and had her feet up as she looked out at the ocean, sipping her coffee. This time *he* got a big thumbs up. "I'll get the address to you in a bit, but you've got my number. Thanks."

Hank took another sip as he hung up. "I think this is a little stronger than Martha's."

"You're darn right. I figure you're going to be shooting video all day, and you needed a little something to get you started."

"Wrong, lovely lady." Maggie pulled down her glasses. "*We* are going to be shooting video all day. Come on, you'll be my grip."

"Oh good." Maggie stood up stretching, smiling, and sipping all at the same time. "Something I have experience in, from last night..."

With Maggie leading him to the most scenic spots in the area, they had time to get to know each other even more than during their most intimate moments the night before. And she learned how to handle cameras, tripods, and microphones. At the end of each shoot, Hank would review the footage, showing her what they had accomplished. She also took the video camera a couple of times, and he loved the shots; she's a natural, he thought. For a few hours, the ghostly events that followed him had disappeared. When they were driving from one location to another, he hadn't realized that he reached out to take her hand until she squeezed it. Life was going to be wonderful, after...

Driving back to her 'enhanced' cabin, seeing her watching the trees go by and smiling, he didn't want to break that mood, but he had to ask; he had to ask about the last remaining accomplice who still alive and who wasn't the father or the son.

Still enjoying the moment, she answered quickly but continued to relax. "Alex. Alex Moon. He was a nice kid just trying to fit in. Great family and the only Asians up here. He lives out here along the coast. Like me, his house faces the ocean."

"Do you all know where each other lives? I mean, don't you have some privacy?" For a moment, despite the smile on her face and the lowered sunglasses, Hank wondered if he had gone too far. But she was once again ahead of him. She was his intellectual equal, and that he had missed.

"When we want it. Don't worry about it. I can read your mind. Actually, it's more your expressions and body movements—they tell me your mind. My degree is in behavioral therapy, so I had to read minds. You'll get so you can read my mind soon, too."

Hank suppressed a laugh. "No wonder you know me so well."

She continued watching the trees roll by. "No, it's just that you're different. I had a problem with you at first, but then I realized it's because you have nothing to hide. I tried to read you, but there is nothing to really read but good. That's when I knew, um, I knew, that I..."

"Liked me? I like you, too. I like you a whole lot." Seeing she sank even lower into the seat and her smile increased, he still pressed. "I think we should try to get to this kid or guy. Let him know what's happening?"

"Yes...we should, but not tonight."

"But don't you think..."

"I know them, the Moons. I will call them, and if we have to we'll go over there."

Hank was hoping they didn't have to, but if they had to...

Two miles away, up the coast from Maggie's house, Alex Moon had talked with Randy and knew Randy was leaving town. Alex knew he was alone now. There would be no support from the Chapmans. He didn't know if he believed Randy's story about the ghost. That was too much to wrap his head around, and he knew Randy was very fragile now and had been having even more problems over the past few months.

Sure, there had been weird things going on and he had heard about the new guy and little bits of his story, but Alex had finally worked his way into acceptance of what had happened, as had his family. He knew right from wrong and that he had done wrong by staying silent and taking money from the Chapmans. But still his family had looked a long time for a place to call home, for some kind of acceptance among others, and he thought that this, too, would pass. Plus he kind of liked being the big guy with 'big' friends. It was a nice change.

It was twilight now with the sun settling into the ocean to the west. Alex needed to think.

"Hey, Mom, Dad, I am going out to get some sunset pics."

"Not too long, honey. Your dad's smoking a tri-tip and it's almost ready!"

Alex sniffed the aroma and agreed. This would be a great dinner. His mom and dad had worked for so long to find a place where they were comfortable, and he had tried so hard to fit in, and eventually he did, regardless. No. Life was good here. Except there was this nagging thought in the back of his mind. It was the sense of guilt that he had tried to bury a long time ago—but it wouldn't go away. He had tried to do the right thing, but no one would listen. It wasn't his fault, he reasoned, so if they wanted it buried, so to speak, that was good enough. But still...

Darkness was coming fast. Alex had promised his girlfriend some new pictures of the ocean from where he lived. She would be coming home from college soon, and he intended to propose marriage. Still, he wondered how to do that with this albatross hanging around his neck and the town knowing he was involved. No! This would end here. And he would be happy. Snapping off a few shots and looking at them on his phone, the sun finally dipped below the horizon. Darkness was not a problem, he knew the way back to the lawn lights, the lights that his dad was intending to put all the way to the cliff. These were ordinary solar lights, the kind you could find or order anywhere.

There was a slight ocean breeze as he began the walk back. *The perfect evening*, he thought, *as this time of year the breezes might be a little stronger*. He tried to reassure himself that all was good. Taking a few steps away from the cliff, he stopped. What was that he heard? Was that a voice? He stopped walking to listen again, and it became clearer.

"Alex." The voice was faint but getting stronger. "Alex. I have come for you. It is time now."

"Wait. Who are you?" Alex knew the answer, but he was trying to delay the inevitable. "What? What is happening?"

"Oh, Alex." The voice seemed to swirl around him with the light breeze. "It's Jenny. You remember. The girl you helped dump in a ditch. The reason no one likes to drive past the cemetery at night."

"No! This is not happening!"

"Alex! Alex, we are ready for dinner!" He heard his mother's voice and for once wished she was the shield she had been in his youth, before he had grown up—ever protective.

"I don't believe in you, Jenny, or whatever you are. I don't even know you are you." Alex stood defiant.

"Really? You don't remember you squeezed my breasts and touched me in other ways as you helped throw me in that ditch?"

Alex knew this swirling voice was the real deal now. "I tried to tell them, Jenny! I tried! No one would listen!"

Instinctively, he began to back up, getting ever closer to the cliff's edge. But he didn't know where he was anymore. How could anyone know?

"You're dead, Jenny! You have to be dead! Ghosts can't hurt anyone!"

"Then why are you afraid of me, Alex?" Jenny crept slowly forward as Alex retreated closer and closer to the edge of the cliff. "All I want is for you to do the right thing, Alex. Join Randy and tell them—tell them all what you know."

Alex couldn't take his eyes off of her as she edged ever closer. He didn't know he was running out of room.

"No! I tried to do that, and no one listened. It took me forever to be back with my friends! I am accepted now. You couldn't understand! Please, go away. I will not go through that again."

"Then I have come for you, Alex. You will join the others. I hope you like heat..." Her voice had become a hiss.

As he watched, she transformed into the hideous creature of his nightmares. The woman's face was gone, replaced by a demonic visage with glistening fangs and glowing eyes. Her flowing white hair was now in flames. Hideous claws extended from her flowing white robes and she moved more quickly than before.

"Alex! Alex!" His mother called as his father moved the sizzling tri-tip to a service plate to take inside. "Dinner! Hurry up!" As she looked toward the end of the coast trail, about a football field distance away, she saw a glowing white light with flashes of red.

"Kim?" she asked. "What do you suppose that is?"

He looked up from slicing the trip-tip, annoyed at his son for delaying dinner. Noticing the flashes of light, his aggravation increased. "He's using his phone to take pictures for his girlfriend. The boy doesn't listen to us anymore. Come on, the potatoes are ready, too. Let's eat."

Reluctantly she followed him inside—stopping to look again, she saw that the light was growing more intense

"I don't think that's his cell phone."

"Come on. He can eat his dinner later, whether it's warm or cold. And I'm not going to reheat for him."

Alex's mom shot her husband an angry look, but she followed him in closing the sliding glass door.

"This is your last chance, Alex," the specter hissed as it grew ever closer. "You can make this right. You can save yourself from eternal damnation. You can help me find home."

Alex hadn't broken his gaze. This was every horror film he had ever seen, every piece of special effects he ever reveled over—only this time it was real. It was here, and it was coming for him. But still, on every ghost show he had ever seen, and all the reality shows, they had always said that ghosts can't hurt you. They can frighten you, nudge you, slap you, but they don't have to power to take your life. He decided to make his stand.

"No. I am sorry for what happened. I really am. I was wrong. But I won't go back. You can scare me, you can slap me around, but you can't kill me. This much I know. It won't change things."

"Did you enjoy touching me, touching my dead body, Alex?"

Thinking he had found a way to hold off this thing before him, Alex began to seethe with his own anger and hatred.

"Yes, I did. That part I am not sorry for, and you can't kill me for it!"

"I don't intend to do it, Alex. You will do that for me."

As his left heel hit some crumbling rock, he realized he had nowhere else to go. She laughed and rushed forward as he stumbled backward over the cliff, screaming as he fell to his death more than 100 feet onto the jagged rocks below.

In the house, Alex's mother looked out the window and saw the light was gone. She waited for her son to come home.

Maggie woke up the next morning to her cell phone buzzing. She looked over at Hank, who muttered, "What? Who?" and then dropped back to sleep. For the first time in recent memory she had switched the phone to silent, to let someone else rest. That felt good. Getting up, she walked to the kitchen, not even thinking about being naked since no one could see; plus she was starting to like her body again. Tapping her phone, she saw Martha had called, so she called her back.

"Hey, Martha what's up?" Maggie still sounded groggy, but not for long. "Yeah, I know I'm usually an early riser but we, I mean I, I mean we, needed some sleep." She couldn't help but grin. "Wait, no!... What?"

"I said, lover girl, the last of the boys, except for Randy and the Chapman kid, is dead. They found his body on the rocks below his house. The deputy said he would like to talk to Hank, probably about not making a big deal out of this. Everybody is so worried about the, you know, *the legend*."

"I can tell you right now, Martha, this is no legend—it's real." Maggie bit her lip, for a moment wondering: If they had contacted Alex last night would he have listened? But she knew him, and she was betting, no. "Martha, you know everything that is going on. Did Randy make it out of town this morning?"

"Yeah. They all stopped by for some breakfast. I've never seen a kid so happy to leave Juniper in my life. His folks didn't seem too broken up about it, though. You know, they never wanted him."

"All right. We'll get down to the rocks. I know the way."

"Maggie, are you serious about this whole thing being real?"

Maggie didn't try to comfort her friend. "Yes, it's real. We all knew something was going on, and now it's coming to some kind of conclusion. Don't you worry though. No one else has to worry, either, except for the Chapmans. Hank has friends in high places, and I hope they get here to end all this."

As she hung up, Hank came in. He was naked, too, but he didn't care, and seeing Maggie, he had thoughts about the morning agenda.

"What's up?"

As Maggie fired up the coffee maker, she answered, "Baby, we have to go to a beach called 'The Rocks.' They found Alex Moon there this morning— dead."

"Damn!" Hank took his coffee...

"Howdy, folks. Deputy Tomlinson. You didn't have to come down here. I don't want this to leave a negative impression, but as long as you are already here..." He stepped in the way to block the view of the broken body. "I understand you've been asking questions about the local legend? I was hoping you could tell me what you have learned. I wasn't here when it all happened."

"Deputy, you don't have to shield the body from me. I was a reporter for 30 years till I got out. I covered a lot of homicides. The cops used to call me 'Ice' and let me in. Sometimes I would see things they didn't see."

"Oh, well, I guess there is no harm... just don't get in the way of the, you know, the coroner. And don't hold this against us. I hope this whole legend thing is over since I live here now, too. We're hoping to really see some good things as we go forward"

"Deputy Tomlinson—it's not over." Ignoring the deputy's stunned expression, Hank walked over toward the body, being careful to not step on anything that looked out of the ordinary. He gestured for Maggie to wait, but she would have none of that. Where he went, she was going.

"Um, Doc Murphy? This is Mr. Wilson, the man who is going to help us." Tomlinson tried to catch up.

"Hello, Hank. I was at your presentation, and I looked into your background. Impressive."

Staring up at the cliff, all of Hank's reporter instincts kicked in. "Thank you, Doc. Deputy Tomlinson, have you looked at the ground up there yet?"

"Well, no. Forensics has been called, but since this looks like an accident, they usually take their time."

"Doc, what have you got?"

"There are multiple fractures. Immediate cause of death seems to be concussive brain failure from the fall."

"How do you account for his face— his expression?" Hank, who was used to seeing trauma, didn't turn away, but Maggie did.

"I would think he was terrified enough that his face froze like that when he fell."

"Did you see anything else?"

The doctor was beginning to rethink his initial evaluation. "Well, there is some strange residue on his shirt. I've never seen anything like it. I took a sample; a couple of samples, actually."

"If you get an answer other than 'we can't explain it' I would love to know. I think it's ectoplasmic in nature. Deputy, I would protect that ground up there. I think you will see that the grass or whatever is burned for a wide radius around the fall point."

"Ectoplasmic?"

"Yeah, Doc...ghosts. I know it sounds weird, and if it's there, it came from him for making contact with another entity. Anyway, will you let me know? I might be able to help."

Doc Murphy looked stunned.

"I'll bet you have seen it before. Will you let me know?"

The doc moved closer so only he, Hank and Maggie could hear. "You've seen and talked with her? Is that true?"

"Yes." Maggie grabbed Hank's hand, a gesture not lost on Murphy.

"I see. OK, then... it will be unofficial, but I will let you know."

"Yes, thank you. And it's time to stop this."

Still holding Maggie's hand, she and Hank turned and walked back toward the trail leading up the cliff.

"So you're an expert on the paranormal, too?" Maggie grinned.

"Back when I was a TV reporter, I did a series of ghost stories for my station. There was a lot I couldn't explain. I worked with a paranormal psychologist back then. He had other degrees, too, but he... well, I couldn't find ways to debunk him. I learned a lot."

Taking a moment to digest more information on a man she was already in love with, she finally asked, "What happens now?"

"We've got to find a way to get to Chapman and his son. She'll go for them next."

"But why the old man?" Maggie didn't have a problem keeping up with this determined man—in fact she moved ahead of him at times. "He wasn't even there."

"No, but he brought that bastard kid into the world, covered up for him, and has held the town hostage. I am told Jenny loved it here." Hank stopped to look Maggie in the eyes. "Sweetheart, Jenny is looking for two things. First, she wants justice. You know that she didn't hurt me or Randy—and she had cause to go after Randy, but he was genuinely sorry. And second, she wants a way home."

"Home?"

"A way to the afterlife; a way to not be in prison here on Earth."

Maggie took a few minutes to digest what he had said, and he waited for her response. He got it. "All right. But, baby, does this mean we'll be chasing ghosts all over the place? Not that I mind that, you know. I just need to know what to pack."

Hank laughed, which is the response she wanted, and then gave her a deep, long kiss. "No, new love of my life—and the last one—we won't do that."

The two, still holding hands, continued up the trail.

Chapman was in his study talking with his son when his "butler" entered. Cody Smith didn't actually consider himself to be a butler, but since he was older and Chapman had successfully cheated him out of his small farm, he had nowhere else to turn.

He had swallowed his pride in order to provide for his family since there was nothing left to do.

For the past few years, Cody had endured the insults and the gloating face of the man he hated. He had thought about killing him; Chapman deserved it. Many people in Juniper had the same thought. But that wasn't Cody's way. Someday, this old devil and his idiot son would get their just rewards. Smith absolutely believed in Karma.

"Sir, there is a Mr. Wilson and Maggie—I think you know her—to see you."

"Didn't you tell them I was busy? Get them out of here!"

"This is *the* Mr. Wilson, sir. The one who is going to make millions for you. He says it's very urgent."

The word money was like *ca-ching* to Chapman. It was the only thing that truly had ever mattered to the grizzled old man. "They could have asked for an appointment! All right, let them..."

Hank didn't wait for an introduction as he and Maggie came through the door. Smith didn't try to stop them and secretly admired their determination.

"Who the hell do you think you are, bursting into my office? You have no right..."

Hank didn't back down. "We are here to save your life, Chapman. You and that sorry excuse for a human next to you."

Chapman sneered. "Well, Maggie... I see you have gone from the town spinster to the town slut."

That was enough for Hank. He lunged for Chapman as Dick backed away from his father, obviously not willing to defend him. *Like father, like son,* Hank thought as Maggie grabbed his arm.

"That is not the way, baby. We're here to warn them." Maggie then turned to the shriveled, leering old man behind the desk. "Chapman, your time here is nearly done. This man, Hank, is the only man who can bring you money and keep you in your horrible, miserable skin long enough to count it. Now, either you listen to him, or we are out of here and you will be dead shortly after sundown."

The word 'dead' caught Chapman's attention. "That's a threat! You heard them, Smith! That was a threat!"

Removing his hated uniform coat, Smith defiantly turned to his taskmaster. "Chapman, I didn't hear a thing. And either you listen to him or you *are* dead."

Chapman coughed, leaving drivel on his chin. "You're fired!"

Smith felt confident for the first time in years. "No, actually, I quit. My family is okay now. I will be fine." He walked out of the room.

For the first time, Chapman appeared to be lost. The last person he could belittle and threaten was gone. He was alone now, and he knew that no one in town would come to work for him and endure his abuse.

As he watched Smith walk away, Hank stepped in the way.

"You've got bigger problems, Chapman. I don't know why I am doing this, but you need to get out of town now. And whatever you do, wherever you go—don't look in any mirrors."

"Wha—? What are you talking about?"

Hank kept moving to stay in front the old man. "She is coming, Chapman. She will be here soon. She wants you and that kid over there. Your son is the murderer. He killed Jenny."

Chapman began to recover from his shock at being left alone.

"If you're talking about that bitch along the road, that was bought and paid for long ago."

During the confrontation, no one had noticed the clouds gathering outside the mansion. But when the first crack of thunder sounded close by, they realized something was happening.

Maggie stepped forward next to Hank. "She's here now, Chapman. And she is coming for you."

"Oh, it's just a summertime storm. Nothing more!"

Seeing the younger Chapman cowering in the corner, trying to stay out of the light, Hank added, "She's right, Chapman. Jenny is coming for you and that punk over there. One has been saved because he confessed and asked for her forgiveness. Three are dead. You two are next."

"Both? Why both? *He* did it. I have tried to help him, but he won't change. *He can pay the price.*"

Hank shook his head. "We tried, you angry old piece of nothing. But it's not about you and this shithole of a life you have created. It's about Jenny. She needs to be free. She needs to go home. She needs peace."

"That slut was just like Maggie! No woman has ever been worth anything!" Chapman was enraged to the point that Hank stepped in front of Maggie, but she stepped around him and stood next to him. Chapman continued to yell. "I am the only one!" He staggered for a moment, and then tried again to yell, "I am the only—" His face blanched white and, clutching his chest, he stumbled a few steps and then dropped in a heap onto the floor.

Maggie rushed to his side taking his pulse. "I think he's had a heart attack." She began to do CPR when Dick's giggling voice interrupted.

"Is he dead? I said, *is he dead?* Well, that's it then. Don't bother. That's it then, right? I'm free."

Stunned at the son's indifference—even joy—at his own father's death, Maggie couldn't continue. What kind of animal was she looking at? What kind of animal was she trying to save?

"This is your father, Richard." Maggie's voice was one of amazement at what she was seeing.

"Oh, he never loved me that much anyway. He didn't love anyone that much. He couldn't. He only loved money." The younger Chapman seemed to almost dance across the room, speaking in a voice that didn't sound... sane. "It's all mine now. All of it! Oh, I'll be better than he was. I want *more* money than he did, and I know how to get it." He stopped for a moment, unsure. "It is over, right?"

Hank had never felt so disgusted in his life. Still, he had come here to end Jenny's misery.

"It is over if you admit to this murder and clear the record. If you don't, you will never be free. It's time to set Jenny free, Richard. It's time to grow up."

Chapman seemed to be sinking even further into delusion. "Of course. I will build her a nice monument, and the town will love her again. I am *not* going to admit to her murder. After all, she did step in front of the truck. But I will show the town that I cherish her and her memory." He walked to the liquor cabinet and poured himself a glass of brandy. "This was his favorite, you know. He would never let me try it. He would just drink it in front of me and laugh." He sipped and then turned to his dead father. "Well, now who's laughing, you ass! I have it all! All of it!" He began to hum while looking around the room, realizing all that he now owned.

"Hank," Maggie whispered. "We need to go."

"But—"

Maggie grabbed his arm and gripped hard. "This is a thing I am sensing now. We need to go, now."

Seeing the fear in her face and watching the surviving Chapman sink further into madness, Hank nodded, and they headed for the front door. As they got into Maggie's truck, Hank saw the garage door was open and one vehicle was missing. Smith had left, and that was a relief.

Maggie turned the key, but the engine wouldn't start. She tried again. Hank touched her arm and pointed out the window. A bright white luminous cloud was rapidly approaching them. Hank, knowing what it was, got out of the truck to meet it, with Maggie close behind.

The light stopped just a few feet from them, pulsating with red and blue bursts of mist.

"Jenny? Jenny?" Hank's voice was calm, as if he were greeting a friend. "Jenny, the old man is dead."

"I know." Jenny's voice was soft and seemed to be all around them, everywhere. "But there is one more."

"Jenny, may we see you, please?"

"All right, Henry."

Watching as the luminous light and mist began to coalesce, Maggie asked, "Henry?"

Hank quickly and quietly answered. "My full name is Henry Wadsworth Wilson. She likes Henry, and for the privilege of talking with her, I am not complaining."

The mist slowly drew into human form, and Maggie had to catch her breath. This *was* real. There *are* ghosts, and they are not all terrible. As Maggie watched, Jenny took form with her flowing hair and white robes, her smiling kind face, even though it was ghastly white, it was somehow warm. She fought the urge to step back as Jenny turned to look at her with pitch black eyes.

"Hello, Maggie." Jenny's voice was soothing, but still, even though Maggie could see Jenny's lips move, her voice seemed to be everywhere around them. "Yes, it's me... Jenny." Maggie relaxed, regretting even a moment of fear. "I am so glad you are in love again," Jenny continued, smiling. "Henry is a very good man, and I know he loves you, too."

Maggie almost never blushed, but she did now.

"It's true, Jenny." Hank smiled. "I believe we are in love, and I will do all I can do to make her happy." Hank paused for a moment, trying to phrase a request—but Jenny already knew his thoughts.

"Henry, there is one left, and you want me to wait. Why?"

"Jenny, I think you already know, my friend, but I will say it out loud. The old man is dead. That part of the evil is dead. His son, the one who hurt you so badly, is insane, and he will be judged as such. I have help on the way. Soon this evil will end."

"Did you just call me your friend?" Jenny smiled again, the lifeless eyes locked with Hank's eyes.

"Yes. I am so sorry that I couldn't help you earlier, but Jenny, you can go home now. You are free. I promise you—I, we, will take care of the rest here. Jenny, your family is waiting for you. You have a good soul, and that soul needs to be free now. Will you do this for me, for us?"

"Henry, I believe you, my friend." Bluish mist surrounded the ghostly figure. "You say I can go home now?"

"Do you see the light in the trees, Jenny?" Tears began to stream down Hank's cheeks. "That is your door, Jenny." He cleared his throat and then began again. "That is your way. Time to find those who love you."

"Very well, Henry, and thank you. Maggie, your children will be just as kind and loving as you both are."

Maggie touched her stomach. "Children?"

"Yes. And you have already started."

Hank and Maggie looked at each other, dumbfounded.

"Goodbye my friends, I... I love you both..."

As her form dimmed and seemed to float toward the light in the trees, they heard one more "Thank you..." Then the light glowed brilliantly for just a moment, and was gone.

Except for the faint maniacal laughter from the mansion, all was quiet for a moment. Then Hank turned to Maggie and held both her hands.

"I was going to ask you this anyway, but would you marry me?"

"Wait. What?"

Hank dropped to one knee. "Will you marry me?"

"What took you so long to ask? Yes!"

In the mansion, the last remaining Chapman reveled in his newfound wealth and in his hatred of his father and everyone else. He had made promises, yes—but would he carry those out? He burped, slugging down some more of his late father's favorite brandy. *If I have to*, he thought, *but only so far. Life is going to be one party after another. I am the king now*, or so he thought.

Hank and Maggie headed down the hillside, knowing they had actually made a difference. And not just for Jenny, but also for their future together.

Dick Chapman decided he wanted a fire in the massive stone fireplace in his father's office, the one he was never invited to sit next to. Standing up and pouring another round of brandy, he weaved side to side, stumbling—wondering where the firewood was. Oh yes, he remembered, the old fool had converted it to gas, saying it was safer. *Well*, he thought, *I'll change that. This will be a place of... of debauchery and pleasure. And the money will roll in.*

Still giggling, he looked for the spigot and, finding it, he turned it up full. Smelling gas, he looked around for the thing—the thing that would light this. Smelling the gas slowed him down. The brandy didn't help either. He could barely walk, and he forgot to shut the gas off and open the windows.

Oh, there it was. He spied the ignitor near the fireplace. Not paying any attention to what he smelled—nothing was going to stop him. He tried to focus on the ignitor button. There it was. As he held it toward the fake logs, he thought he heard the hideous laughter of his dead father. It seemed to be everywhere. He stopped and turned to see his father's body near the desk, and he smiled. *He never loved me, and I never loved him*, he thought and that brought an even greater smile. His head was beginning to spin. Time to light the fireplace and sleep in the old bastard's office. As he turned, he leaned into the fireplace and clicked the ignitor button.

The resulting explosion ripped through the entire ground floor, knocking down old walls and weakening the entire mansion. Richard felt the horrible pain as he realized his entire body was burning. He looked at the fireplace, only to see his father's laughing face. That hideous laughter was the last thing he heard as he screamed in agony and the house collapsed around him in roaring flames.

The explosion was loud enough to stop Hank and Maggie just as they were exiting the road from the mansion. Getting out of the truck, they saw a towering ball of flame and watched as the old house—all 24 rooms—collapsed on itself.

Hearing distant sirens, Maggie grabbed Hank's hand. "Jenny?"

"No. She didn't have to. She went home. It was them—they made that happen. That kind of evil feeds on itself." They had pulled off to the side of the road, and watched as trucks from the volunteer fire department went roaring by.

"Lady In the Lights" is ©2021 by Bill Brown. It previously appeared in

The ACES Anthology

"A Walk in the Twilight," a collection of short stories published by the author. Bill Brown is an Emmy Award-winning retired anchorman who lives in Northern Nevada. At the time of this printing, he had 17 books in print and was working on his 18th. "Blood Mountain," his first novel, is a story based on fact and legend that he first wrote 40 years ago. "The Alien" is also based on an actual incident but asks the question, "What if?" His other novels include, "The Beasts," "Gabriel's Horn," "The Ghost Within," "It Waits," "A Walk In The Twilight," "The Return," and "Lightning." All the novels begin with an actual occurrence and are supernatural thrillers with proven scientific twists.

The ACES Anthology

Paul Clayton

Flysense

After I tied the radio to my rucksack and pulled it on, I realized that just carrying all my equipment was going to be a challenge. I walked up to the Command Post bunker with the other new guy, Glock, short for McLaughlin. Our squad leader, Papa, and his assistant, Ron, sat leaning against the bunker, studying a map sheathed in acetate. Ron was one of the two black guys in the squad. Papa had been preparing him to take over the squad after Papa rotated back stateside.

Glock and I took off our rucks and sat down. Ted, the company clerk, came out of the bunker with B-O-B, another new guy like Glock and me. He was a rebel from down south somewhere, North Carolina, I think. He'd come up on the same chopper as me. The guy could talk your ears off.

B-O-B was chewing gum nonchalantly. His rucksack was stuffed and bulging, and he had his M16 slung over his shoulder, barrel down. He was obviously going with us.

Ted nodded to us and said to Papa, "This is one of the new men. His name's B-O-B. He'll be your gunner on the patrol."

Papa reached up to shake B-O-B's hand. Ron ignored him, looking instead at the map. Ron turned to Papa, frown lines etched deep into his forehead and said, "They're giving us three 'cruits for a six-man patrol? You think that's right?"

Ted blinked thoughtfully but said nothing. Papa's face reddened. "Look Ron, you're not squad leader yet, okay? Not until I go home. And they don't pay us to think either. You better get used to that. This is the darn infantry not the Pentagon."

"That's right, Ron," said Ted, "and B-O-B's already served a tour with the 1st Air Cav down in Cu Chi. He ain't no 'cruit."

Ron's voice rose in pitch. "I don't give a shit, Ted. That don't make him no expert in this AO! Shit!" Ron pronounced it, 'shee-it.' He turned and looked off into the distance in frustration.

B-O-B casually daubed the sweat from his face with his olive-drab handkerchief.

"Look, Ron," said Papa, a hurt look in his big, brown cow eyes as he tried to take control of the situation, "just take it easy, okay? Let's not get all bent out of shape over this."

Ron smiled thinly in exasperation. "Hey, it's your patrol."

Ted patiently watched the two of them as he waited for things to settle down. After a moment, Ron went back to studying the map. He said nothing, and with his dark sunglasses on, there was no telling what he was thinking. The other black guy in our squad, Mike, approached. He'd been in-country about six months. He took off his steel helmet and smiled at everybody, having missed the angry exchange of a moment before.

Ted sighed dramatically and shook his head. "Okay then. I guess you're all ready to go." His face took on a stern cast. "Be careful fellas."

Ron walked point as we descended the hill on the main trail. The guys talked and joked till we got about a hundred yards down the mountain. Under the tall trees and vines that blotted out the sun and sky completely, it was awfully hot and humid, like being in a sauna, and everyone grew as quiet as the jungle.

On the valley floor, the vegetation grew even thicker, and the trail became a barely discernable thin passage. Our rucksacks caught on the vines and bushes that crowded together fighting for the anemic light.

After a while, Mike took the point and Ron's course took us off the trail. We now had to almost tunnel through a six- or seven-foot-high tangled mass of bamboo and elephant grass. It was rough going, and both B-O-B and Glock wondered aloud a couple of times if maybe we had somehow gotten off course. Ron said nothing, and Papa didn't get into it either, evidently not wanting to take sides. Mike angrily threw himself up against the tall grass, mashing it down with all his weight, as if sacrificing himself to make up for any mistake Ron might have made. The heat was oven-like, and every now and then we'd knock down some bullhead ants nesting in the trees overhead. They'd get on our faces and down the backs of our shirts and bite stingingly like bees.

The going got rougher and slower, and I thought we were making way too much noise, but nobody else seemed to care. After an hour or so of fighting the brush, just getting out of it seemed to have become more important than how much noise we made. I relieved Mike on point as the "masher-downer," and after twenty minutes of that I was so exhausted I could hardly stand. Finally, we burst out onto a trail.

Ron knelt to look at his map. Mike and I crouched low on the ground, exhausted. We each broke out one of our canteens. I was carrying five of them, and I drank half of one in a long swallow.

B-O-B crept up behind Ron to look over his shoulder at the map. "You see, Ron," he said, pointing at the wavy lines of elevation, like thumbprint smudges on the map, "these here ridges all have trails. We could've taken this one around to here, picked this one up, and been here a half hour ago."

Ron turned to him wearily, his face beaded with sweat like a cold bottle of Coke taken from the refrigerator on a hot, humid day. "We're here, ain't we?"

B-O-B pulled out his handkerchief and daubed it quickly over his face. "Well, suit yourself. I was just trying to help, that's all." He moved away and crouched down.

We moved out again, B-O-B on point, then Papa, Ron, then Glock, me and Mike, bringing up the rear. We hiked along the trail without incident for another hour or so, and Ron's course again took us off the trail and through some really thick stuff. We were bulling our way through that when Glock accidentally bumped into Ron.

Ron jumped visibly and turned to him. "What the fuck's with you?" he said in a loud hiss. Glock was a big guy, a boxer, and by the look on his face I thought they'd fight right then and there. Papa glared at the two of them, his finger to his lips, and switched their positions. We began humping again at a very quick pace.

I was really pissed. We all were. We had to be at our night location by five o'clock, and now we were really moving down the trail. With the weight of the radio and everything, I was having a hard time keeping up. And with all the noise we were making, I didn't think it was safe either. By the time we finally slowed down, my clothes were soaked and sticking to me, and sweat was stinging my eyes. Suddenly, Ron stopped, and I staggered and bumped into him. He turned his sweaty face to mine and put his finger to his lips. I marveled at how bug-like his dark, wrap-around sunglasses made him look, like he was right out of the movie, The Fly. I tried to see what Papa and the others were up to, but they were out of sight around a bend in the trail about forty or fifty feet away. Maybe they'd discovered we were going in the wrong direction again. It wouldn't have surprised me.

Ron and Mike and I stared out into the brush. It was very quiet. Even though it was Papa's last patrol, and everybody wanted him to get home safe and sound, I wished something would happen. Nothing dangerous, of course, but something, like maybe finding a deserted tunnel complex. Mike had told me about a patrol he was on that had stumbled on one of them. Or, better yet, I wished we'd just set up here for the night so I could do a little reading before it got too dark.

A single shot rang out and we hit the ground, pointing our weapons out. We waited, watching intently. Nothing happened. Everything grew quiet again, and then Glock came crashing through the bushes. He held a hurried, whispered conference with Ron.

My God, I thought, Glock makes as much noise as a herd of drunken elephants and then he whispers in Ron's ear, so the enemy won't hear him?

Ron turned and whispered to me and Mike to watch the rear while he went forward. We sat and watched, but nothing further happened. Maybe B-O-B's or Papa's weapon had gone off accidentally. That sort of thing happened.

The rucksack dug into my shoulders. I leaned back, using it as a backrest. I took a swig of water and felt better. The patrol seemed like it would go on forever, and my load was beginning to kick my ass. But I'd rather my goddamned heart burst than ask somebody to help me. Why the hell did they have to go so fast? Shit!

A fly buzzed my face, made a quick turn, and landed on the hand that held the canteen balanced on my thigh. I watched it suck at a drop of sweat through its straw-like snout, and I thought about slapping it, but luckily for it I was way too tired.

Any other time and I would've smashed it immediately. It sucked that sweat drop to half of what it had been, and I was just getting ready to swat it when it took off. I almost had to laugh as I realized that even flies had karma. Karma was what the Buddhists called luck. This fly evidently had good karma. I heard a noise and Ron came down the trail. He waved us to follow him.

In a little clearing, B-O-B and Glock were talking to Ron and Papa in excited whispers. B-O-B's helmet was off, and his almost-bald head shone with sweat. "It was damn near the easiest shot I've ever made, Ron," he said, pausing to daub his sweaty face.

I looked around to see what they were talking about and saw some guy lying on the ground. B-O-B returned his handkerchief to his pocket and continued, "I just waited till he was about a hundred feet away and let him have it, just squeezed a round off."

Ron's face was expressionless, his eyes hidden behind his black sunglasses. I swear he must've been born wearing sunglasses.

Papa nervously rubbed his dark, smudgy beard stubble and looked over at Glock, who was now on his knees beside the enemy guy, going through his pockets.

"He didn't try and run?" Papa asked B-O-B.

"Hell no. Why would he run? With me behind all this brush here, there was no way in hell he could see me."

I moved away from them to see the dead guy. I looked down at him. His skin looked clean, almost scrubbed, and his fine, black, hair was cut nicely, not long and matted with dirt like mine. His fatigues were clean too. Christ, he didn't look dead, but then again, I'd never seen anybody who'd just died. The only dead people I'd ever seen had been to the undertaker and looked horrible, like wax figures. This guy looked like he was asleep and might wake up any second.

"Are you sure he's dead?" I said.

Ron cursed with an exasperated hiss, and Papa gave me a sad, understanding look.

B-O-B came over and knelt beside Glock. "Look at the goddamned entry hole if you don't believe it, Carl." He ripped the dead boy's shirt open up to his armpits, popping the buttons off and exposing his belly and chest. Then he turned him a bit and pulled the shirt back over his arms, tossing it aside. I didn't think it was right to treat him that roughly.

"See," said B-O-B as he pointed. Right below the rib cage there was a small, pink hole, like a birthmark.

"That's the entry hole," said B-O-B. He looked at Glock. "Let's turn him over. I want to see if the bullet exited."

They rolled him over like a sack of potatoes. There was nothing, no mark on his back. B-O-B said the bullet was still inside him. The guy's belly was distended now, as if he were pregnant. B-O-B said it was because of the internal bleeding the round had caused when it ricocheted off his ribs, whipping his insides to jelly. Then I noticed the thin red line his blood made as it oozed from his wound like a stream of gleaming nail polish, coursing down his tan belly and onto the brown earth. I felt bad about the whole thing, like there'd be hell to pay. It reminded me of the time, about five years earlier, when my cousin Bobby and I had been over at my friend Lou's house. Bobby and I were boxing around, and I backed up into a table and knocked a lamp onto the floor, breaking it. It was Lou's mother's favorite lamp, an irreplaceable antique. I felt terrible about it because I knew that no matter what I did, I could never make amends. I had the exact same feeling now, that panicky feeling of never being able to make something right again, no matter what you did. I looked at the others and wondered if they felt it too.

B-O-B moved away and then came back with an AK-47 rifle. He lovingly ran his hand up and down the wooden stock. "This here's one of the best fightin' rifles made, Carl," he said to me.

Glock looked at it. "Let me see it, will you?"

B-O-B handed it to Glock, and he brought it to his cheek smartly, sighting along the barrel. "Pretty nice," he said, as he handed it back.

"Sure it is," said B-O-B. "It's a damn sight better'n that piece of shit M16. The AK ain't got no plastic in it. It's all wood and steel, got a good weight and balance, and it don't hardly ever jam." He smiled suddenly and turned to Ron and the others. "I'm sending it home to my daddy to shoot squirrels with."

Papa tried to smile but couldn't. Ron's face was inscrutable.

B-O-B hefted the AK over his head triumphantly and smiled at me. Just meeting his look was all the encouragement he needed, and he continued bragging.

"You should'a seen it, Carl. He was just coming down the trail with his eyes on the ground, his rifle slung over his shoulder, like he was on leave in Hanoi or something!"

I listened to him for a while, and then he went over to the dead soldier's ruck and started going through it.

Papa watched him and said, "I think he's NVA regular forces; they usually carry nice equipment like that."

"Is that right?" said Ron.

B-O-B looked up. "He's right, Ron. He's NVA all right. He was a medic too. Just look at this equipment. It's all made in Czechoslovakia." B-O-B laid them down in a neat row—shiny, stainless-steel tools, scalpels, scissors, and clamps. They looked odd against the dust of the trail. There were vials of pills, letters, and papers with official-looking stamps.

Papa waved me over so he could use the radio in my ruck. He called in to the Command Post and told them what had happened. I couldn't hear what they said to him, and after a moment, he put the handset back. He turned to the others. "Pack the tools and letters up and let's get moving. He may've been lost, but I doubt it. Chances are his unit is close by and that's why he was so careless."

The other guys quickly put on their rucks. The guy looked so cold lying there in the shade I picked up his shirt and laid it over him. As I put on my ruck, B-O-B and Glock dragged him by his arms and legs into some bushes off to the side of the trail, hiding him.

As we started down the trail, I kept looking back, half expecting him to get up and try and run away.

We sat in a circle on the ground in the dying light, playing cards. After a half hour or so, I quit the game and tried to read. But I had to put the book down. There was still enough light, but I kept thinking about the NVA medic. There had been a lot of radio traffic earlier, with different people from the Command Post calling every so often to ask about the medic and what we'd found in his ruck. They told Papa that there was a battalion of NVA in the area, and to be careful. Just before I fell asleep, I imagined the medic suddenly sitting up and yawning. He got to his feet and put on his shirt. His face grew worried, and he quickly walked off.

The hump back the next day seemed to be all uphill. Carrying the radio was killing me. I wondered if we'd stop and look at the medic. I wasn't so sure he'd be there. When we came to the place where they'd hidden him, a noisy cloud of flies swarmed us. We waved them away as we passed, nobody saying anything. That feeling of payback came over me again. I still couldn't believe it. The others rushed on as if the jungle would close in and swallow us up. I had to run to keep up with them or they would've left me behind.

The ACES Anthology

Jay Crowley

The Lady of the Lake

The Lady of the Lake,
Queen Noe Hoe
Mistress of the Fairies and the Mists.
Coming forth to meet me.
She is here, reaching out to save the Lake
as she looks into men's hearts.
I cry for the Lake and all that is
Fantasy.
Everyone needs to believe.

She walks to the base of Cave Rock every day, just her and her dog. She sits on the bench and looks across the lake. The weather does not deter her from visiting the lake every day, even when it is snowing. She brushes the snow off the bench and sits holding an umbrella. She lays a blanket and sets up an umbrella for her dog. The love for her dog shows. She spends hours sitting there, not reading, just looking out across the lake. Sometimes a tear rolls down her cheek.

The park rangers do not know her name, where she came from, or how she got there. Worst yet, they never ask. The dog lies at her feet. Seeing the dog does not bark at passersby, the rangers do not care who she is. Visitors to the lake never even notice the old Indian woman and her old dog. They are like two statues sitting on the bench.

Mary has watched her for a long time. Last winter, she was going to talk to her, but she was too shy. Mary is afraid of humans.

Today was a sunny fall afternoon, as the woman sat on the bench with her dog by her feet. Mary decides that today is the day she will talk to her. She flies over to the left side of the woman to say hi. (Oh, by the way, Mary is a young fairy, by fairy standards: She is only sixty years old.) Mary lands on the back of the bench, not wanting to scare the woman.

Quietly, she whispers, "Hi, I am Mary. What is your name?"

The woman turns and stares at the fairy with wide eyes. She stutters, "Wwwhy, hello."

Mary is ecstatic.

The woman replies, "Humans call me Georgia. My real name is Queen Noe Hoe of the Washoe tribe, though. I have never talked to a fairy before... you are a fairy, right??"

"You can see me?" Mary asks excitedly. "Yes, I am. What are you?"

The old woman laughs. "Well, I am the Lady of the Lake; see my face in the rock up there?"

"I have heard stories about you," Mary replies in awe. "Are they true?"

"Maybe they are." A tear flows down the old woman's face. "I am so upset with how this world is treating my lake. I sit here every day, hoping things will get better."

"Would you tell me your real story?" Mary asks.

"Well, Mary, I will tell you the myth, and you decide if it is real or not," the old woman says.

"My story or legend goes like this: I am a descendant of Queen Noe Hoe. She was the key reason the mountain people were healthy and prosperous. Mainly, she represented the strength and presence of the Washoe tribe. Seeing I am a direct descendant of Tahoe's first woman, my namesake, Queen Noe Hoe, my task now is to take care of the lake. But I digress...

"Queen Noe Hoe was as steely (at times) as she was striking in her effervescent beauty. She was also something of a geological genius with a profound knowledge of how nature's forces worked.

"There had always been rumors that she spent time alone in the Sierra Nevada mountain range and had inherited ancient secrets from Pangaea, the supercontinent. Pangaea is derived from the Ancient Greek pan (πᾶν, "all, entire, whole") and Gaia (Γαῖα, "Mother Earth, land"). Queen Noe Hoe loved and cherished Mother Earth, as did the Washoe tribe.

"There was little peace among the different tribes in the area, so Queen Noe Hoe requested a summit meeting of the various tribes. The Chiefs with No Name were initially skeptical about the meeting. Finally, they decided to attend after an earthquake rumbled through the river's fault line and shook their community for an hour. They knew of Queen Noe Hoe's reputed relationship with nature.

"Queen Noe Hoe is known as the Lady of Lake Tahoe, which is 6,200 feet—a half-mile higher than their Lake with No Name, which is 3,700 feet in elevation. Supposedly, the Truckee River and a fabled fault beneath the river connect the two massive lakes.

"The summit meeting was called. The No Name people traveled for two long days to arrive at Emerald Bay, a portion of

Lake Tahoe. This was the ceremonial site for all the mountain people's important events. The No Name Chiefs came in their finest regalia, accompanied by a full contingent of warriors. They passed through the entrance to Emerald Bay in large canoes painted with bright colors symbolic of the chief's rank and status.

"To their surprise, the No Name Chiefs and their tribe members were greeted with elaborate hospitality and honors as though they had won a war, which they had not. In fact, they were poor in relation to the mountain people. Their constant war efforts against the mountain people, while annoying, had not interrupted the great fishing on Tahoe or the prosperity of the tribe.

"That evening, on a small knoll near the bay's entrance, Queen Noe Hoe greeted the No Names tribe members graciously at the start of a sumptuous dinner. Young mountain tribe women served fish, deer, and wine. The No Names tribes had seldom experienced wine, living as they did in the high desert far from grapes and rich soil.

"Queen Noe Hoe rose as the sun set and walked to the camp's large, crackling fire. She merely signaled for silence by pressing her ring finger to her lips. On her finger was the Sacred Ring. The ring reflected the entire scene back into the upturned faces. She then appeared to float effortlessly in a complete circle around the fire. Queen Noe Hoe stopped at the point where she had begun. She then extended her arm and ringed finger to the far western end of the bay.

"Everyone's head turned toward the water, and they watched her gaze as she steadily swung her arm in an arc that moved up to the opening in the bay and across Lake Tahoe. On the far side of the lake, the moon was peeking over the mountains. The sight of all of this transfixed even the hardened warriors.

"The moon increased its speed as it climbed higher and higher. Queen Noe Hoe kept pointing at it. When it was above the brim of the darkened mountains, the moon became a beacon in the sky whose yellow path lay on the lake and reached precisely where the summit was gathered.

"Now the queen moved her arm in a reverse course, back down to the middle of the bay... until her hand pointed right at an island in the bay that had not been there only moments ago. The island was illuminated by moonlight and still wet from the depths. It was a pointed, craggy little island, complete with dripping trees. On one end of the island—the end closest to the assembled enemies—sat a miniature castle. A shiver of emotion ran through everyone present.

"There was no sound.

"The queen let her arm fall to her side. 'People of Lake No Name... name... name... name...' Her voice echoed from the other end of the bay. 'That island now before us is a sign of our desire for harmony with our neighbor and Mother Earth... That castle is where we pledge our commitment to peace tomorrow jointly when the sun is the highest... high... high... high.'" She stopped and raised her clenched fist, with the Sacred Ring toward the sky.

"'Given this commitment to peace, you, People of No Name, an island will appear in your lake.' Everyone gasped, followed by a murmur among the tribe members.

"'These symbolic islands will stay in place within our two lakes for as long we stay true to our commitments to each other and share our food, as neighbors should.'

"To this day, the island remains in Emerald Bay."

Sure enough, Lake No Name has an island shaped like a pyramid. The lake now has a name: Pyramid Lake. The No Name tribes became known as Paiutes and Shoshoni. The queen told them that if they took care of their Lake, Mother Earth would bless it with lots of fish, which she did.

Mary sits in awe as the older woman told the story. "I believe most of the story to be the truth," Mary says.

The old woman smiles beautifully, and her eyes glisten, "Thank you, Mary."

"I have a question, if the summit was at Emerald Bay, why do you, the queen's descendant, sit here at Cave Rock?"

The old woman speaks very softly and replies, "One of the reasons the Washoe tribe considered Cave Rock sacred is because the rock is 'The Lady of the Lake.' The 'Lady' that appears in the rock formation is the profile of my face gazing out toward the whole Lake. That is my profile, Mary. Mother Earth gave me the responsibility to care for the Lake.' She starts to shed tears down her old weathered cheeks. "As the Lake dies, so do I, and there will be no new descendant."

"What can I do to help?" Mary asks.

"I am not sure; the lake at one time was so pristine you could see over one hundred feet deep. Now, you are lucky to see thirty. There is an algae bloom in Emerald Bay from too many people and boats. Also, algae is growing on the west side of the lake due to too much growth. I have tried everything to rid the basin of so many people. I have produced heavy snows, fire, drought, and even small earth earthquakes. Nothing seems to work. I even woke Tahoe Tessie to scare them off the Lake."

Before Mary can ask a question about Tessie, Noe Hoe says, "We better go. The sun is going down. Come on, Eish Keen." The old dog gets up and started following Noe Hoe. "Will I see you tomorrow, Mary?"

"Yes," Mary replies, looking down, deep in thought. When Mary looks up, the older woman is gone.

For several days, Mary and Noe Hoe discuss what they can do to resolve the lake's situation. Noe Hoe's last resort is to create a massive earthquake and empty the Lake. Mary is opposed to this, as it would kill many humans.

"They have brought this upon themselves, their greed," replies Noe Hoe. "Look what their greed has done to my lake." A handful of algae floats up to the queen.

"What if we plant a fish that would eat the algae?" Mary suggests.

"That is a thought." With the flash of the Sacred Ring on her finger, she plants algae-eating plecostomus catfish to eat the lake's algae. She plants hundreds.

Mary is a very smart fairy. She knows natural algae control results from nutrient reductions, and algae-eating fish will not eliminate all the algae. The cause of what nourishes it must be found. In this case, its nutrients are coming from too much growth: homes, and businesses with septic tanks. Then, the nitrates get into the lake and create the algae.

So, how do I stop the nitrates?

A thought comes to her.

She knows people she can talk to... well, not really. She will whisper in people's ears about the problem. She explains her plan to Noe Hoe and tells her to be patient.

"I like your idea, Mary," the queen says. "I will help you."

So Mary sends thoughts to the people living around the lake.

Surprisingly, the states of California and Nevada, which control the lake, suddenly see the problem and start creating procedures to curtail the pollution. Over time, growth starts being managed, bringing the lake back to life. By the end of several years, the visibility in the water goes to seventy and almost eighty feet in places. Mother Nature does her part with lots of rain and snow to help cleanse the soil.

The lake's improved clarity makes the Queen jubilant. As she and Mary stand looking over the lake, the queen raises her hand with the Sacred Ring toward the heavens. She says a prayer to bless the lake. In doing so, you can see her grow younger, along with her dog. When she finishes the prayer, she is a beautiful young woman, and Eish Keen is a young dog. Mary then knows this was the real queen and not a descendant.

"Thank you, Mary, for your assistance; I couldn't have done this without your help. Life will be good for you." With that, the Queen and her dog walk off into the mist of the lake.

❧

Queen Noe Hoe, however, never leaves her lake. She is still in the rock formation at Cave Rock, watching the lake's future, with her dog lying down beside her.

Mary still works with the Queen occasionally. However, the remainder of her life is spent preserving Mother Earth. She travels to Yellowstone, Yosemite, and Glacier Park, as well as to other places—wherever she is needed to keep the Earth safe.

❧

As humans, we have all benefited from Queen Noe Hoe and Mary's caring; now, it is our turn to help them. Do not dump garbage from your boat in the lake or any lake. When hiking or camping, leave the land as you find it... Protecting Mother Earth will save us all.

Martin A. David

Bendl the Goniff and the Great Baby Exchange

Bendl, our shtetl's crafty thief, prankster, mischief-maker, and carrier of clandestine messages, has stolen many things. However, let it be said in his defense, that he has never, ever stolen—or even really borrowed—a baby. In fact, he has never, as far as he knows and I know and the people of the town know, made a baby.

So then, how did our dear Bendl get involved with more than a dozen babies? Well, it's not a long story, so if you sit and have another cup of tea, I might be able to tell you.

To begin at the beginning, it began with a wedding. Now, a wedding is a good beginning—both for a story and for a life. When two people stand together under the bridal canopy and then make their marks on the *ketubah*, the marriage contract, it is cause for celebration. If the bride's parents are living, they feel blessed and relieved to see a daughter leave their room-and-board and join the mainstream of the community. Similar feelings can be observed in the groom's parents.

The community celebrates to welcome the couple over the threshold between childhood and the responsible existence of adulthood. The community, if the truth were known, also celebrates because life is not always easy and everybody likes a party.

The size and shape of the party depend on many things. If a rich man's daughter marries the son of a wealthy man, then the party becomes the subject of shtetl reminiscences and legends for many years to come. The daughter of a well-to-do father who is joined with the scholarly son of a great rabbi can also expect to see her parental house filled wall to wall with people on the day of her wedding. To be invited to eat, drink, and dance at such a wedding is a great honor and is usually preceded by the construction of a huge appetite.

Another large wedding, one where everyone who is well enough to walk may assume himself or herself to be invited, is the uniting of the son or daughter of someone particularly beloved by the community. At such a wedding, there is also great feasting. It may not be on the same slaughter-the-fatted-calf level as the event hosted by the prosperous parents, but who wouldn't want to come and celebrate the joy of a well-loved rabbi or teacher? Of course, it is interesting to point out how the adored are not often affluent and the affluent are seldom adored, but that is the matter for another story.

A third kind of wedding is the joining of orphans or the offspring of families with little or no means. At these nuptial festivities, it is the guests and neighbors who supply most of the food and drink, but the size of the feast never seems to shrink the magnitude of the joy.

It was the middle kind of wedding that provided a background for this story. The children of two beloved, learned, wise, compassionate and very poor rabbis were being brought together. The son of Moshe ben Beryl, the rabbi of our Narodny shtetl, was signing a marriage contract with the daughter of Rabbi Jacov ben Itzkhak, from the town of Dołek, which lay over some rolling hills just several hours' wagon ride from Narodny. The most commonly heard blessing being bestowed on the engaged couple was "May your progeny bring forth a dynasty of great Talmudic scholars." The spouses-to-be had gotten a glimpse of each other at the betrothal ceremony and, although they both were too young to understand what marriage really meant, were neither frightened nor horrified by what they saw.

When we say the fathers, Rabbi Moshe and Rabbi Jacov, were poor, we do not mean they lacked for any of the necessities of life. Food and firewood, and used, but quite presentable clothing, all arrived on their doorsteps whenever such things were needed. Their neighbors, Jews and Poles alike, made sure that want never cast a shadow on them.

Piotr-son-of-Piotr, a Polish landowner for whom Rabbi Jacov had once helped settle a dispute, made sure the bride had a respectable dowry. Benesh-the-Merchant from our own shtetl made sure that barrels of wine stood ready, and that chickens and a well-fattened sheep arrived in plenty of time to be slaughtered in the ritual manner, koshered, and prepared to be served to the guests. Musicians arrived from all sides, ready to play just for the joy of playing. There were almost more volunteering hands than there were tasks to busy them.

And the guests. There was no lack of guests. It is a mitzvah, a good deed, to attend such a happy occasion. It was, if such a thing is possible, even more of a mitzvah to dance at the wedding linking the houses of two such prominent scholars as Rabbi

Moshe and Rabbi Jacov. The guests came from every corner of the shtetl, they came from the surrounding countryside, and they came, in a long line of wagons, droshkies, and ox carts, from the town of Dołek where the bride had grown up. Whole families came to share the joy. Fathers and mothers and older children sang songs in the fronts of wagons while old grandmothers and grandfathers held on tight and hoped their bones would not shatter from all the rattling. Younger children swatted and punched each other and ended up looking and smelling nothing at all like the clean little angels that had been loaded into the vehicles hours before.

Weddings such as this tended to last from early in the day to late into the night. The dancing and eating and drinking went on as long as there were supplies to be had and guests there to enjoy them. A few people from outside the shtetl stayed with relatives; others wedged into crowded spaces with strangers or, in the case of the more rambunctious drinkers, just slept where they fell. However most of the guests had work to do in the morning. Just before midnight, there was the sound of horses being set in motion, wagon wheels creaking, and goodbyes being shouted. The horses knew the way, and the drivers dozed most of the way home. They arrived in time to gather in a precious few hours of sleep and then to say the morning prayers in their own, familiar surroundings. Of course, weddings like this took place only once every few years, and so the arrangements were hardly ever a problem.

Hardly ever, but not never.

You may have met Bendl-the-Goniff. In a shtetl, there is usually someone for every task. Yochnan, the Polish miller made his living by grinding wheat and other grains into flour or meal, Menachem-the-Tailor made his living by sewing fine jackets and caftans, and Benesh-the-Merchant made his living by trading one thing for another. Our Bendl made his living by running in between the raindrops and never getting wet. Yes, it is true that the word *goniff* means thief, and yes it is true, though shocking to admit, that Bendl sometimes took things that were not his. Mostly he lived on the small commissions he received for running the unpleasant errands that needed to be done. If one needed to carry three plump chickens to express one's friendship to a police magistrate, one merely gave them to Bendl and, as quick as a puff of smoke, the two plump chickens arrived safely at their destination. Superstitious folk whispered that Bendl could shrink himself down to nothing more than his smile, slip through the crack in a door and materialize again on the other side. Others countered that it had more to do with doors and windows being left unlatched than with magic, but who's to argue with superstition?

Bendl-the-Goniff was both lazy and industrious, honest and dishonest, clever and foolish. He was also a prankster. His sense of humor knew no bounds, and when he wasn't using sleight of hand to conjure up a few bits of food or a silk scarf to sell, he was plotting jokes and tricks to play upon friends and strangers alike. If Jews believed in leprechauns, Bendl would have been called a leprechaun.

The adventure of the babies started innocently enough. When darkness fell, while the parents were still dancing and drinking and the older children were standing on the edges of the merriment, struggling to stay awake, the little ones were tucked away in wagons and carts to sleep until it was time for the ride home. Bendl was wandering through the shadows, looking for bits of this and that when he encountered one of the children. The child, a little boy, had been roused by a bad dream, called out for his mama and, not finding her nearby, climbed, more asleep than awake, out of the wagon. He was straying among the wagon wheels, munching horses and grunting oxen when Bendl found him.

1. "Well, well, well, little gentleman and what is your name?"
2. "Mama."
3. "And who is this mama of yours?"
4. "Mama."
5. "Do you know your papa's name?"
6. "Mama."

The conversation was not progressing well. Bendl studied the little face in the moonlight. Ah, he thought he knew whose child this was. This sleepy urchin must belong to Gittel-with-a-limp's cousin Miriam who, with her husband, Red-headed Kuppel, had a farm a few miles out of town, by the river. Bendl knew their wagon. He gathered up the small creature and carried him to the wagon. He lifted the canvas cover and started to put the now sleeping boy in the wagon. One, two, three... there were already three breathing lumps asleep in the straw. Adding the boy would have made four, and four was one more than Miriam and Kuppel had produced. The boy belonged elsewhere.

That is when the idea struck the impish Bendl.

Three was the proper number, *and three it shall be*. He put the boy in the wagon and took one of the sleeping lumps out. The lump did not wake up. He carried the moist bundle to another wagon and set it there. Then, for the next hour, he tiptoed from one vehicle to another, carrying his little packages, some of them dripping with the childish accidents of night, and depositing them here and there. Some woke up and complained, but Bendl charmed them back to sleep again with his rocking and lullabying until the mixture was complete. At the wedding, music was playing. Outside the wedding, Bendl danced to its melodies. Each of his little partners ended up in a different place from that in which he or she started.

When the first sets of tired and slightly tipsy parents headed for their wagons and carts, Bendl was lurking in the shadows. The first cautious mother, in a scene that would be repeated many times, lifted the canvas that covered her family's wagon, counted the sleeping bumps in the straw, listened to make sure all were breathing, and climbed wearily into the wagon seat for the long trek home.

After a few families had headed home, Bendl faded into the shadows and disappeared. Some things are better pondered and imagined from a safe distance.

The first discovery took place some miles outside of town. Jacob-who-squinted stopped his wagon and climbed off to drain some of the extra liquid he had consumed. At the same time, he thought it might be prudent to wake his oldest child, a son, and have him perform the same act of discharge. He lifted the largest sleeping bump out of the back of the wagon and stood it on its feet.

"Kom, kom, gayn pishn," he coaxed.

The sleepy child complied, but imagine Jacob's shock and consternation when the small creature beside him squatted down and did it like a little girl. It took only a quick glance to reveal that she was, indeed, a little girl.

His wife, Faygl, a very superstitious woman, became nearly apoplectic.

"It is you, it is your fault," she screamed so loudly that birds in trees a half-mile away began to stir. "Because you are always drunk. God has decided that we are not worthy to have a son. He has taken away our son as punishment and given us another girl to try to marry off without a dowry."

Similar scenes, some with more yelling and screaming, some with less, were taking place from Narodny to Dołek. Imagine going to wake little Herschel and finding out that he had transformed overnight to a little Hindeleh, or from a dark-haired boy to a red-headed one. Everything from sleep-walking to divine intervention was blamed. Some of the exchanged children simply looked around at their new surroundings, new siblings, and new situations and declared, "I'm hungry." Others of the temporary changelings began to squall for their mamas—their real mamas—and set up a wave of noise that could be heard almost all the way back to Narodny.

Soon there was a great traffic of wagons and carts heading back toward the scene of the transformation. Neighbors met neighbors on the road and inspected each other's children. By the time they all got to the Narodny marketplace, it was not a market day and the large, empty square seemed like an excellent place to meet, they all had realized that they were the victims of a colossal joke. An air of hilarity prevailed. It was annoyed hilarity, but hilarity nonetheless. Uninvolved townspeople stood around and roared with laughter, or whistled, stamped and applauded as groups of bewildered children were gathered in the marketplace and parents walked up and down holding joyous reunions with their own or bartering a child for a child as if they were trading goats.

At first, the happiness they felt in straightening out the tangled muddle was the only thing on their minds. After a while, thoughts drifted to questions of who might have been the perpetrators of such a scandalous practical joke. Could it have been a drunken Pole or a gang of young boys from the town? Were there demons lurking nearby whose earthly pleasure w. causing great confusion? By late afternoon there was only c name on everyone's tongue. It was the right name; it was Bendl the-Goniff. Nobody but Bendl could have played such a trick.

And where was our shtetl's goniff? He had made the very

wise decision to go out and explore the countryside. At the moment he was lying out of the hot sun on the cool, moist earth under a bridge many miles from Narodny and chortling so loudly that any passersby would have thought he was mad. He often wandered out to live among the trees and hills. He would be back before the cold winds began to blow.

Michael K. Falciani

The Christmas Spirit

L ouise Forsythe sat in her late grandfather's mansion staring up at her freshly decorated Christmas tree. She poured a cup of hot tea in contentment and stared out the French Victorian bay window. Settling in her chair, she smiled, watching as flakes of snow fell, carpeting the grounds outside. With a wan smile, Louise lifted the cup and inhaled the tea's herbal aroma while the glowing embers of a fire emanated heat from a coal-black stove beside her. Four days till Christmas, Louise took in her surroundings one last time, luxuriating in the warm serenity of her home.

In the distance came the low rumble of thunder.

Moments later, Louise heard the front door open, and slam shut. Angry footsteps pounded down the hallway leading into the living room. Looking up, Louise saw the stony face of her brother, his eyes burning with rage. In his left hand was a metal flask that carried the unmistakable nutty aroma of his preferred drink.

"Where is it?" he demanded, his eyes flicking about the room.

He took a long pull from his flask and wiped his mouth on the sleeve of his coat. "I know you've taken it. My son said he saw you open the family safe."

"Yes," she replied. "I retrieved the item while you were passed out drunk, despite your offspring's protests. A monster of a child, I never cared for him. Tea, Mathias?" Louise offered, nodding at the porcelain teapot in front of her.

"The hell with your propriety," he roared drunkenly, ignoring her offer. "What have you done with it?"

Louise frowned at him. "I thought you to be a preacher. Are you not a God-fearing man of the cloth? You may do what you like in your home, brother, and your church—but I'll not tolerate drinking, nor the use of the lord's name spoken in vain inside the Forsythe Mansion."

"I don't care what you'll tolerate, you ungrateful bitch," he snarled. "Grandfather left it to me!"

"He left it to the both of us," Louise chided, frowning at her brother with disapproval. "I doubt he'd be happy knowing you've lost half his fortune gambling in the stock market. I'm certain he'd not want you squandering his most prized possession to settle your debts. I have it now, and I've hidden it away for safe keeping."

Mathias's face burned with fury. "It is *my* birthright, you... you... childless whore!"

Louise flashed him a look, one filled with both pity and disgust. "I have nothing left to say to you, little brother. It is time for you to go."

Mathias removed his hat and threw it across the room. "Goddammit, Louise, you'll not dismiss me so easily! You are nearly seventy years old, teetering on the brink of death. Tell me, woman, where is it? Tell me or... or... so help me..." He took note of the embers glowing inside the stove. His face took on a cruel look, one borne from the fervor of desperation. "I will burn the answer from your flesh."

Louise began to laugh until the sound filled the room.

"There is no need for threats, brother," she said, once her mirth had subsided. "I visited both the doctor and the apothecary today. It seems I am shorter for this world than you know."

She tapped a finger to her temple. "Brain cancer; there is no cure."

Mathias snorted, unable to conceal his smile. "How apropos," he sneered. "It serves you right. Whatever time you have left, I hope you spend it in agony."

He stepped forward, towering over her. "Now give it to me, sister, and I will leave you to die in pain."

Louise set her cup down on the table next to her and nodded at the cabinet sitting across the room. "There will be no pain for me," she said, her words turning lethargic. "Not anymore. Soon, I will pass into the beyond, via the apothecary's mixture of opium and honey."

The old woman looked up and pointed to the top of the Christmas tree. "I have been given a gift, you see, from the Christmas Angel. It is only right that I return the favor."

"What the hell are you talking about?" Mathias hissed, lifting the empty bottle from the cabinet, inhaling its contents.

"The essence of poppies?" he snorted; his voice incredulous.

"Good-bye, little brother," the old woman managed, her eyes grown heavy. "May grandfather's gift go to someone more worthy than you... or your son."

Her head lolled to the left and came to rest against the side of her cushioned chair.

Louise Forsythe closed her eyes forever.

His face mottled with rage, Mathias threw the empty bottle across the room, shattering it against the wall. "Damn you, woman," he howled, clutching the silver cross around his neck. "I condemn your soul to rot in this place until the end of days! May you never know the rest of eternal peace until one of my blood finds what you stole!"

Lightning flashed outside the Forsythe Mansion, followed immediately by the ominous sound of thunder.

Friday, December 20th, 1996,
Carson City, Nevada
The Carlson House Restaurant

Dean glanced at his watch, seeing it was 9:45 p.m., a good 15 minutes past the restaurant's closing time. The POS machine next to him began spitting out a new order, its high-pitched printing grating on Dean's nerves.

He tore the paper from the machine and looked at it with a sigh. Footsteps came from around the corner, and a tall server with long blonde hair tied back in a ponytail entered the room.

"My guests want one for the road," the server announced, his face grinning smugly. "Gotta up sale if you want to make the big money, aye boss? I'll see if I can talk them into a dessert."

"The kitchen's closed, Cole," Dean reminded the long-faced server, pulling a bottle of Beefeaters from the well. "Gently remind your customers this is last call."

Cole shook his head. "Whatever you say," he sniffed, running a finger along the top of the bar. "Did you wipe this down? It feels sticky."

"I'll get to it after hours," Dean answered, scooping ice into a glass. He lifted the bottle and poured a generous supply of gin into it before adding sour mix and a dash of club soda from the gun.

"I thought you were going to decorate the Christmas tree today?" Cole drawled.

"I ran out of time," Dean replied, painfully aware of the empty tree standing in the bay window. "I'll get the ornaments tonight."

"Umm... a Tom Collins gets a lemon garnish," Cole scolded, seeing Dean reach for a wedge of lime. "No wonder you can't afford your last semester of college, you can't even make a drink correctly."

Dean gave him a hard stare. "Last time I checked, I was the bartender... and acting manager. Don't tell me how to do my job. You had your chance to impress the owner all last month. Rob selected me to run things while he was away, not you."

The younger man took a deep breath, trying to calm himself. "As to the other matter, the spring semester hasn't started yet. I still have time."

Cole gave the bartender a sneer. "You'll never be able to afford the tuition. Rob only put you in charge because you are a kiss ass, doing everything he asks..."

The red-faced server trailed off as a young woman entered the room.

"I'm sorry to interrupt, but," she looked at Cole, "your customers are getting antsy."

"Of course, Kacee, thank you," Cole replied, his angry look replaced with a smarmy grin.

Cole lifted the Tom Collins and made his way across the room. "What are you doing later?" he asked the girl, stopping directly in front of her. "If you don't have any plans, I thought you might like to swing by Joe Garlic's? They have a new drink I've been dying to introduce you to, the Molten Sunset. It's supposed to be downright devilish—an aphrodisiac, if you will."

"Thank you, but... I'll be heading home as soon as I'm finished here," Kacee replied, edging away from Cole.

"Suit yourself," the tall server said, shooting Dean a look of embarrassment. He turned away and left.

Kacee gave the departing server a disgusted look and made her way over to the bar. "The kitchen asked if you wanted anything before they leave," she inquired, brushing bread crumbs from her apron. "There's a leftover plate of beef stroganoff if you are interested."

Dean blinked and gave her a small smile. A wave of nerves knotted his stomach. "Thank you, that is kind of them to offer. A full plate is too much for me, but if they want to wrap a portion of it, that would be appreciated."

He swallowed his nerves and looked at her shyly. "Perhaps you would like the rest? Caesar is a talented chef; I highly recommend it. His beef stroganoff is to die for."

Kacee returned his smile. "I'll tell them... and thank you... for thinking of me, I mean."

She turned and walked out of the room.

Dean let out a breath he hadn't realized he'd been holding. *"She's out of your league, dummy,"* he thought to himself. *"If that Casanova Cole can't capture her attention, what chance do I have?"*

Annoyed with himself, Dean searched under the bar. He grabbed the bottle of cleaner and began to spray the top in preparation for closing the Carlson House Restaurant for the night.

Half an hour later, Dean was heading downstairs, carrying a box of ornaments he'd found in the attic, when he heard a knock at the front door. Peering through the window was the anxious face of Kacee. Giving her a confused look, Dean set the box at the bottom of the stairs, undid the lock, and let her in.

"Thank God you're still here," she gasped, shooting him with a grateful smile. "I forgot my car keys in the drawer under the computer."

"I see," Dean said, lifting an eyebrow curiously. "You're in luck. I'm nearly finished for the night; I was just about to leave."

She looked up at him and managed a shy smile. "How come Cole didn't ask you to go tonight? I thought you two were friends?"

Dean shook his head. "I made the mistake of tagging along once. I won't do that again. He spends all his time hitting on girls he used to know in high school. Besides, he knows I don't drink."

"But, aren't you the bartender?" she asked, while pulling the drawer under the computer open, fishing for her keys.

"It's ironic, I know," he nodded. "Like a fish that can't swim."

Kacee gave Dean a tinkling laugh and his spirit soared.

"Found them," she stated, pulling her keys from the drawer, tucking them into her purse. "It's so quiet here at night," she noted, looking up at the curving staircase overhead. "Don't you get scared? Or does your desire to raise money for school override any fear?"

Dean shrugged. "I'm so busy with work, I just finish and leave. I don't think about being alone here... besides," he smiled, "I quite like the old place. There's something comforting about it. My understanding is that it used to be a private residence... or so I've been told."

Kacee pursed her lips. "What do you have left to do?"

"Not much," he shrugged. "Just put these ornaments in the bar and head out."

"Here, let me help," Kacee said, grabbing hold of the box. "It's the least I can do."

"That's OK, I'll take care of..."

He was cut off by a surge of electricity, immediately followed by a high-pitched screeching of the POS machine in the bar.

Dean glanced at Kacee and ran a hand absently through his dark hair.

"What was that?" the waitress whispered, setting the box back down.

"I... I don't know," Dean stammered, eyeing the computer. He had shut it down more than ten minutes ago. The power was off, and there was no other way to send an order. "Better go check it out," he murmured, walking into the bar.

Everything was as he'd left it. The chairs had been tucked under the tables and the floor swept clean. Dean moved behind the bar and tore off the paper sticking out of the POS machine.

"What is this?" he muttered, reading the words to himself.

The blood of my kin is nigh, true heart.
For long they've searched and failed.
The time has come to reveal all,
So that my spirit may pierce the veil.

This house is steeped, long in lore.
Countless secrets it does hold.
Ware those you trust, true heart,
What they seek was hewn from gold.

A gift was given years ago
By a man who ran the Mint.
Three there were, bright as noon,
A tale, ne'er seen in print.

The second for Blasdel, the third to Grant,
But the first will best them all

A gift he gave to his truest friend
When he walked these hallowed halls.

"What is it?" Kacee asked, scooting next to him.

Wordlessly, Dean set the paper on the bar top, as he scanned the words a second time.

"Wh...what do you think it means?" Kacee asked, her eyes alight with curiosity.

"I don't know," Dean answered, casting his gaze toward the POS machine. "I'm more interested in how this note printed at all."

"Maybe there is another explanation," Kacee suggested, her eyes dancing playfully. She dropped her finger, pointing at the last line of the first stanza. "Look here, it says, 'so my spirit may pierce the veil.'" Her smile brightened. "Looks like we have a ghost inside the Carlson House."

Dean gave Kacee a sidelong look. "A ghost?" he scoffed lightly. "I've heard that this place is haunted... a few of the regulars like to pull my leg... but those conversations are mostly tongue in cheek. The week before last, Stephanie, the waitress you replaced, swore up and down a spirit from the beyond had trapped her in the bathroom."

Dean shook his head ruefully. "Turns out the door was jammed at the top and she was high on crack. The owner let her go and hired you." Dean let out a sigh. "Then there was a year ago when Cole swiped the television remote without me knowing."

Dean nodded toward the bay window, past the still undecorated Christmas tree. "He stood outside for twenty minutes turning the television on and off until I saw him. He thought it a great joke."

The young bartender turned back toward Kacee. "Don't get me wrong, I love the idea of a ghost haunting these hallways. It's fun and always proves to be an entertaining topic to discuss with the guests. But I've been here nearly a year and a half now, and I've never seen anything that would make me believe..."

His voice trailed off as the POS machine buzzed to life anew and began printing once more.

Dean stared at the far side of the bar as a new message appeared. Frowning, Dean eased his way over to the machine.

"What does it say?" Kacee asked.

Dean licked at his lips, suddenly gone dry.

Find the gift that was given, true heart,
Else I'm bound forevermore,
and you, Dean Crawford, won't last the night,
unless you lose what you once adored.

~Louise Forsythe

Dean's breath caught in his throat. "What is going on?" he asked, studying the words again.

"Dean," Kacee gasped, backing into the corner of the bar, pointing at something near the television.

The bartender's eyes widened, as the hair on the back of his neck began to rise. There, not two feet in front of him, was the television remote, floating in the open space of the bar, five feet off the floor.

"What the...?" Dean whispered, in a mix between shock and horror.

The television switched on, the channel showing nothing but static.

"Dean?" Kacee whimpered, her back pressed tightly against the wall.

The volume on the television was turned up. Slowly, pushing

past the noise of static, came a voice from beyond the grave.

"Find the treasure true heart, or you will suffer the same fate as I..."

In an instant, the buzzing of the POS machine disappeared, the television powered off, and the remote dropped to the wooden floor with a clatter.

Dean glanced at the bar and swept up the original message. "Come on," he shouted, grabbing Kacee by the hand and running out of the room.

"Where are we going?" Kacee demanded, her face a pale green.

Dean did not bother to stop and lock the door. "To see a friend of mine. A man who I'm hoping, can help us out."

Dean pulled up to an old house located less than a mile away. It was a poorly built, one-story structure with a dilapidated wrap-around porch. A rundown Volkswagen was parked in a driveway, cracked with age. Covered in rust, the vehicle looked to be in even worse shape than the house.

They exited the car to the sound of distant thunder. Snow began to fall from the starless sky.

"How... why are we here?" Kacee asked, her eyes taking in the surroundings.

Dean shoved his keys in his pocket and strode determinedly up to the front steps. "There's a man who lives here, Ron. He... watch your step," Dean cautioned, pointing at a hole in the stairs.

"Thank you," Kacee murmured, taking care to step around the danger.

"Ron comes into the bar at the Carlson House sometimes," Dean continued. "He always orders the same drink, a sherry." Dean shrugged. "He knows all about the place, before it was a restaurant. Ron used to be the curator back in the day."

Dean took a deep breath. "He invited me back here once this past summer. Ron spent nearly an hour talking to me about the Forsythe Mansion. He has a ton of furniture and knickknacks that used to be at the mansion."

Stepping on the landing in front of the door, Dean raised his hand and knocked. He ran an anxious hand through his hair. "I figured if anyone knows about what the... ghost wrote," he swallowed nervously, "it will be Ron."

From inside came the shuffling of feet and the doorway cracked open.

"Who is it?" a tentative voice asked.

"Ron, it's Dean, the bartender from the Carlson House," Dean replied. "I'm sorry to bother you like this, but, it's something of an emergency."

"Dean," the voice from inside repeated, as the door opened wider. The round head of an old man appeared, his face covered with a well-groomed silver white goatee. Hazel eyes shifted from Dean to Kacee.

"Who is this?" Ron asked, giving the girl a distasteful look.

"This is Kacee," Dean explained. "She works with me at the restaurant."

The old man studied her for a long moment before turning his attention back to Dean. "It is late," Ron sniffed. "I don't normally entertain visitors at this hour."

"I understand," Dean said, digging into his pocket. "But something happened at the Forsythe Mansion tonight... something I thought you might be able to help with."

Ron shook his head. "I was just about to go to bed. Perhaps tomorrow, or the day after..."

"Please, Ron," Dean said, holding the note out in front of him. "There is no one else I can go to. No one else I might trust with this. It will take only a moment of your time."

Ron let out an annoyed breath, blowing past teeth yellowed with age. "It is past ten on a Friday night..."

"Please, sir," Kacee said, her eyes imploring. "It is a matter of some urgency."

Ron fixed the girl with a hard stare and rolled his eyes. "Come in," he offered at last, unlocking the door. "Close the door behind you. It's started to snow, and I'm on a fixed income."

Once inside, Dean stared for the second time in his life at one of the most eclectic and fascinating collections of antiques he'd ever seen. Translucent floor lamps with shades of rose-colored glass stood in the corner. An old davenport of red velvet lay next to a chartreuse lounge chair tapered in white. Twin vases with mother of pearl inlay sat on maroon carpet that rested atop an inch of sawdust. Fine china painted with cherry blossoms lined the wall. Everywhere he looked, Dean saw the former trappings of the Forsythe Mansion. It was as though he had stepped through a portal and traveled back to a time when the most luxurious building in Carson was in its glory.

"What's this about?" Ron asked, his high-pitched voice filled with annoyance, as he sank into a chair in his dining room, pouring himself a snifter of sherry.

"Here," Dean offered, handing Ron the paper. "It came out of the POS machine we used to fill drink orders. The power was off and... well, that note appeared out of nowhere."

Ron took the proffered paper and moved his bifocals down the bridge of his nose. "The lighting is too dim in here," he muttered. The old man snapped his fingers, "You, Kacee, be a dear and turn on the lights for me."

Kacee moved over to the far end of the room and clicked the light switch located on the back side of the wall on.

"That's better," Ron said, giving the girl a swift nod. "Now, let's see what all the fuss is about." As he began to read, his face turned in confusion. "Well, it doesn't seem to make much..." Ron's voice trailed off and his eyes widened as he read further down the page.

"My god," he whispered, finishing the note. "When did this happen?"

"Ten minutes ago," Dean answered. "Do you know what it means?"

Instead of answering, Ron's face glossed over, and tears brimmed in his eyes. "After all this time," he whispered, speaking more to himself than Dean.

"Ron," Dean said, his voice louder. "Do you know what it means?"

"Maybe," the old man said, giving Kacee a sidelong glance.

Seeing how Ron looked at her, Dean placed his hand on Ron's shoulder. "I trust her implicitly. She was there when the... message came."

Ron turned his eyes toward Dean, looking at the young man intently. "Are you certain of this? What of that oaf you work with? Could he be playing a trick on you?"

Dean shook his head. "All the computers were powered off. There is no way that message came from anyone other than..." he trailed off a moment shaking his head. "Who is Louise Forsythe?"

"It doesn't seem possible," Ron stated. "It must be a prank of some kind. There is no way that Louise..."

"She turned the television on right in front of our eyes," Kacee, snapped, cutting him off. "The remote was floating five feet off the floor! You two keep tiptoeing around the obvious. It *was* a ghost! She was right there, in the room with us. For Christ's sake, she *spoke* to Dean through the television!"

Ron looked shaken. "You saw the same?" he asked, his eyes shifting to Dean.

The bartender nodded. "It happened exactly as Kacee described. It was as clear as me sitting in front of you now."

Ron's hands began to shake. "So, the stories are true," he said softly.

Dean let out a pent-up breath. "What stories? What does that note mean... and why did it come to me?"

Ron gave the younger man a rueful grin. "I will tell you, though I never thought I'd live to see the day."

The old man sat back in his chair, a serene look upon his saintly face. "Mathias Forsythe settled in Carson City in 1864 along with his new wife, Marcella. It was the same year Nevada was admitted to the union. Gold and silver were flowing from Virginia City, and there was money to be made. Mr. Forsythe made millions in the meat..."

"We don't need a history lesson," Kacee interrupted. "What does the note mean?"

Ron gave her a sharp look. "I'm getting to that," he snorted, no longer saintly. "Mathias had his mansion built and finished for his wife in 1876. However, as a man of means and one of the pioneers of the area, Forsythe knew many of Carson City's founding fathers. One such man was Abraham Curry."

"The Carlson House is on Curry Street," Dean said with a jolt. "I had no idea the name was tied to one of Carson's forefathers."

"Yes," Ron nodded, growing excited. "What building is located behind Curry Street today? I'll give you a hint. It is prominently mentioned in this note."

Dean frowned and peered curiously at the paper. "The courthouse?" he guessed, knowing that was wrong.

Ron shook his head. "A fine conjecture, but no."

"Just tell us," Kacee said, frowning at the old man.

"Here," Ron offered, placing a wizened finger under a single word.

Mint.

"The Carson Mint?" Dean offered.

"Yes," Ron replied. "The man who ran the mint was none other than Abraham Curry."

"So?" Kacee scoffed. "I still don't understand. What does he have to do with anything?"

Ron shook his head. "I swear, youth is wasted on the young."

"What is Curry's significance?" Dean asked.

Ron smiled, took off his spectacles and began to polish the glass. "What did they print at the Carson Mint?"

"Coins?" Dean guessed.

"Precisely," Ron beamed. The old man moved his hand toward the bottom stanza. "What I'm about to tell you was never reported to the newspapers... but I, and a select few others close to the family, knew the Forsythes' greatest secret."

He leaned forward and tapped his finger on the paper. "You see here where it says, 'The second for Blasdel, the third to Grant?'"

"Yes," Dean nodded. "But... I don't know what that means."

"You need to learn about this state's past," Ron sniffed. "Henry Goode Blasdel was the first governor of Nevada from 1864 to 1871. Ulysses S. Grant, was the President of the United States back in 1870, when the printing press began minting coins."

Ron paused, giving his listeners a moment to soak in the information. "Known to very few, Abraham Curry printed three gold coins that first day. One of them, the second coin ever made here in Carson City, went to Governor Blasdel; the third was given as a gift to President Grant."

Dean glanced at Kacee, who absently ran her tongue over a

pair of full lips.

"What about the first coin?" Dean inquired.

A smile that would have made the Cheshire Cat envious crossed Ron's face. "The first, made from the purest gold mined in Virginia City, was given to his good friend, Mathias Forsythe."

Dean blinked in wonder. "*Find the gift that was given,*'" he whispered. "That's what the ghost of Louise Forsythe said through the television." His eyes widened further. "She wants me to find the first coin... it must be hidden somewhere inside the Carlson House!"

"That would appear to be the case," Ron said in satisfaction.

Silence descended upon all three people in the room, as the snow continued to fall outside.

"How much would such a coin be worth today?" Kacee asked.

Ron rubbed his hands together. "Who can say? I know a 1849 Double Eagle Gold Coin goes for millions. I'd wager the first coin ever minted in Carson City would fetch a steep price."

"My god," Kacee whispered, her eyes flashing toward Dean. "Millions? All we have to do is find it?"

"Yes," Ron agreed.

"All right," Kacee said, standing back up. "What is our next step?"

Ron rubbed the side of his whiskered cheek absently. "We should go to the Forsythe Mansion... tonight... strike while the proverbial iron is hot."

The young bartender hesitated, uncertain of what to do.

"I... I don't know," Dean stammered, eyeing the pair in front of him. "Maybe I should contact the owner, Rob. He might not..."

"We can't tell anybody about this!" Kacee exclaimed. "Think about it. If a whiff of this gets out, the place will be crawling with treasure hunters. Right now, only the three of us know. I say we keep it that way and split the money."

Dean was torn. He did not want to desecrate the mansion, but he desperately needed the money to finish college.

"Think of it this way," Ron said kindly. "The spirit of Louise still endures in the old place. It must have pained her all these years to be trapped in the home of her youth. We can help her pass to the other side. She even says so in her note."

He pointed to the last line of the first stanza.

So that my spirit may pierce the veil.

Ron placed his hand upon Dean's. "She revealed herself to you for a reason. She's asking for your help. This." He motioned to himself and Kacee. "The three of us working together to find the coin... I'm certain that is what Louise would want."

Dean gave Ron a long look. "You knew Louise, didn't you?"

Ron let out a sigh. "Yes," he admitted. "In my youth. That is why I know the secret of the coin."

Dean glanced at the parchment once more. "All right," he said, his eyes scanning the paper. "Let's do it. Any reward offered, we will split in three ways, agreed?"

"Yes," Kacee said, leaning forward, hugging Dean impulsively.

"You have my word," Ron swore, lifting his snifter, finishing off his sherry. "Let me get my coat," he said, rising to his feet. "I'll just be a moment."

"Can I use your phone?" Kacee asked. "I need to let my..." she flicked her eyes at Dean. "Roommate know I'm running late."

"Make it quick," Ron grunted, shambling off to the other room.

Kacee nodded and walked through a side door into the kitchen. Dean could make out a dated, yellow, rotary phone. He watched curiously as Kacee dialed the number. Her discussion was brief, taking less than a minute. She hung up the phone and made her way back over to Dean, popping a Tic Tac into her mouth and dropping the container back in her purse.

"This is so exciting!" she breathed, drawing close to him. "I never thought I'd be part of a treasure hunt."

"Who did you call?" Dean asked, drawing away from her.

Kacee's face turned in confusion. "My roommate, like I said."

"What's his name?" Dean asked.

Kacee gave Dean a smile. "It isn't like that. I'm only staying with him until I get settled. I've only been in Carson for a couple of weeks."

She leaned in and kissed Dean on the lips. He could taste the cool peppermint of the Tic Tac on her tongue and feel the supple leather of her purse pressing into his ribs. Thirty seconds later, she pulled away, looking at him with longing.

"Enough for now," she exhaled. "We can take it back up again... after."

Dean's head was spinning, unsure of what to make of this new wrinkle in his life.

"Are we ready?" Ron asked, re-entering the room.

With a final glance at Kacee, Dean nodded his head.

"Let's go."

More than an inch of new snow had fallen by the time they had arrived back at the Carlson House. Crunching their way up the stairs, Dean led the trio onto the landing. Dean turned the knob and opened the door, turned the main light on, and led the way into the bar.

Ron squinted through his spectacles, his eyes taking in the entire room. "Gads, it's so different now," he stated, his mind in the past. "This was Louise's bedroom once... She'd be furious to see it has been turned into a bar. She was a prohibitionist you know—couldn't stand drinking of any kind."

Ron noted the box of Christmas ornaments sitting on the bar.

"What's this?" he murmured, sticking a hand inside the box. "I haven't seen these in years. Not since..."

The walls of the mansion began to shake as a surge of power buzzed through the room. The old curator ceased his examination of the box, grabbed his cane, and took refuge behind Dean.

The lights flickered momentarily and went out. A dull wailing came from the ceiling above them, and the walls ceased to shake.

"Stay calm," Dean urged, trying to keep his nerve.

A heartbeat later, the lights flickered back on, shining brighter than before. Despite the building's warmth, each of them felt a trickle of fear race down their spines.

A presence from beyond the grave had come.

"My god," Ron gasped, his voice soft, trembling. "She's here."

Dean moved forward, raising his hands to appease the spirit. "It's all right, Louise," he said, his voice unsteady. "I've brought help." He pointed at the old man behind him. "Surely you remember Ron. He was the curator here for many years. He knows about the coin. He wants to help find it."

There was a moment of silence, followed by the hum of electricity. The POS machine activated, and the room was filled with the screech of ink printing on paper.

"I'll be damned," Ron whispered in awe. "It *is* true."

"Well..." Kacee laid a hand on Dean's shoulder, nudging him. "Go see what it says."

The bartender took a deep breath and strode forward. He tore the paper from the printer and read the words to himself.

"Well?" Kacee asked, her voice filled with hope. "What does it say?"

Dean folded the top of the paper back and held it forward. "Take a look."

All eyes fell upon the receipt, drinking in every word.

Find the nook where I last took breath,
It conceals what you do seek.
Fair warning to you, my trio of souls,
Character tests both the strong and the weak.

"What does it mean?" Kacee asked, her face twisted in confusion. "Is there a hidden nook someplace in the building?"

"Not that I know of," Dean said, looking at Ron. "Well, Mr. Curator, this is your department. What do you know?"

Ron was staring at the words, his face thoughtful. "I don't know anything about a nook, but..." he trailed off and looked at the back of the barroom wall. "There used to be a door right there." He pointed, staring at his reflection in the mirror. "I know Louise died sitting in her chair..." He moved his eyes down and pointed at the narrow space behind the bar. "In that spot."

Dean's mind jolted with recent memory. "I've got it," he whispered, staring at the floor.

"What?" Kacee asked.

Dean looked at her, his voice excited. "One time last year, I had a drunk customer throw a drink at me. The guy was bombed out of his mind, and I wouldn't serve him anymore."

The bartender shook his head. "He got upset and tossed what was left of his drink at me—there was frozen peach margarita everywhere."

Dean bent down and lifted one of the anti-fatigue mats that lay on the hard wooden floor behind the bar.

"I distinctly remember it because he left his bike here and had to come back and get it the next day. He got an earful from me, I can tell you."

Dean lifted the mat and set it on top of the bar. Swiftly, he bent down and grabbed the second one. "It was a mess. There were bits of minced peach everywhere. It spilled all down the back of the bar here, and the owner made me scrub every inch."

Dean lifted the second mat and placed it on top of the first one. "You see this?" He pointed downward at a tiny hollow in the floorboard. "I remember scrubbing around it that day and thinking it was the only blemish I've ever seen in the entire floor of the restaurant. I'd forgotten about it... until now."

"You think this is the nook?" Kacee asked.

"We are about to find out," Dean answered.

"Careful now," Ron cautioned. "You don't want to damage anything."

"I'll try not to," the bartender replied, wedging his finger into the empty knot of space.

Dean pulled upward, straining against the wood for a few seconds. The outline of a crack appeared in the floor.

"It's moving!" Kacee yelped, her eyes widening in disbelief.

"Almost there," Dean grunted.

A moment later, it was done. A foot-long portion of the floor popped out, leaving an empty space underneath.

"What do you see?" Ron asked, his excitement boiling over.

"Nothing yet," Dean answered, peering downward. "It's too dark."

He stood up. "Kacee, can you grab the flashlight out from under the computer? It's on the shelf under the drawer."

"I'm on it," she said, plopping her purse down on the bar, striding out of the room.

"What was that?" Dean asked, nodding to the window

behind Ron.

The old man looked outside, peering into the darkness. "I don't see anything."

"Hmm," Dean grunted, watching as the snow continued to fall. "I thought I saw..."

"I've got it," Kacee interrupted, coming around the corner, holding the flashlight out to Dean.

"Thank you," the bartender said, clicking the button, turning it on. He bent down to one knee and shined the light inside.

"It's just the ground underneath," he said, moving his head closer, seeing nothing except loose earth. "I don't see any..."

His voice trailed off as Dean ran his hand along the backside of the floorboards.

"I've got something," he said, grabbing hold of a small, boxlike object attached to the floor. Carefully, he slid it free from its binding and brought it into the light.

"Oh...my...*god*," Kacee gasped, her eyes as wide as saucers. "Is...is that it?"

"Can it be?" Ron whispered, his voice reverent. "After all these years?"

Dean stood up and placed the wooden box on the top of the bar. The trio looked at it in wonder.

"Shall we open it?" Ron asked, flicking his gaze at Dean.

"Kacee?" Dean offered.

"I can't," she answered. "My hands are shaking."

"I'll do it," came a voice from across the room.

Looking up, Dean saw Cole standing at the entryway. He was dripping wet with melted snow. One hand was in his pocket. In the other was a pistol, pointed at Dean.

"Cole?" Dean asked, his eyes widening. "Wha...what are you doing?"

"Taking what's mine," the lanky server replied. "Do you

know how long my family has been looking for that?"

"Your family?" Dean asked, not understanding.

Cole gave him a sharp smile. "Yes, my great aunt Louise hid our family heirloom from my great grandfather. She stole it on the night she died, never revealing its whereabouts."

Kacee took a step forward. "There is no need for the gun. We are all friends here."

"Put that thing down," Ron admonished. "What do you hope to accomplish?"

"Ahh yes," snickered Cole. "Play the victim if you will, old man... Lucky for me I was tipped off about this midnight rendezvous."

"What are you talking about?" Dean asked, inching his way toward the POS machine. "We only just found out about it," he pointed at the box, "a half an hour ago."

Cole laughed, with genuine humor. "I forget, Dean, you are the proverbial white knight."

He pointed the pistol directly at Dean's chest. "Don't go for the silent alarm behind the bar. Did you think I forgot about it? Hell man, I'm the one who showed it to you."

Dean stopped and slumped his shoulders in defeat.

"Tell me something, choir boy," Cole barked. "Did you think it was an accident Ron here knew all about this place? I bet he's still telling people he was the curator." He looked back at the old man. "Why don't you tell him who you really are... Grandfather Forsythe."

"Grandfather... *Forsythe*?" Dean said in surprise.

Ron gave Dean a quick look. "Yes," he said bitterly. "Nephew to Louise. The old bat never cared for me—or my father." He paused, looking back at his grandson. "Enough with the gun Cole. Let's walk out of here together, treasure in hand."

"Oh no, old man," Cole said, cocking the hammer. "The colt

2000 and I are taking what's mine and leaving you behind."

Ron shot Cole with a venomous look. "You lazy little shit. Where would you be without me? *I'm* the one who told you of the treasure. *I'm* the one who kept the family history all these years! *I'm* the one who solved the riddle written by the..."

"You were trying to cut me out of my share!" Cole roared. "You always were a greedy old man... too scared to do what was needed to secure our family treasure. You lived in this house for years and never figured out where the coin was."

Cole shifted the pistol toward Dean for a moment. "The bartender here found it after only one night!" The lanky server gave his grandfather a look of disgust. "Without me, you're nothing but a hack, spouting useless knowledge about a legacy that was never your own."

Ron glowered at him. "You son of a..."

His voice stopped as the walls of the building began to shake once more. A bolt of lightning flashed in the bay window through the falling snow, followed by the boom of tearing thunder.

"What the fuck..." Cole hissed, his eyes darting around the room.

The lights went out, leaving them all in pitch blackness.

Knowing he had little time, Dean placed his hands upon the bar and vaulted over it, landing softly a few feet away from where Cole had been standing. Hoping the lanky server had stayed in the same spot, Dean lashed out with his fist, feeling it smash into Cole's jaw. A jolt of pain ran through Dean's hand as he struck flesh and bone. His punch, while painful, had the desired effect. The taller man fell to the floor with a groan, the gun tumbling from his hands.

The lights came back on, and Dean scrambled across the floor, his knuckles throbbing in pain. He swept up the gun and held it at the ready.

"Kacee," he called out, as Cole was groaning on the floor. "Call 911." He shifted his gaze from Cole to Ron and walked over to the bar. "Tell them we have two men for custody."

Ron was wringing his hands together, eyeing the gun. "Please," he hissed, nodding at the wooden box. "Can we at least open it? I must know what's inside... you... you owe me that."

Dean lifted the box and placed it behind the television. "Not after what you did. You could have told me the truth back at your place. Instead, you used me. You let your grandson point a gun at my head. I don't owe you a thing."

"They are on the way," Kacee reported, licking her lips nervously, hanging up the phone.

"Then we wait," Dean replied.

Minutes later, the police arrived and took Ron and Cole away in handcuffs. It was nearly midnight when Kacee and Dean finished their statements. Cole had been booked on charges of attempted robbery and assault, while Ron was taken in as an accessory to both, though he vehemently denied the charges to anyone who would listen.

Neither Kacee nor Dean felt it necessary to mention the ghost, or the treasure box.

After a whispered conversation with one of the police officers, Dean bid them farewell. Alone at last, the pair trudged upstairs into the main office and closed the door. Dean took out the box and laid it on the desk

"I wish I'd never heard of this stupid thing," Kacee said, her voice tired. "Let's just open the box and be done with it."

"In a moment," Dean said, pursing his lips in thought. "Bad luck having Cole come in like that, don't you think?"

"Very," Kacee agreed, brushing the blonde tresses away from her eyes. "We could have had this opened and gone home to celebrate by now." She smiled; her eyes suggestive. "We still could, if you are game."

Dean smiled back. "You are good, Kacee, you really are."

The serving girl's forehead furrowed in confusion. "What do you mean?"

"The way that you tried to play us all. That bit with the suggestive eyes right now, that was a nice touch."

Kacee clutched tightly at her purse, staring at him. "I'm sure I don't know what you are..."

"Your first mistake was claiming you left your keys," Dean explained. "There was nothing inside the drawer when I emptied it earlier; I always double check. You must have been palming them before you stuck your hand inside."

"That's not..."

"You made a bevy of mistakes at Ron's house," he continued, cutting her off. "How would you know where the living room light was, for example? It was on the far side of the wall, completely out of sight. You found it easily, without a moment's hesitation."

"What are you saying?" Kacee asked, her face growing red.

"That you'd been in that house before."

"That's nonsense. I didn't even know Ron until you introduced us tonight."

"Really? Then how do you explain the phone call to your roommate?" he queried. "I may have been standing in the living room, but I recognized the number you dialed. It wasn't to your roommate at all, was it? It was a call to Joe Garlic's. I've had to dial that number myself on any number of occasions since I began working at the Carlson House. There is only one person you might call that was frequenting Joe Garlic's—Cole."

Kacee's face went from abject confusion to an amused superiority. "Well, well," she tsked. "Who would have thought the bumpkin from Podunk Nevada would have figured it out. I must say, I am impressed."

"Don't be," Dean replied, slipping a hand into his pocket. "Even with all that, I wanted to give you the benefit of the doubt. That is, until I read this."

He pulled the last note Louise had sent through the POS machine and unfolded it so Kacee could read what had printed at the top, words he had folded under earlier.

Trust none of them. They are all in it together.

Kacee read the print and flashed her eyes dangerously.

"Well done, bumkin," she hissed. "I've been sleeping with that idiot, Cole, for six months now, trying to get a lead on the treasure. Do you know how obnoxious he is? Do you have an inkling of how much of his shit I've had to put up with? And his grandfather, Christ almighty he's been even worse. Getting this job, putting up with their crap... you have no idea of the sacrifices I've had to make."

"But you sold them out," Dean said quietly. "Didn't you? All three of you had the treasure in your grasp, and decided to cut each other out for the money."

Kacee let out a barking laugh. "Cole was right about you. The Boy Scout—always doing the right thing. Well, now it is just you and I, Dean. We can take the treasure and run off together. Ron said it's worth millions. What do you say?"

Dean stared at the beautiful girl in front of him and shook his head. "I'm sorry, Kacee, but the idea of trusting you makes my stomach turn. I think it best if you leave."

Kacee's beautiful face turned with an ugly scowl. "You think I'm walking out of here without that coin? Fuck no. I put in too much work to go unrewarded."

Dean picked up the box and held it close to him. "I'm not letting you take it. As far as I'm concerned, it belongs back in the Carson Museum, right where it was made."

He paused and gave her a tired look, picking up the phone. "As for you, I think I need to call the police."

Kacee's eyes narrowed, and she slipped a hand into her purse. "I don't think so," she rasped, pulling out a double-stacked Derringer. She leveled the pistol at Dean, who froze at the sight of the gun.

"Are you sure this is the route you want to choose?" he asked, making no move to drop the phone. "You could just walk away."

"Not without my treasure," she hissed, pointing the gun at his head.

Dean let out a sigh. "Then you leave me with no choice."

His fingers dialed 9-1-1.

Kacee pulled the trigger.

Click.

"You can come on up," Dean said into the receiver, his voice calm, pushing the Derringer away from his head.

"What the fuck?" Kacee snarled, re-aiming, pulling the trigger again.

"Oh, I forgot," Dean said, reaching into his pocket. "Are you missing something?" He held out his hand and showed her two bullets resting in his palm. "I was on to you at Ron's house," he explained. "When you kissed me, I pulled your Derringer out of your purse. I swapped it back in when you ran to get the flashlight. I took the bullets out as a precaution."

Downstairs, the front door opened and was followed immediately by the heavy tread of footsteps approaching up the stairs.

"You... you bastard!" Kacee screeched, looking like a cornered rat. "It's not too late... you don't have to do this!"

"You just pulled the trigger of your gun while it was aimed at my head," Dean snapped back. "I'm no lawyer, but it is my understanding that attempted murder in the first degree comes with a life sentence."

A pair of burly police officers strode through the door, handcuffs in hand.

"Dean, please," she cried, falling to her knees.

"I adored you once," Dean said bitterly. "Good-bye Kacee."

Saturday, December 21st 1996
Carson City, Nevada
The Carlson House Restaurant

Dean left the box unopened until the next morning. It had taken another two hours to get his statement the night before, and by the time he had stumbled home, he was exhausted. Bleary-eyed and dragging his feet, it wasn't until 10 a.m. the next day that he staggered through the restaurant door.

Moving behind the bar, Dean took the box out from where he'd hidden it the previous night and set it on the bar in front of him. All alone in the building, he had time to himself at last.

Carefully, Dean opened the lid.

Inside was a tiny brass key, no larger than the length of a paper clip. Under the key was a four-word note, written in beautiful calligraphy.

For the angel's gift.

Dean began to laugh to himself. "All that nonsense last night, for this?" he whispered.

Gently, he placed the key and the note back inside the box.

The phone rang.

"Hello?" Dean answered, closing the box once more. "Hey Rob, I was just going to... yeah, I know, it was kind of a crazy night. I didn't get a chance to... I'm getting to the tree right now, that's why I came in early. No, I think we are going to be a little short staffed today, but we will manage. Tomorrow? Sure, no problem. I'll fill you in when you get here. Hey, we are going to have to hire two new servers. Cole and Kacee are not coming back. It's a long story... OK man, I'll see you then."

Dean hung up the phone and put the box back under the bar. With a sigh, he grabbed the box of ornaments from last night and began the tedious chore of Christmas decorating.

It was nearly an hour later when he was putting the last touches on the tree. Only two items remained in the box. The first was the tree topper, a delicate angel made of fine porcelain. Dean meticulously placed it atop the tree. The last item was a red laced ornament tied with gold ribbon that looked like an unopened present. Dean lifted it up and hung it at the angel's feet.

"Done," he grunted, glad to be finished. He was about to walk away when something caught his eye. Leaning in, he took a closer look.

There, on the bottom of the present, written in the same hand as the note in the box, were three words.

The angel's gift.

Eyes widening, Dean took the ornament off the tree and studied it closely. There, on the front of the gold ribbon, was a tiny keyhole.

"You've got to be kidding," he muttered, his weariness evaporating.

Dean walked back behind the bar and retrieved the box. Taking out the key, he took a deep breath and pushed it inside the keyhole.

It was a perfect fit.

He turned the key, and the top of the present popped open.

Before he could look inside, the POS machine began to buzz, and a new message began to print. Tearing his eyes away from the ornament, Dean ripped off the message.

I am finally free. Thank you, true heart. Merry Christmas.
-Louise Forsythe-

Dean noted a movement out of the corner of his eye. He looked to his right. There, in the mirror behind the bar, he saw the kind face of a ghostly old woman.

"Louise," he breathed, giving her a smile. "May you finally be able to rest in peace."

The apparition gave him a nod and pointed at the box.

Grinning, Dean turned back to the ornament and looked inside. His eyes widened as he saw a flash of gold.

"Damn," he whispered in awe, glancing again at the mirror behind him. "I'll drink to that."

The apparition rolled her eyes, gave him a rueful smile and dissipated into the beyond.

Dean closed the lid of the box and walked over to Ron's favorite drink. He opened the bottle of sherry and breathed in its unmistakable nutty aroma. With a look of distaste, Dean raised it and looked up to the heavens.

"For the Christmas Spirit, Lady Forsythe," he said, dumping the contents of the bottle down the drain.

"The Christmas Spirit" is ©2024 by Michael K. Falciani. It appears here for the first time. The Carson City resident is the author of the ongoing fantasy series, "The Raven and the Crow." His novels "The Dwarves of

Rahn" and "The Raven and the Crow: The Gray Throne," won Imadjinn Awards for best steampunk novel and best fantasy novel, respectively, at the 2023 Imaginarium Convention. His books are available on Amazon.

L.F. Falconer

Asmund
Here and There

The squeal of pigs in slaughter still skewers me with dread, yet as long as I'm not doing the killing myself, I pretend it's not real. As one utters its final cry, slowly, I peel the lone remaining poster from the barn wall, a yellowed advertisement for a movie I declined the opportunity to see. It might have been entertaining. I will never know.

For as long as I can remember, this outer barn wall has been used by the villagers to post notices, and no one ever bothers to remove them. They are stacked layer upon layer. Decades of layers. Forgotten relics no one cares to dispose of once their usefulness is past until they simply become padding beneath newer postings. Pappa has not minded. He says they help keep the barn insulated. But yesterday he decided the wall needs sprucing up, and has tasked me with that duty. I am happy to do it. It keeps me free from the slaughter.

Pulling the movie poster down, I'm met with a face I haven't seen in 20 years. Pigs and barn walls vanish from my thoughts. The "Missing Child" flier has remained pristinely protected by the layers tacked atop it. The face, photocopied in all its varied shades of gray, sparks a knot in my stomach, rendering bittersweet memories. Thoughts happy. Thoughts sad. Thoughts of fairy tales and reindeer. Of terror and regret.

"Asmund," I whisper, tracing my fingers across the photo. "Are you still there?"

The clank of the pulley chain inside the barn precedes my father's shout, "Dahlia, are you finished? That wall needs to be ready for the paint tomorrow."

I crumple the movie poster into the trash bin. "Do not worry, Pappa," I answer. "The wall will be ready."

"I could use your help in here, then. Be quick now."

I do not want to help with the pigs. But it is what I do. I do whatever Pappa expects me to do, because that is what we do here. Whatever is expected. Whatever is necessary. Today. Tomorrow. Yesterday. Every day. Nothing ever changes here. Asmund knew that long before I did.

I met Asmund two days after Pappa and I resettled here in Hǫrgr after Mamma died. "I'm sorry to meet you," Asmund had said upon our introduction, yet before I could judge his remark as rude, he laughed and clarified, "Sorry that you are here now, instead of there. Here, it is only the same. Every day, the same. There, it is different." I liked him immediately.

He was a boy born of wanderlust, never satisfied to simply be. He was swift to laugh and thought he was clever, holding me rapt with his tales. I was bound to follow him anywhere, even to my doom. Yet I did not. Only one could go on that journey.

Carefully, I remove the flier from the wall, staring up at the July long-days' sunlight streaming in through the treetops. I gaze back to the paper quivering in my hand. It was in the season of the long-nights that I had last seen my friend. In the nights of the aurora.

Here in the land of the midnight sun, in the land of trolls and the snow queen, Hǫrgr nestles within the forest, not in a glade but deep within the shelter of the trees. It hides in such seclusion that one could, if they did not already know it was here, pass the village by without notice. Such seclusion entices certain folk to settle here, like my father. Like Asmund's family. But being forest-bound does not benefit the arrival of sunshine into the midst. It does not allow for adventure. Nor does it allow for optimal viewing of the aurora. It was in the month of November, while Asmund and I gathered wood for the fires, when I first spotted the lights of the north peeking greenly through the treetops.

"I so wish I could see them better," I'd remarked.

"You can," Asmund had told me. "But you have to get away from the trees."

"It's impossible. The trees are everywhere."

The gray flecks in Asmund's eyes flickered like starshine. "There is a place not far. At Trǫllsborg the sky is wide open."

"Pappa would not allow me to go to another village." The ominous churr of a late-season nightjar echoed through the woods and I shivered, wondering whose death the bird augured.

Asmund plucked a fat limb from the ground. "No one lives at Trǫllsborg. It's a small lake, but one rarely visited."

"Pappa would not allow me to go on such a lark. Especially in winter."

The nightjar's churr wavered once more. Asmund's smile brightened the afternoon twilight. "Then do not tell him, Dahlia. If you want to see the aurora at its finest, Trǫllsborg is the nearest place."

"I couldn't not tell him." I had been taught not to lie.

Mischief twinkled Asmund's eyes. "I'm certain there's much you do not tell him."

I shook my head. "No, I tell him everything."

"Then you are a silly goose," he laughed. "Rules are meant to be broken, Dahlia. If you wish to see the aurora, you might have to break a rule or two. That's up to you."

My life with Pappa did not leave much time for recreation. With Mamma gone, my duties to the home life as well as to the slaughter kept me occupied. So much of this far north was new to my eyes: the reindeer, the long long-nights, even the famous aurora. How I wanted to see it all. But could I disobey my father? What would the consequences be?

"We can ski there and back within a few hours," Asmund assured me.

"I don't know. I'm afraid."

"If you give in to your fears, you will never be anywhere but here."

"Pappa says fear is what guides us away from consequences."

Asmund put a hand upon my shoulder and stared me straight in the eye. "Not all consequences are bad. Your pappa will forever be stuck here. But you do not have to be. Be brave, Dahlia. Dare to live a little. Come experience the lights in a way you can never experience them here."

I'd gazed at the virescent glow in the darkened sky above. As if it called to my soul, the allure of an unimpeded view of the dancing lights dredged deep. Once again the nightjar churred, yet I chose not to hear. Like Asmund, I would not listen to my fear.

"Let's do it," I said. And like a pair of conspirators, we made our plan. We could leave by 9 p.m. and reach the lake by 10, when the lights would show us their peak performance. We'd be home by midnight. It was a simple plan, a solid plan. It was our adventure. Our shared secret. I felt empowered by the rebellious, unsanctioned plot. By the defiance of my father's heavy hand. It sweetened my soul with drops like honey.

A week later, we set out.

"Won't the woods be dangerous?" I trusted Asmund to tell me the truth, and he did.

"There's always danger, Dahlia. Everywhere. We could come upon wolves. But the angry reindeer will keep them at bay for us. The road is safe to pass."

I tried to picture the reindeer in the woods fending off the wolves who might hunger for children skiing in the night, but kept all thoughts silent so no one in the village would hear. We strapped our headlamps on and slid silently out of our civilized haven, onto the crusted snow of the forest road to Trollsborg.

The air was brittle, dry, honed to a sharp edge, and I was grateful for the protection of my balaclava. I did not have as much experience with the skis as Asmund. He kept pulling far ahead of me in the dark, the frozen snow like grit beneath my runners. We had only progressed beyond the fringe of the village, and already my legs were burning from the effort.

Except for the swish of our skis against the snow, the woods surrounding us were silent and still. I would have preferred Asmund stay closer to me. I would've preferred some conversation, even if it would've been a breathless struggle, impeded still more by the balaclavas wrapped around our faces. Pappa had not allowed me to wander far from home in the dark before, and I did my best to remain brave. Despite that, with Asmund straying so far ahead of me on the road, the night seemed like ill company for a lone girl unaccustomed to such things.

I began to notice dark shapes rushing through the trees beside us on silent feet, keeping time with the movement and noise of our skis as we slogged across the hard-packed snow. We were not alone in these woods, but what accompanied us was beyond my vision. I could only hope it was reindeer. I stopped for a moment to listen—to look—my headlamp providing a dim light in the mossy-hued darkness. The night stopped with me. Only Asmund continued onward, his skis swishing through the dead-silent night. I could see nothing in the woods but the darkness of the trees. Whispering through the branches came a distant, familiar churr, and I shivered. I looked back to the road home, then around to Asmund on the road ahead. The churr of the death-bird ebbed away, and the night grew silent once more.

Taking a deep breath, I quickly moved on, struggling to catch up with Asmund. Exertion got me there at last, but the heat and clamminess inside my shirt I knew to be dangerous. I had to stop again to remove my outer jacket in order to cool myself against the dangers of overheating in the frigid night air. This time, the night was not so silent. Oh, how the trees whispered in the dark, like muted voices speaking a language I could not understand, telling tales only they could know. Above, the northern lights snaked across the blackened sky, teasing me with ribbons of splendor. Yet I heard no birds, and that eased my fears, if only for the now.

I glanced back at the road south. How much farther did we have to go? I gazed north to Asmund. He appeared as a dim point of light in the distance. Why was he in such a hurry? Why wouldn't he wait for me? Was the effort of trying to keep up with him worth the show the aurora promised? I prayed it was as I pushed off once more, struggling to catch up to my friend.

At last, we reached a point where the trees began to vanish into emptiness, the snow-covered plain, an eng, stretching like a vast sea that melted into darkness. Out here, there were no lights—only the aurora and the stars and the two headlamps that lighted our way. A sound like a distant church bell tolled through the dark, haunting and relentless. Yet there were no churches out here. There were no church bells in Hǫrgr. Was there another village nearby? Or was it something borne of the trees? Something joining their own macabre choir of endless, muffled murmurs that poured into the open eng?

The unimpeded land before us shimmered in shades of lilac and clover, reflecting the languid sky waves overhead. I slowed my progress and removed my balaclava in order to freely gape at the wonderous sight. Asmund had stopped as well, awaiting my arrival. When I reached his side, he peeled off his balaclava and pointed to the sky. I gazed up again, watching the aurora cavort across the heavens. When I brought my eyes back to Asmund, his broad smile proved he was pleased that I was pleased with this secret we were sharing. Yet the very air around us seemed fat with aggressive malice. It gathered thickly in my chest.

"Are the lights truly better at the lake?" I asked, repositioning my headlamp.

"We're already on the shore." He pointed with his pole, and I noticed then the flatness behind him, frosted with snow, broken only by one large uplift of dark and craggy spires of stone. From what I could see, it was not a large lake, more a good-sized pond, and well-frozen through this close into winter. The rocks were an island, now accessible without a boat. Truly this is what gave the lake its name, for the island uniquely resembled a fortress grotesque enough for trolls.

Asmund pushed off again, skiing out onto the surface of the lake. I readily followed, more thrilled by this adventure with my trusted friend than heedful of any possibility of danger.

"Now you cannot say that you've never skied on a lake," he said with a laugh.

"It is no easier than skiing on the road."

The ice below us rumbled with a long, echoing gurgle. My sudden dismay must have shown in my eyes. Asmund laughed again. "The lake is protesting our presence. It's nothing to fear. Unless it awakens the trolls. Or something worse." He turned then and headed for the stone island.

Not that I believed in trolls, but I glanced around in cold panic, becoming aware of how helpless and vulnerable we were to this wilderness. To this night.

The same boreal wind that crept through the trees and caused them to wail made the lights overhead squirm and batter the sky. It made the rocky spires of the island undulate like tall pines. Except there was no wind. The night was calm, though hardly serene.

My imagination was fueled by the depth of the long-night, by the fury of the aurora, by the oddness of the stones gleaming in the glittering darkness. Fueled by the faint and distant church bell knell. By the whispering trees. The frigid air. The groaning lake. By the heat of excitement captured against my flesh as it lay buried beneath layers of protective clothing. Digging my poles into the ice, I pushed off, following Asmund, whether I wished to or not. I only felt at ease when by his side.

He shed his skis at the island shore while waiting for me to catch up. "I'm going to climb to the top," he told me.

I was fairly breathless by then. The towering rocks inundated me with great presence, as if they were living, breathing things upon which we had dared to intrude. "Is the view better up there?"

"I can't say. I've never been up there. No one has."

"No one?"

"No one that I know of. This island is forbidden. No one is supposed to be on it."

I slipped off my final ski, my heart quickening. "Then why are we here?"

He scrambled up on rocks that rose roughly like a staircase.

"Because, Dahlia, it is forbidden. Because it is different. Because it is *there*."

He needed no other reason. So, neither did I. Yet I followed him up the stones with a tight coil in my belly. The voices from the woods carried well out to the island and to the rocks that surrounded us, those overbearing spires, those twisted crags, those bulbous boulders glistening with rime and reflected aurora, which all seemed to come to life with our trespass. By my sanity, I swear the rocks were moving. The ledges and cliffs shored up and hedged their way in as if crawling inland on the snow-hushed paws of Laikas. Imperceptible when watched. But glance away and then look back, their advancement was noted without question.

The thought was absurd. Rocks cannot move on their own. Asmund showed no signs of fear. The terror I perceived was mine and mine alone. Yet it felt...so real.

Like towers in a storm, the spires swayed. The boulders swelled. And the voices of the woods that drifted in resembled words now more than ever, punctuated with occasional animalistic expressions, much like Pappa's pigs and lambs awaiting slaughter. Confused, agitated sounds, titters and squeaks.

"Do you hear that?" I asked Asmund as he ascended the rocks.

He stopped and gazed out at the surrounding lake and glade, his face taking on a greenish hue from the lights in the sky. "Yes," he said quietly. "Yes, I do hear it. But the song—I've never heard that song before."

I did not know what song he referred to.

He gazed up toward the stony crest illuminated darkly against the night sky. "I wonder, Dahlia, can it be? Can it truly be the song of Snedronningen? She is rumored to be imprisoned here."

I scoffed. "The snow queen is only a fairy tale."

He continued to stare at the crest. "Is she?" He then raised his face to the lights overhead, his voice dropping solemn like a man of God. "Hundreds of years ago, before she could freeze the world again, Snedronningen was captured and locked away in the fortress of the trolls." He waved his hand to indicate the rocks we stood upon. "She sings her loneliness in a song that can only be heard by those she deems worthy of hearing it."

"What does that even mean?"

He started climbing again. "She likes us," he said, looking back at me with a grin. "So there is nothing to fear."

Beneath the raucous voice of the woods and the distant bell, I began to hear it too, a musical tone. A song that grew more clear with every step we ascended. My heart beat faster, my breaths growing tight. The aurora above grew more frantic and convulsive, the colors pulsating, flashing with tinges of fiery red at the edges and reaching down like the hands of falling angels. My awe morphed into terror. I could not say why. It was simply a feeling that I tried to shake away. I had seen what I came to see. I wanted to go home now. But Asmund was my guide, and he held no fear. I trusted him, so onward I went up the hill, keeping the terror I possessed to myself in silent admonishment for possessing it at all.

A great rumble then shook the night. We came to a halt upon the stony steps, caught in frozen surprise. From the trees below came the reindeer. With thudding thunder, the ground-shaking reindeer streamed. Hundreds of reindeer, loping out from the trees and into the eng, pacing about the shore, yet never venturing a single step onto the frozen lake. As if knowing their combined weight might prove deadly on the ice, they stayed upon the shore, circling in droves, further packing the hardened snow beneath their wide, flat hooves.

I turned to Asmund. His gray-flecked glare cut me to the bone. There it was. Fear. His eyes could not hide it, no matter how often his mouth denied it. I hated him at that moment. His fear validated my own, and I desperately needed my own to be only imagination. Was it the reindeer that struck him cold, or something else? I could not explain my terror. I only knew it held me in a tight embrace. But the fear that was his gripped me much more strongly, with suffocating constriction.

"I don't want to be here anymore, Asmund."

"Where do you want to be?" He turned away, bounding farther up the frosted steps. "What do you want to see in life, Dahlia? The pyramids? The rain forests? Perhaps some kangaroos or penguins? Or are reindeer and slaughter enough for you?"

Who wouldn't want to see those wonderous things? But it wouldn't happen this night. This night, I was only here. Here, on a forbidden island. Far from home in the frozen dark. Here, with Asmund, who was beginning to frighten me. I could no longer trust him. How could I when he could not even admit his own trepidations?

Below, the reindeer ran circles on the shore. From above drifted a haunting melody. Beyond the darkness, the forest cried, and all around us the lights swirled like a swarm of angry hornets. I wanted to go home, but did not wish to go alone. Asmund had thoroughly buried his fears. I, too, could be brave. I had no wish to listen to his mockery of my fear.

Swallowing my reticence, I continued to trail Asmund up the hill.

Near the top of the rough-hewn staircase, his footsteps slowed, and I caught up to him at last. Before us, wedged between two cylindrical pillars of stone, was a mirror, gleaming a bluish silver in the dark. From this mirror, the song emanated in tones remote and hollow. Asmund leaned in for a closer look, and I realized I had been mistaken. The silver face reflected nothing: not Asmund, not me, not the dancing aurora overhead, which even the frosted stones chose to imitate. It was more like a window than a mirror.

Above us, the aurora brightly flashed, nearly neon in essence, lighting up the night to a gloaming. The surrounding rocky spires continued to swell and sway. The cracks and holes upon them took on a beastly visage. The echoes of the night roared.

Asmund reached for the glassy stone.

"Don't touch it!" I shrieked, rushing forth to stop him. I grabbed his arm, but he did not listen, instead lightly tapping the smooth, gleaming surface with his gloved knuckles.

"It's terribly cold," he stated, taking a step back, eyeing his gloved hand suspiciously.

Releasing my grip, I stepped back as well. "What is it?"

"I don't know." He leaned close and tapped the surface again. "It feels like stone, but sounds hollow."

"And there's someone behind it singing," I said. *Snedronningen*, but I did not say the name aloud as if I feared she would hear. As if I feared she *could* hear. She, who was but a myth.

Asmund tapped the surface again, harder this time. When he pulled his hand away, the surface in the center of the window wavered and began to ripple.

He juddered back, and I scurried down several steps, preparing to race to the bottom if he said to run. But he did not say it. He stared at the silver stone's face, and I, too, watched in fascination the expanding movement in the center. It continued to grow until we could see the figure of a woman dressed in white walking toward us, yet far off, surely in the distance. Each step she took brought her closer, larger. The bewitching song intensified.

The surrounding night grew more calamitous, the aurora writhing wickedly above in strange and exotic contortions. The woman within the silver stone drew ever closer. I dared look behind me to the forest with longing. How I wished I had obeyed my father's rule and remained safe in the haven of Hǫrgr. I had seen enough of the aurora. I had seen enough of the silver stone. Enough of the black rock towers around us, which, like blossoming flowers, continued to quiver with new-found life.

"Please, Asmund, please, let us go home. Now."

My voice was overshadowed by the intensity of the encroaching song, the relentless bell, the furious murmurs and the frenzied lights in the sky, the thundering hooves of the reindeer circling. Circling. Asmund paid me no heed, staring transfixed at the approaching figure in the silver stone.

"I will go home without you then." I wasn't accustomed to issuing threats, but he was leaving me little choice.

"Don't go yet," he stated with a chilling calm. "I only want to see her."

"What if she gets out?"

"I think if she could get out, she would have done so long ago. Don't you want to see her? How many people get this opportunity, Dahlia?"

"Why is this island forbidden, Asmund? Think about that. What if she simply needed someone to come and set her free, and guess what? Here we are!"

The woman in the stone drew nearer, her white dress long and flowing like drifted snow, studded with glittering crystals. Her coat and hat were ermine, her skin as pale as the aspen bark. Like glacial ice, her eyes shone cold and blue, sparkling with streaks of silver.

Now large as life, she stopped her steps. A smile curled her blushing lips, and she reached out, her white hand beckoning.

Her song went silent, and with its hush, so went the world. A silence suffocating. Deafening. A silence we could drown within.

I shot one terrified glance upward. Beneath the raging aurora, the stone spires bent inward, bowing in reverence.

"She wants us to go with her," Asmund said. "Maybe we should."

"I-I don't want to."

"If we don't go, what will we know?"

"She's evil."

"Is she? Or is that merely what we've been led to believe? Is it only the tales we've been told?"

Yes, she is evil, my soul screamed inside, terrorized by the accoutrements of her appearance. If she was not evil, why had the forest wailed? If she was not evil, why did the reindeer dance? Why had there been a relentless knell pealing from the edges of the world? If she was not evil, why was the sky above contorting in throes of agony? Why had the nightjar cried?

Tears filled my eyes. "Please, Asmund, if you care at all, let us return to Hǫrgr."

He gazed into the shimmering stone. "I have been to Hǫrgr. It offers me nothing."

His words cut me deeply. "But it's my home now, too. Am I nothing?"

The woman in the stone continued to beckon in silence. Asmund took a step closer.

"Am I nothing?" I shouted through my gathering tears.

Asmund said not a word as he stared into the stone. He then turned and looked at me like a most ungodly beast. He stepped toward me, grabbing hold of my hand. "Be brave, Dahlia. Let us go there together."

I quivered in a solid stance. "No. Stay here, Asmund. With me."

"There is nothing here, Dahlia. You can stay and devote your life to the blood of pigs if you wish. Stay and fade into your father's shadow. Or come with me."

"No!" My heart tried to leap free of my chest, pounding so swiftly beneath the pain and shame of betrayal. "I will not go, but you can. You go. It's where you always want to be, isn't it? There? Never here. Not with your family. Not even with me!"

I wrenched my hand free and shoved him away, hard. He staggered back against the silver stone. Two white arms shot through the stone and wrapped around his shoulders. With eyes agog, Asmund squealed like a pig in slaughter as he was dragged inside, sucked into the silver. For a moment, the stone shimmered brightly, blinding me before turning blacker than the blackest night.

"No, Asmund," I reached out for him, but far too late. "I'm sorry!"

Asmund was gone. Vanished. His final shock, his terror, his scream though, is forever etched into my memory.

I had cried out, pounding my gloved fists against the cold black face of the stone. I beat it while begging for him to return until my fists turned to throbbing putty. But Asmund was no more. And I was left alone upon the forbidden fortress of the trolls, alone beneath the writhing aurora in the long-nights with ghastly stones that shifted and struggled to come to life. Yet the forest had silenced itself, the lakeshore deserted, the frantic reindeer no longer to be seen.

As if in a dream, I'd raced down the hill, returning to Hǫrgr in stunned and shattered silence, creeping desperately into a cold bed from which I hadn't been missed.

Over the next few days after my return, Asmund's parents tacked fliers upon every flat surface in Hǫrgr and beyond. And I remained silent, never revealing why Asmund was no longer here. It was my secret then. It is my secret now. But for my fear, I might have joined him. My fear, which either imprisoned me, or kept me free. Yet not quite free of consequences. Everything ends in consequences.

I have never returned to Trollsborg. I imagine, to this day, Asmund's skis still remain upon the forbidden rocky shore. To this day, his parents still mourn his loss. To this day, I do not care to see the aurora. I do not care to leave the shelter of the forest. I do not care to listen to stories or song. To speak of reindeer or fairy tales. I do not think of Asmund. I still have no desire to go *there*.

"I'm sorry to have met you." I take a binding look at the dashing, youthful face upon the flier in my hand. "I am sorry you are there. There, instead of here to share a life of sameness with me in the shadows. It might have been entertaining. We will never know." Gently, I place the paper into the trash bin. In the treetops above, the soft churr of a nightjar scampers through the air and as I cross the threshold of the barn to aid my father, another pig squeals its last and final cry.

"Asmund Here and There" is ©2024 by L.F. Falconer. It appears here for the first time. A lifelong resident of Fallon, Nevada, L.F. Falconer's works veer toward the dark and the weird as she pursues her fascination with words and the unknown. She enjoys getting off the beaten path to explore the forgotten places, and is an avid collector of interesting stones. Her novels and short story collections can all be found on Amazon.

Jade Griffin

The Bowers Ring

1956

"**G**rand-Auntie!"

The seven-year-old female relative ran at Virginia as soon as the door was flung wide. The youth stopped herself just before colliding. Good, as the old doctor's femur still gave her issue. Falling could break it again, and she'd prefer no more time in the hospital as a patient.

"Calm yourself, child," she advised, but smiled down at the boisterous youth.

"We haven't seen you in forever!"

"Less than a year is not forever. Precise over exaggeration."

The youngster rolled her eyes. "Will you tell me this time?"

"I may, but I haven't even stepped inside. Have patience."

With a gusty sigh, the girl plopped herself down on a couch, swung her legs, and generally made a scene while Virginia drew out the quiet process of setting her things upon the dining room table, applying an expected cheek kiss to her nephew, Robert III, and a more formal greeting to his wife, Laura, while Robert III took her bag to the guest room. Refreshments were offered, but politely declined. Honestly, she just wanted to stretch out on the bed and nap after her journey abroad, but around the doorframe crept her excitable grand-niece's face.

"Yes. Come, but sit," Virginia added quickly as the girl launched herself atop the guest bed. Virginia braced for the jostling, a brow raised until the child did as commanded.

Giggling, hands clasped in an effort to contain herself, the girl tried to mirror her grand-aunt's poised posture. Her socked feet dangled over the edge and swayed gleefully. "May I please, pretty please see your ring, Grand-Aunt Virginia?"

She splayed her hand for the inquisitive youth to inspect the jewelry in question.

"Did a handsome prince give you the ring and you told him to shove it? Oh, it doesn't have any diamonds but a weird symbol. Are you under a curse and have to wear it, and that's why you aren't married? Is it a secret society of super-secret women doctors and that's your special ring?"

"None of that, no. This silver ring has been in our family for two generations before mine. It has no diamonds but is special for other reasons. The star symbol on the top is an Elder Sign and keeps evil away."

"May I please please *please* hold it while you tell the story?"

Virginia pulled the ring slowly over thickened knuckles and slipped it onto the waiting finger of her youngest grand-niece. "Be careful with it."

The child played with the oversized loop, distracted only momentarily before engaging in the next query to pop into her young head. "Grand-Auntie... Are you a witch?"

"Of course not. You know I'm a doctor. I don't have time for witchcraft, Susan. I do have time for a promised story, though it is quite short. My grandfather knew magic but wasn't very clever about hiding it in his youth. Half the town ran him off. He wound up in a smaller town, set up shop as a veterinarian, but his reputation in the prior town traveled to the ears of a very powerful and evil family. If not for the warning of a local young lady, they'd have killed him, but her warning allowed him time to craft the ring and cast the spell. He made an identical one for her, as a wedding gift. This one was hers. It has been used by many to hide from evil magic-users ever since."

Little Susan's mouth trembled in fear. "Are they going to come after us?"

"No, child. They don't even know you exist. Best to keep it that way and not dabble in magic."

With quick nods, the youngest grand-niece dashed from the room.

Watching her long brunette hair fly out the door, Virginia caught the gaze of her eldest grand-niece, sitting up in bed, reading in her room, pretending not to listen. Christine, eldest child of Robert III, flung a single glance her way; neither invitation nor welcome.

Virginia saw it as a challenge and rose to say hello as well as gather more information on the quiet twelve-year-old.

"If you wanted her to leave, you didn't have to scare her," Christine said before she'd crossed the threshold of the open door, painted green and blue with pictures of ocean animals tacked up.

Virginia cocked a brow and a grin at her eldest grand-niece. "There are a great many things under the sun and the sea than even I have beheld. You don't believe magic exists?"

Christine produced the most dubious of glares before returning all focus on her book. "I'm not a little kid, Grand-Aunt Virginia."

"So I see." The pre-teen was reading a rather worn copy of *The Sea Around Us* by Rachel Carson. Familiar with the book and its poetic descriptions of the beginnings of land life and the sea environs, it was not something most children would pick up, let alone remain engrossed in. Nor was her eldest grand-niece's last favorite read: *Principles of Genetics* by EW Sinnott & LC Dunn. That, she'd learned, was very much Christine's way. Precocious, serious, and hungry for science fact, not science fiction. A dangerous combination if not schooled properly—something of which Virginia was intimately aware. The problem sat in the generational gap, and the fact that Christine started avoiding her grand-aunt last year for an as-yet-unknown reason. Time to pry the lid off that box.

"Christine, I believe you've taken some sort of issue with me, and I'd like to know what it is. Feel free to speak candidly without reproach."

The young female relative gave a little sigh, set the book down, faced her grand-aunt, and said, "The reason is simple: You are a liar."

Blunt, unexpected, but Virginia did not have feathers to ruffle. She herself was all scales and saw much of her own calculating coolness in the girl.

Easing onto the bed, she regarded her grand-niece with a clever smile. "What specifically do you believe you've been lied to about?"

Christine scowled, as if Virginia should already know the answer and it angered her to point out the facts. "Not counting the lie you just told about our family history, I overheard you talking with my dad last year, telling him where you'd been and what you'd done. All that stuff about magic and old gods and monsters. It's all lies."

Ah, there it sat. The difference between her and Christine. Her eldest grand-niece took grand offense at presumed lies, whereas in Virginia's experience, she'd simply move away from liars and charlatans. Christine also appeared to be a young person only believing what was presented in a book or that she could see. Pity. Perhaps there may be time to change that.

With patience, Virginia explained, "I've lived quite an extraordinary life in my nearly seventy-three years, Christine. I'm sure in time your own experiences will grow—and I hope it shall not be a painful growth, but it will if you do not curb your thirst for knowledge and that start of a superiority complex."

"But I *am* superior!" Truly affronted, the girl shot to a stand.

Virgina's brows crested in a fine arc of surprise. "Superior in your ignorance, yes. The truly learned do more than spout supposed facts and read along the line. But, it is much safer to not stray off the visible path."

A puzzled frown overtook Christine. "You really believe the things you told him?"

"I am neither delusional nor a liar, child, but my past is also not something I share outside of chosen family. You were not to hear of it for a reason, and not because you are too young. You have proven a great capacity to absorb knowledge, but your reactions and biases remain at or below your age."

She took great offense, that eldest grand-niece, and sputtered such indignations until Virgina held up a hand. To her credit, Christine quieted, though her eyes burned.

The old doctor continued. "I lived the things you heard me caution him about. I only told him because your father, unfortunately, sought other means to aid the family three years ago, so I brought a warning to him against such tactics. I return, yearly, to make certain he followed my advice, or to aid in correcting any threats created."

Dubious, Christine searched her grand-aunt's face for any hint of falsehood. Cautious, she queried, "Do you mean he sought the help of mobsters?"

"Mobsters, no. Monsters, yes."

"If they're real, prove it to me."

"With luck, child, there are no monsters here. I have to determine that, however. Tomorrow, we shall see."

Oh, the look of condescension from the twelve-year-old!

"Just as I thought. There is no proof." Her snideness came as no surprise.

"There is always proof if one goes after it," Virgina said, meaning it as a warning.

Indignant, Christine crossed her arms, a challenge.

"Very well, child. Three years ago, your mother was very ill. She had an inoperable tumor. Not even I could help her. So, your father turned to supernatural forces and summoned a creature to eat the cancer out of her. It might have eaten both of your parents as well, if I hadn't been there to help him stop it."

The wide look of shock caused Virginia to chuckle. "If you're wondering why you don't remember, it's because you and your sister stayed that night at your Aunt Lucille's house."

"But... but my dad is a librarian."

"An accomplished one, knowledgeable in more than just card catalogues and maintaining silence."

"And... you claim this is all real?"

"I do."

Christine edged closer, a sudden excitement prodding her. "Take me, the next time you go traveling. Or when you leave. Dad won't even tell us where you live. Let me come with you!"

"He doesn't tell you because I've never told him. Not even your grandfather, my brother, knows where I reside."

The youngster expressed concern. "You do have a home... Don't you?"

"Of a sort. As to your request to join me on my travels, I shall see if there is any further traveling left in my old bones, and if your parents might be inclined to allow it. Perhaps in the summer."

"But it's November now," Christine groaned, flopping bodily onto her bed.

"Yes, and it is school-time in two days."

The preteen sat up in a rush, affixing her eyes on her grand-aunt. "But you will ask my parents, won't you?"

"If your father has kept out of certain affairs, you may ask them yourself. It is not my wish but your own."

Her shoulders sagged, a sign of defeat, or perhaps in preparation to plead. "Grand-Aunt Virginia, I didn't like calling you a liar, but I—"

"You need to see for yourself. I understand, as I understand the consequences of granting your request. Those who are not ready for the truth, not open enough to accept what lies past their perception... That truth may break them. I've seen it happen."

"Children are often more perceptive and open to the broader truths of the world, as well as the forces which wield them," Christine stated confidently.

Again, Virginia's brows rose. "Do not think it impossible for children to be driven insane. Sadly, they can."

"You've seen that, with your own eyes?" The dubiousness returned.

Virgina nodded. "Once. Not something I'd care to see again, and most assuredly not to family. But my journeys have left me quite spent. I shall retire for now, speak to your father later, and determine a course from there."

As she started out, Christine spoke up. "Grand-Aunt? Don't you think you should get your special ring back before Susan loses it?"

Virginia looked back at her eldest grand-niece and gave her a smile reminiscent of the ones she'd give her patients. "Oh, I fully intend for her to wear it the whole length of my stay, just as I'd planned. Beside which, I have the other here." She pulled from under her shirt front a simple silver chain which hung around her neck, wherein a similar larger ring dangled.

"You scared her to get her to wear it?"

A measure of appreciation reverberated in the youth's tone. Good. Respect was, after all, due. "Of everyone in this house, children are the most vulnerable when it comes to monsters. My visits here are pleasant company, but I come to ensure the safety of both of you, as well as your parents. Your father is proof that some should not meddle in things they are not prepared to understand. If you truly want proof, look on his face when you ask where he got the scars on his arms. Look and tell me if you see a lie."

Christine gave a meek nod.

She again started out of the room.

"Grant-Aunt Virginia?" Again, the eldest grand-niece stopped her.

"Yes, Christine?"

"Could I... May I borrow that other ring? Just until I get answers."

"Yes, child." Virginia hid her grin as she lifted the jewelry from off her neck and placed it around Christine's. Everything falling right into place, the elder female child need not require much schooling after all.

In 1956:

Christine Bowers—future "Nurse Stabby", Virginia's older grand-niece, 11

Susan Bowers—younger grand-niece, 7

Laura Bowers—niece-in-law, 32

Robert III Bowers—nephew, 36

Robert II Bowers—older brother, 77

Virginia Bowers—previously Paisley Foundation medic, traveling doctor, age 73

The ACES Anthology

Norm Halverson

Blood Lake

The 20-year-old faded orange and primer grey Volvo sped down the road. Malcom's heart beat in concert with the wipers as they struggled to keep up with the pounding rain. Malcom, the 19-year-old, ginger-haired driver, barely 5 foot 2 inches tall, and often mistaken for an underfed 15-year-old, worked frantically to see the road. The full moon did little to light the way through the thick clouds and heavy rain. A river of water flowed down the road, obscured the lines, and deposited debris on the blacktop. To make matters worse, Malcom's nearly legal, hubcap-less, bald tires provided limited traction.

Malcom checked his watch, shook his head, and pressed the accelerator a little harder.

A flash of lightning struck a nearby tree. Thunder immediately followed, shaking the car. The windshield turned opaque, blinding Malcom. His vision was slowly returning when, out of the darkness, a hard left hand turn suddenly appeared. Malcom locked up his brakes and spun the wheel hard left.

Rather than turn, the car decided to hydroplane and slide straight into the ditch.

Malcom was uninjured. His car was undamaged. Fearing for his safety and the safety of anyone walking invisibly down the road, Malcom knew he had to abandon the car somewhere and continue on foot. He also knew time was short and the only place in the area to leave his car was Blood Red Lake, or Blood Lake as it had become known to the locals. Not his favorite place, but tonight it would have to do. Malcom started the car, nursed it back on the road, and headed to the Blood Lake parking area.

Blood Red Lake, as legend has it, was originally named Crystal Pines Lake and was a crystal-clear alpine lake. It was rich in fish and a favorite camping destination for locals and tourists alike. Nearly three decades ago, that all changed.

One night, three college students, intent on doing some early morning fishing the next day, set up camp at the base of Red Mountain, a mountain rich in deep red soil. As the night wore on, a storm appeared. The storm grew and raged on, the townspeople reported the ground rumbled and shook. The next morning, the three students and their camp were gone, and the lake had turned blood red.

Search parties were formed, but no sign of the students or their camp were ever found. Over time, the story grew. Now the speculation is the college students did more than prepare their fishing gear. They opened a portal to hell.

Not wanting to lose the lucrative tourist trade, the people of the town changed the town's name to Blood Red Township, the mountain to Blood Red Mountain, and the lake to Blood Red Lake. It attracted a few curiosity seekers, but for the most part, the tourists were gone and never returned.

However, the Blood Red Lake story became popular among high school students. Every new storm prompted challenges for students to spend the night at Blood Lake. Few challenges were accepted, but when they were, new incidents were reported. The reports ranged from new flashlights with new batteries going dim as they walked into the woods, to students emerging with specks of blood all over their clothes, to a creature roaming the woods.

Rounding the curve, Malcom saw a sign, "Welcome to Blood Red Lake."

Malcom let out a sigh as he turned into the parking lot.

Unsurprisingly, the parking lot was empty: no cars, no trucks, not even a bicycle. Malcom selected a parking space near the Blood Red Mountain trailhead and checked his watch. Time was short and getting shorter. Taking the trail would trim miles off his journey.

Preparing to leave the shelter of his car, Malcom took a deep breath. He looked out at the white caps—or pink caps, rather—breaking over the lake.

Malcom grabbed the flashlight from the glove box. He turned it on and off several times, ensuring that it was functioning correctly and the batteries were good. Wearing the slick yellow raincoat he had grabbed when he left home, Malcom exited the car. Fighting the wind and pouring rain, he reached back inside and retrieved the 20-by-20-by-6-inch black vinyl pouch from the passenger seat.

The waves slapped the rocks along the shore and made a loud rhythmic clapping. Torrents of raging water thundered down the hill, where small streams had once been. The wind whistled through the forest. Together they made a cacophony of sound, a deafening, unharmonious combination of water and wind.

Malcom had never been up Blood Red Mountain, but his destination was just a mile down the trail. He checked his watch, tucked his head and started jogging down the trail.

Each step Malcom took sank in the soft, rain-saturated ground. The mud oozed up, grabbing his feet. The footsteps behind him immediately filled with blood-red water and created a trail of mini-blood lakes.

Malcom trudged along the trail. Finally, the rain lightened up and the sky started to clear. The rain was replaced by a low-hanging fog. Unable to see the brush through the fog, Malcom repeatedly snagged his pants on every bush he passed. Each limb felt like a hand grabbing him. His flashlight was growing dimmer and dimmer. The lush leafy trees and shrubs at the beginning of the trail turned to a leafless forest of dead or dying timber and bushes. The dark silhouettes of the trees swayed back and forth in the wind, creating the illusion that they were alive. Malcom kept going and going. He finally stopped when he thought he heard a rustling in the brush.

When he stopped, it stopped. When he ran, it ran.

Hell Hound! It's real! Malcom thought, running as quickly as he could and only slowing to take a quick glance at his watch.

Faster and faster, he ran. Snagging his clothes on the brush, splashing in the puddles and slipping on the mud, he ran. His lungs burned. Every time he felt he couldn't go on, the thought of the creature in the brush or a glance at his watch rejuvenated him.

At long last, Malcom turned a corner and the fog parted. The wind calmed. The clouds disappeared. The stars became visible. The combined smell of rain-freshened air, wet thigh-high grasses, and yellow, red, and purple wild flowers filled his lungs. Malcom found himself at the edge of the forest and gazing at a small dimly moonlit meadow, with an old Victorian house about 100 feet ahead.

The three-story building had multiple roof lines, a porch that ran the length of the house, and large windows on every side and level. Unfortunately, the once-grand house had succumbed to the passage of time. The peeled paint exposed grey weathered wood. The windows were poorly boarded up and coated with filth. The porch railing leaned, and sections had fallen. All these things and maybe more went completely by Malcom as he, nearing exhaustion, continued to run. Time was running out.

Malcom spied light moving from room to room and flickering between the gaps in the wood covering the windows as he ran across the meadow. Moments later, he reached the house. Bent over near the door, Malcom worked to regain his breath. Mustering all the energy he had left, Malcom pounded on the door then checked his watch.

"COME ON! OPEN UP!" Malcom yelled, gasping for breath. "I know you're in there."

Malcom detected footsteps approaching the door and saw light sneaking out around the edges. Then the sounds stopped.

"Who is it?" asked a deep male voice from inside the house.

"It's Malcom from Blood Red 24 Hour Pizza, 30-minute delivery or it's free," said Malcolm. "I have a large cheese with triple garlic pizza for a Mr. Van Helzing."

The hinges creaked as the door slowly opened halfway. A middle-aged man dressed in a long black coat with a large silver crucifix around his neck stood before him, holding a lantern in his right hand. His black wide-brimmed hat obscured much of his face. He hung the lantern on a nail by the door, freeing his right hand to retrieve his pocket watch from his vest. He looked down at the watch, but Malcom, still panting, couldn't take his eyes off the large, sharp wooden stake in the man's left hand.

The man looked up.

"Twenty-eight minutes. In this weather... good job young man," he said.

The man put his watch back in his vest pocket, tucked the wooden stake into his belt, and retrieved a large roll of bills from inside his coat.

"Keep the change," the man said as he peeled off three twenties and handed them to Malcom.

"Thank you, sir," Malcom responded, still breathing heavily.

He knew good manners could mean a bigger tip next time.

Malcom opened the insulated pizza delivery pouch. The smell of garlic forced him back and made his eyes water. He slid the pizza box out of the pouch and gave the pizza to the man.

The man grabbed the lantern and began to turn to go back into the house when he saw the dim flashlight in Malcom's hand.

"Let me see that," the man said, taking the flashlight from Malcom.

He put the lantern down on the porch and pulled out a handkerchief. Wiped the lens. The flashlight got brighter.

"That dang iron rich dirt is everywhere, even in the leaves of the brush," the man said, returning the flashlight to Malcom and bending down to pick up the lantern. "And look at your pants. It's all over them. You need to wash them before they dry, or you'll never get it out."

Malcom looked down at the blood red specks and splashes on his pants.

"Ever since that avalanche killed those poor college kids and turned the lake red, that iron rich soil from Red Mountain is everywhere. It killed all the fish and half the forest." He again turned to go in the house.

His retreat was stopped abruptly by the rustling in the thigh-high grasses about 20 feet from the house.

"Oh, no, It's a Hell Hound. He followed me," Malcom yelled out with all the energy he had left.

"Hell Hound?" the man said, trying not to break into

laughter. "No, that's my puppy, Lucian. He bolted when the lightning struck. He probably couldn't find his way home so he followed you. Thanks for bringing him back.

"Come on, Lucian. Come here."

A medium size, long-haired, jet-black dog came bounding onto the porch and greeted his owner.

The man, petting and praising the dog frantically, said, "Where have you been?"

"He doesn't like thunder," the man said, directing his comments to Malcom and still petting his dog.

"Now you should be getting on home young man... It'll be midnight soon," the man added as he and Lucian slid into the house, closed, and latched the door.

Malcom looked to his right toward the trail then to his left toward the road.

My car is only one mile by trail and three miles by road, he thought.

He stepped off the porch and took a step toward the trail.

Malcom paused.

No, no, not a chance, Malcom thought.

Pivoting to his left, Malcom started down the road, still thinking about the really, really, big, sharp, stake.

"Blood Lake" is ©2024 by Norm Halverson. It appears in print here for the first time. The author is a long-term resident of Nevada and Lyon County. Upon his retirement he started writing for the sheer enjoyment of it and is a member of the Dayton Writers Group.

Kelli Heitstuman-Tomko

Deliveries

T op Copy. Copy Cats. Dean and Ted's Excellent Copies.
I didn't like any of them. Well, maybe Copy Cats wasn't too bad. *Hey, boss, why don't we go down to Copy Cats to get our copies done?* Yeah, Copy Cats wasn't too bad. I'd bounce it off Dean the next time we talked.

There wasn't a print shop in town, and most folks who wanted major printing jobs done had to drive a half-hour to the city. I thought about how often people ran to the library to pay a dime a copy of whatever small jobs they needed, and the way I saw it, they should be giving all that money to me, ten cents at a time, and I wouldn't even have to work for it. What did they call that? Passive income?

I sat at breakfast one morning and told my parents my plan. I hoped anything I said that didn't involve sitting in my room or Dean's playing video games would make them happy, but Mom just rolled her eyes and muttered something patronizing. Dad glared at me over the top of the morning paper.

"Does Dean have anything to do with this?" he demanded.

"Well, yeah, we're planning to do it together," I said, and he snorted. I didn't bother telling him I hadn't actually talked to Dean about it yet.

"Why don't the two of you just get a God damn job," he growled at me. "Only college graduates start businesses. You two idiots were lucky the high school decided to give you a diploma."

Mom shrugged apologetically, but, I'd gotten the response I expected from my father. It could be he was right. Maybe we were wasting our time. Dean and I were four years out of high school, and neither of us could hold down a job. But then I'd think about all those dimes going into the library copy machine. I could do this. I knew I could.

The only time I ever hit the library was when I wanted to make copies or flirt with the cute new library assistant who'd moved in from out of town. But I'd heard about this thing called "market research," and libraries were for research. I didn't know what market research was, really, but my version was to sit facing the copy machine at the library while looking through some books on how to start a business. There were books for dummies, for starting businesses on a shoestring, for creating a business plan. While I wrote things down I figured I had to remember, I kept a tally of how many people came in to use that one copy machine.

After four days of pretending I knew what I was doing, I'd counted thirty-two people making copies. I did some quick figures on my notepad and realized that with only one print per person, the grand total of dimes in the machine was a whopping $3.20. Most people made more than one copy, but the Sunday school teacher made a boxful. I'd sauntered over to peek at the meter after she left and found she'd only spent $12. I started to think this wasn't a good idea after all, but something in the back of my head told me not to drop it.

I went home and pulled out my laptop. I typed in the name

of the print shop in the city and found they did more than make copies. A lot more. There were rates for binding, for business cards, for different weights of paper. I thought about the Sunday school teacher. She'd told the librarian she was making ten-page booklets. Twelve of them. I followed the pricelist on the computer screen and realized that, if she'd had it all done at a print shop, it would have cost $336.

I didn't know how to bind books or cut business cards. That only meant I had to learn to do a few things. I decided I was done with the first phase of my research. It was time to talk to Dean.

I'd known Dean since kindergarten, and, together, we'd been at the bottom of all our classes throughout our entire school careers. No one expected us to go anywhere, and, in high school, we were voted the most likely to still be living at home with our parents after thirty. We'd left high school with plans, though. We weren't going to waste four good years on college. We were going into business for ourselves. We just didn't have any idea what business that would be. In the meantime, we just worked odd jobs around town.

But now, I had an idea, and I finally connected with Dean at the one burger joint in town at the end of the week. He'd been with a girl, which was par for the course.

"I cleaned out her dad's garage all last week," he said. "I didn't make much, but I got what I wanted out of it."

"Her room, or yours?" I asked.

"Dad was on a bender. We used the bed of my pickup."

"Have a little class, man," I said. "You should have taken her to your bedroom, at least."

"I told you Dad was on a bender. Besides, have you seen my room?"

He had a point. I shrugged. This wasn't what I wanted to talk about. So, I told him my idea about the print shop, and he listened, nodding. We'd both talked over business possibilities before, but this was the first one that had both of us firing on all eight cylinders. If we could find a place to set up just one machine, I told him, we could start at any time. The only thing standing in our way was capital.

"I tried talking to Mom and Dad," I told him. "I can't expect any help from them."

"My dad just drinks all our money," Dean said. "There's no way I'm getting any from him. Maybe we can find someone to front us some cash."

"No, no, bad idea, buddy," I said quickly. "We don't want anyone stealing our idea. Don't tell a soul."

"Yeah," Dean said. "You're probably right. So, what have we got?"

"I have about $350 in the bank left over from that painting job I did."

"I have $500. I don't think that's going to get us far."

"It's a start, though. I did some research and read that we need $100,000 to start a business. We need to find a way to make money until we have that much."

"A hundred grand? Where the hell are we supposed to get that kind of money?"

I put a hand on his shoulder. "Dean, I hate to break this to you, but I think we're going to have to find jobs."

I started looking for work immediately. My reputation as a slacker preceded me, though, and no one seemed willing to give me a chance. Everyone in town knew Ed Slocum's kid was worthless, including Ed Slocum. When I told him I was looking for a job, he laughed that bitter laugh with no humor behind it.

"That won't last long," he said. "It never does."

But two days into my search, I found myself on the doorstep of the town's one and only Asian restaurant, Nanjing and Nagoya. Chen Ling, the owner, decided I was worth a try. He needed someone who was familiar with town to deliver food, and I knew every nook and cranny. I started work that Friday night.

The restaurant was run by Ling and his brother, Huang. There were three Chinese cooks in the kitchen, and Huang's girlfriend waited tables. I sat at a table in the back and waited until Ling told me to take food to a customer, and then I was off and running in my beat-up Jeep. By the end of the night, I had $30 in tips.

By Sunday morning, Dean also had a job. He was pumping gas for his uncle. He didn't figure he would make much money because his uncle was tight-fisted, but he also made tips on top of his pay.

It didn't take me long to learn who the restaurant regulars were, who tipped and who didn't, and who had yappy little dogs that would bite my ankles. I dealt with the dogs immediately by carrying dog treats. I learned that old Mrs. Grant ordered Tangerine Chicken every time she called. The high school principal ordered a PuPu Platter and tons of fried rice every Wednesday, laughed and called me a loser, and never tipped. The cute librarian's assistant ordered steamed vegetables three times a week. I had a lot of calls to the one little motel in town, but if the office called, rather than a guest, the order was always won ton soup and chicken wings.

When I got my first paycheck it wasn't huge, just a few hundred dollars, but I'd made almost four times that in tips over the course of the week. I put the paycheck and half my tips into my savings account and didn't touch it. The rest of my tips put gas in my Jeep.

Dean and I both managed to have Mondays off, so we got together every week for some brainstorming. Two months into our jobs, we were developing some working and social skills. We were always on time for work, always smiled for the customers, and always took the chance to learn something new. Dean griped about it a lot, but I found I was enjoying the experience, and I usually looked forward to work.

One Monday, we were sitting in his dining room eating pizza and chilling when I started onto an idea. Dean's dad had passed out on the couch, and the news was blaring something about an accident on the interstate, some rich guy's grandson getting kidnapped, and a body being found in the local pond. Dean was on the phone, arguing with his mom over a bill that wasn't getting paid. The clock was striking the hour. I lived in a fairly quiet household, and the noise at Dean's was getting on my nerves. I finally got up, went into the bathroom and shut the door, and relaxed in the quietness so I could think.

Why would our print shop be different? Delivery. I learned that people were willing to pay more to have their dinner delivered to their door. They paid more to have their gas pumped so they didn't have to get out of their cars. What was the chance businesses might do that same thing with print orders?

Dean banged on the door. "Ted, man, are you having a problem in there?"

I threw open the door. "No way, bud. I got me another idea."

"Still with the print shop, though, right?"

"Absolutely. Dean, we could deliver orders to businesses. They would send some stuff and say, 'We need 300 copies,' and we'd be, like, 'You'll have them by five.' We copy. We deliver. We get paid *and* tipped."

"I dunno, Ted. What if we both need to be at the shop?"

"If we both need to be at the shop then we'd be generating

enough business to hire someone to deliver for us."

"An employee?"

"Yes, an employee. That's what businesses do. They hire people to work in them. We could even have one of those bicycle couriers like they have in the big city."

Dean rubbed his chin and nodded. "Yeah," he said. "Yeah, I like that idea." He reached over and clapped me on the shoulder. "Keep 'em coming, man. You think better than I do."

Three months into my job I was learning more about customer service by watching my boss. Ling remembered just about anyone who came through his door. He taught me to bus tables while I waited for deliveries so there was little waiting for seating customers. I learned to take credit cards and orders over the phone. Customers who had been accustomed to seeing me loaf around town began to speak to me differently, and I liked it. They would watch me work around the floor of the restaurant until Ling would bring me a bag of food and politely ask me to deliver it.

"Ted is one of our most important employees," he told customers.

Unfortunately, three months in was also when there was a snag in the print shop plans. Dean met a girl. She was a pretty but brainless thing, and she was sure he'd make ever so much more money at her father's service station—700 miles away. I laughed when Dean told me about it until he told me he was packing up.

"Excuse me?" I demanded. "Did you say you were going to take her up on it?"

"Yeah, man," Dean said. "I already talked to her dad on the phone. I'll be doing lube jobs. I've been doing them here for two months now, and my uncle gave me a great reference."

"I don't believe it!" I snapped. "I sleep with a girl, and her father threatens to shoot me. You do it and you get a job offer? What about the copy shop?"

"Look, Ted, we were never going to make enough money to open that shop, and we both know it. It's never going to get off the ground. I'm not going to waste any more time on a pipe dream. I can make more money in another state. Why should I waste money on something that will never happen?"

"So, *partner*, when are you leaving?"

"Don't be a jerk about this, okay? I'm going with Brandy. I took all my money out of the bank, and we're leaving in the morning."

I stood there for a moment and processed what I was hearing. Then I turned and walked away. I didn't even tell him goodbye.

I was having a late lunch before work when my mother sat down next to me. She put her hand on my arm, which surprised me. I hadn't had any kind of personal relationship with my parents for a long time. I was an only child, and I wasn't exactly their pride and joy.

"I heard Dean is leaving in the morning," she said. "I know we've never had anything good to say about him, but I also know he was your friend. I'm sorry."

"It's not that, Mom," I said. "We had plans to open a print shop here in town. We were working toward it. The money we got from our jobs was going to help us get what we needed to open. Then some girl comes to town and hops into his bed, so he pulls his money out of the deal and runs off with her. He always talked like he was with me all the way. Now, all of a sudden, he's saying he knew it was never really going to work."

"You honestly were going to do this?"

I looked over at her, surprised. "Well, yeah. That's what I've been working for. I've got plans. I know who to contact for some of the machines. I know how much money I need to start. But my partner and a large chunk of that money is following some bimbo out of town."

"I didn't realize you were so serious about this."

"I've been saving for it for the past three months. That's why I got a job. I'm putting away money. I'm working for a plan."

She just looked at me for a moment. "Then I really am sorry, Teddy."

I frowned into my soup bowl. "Don't be. To be perfectly honest, I'm more upset about losing the money than about Dean being gone. It will just take me a little while longer to get set up, that's all."

"You're not giving up the copy shop?"

"No, Mom. I can do this. I can make it work, and I can do it without Dean."

She patted my shoulder. "I'm sure you can."

I was back to work that night, and it was busy. Mrs. Grant's son was visiting so she ordered Tangerine Chicken and Beef and Broccoli. The principal didn't call me a loser this time, but he still didn't tip me. The cute librarian's assistant smiled and said she hadn't seen me at the library in a while. I took orders to nearly every room at the motel. And that night, I got a call to the seasonal RV park that was just opening for the spring.

I arrived at an older fifth wheel and knocked on the door. A tall dude with a cigarette opened the door and nearly dropped ash from his cigarette onto my head. He was wearing a V-neck T-shirt and jeans, and any visible skin was covered in tattoos. His hair was long and dirty blond, and he looked like he'd seen a lot of bad road.

"That will be $42.35," I told him.

"Is the General Tso's really spicy?" he asked in the lisping voice of a child.

Huh?

I glanced past the tall dude and saw a clean-cut kid. He looked about 6 years old and completely out of place.

"Mom always orders it spicy for me," he said.

"Did she order it spicy for you this time?" I asked.

"You get back," the tall dude said to the kid as he shoved a handful of money at me. The kid ignored him.

"My mom isn't here right now," he said.

"Well, if it isn't spicy enough," I said as I backed down the steps, "you just let us know and we'll make it spicier next time."

The tall dude slammed the door. I was putting the money in my bag when I realized he'd tipped me way too much. I started to get out of the jeep to return some of the money but stopped. He was a jerk. If he miscounted his money trying not to bother with me, that was his problem. I was just doing my job. But I was worried about repercussions to the business, so I talked to Ling after the restaurant closed.

"You didn't do anything wrong," Ling told me. "If he calls, we'll deal with it, but he gave you the money. You are not unreasonable in thinking you can keep it. But it's good that you brought this up to me. It means you have concern for our customers and for the business. That's always a good thing."

I dipped my head to him, but I wasn't sure what to say. I wasn't accustomed to being told I was doing a good job. For that compliment, I almost didn't care if I couldn't keep the money.

On my next day off, I was back at the library looking up numbers and reading business books. I still wasn't entirely sure I knew what I was doing. I didn't even look at the copy machine. I knew that it only printed black and white and only on one side of the paper. I knew the cost of copies. I had a general idea how many people visited it. I wasn't going to learn anything else from it. I wondered if that was market research enough.

I worked on reading books I barely understood, but I found that if I reread something a few times it would start making sense to me. The cute librarian's assistant smiled at me while she shelved books.

"Are you finding out what you need to know?" she asked.

"I don't know," I said. "I'm trying to do 'market research.' I don't know if I've done enough."

"A poll might help," she said.

"A poll?"

"Sure. Work out a poll asking if anyone would be interested in visiting whatever business you want to open. You can set it up on the local town information page, and you can do it anonymously. If you get a positive response, you'll know you're on the right track."

"How do I do that?"

She sat down next to me and pulled out her phone. She showed me what page I needed to visit and how to set up a poll.

"Thanks," I told her. "Any other advice?"

"Well, you do look out of place in this section," she said. "You need a haircut."

"You think so?"

"And some new clothes. Some slacks, maybe, instead of jeans. And shirts with collars."

"Then would I look like I fit in this section?"

She smiled at me again. "It would be a start. My name is Emily, by the way."

"I'm Ted."

"I know. Whenever I order from the restaurant, Ling always tells me he's sending Ted to me, and that you are his very best delivery driver."

"Emily," I said, "I'm his *only* delivery driver."

"Well, he likes you. He thinks you do good work. If you spiffed yourself up, I'm sure he'd be happy about it, too."

The long and short of it was that I found myself down at the barber shop getting a decent haircut. After my haircut, I hit a department store and bought some clothes. Three pairs of slacks, four shirts, and a pair of boat shoes later, I headed home somewhat poorer but looking pretty good.

I was walking through the house and up the stairs to my bedroom when my father stopped me.

"What is this?" he asked.

"Someone suggested I could do with an upgrade," I said.

"Was it a girl?" he asked.

"Um, yeah. It was. She works at the library where I've been doing some, I don't know, market research. She just recommended that I might want to get a more respectable look if I wanted to get into business."

Mom walked into the living room to call us to dinner and stopped. "Teddy," she said. I could hear the approval in her voice. "Both of you wash up for dinner."

I put my new clothes away in my room and then went downstairs and sat at my place at the table. As Mom was dishing up our plates, my father turned to me and said, "I heard you were going to go on with your print shop even with Dean gone."

I nodded as Mom set a plate in front of me. "That's the plan. It will take me a little longer to get the money together, but I'll keep at it."

"I think I know a place where you can set up."

I stared at him. To say I was shocked was putting it mildly. "Really?"

"I have that old place on Ash," he said. "It used to be a storefront, and I was going to rent it out. It has its own parking. If you want to start cleaning it out, you can use it. You would have to use your own money, mind you, but it's a good place, and it's paid for."

"Dad," I said, "thanks. Really. I appreciate it."

He grunted at his fork and continued eating.

The principal still wasn't tipping me, but I didn't care. He wasn't calling me a loser anymore, either. In fact, he almost didn't recognize me at the door. Ling was also happy with my cleaned-up look, and I wondered why he hadn't suggested it himself. We were in the kitchen bagging an order, and I asked him.

"You had a reputation, Ted. No one expected you to stay. You did, but you needed to move one step at a time. Learn to work first. Then learn to improve. You don't need a big change thrown at you all at once."

He held a bag up to me. "For the boy in the RV park. We made it spicier."

I drove out to the RV park, and the kid was standing right there next to the tall dude waiting for his food.

"I made him order it extra spicy this time," the kid said.

"Because it wasn't spicy enough last time, eh?" I asked.

"It won't be spicy enough this time," he said. "My mom knows how to order it. She'll order it right when she comes."

"That's good," I said. "Then we'll know just how to fix it." Then the tall dude gave me money and slammed the door.

When I got back to the restaurant, I set up the poll on my phone, anonymously, like Emily showed me. I looked up at Ling while I worked.

"Did the guy at the RV park ever call about that money?" I asked.

"He didn't," he told me. "You're all good, Ted."

I checked out the property on Ash the next morning. It was an old building, just like my dad said, but it was set up for some kind of business. When I looked through the window, I saw a long counter in the front of the store and a lot of space in the back. It wasn't as much of a mess as I thought it would be. Well, the front wasn't anyway. I had no idea what the back looked like.

"Is this where it's going to be?"

I looked over my shoulder, and there stood Emily from the library. She smiled at me, and I probably blushed, my face felt that hot.

"Where is what going to be?" I asked.

"Whatever business you're planning to start." She looked me over. "That's why you're reading all those business books at the library, isn't it? And doing market research?"

"Well, yeah. My father just gave me this building, but it's going to be a while before I can do anything but clean up. I'm still getting the money together."

"What's it going to be?"

I looked at her and tried to judge what I should tell her, but she laughed. "I'm not trying to steal your idea, silly," she said. "I'm interested in you. I've watched you change so much over the past several months. I want to see where you go with this."

I took her to lunch and told her my plans and found out she had a degree in business administration. She told me to call her if I had any questions that needed to be explained, and if I needed any particular books she'd try to set them aside. Then she pulled up my poll and showed me I had a lot of positive feedback. Someone mentioned incoming businesses, schools, and neighborhoods in the comments and suggested a print shop was a great idea for a growing town.

We made a dinner date for Monday, and then I walked her home. We'd spent a lot of time at lunch, and I was cutting things a little close, but I stopped at the hardware store and spent the previous night's tips on brooms, trash bags, brushes, and paint. I dropped it all off at the storefront and went to the restaurant to work.

Emily and I began spending Mondays working at the building on Ash. About a month into our work, she asked me to come to her apartment because she had something to show me. When I arrived, she showed me some older but functional binding machines for making various types of booklets.

"Where did you get these?" I asked her.

"My cousin is helping clean out a storage unit, and all this stuff was in there," she said. "And there's more. This is just the stuff that's easy to carry. The guy who owns the unit said you can have anything you want. There are cutters, and tables and boxes and boxes of different kinds of paper that we'll probably have to mostly throw away, but they'll be great to practice with." She led me to an odd hand-cranked machine. "This cuts business cards, Ted. That's huge, to be able to make business cards."

"This is great," I told her. "How much does he want for all this?"

"That's it," she said, and she started jumping up and down and clapping her hands. "All we have to do is haul it away. It was his father's storage unit, and this guy is cleaning it out, and he said you can have anything you carry out of there. My cousin has a truck. I told him you worked at the Asian restaurant, and he said if you brought him a huge order of lo mein, he'll do the hauling."

"Tell him it's a deal," I said.

I took an order of food to a condo in a new neighborhood under development. I recognized the guy who opened the door. I'd seen him at the restaurant many times, and he seemed to be tight with Ling.

"Ted, isn't it?" the guy said. "Ling tells me you're interested in going into business for yourself."

"I'd like to."

"You should come around to the office building down off Polk Street on Thursday mornings. There's a entrepreneurs' meeting there. It's a great place to network. And I'd recommend joining the Chamber of Commerce."

"Thanks," I said. "I'll check it out."

It was three weeks before I saw the kid in the seasonal park again. He looked tired, and it bothered me. I asked him if we'd gotten his General Tso's hot enough yet.

"No," he said. "And my mom isn't coming anymore, so she can't tell you how to make it."

"I'm sorry, little dude. We'll keep trying, and you tell us when we have it right."

The tall dude grunted, threw too much money at me again, and slammed the door.

I asked Emily to go to the entrepreneurs' meeting with me. She warned me that I was going to have to discuss my plans with people or there was no point in going.

"These people help each other, Ted," she said. "They may have ideas about products or training or funding. They aren't there to steal your ideas."

She was right. We talked to a member who understood what kind of machines we'd just picked up and talked about where we could find manuals for them and places that might offer training in different skills I might need. Another member helped me realize I had to stop thinking about only paper and ink.

"A print shop performs tasks people don't always think of," he said. "There's faxing, laminating, document scanning, even document shredding. Go check out the print shop in the city and find out everything they offer. Sometimes it's about more than just paper."

By chatting with others, I learned about permits and banking and numbers. I told Emily on the way home that I was overwhelmed.

"It's okay," she said. "I'm here for you."

I spent the night with Emily, and the next day we both went to the property to work. We cleaned the floors and walls of the storefront and pulled the older back counters away from the walls. We worked on the building on some Friday mornings and all day on Mondays. On Wednesdays, she went over business plans with me, so I had a better understanding of what I was doing before we went to the entrepreneurial meetings on Thursday morning. I finally came to a point of wishing I'd paid better attention in school. Emily and I took classes or watched online instructions on how to use a few of the machines I'd gotten from the storage unit, including the business card cutter. We'd tried it twice. We laughed as we sent dozens of cards flying all over her living room.

One Friday morning, we were dressed in paper jumpsuits and standing on drop cloths in the building on Ash painting the walls while we talked about bookkeeping. I told her that maybe college wouldn't have been a bad idea.

"College isn't for everyone," Emily told me.

"I was too lazy for college," I said.

"I don't know that you were lazy," she said. "Let's just say you were unmotivated."

"I'm pretty sure that's just a big word for lazy."

"No, it's a big word for 'I don't know what I want to do with my life.'"

"I wasn't looking that hard," I told her.

"If you don't stop," she said, "I'm going to paint a big stripe down the back of your suit."

We were in a paint-roller face-off when someone tapped on the door frame of the back door. I saw my dad standing in the doorway and figured it would be just like him to show up while I was fooling around rather than working. I introduced him to Emily. He looked around at the work we'd done and nodded without saying anything about it.

"You should know that Dean showed up on our doorstep

twenty minutes ago," he told me. "I didn't tell him where you were. I thought I'd give you time to do that yourself."

"Did he say if he was just visiting?" I asked.

"He just said to tell you he's back."

"Of course, he is," I muttered.

To be honest, I hadn't even missed Dean. He'd been my best friend for seventeen years, but, when I stopped to think about it, I hadn't had a single text or phone call from him in six months. It was true that I hadn't called either, and that had me re-evaluating my relationship with him. I looked around the building and saw how much I'd accomplished in a few months, and I realized I didn't want Dean in my business.

Now I had to tell him that.

When I got a call to the seasonal park, to the same spot as always, I almost expected to see a different RV. I had a seafood dish in the bag rather than General Tso's. But it was the same RV as always, and the same tall dude answered the door. I didn't see the kid at first, but when I did see him, he was sitting on the floor between two chairs. We locked eyes for just a moment, and he looked helpless. I had only a moment before the tall dude paid me and slammed the door.

After work, I went to Emily's, where she was going over logo designs. I hadn't exactly chosen a name for my shop yet, but I told Emily about a few of my ideas, and she told me she'd see which ones worked the best. She had a few designs laid out for me when I got to her place, but I was having trouble getting excited about them.

"What's wrong, Ted?" she asked. "Is everything okay?"

"There's this kid," I said, and I told her about all my trips to the seasonal RV park leading right up to tonight's run. "I'm worried about him."

"I don't blame you," she said. "Something doesn't sound right. Do you think he's being trafficked?"

"I don't know. I know he was waiting for his mom to show up, but he told me last time I was there that she wasn't coming."

"Poor little man," Emily said, and I thought it was a perfect way to describe the kid. He seemed like a little grown-up when I first saw him. "Was he looking forward to her arrival?"

"He was looking forward to her ordering his General Tso's chicken properly," I said. "We never did get it spicy enough for him. But I think he's given up. They ordered something else tonight."

"He's probably depressed about his mother," she said. "But we need to consider other possibilities. Did he seem abused?"

"No," I said. "He isn't afraid of his father, if that's who he's with. He was talkative when I first met him, but these last two calls he's been unhappy. Tonight, he seemed... finished."

"I don't know that we can call the authorities based on that," she said, "but I'd just pay attention to him when you deliver there. Look for other red flags."

We sat for the rest of the night and went over logos, but I couldn't get that kid out of the back of my mind.

Two nights later, I was sitting in a parking lot counting my tips and putting my money in order when someone tapped on my driver's side window. It was Dean, waving at me and grinning like a damn fool. I didn't smile back.

I rolled down my window. "What's up, Dean?" I asked.

"You look different, man. Smile! Aren't you happy to see me?"

"I guess. Where's Bambi?"

"It was Brandy, and I dumped her, man. She was trying to run my life—what to wear, where to go, what to eat, how much to drink." He leaned in on my window. "She wanted me to entertain her day and night. Just nuts, man."

I looked down at the clothes I was wearing and thought about Emily. Had she changed me? Not really. She just gave me some friendly advice, and I acted on it.

"What are you planning to do now that you're back in town?" I asked.

"Well, I'll have to find a job again. I spent all my savings on moving and keeping a diva happy. The print shop is still a go?"

"I'm afraid that ship has sailed," I said.

"Yeah, I told you it wasn't going to work. So, Monday? We hang out, have a few beers and a pizza? You might have to spot me twenty bucks or so."

"You don't get what I'm saying," I said. "I am still opening a print shop. But I'm doing it without you."

Dean pushed back from my car. "You cutting me out, Ted?"

"Cutting you out of what? You just said you knew it wouldn't work. No, I'm doing this without you because you left. I've spent the last six months working on this without you, and, when we're down to brass tacks, I'm the only one who has ever worked on this. You haven't done a damn thing for this shop other than get a job and presumably learn to work. I intend to open my print shop, but I need to work with someone I can trust. I don't need to worry about my partner taking all his money and running off with whatever female is sharing his bed at the time."

Dean slammed his hand down on the roof of my car. "You

stupid jerk. You think you're so much better than I am. You're not. You're a loser. Everyone in town says so. Your problem is that you're jealous. You couldn't get a woman if you paid one. When was the last time anything with any quality even looked your way? You can't do it alone, Ted. This was both our idea. You can't make it by yourself."

I thought for a moment about Emily again. "It was my idea, and I didn't say I was opening this shop by myself. I just said I was doing it without you."

I rolled the window up and left him standing in the parking lot. As I walked into the restaurant, I grabbed a newspaper to read while I waited for orders, and I caught sight of a sidebar, an update to a current news story. Some rich guy three states over had raised the reward from $100,000 to $250,000 for news concerning his kidnapped grandson. The article was accompanied by pictures of the kid and the tall dude in the fifth wheel at the seasonal RV park. I looked up at Ling, who was standing at the register.

"I need to make a phone call," I said.

It's been a year, and I still think about that night—the lights, the sirens, the grilling by the FBI to make sure I wasn't complicit. A helicopter came in and whisked the kid away, and I've always felt bad that I could never deliver him General Tso's that was just right.

But the result of all that chaos is that I'm standing behind my own counter taking orders. I greet each customer personally. I remember everyone's name. I even have a kid who delivers for me. I know how to work every machine behind the counter, I cater to nearly every new business that moves into town, and I print Ling's new menus every season. The Copy Cat is in business.

I will admit I never did get the hang of administration, but that turned out to be just the kind of thing Emily would leave the library for.

"Deliveries" is ©2024 by Kelli Heitstuman-Tomko. The author is a resident of Fallon and has published eight works, including the Johnny Lister mystery series, which are available on Amazon. Kelli is a former journalist who has written for newspapers in Wyoming and Colorado. She has also written biography blurbs for Ted-X pamphlets.

Lisa Kirkman

Infinity Necklace

To exist is to change, to change is to mature,
to mature is to go on creating oneself endlessly.

– Henri Bergson

"Don't slam the—" I called after my daughter as the door slammed. I fumed. "Dammit!" *Why is she always storming off like that?*

I forced myself to breathe in. And out. I sighed. "Because there was nothing else she *could* do. That's the way it goes: I yell, she stomps. I threaten, she slams," I explain to myself.

My knees weakened recognizing the chronic pain from our patterns. My patterns. I rubbed my lower back and bent to pick up the stack of folded towels from the floor.

"But I didn't need to get so mad. They're just towels."

"Well, *she* didn't need to get so mad, either!" I retorted to myself, smoothing the towels, casualties of our fight. "I've *told* her before how to fold them. I'm *not* wrong."

I scowled at my own rigidity. "Why can't I just let these things slide?"

The doorbell rang. I breathed in deeply, touching a finger to my collar bone and thought, *Maybe she just went around the block. Maybe she already calmed down.* I trotted to the door. *But why would you ring the doorbell, Anna?*

I expected a familiar face and a resumption of our fight when I opened the door, but got neither. "Oh. Hello. Who are you?"

"I'm Lizzie," with a thirteen-year-old's natural aversion to eye contact. A handshake was out of the question. The sky darkened, and it occurred to me Anna might not have taken a jacket.

But I was drawn to this girl on my doorstep. Awash in a desire for the simplicity of the beginning of life, I leaned on my door. I ached to be in her moment and start everything over.

"You came to see Anna?"

Her backpack dangled from a shoulder, her posture insouciant. She nodded. A lock of blond hair flopped over her eye.

"Oh, are you her new lab partner?"

She adjusted her slouch in a way I took as a full-body nod.

"Anna, uh, just went for a walk," I said. Hoping it was true, I offered "She should be back in a few minutes. You can come in and wait for her."

I opened the door and led the girl to the kitchen.

"So, uh... Welcome! So, you're new at school?" I asked, then chided myself for being overly friendly, reminding myself not to make her uncomfortable. I expected the girl to object to my politeness with outrage like my daughter would. I may never know what eighth-graders want, but a pleasant small talk was not it. Lizzie seemed different.

"Yes, I'm new, Mrs. Bradbury," and steadied herself under the awkward weight of her identity. "My parents got divorced over the summer. My dad moved here. Then my mom and I moved here in January so I could still see him," she said matter-of-factly. It was only March. She was *really* new.

"Few things worse than settling in at a new school," I said, remembering my own dark days of being the new kid.

She looked around. "I like your house," as if she hadn't mentioned her family upheaval. "It's nice. I like all the colors, they're calm. I feel calm here. Nobody is sad here, I think." Her eyes were bright blue. Her nose still had freckles.

Nobody is sad. My neck itched where my necklace pinched. *Did she mean me? Did she mean her?* I blindly reached back to soothe my neck. *Everybody is a little sad,* I wanted to say.

"Uh, well, thank you. Right. Well... uh, I hope *you're* happy here," I said, wobbled by the likelihood she was wrong. "We all have our moments," and laughed too loudly.

Lizzie smiled politely. I got her a glass of juice and a bowl of goldfish crackers without asking if she wanted any. She sat down at the kitchen counter readily, still young enough to welcome afterschool snacks without question. "Thank you, Mrs. Bradbury."

"Please, call me Elizabeth," I offered as I fussed with the napkin holder. "We don't need to stand on formalities here," and smiled.

She smiled back and shrugged as if to say, "I don't have anywhere to go with that."

I'm not usually inclined to entertain my daughter's friends, but it seemed rude to leave this new girl to wait alone in a strange house. And I didn't feel the usual teenage impatience and dread spilling off Lizzie. I pretended it was normal to sit with her.

"So uh, how are you feeling? With the divorce?" I touched my throat in regret. Divorces and feelings about divorces were too-much-too-soon for a light conversation. *Why can't I just ask about school?* "I mean, uh..." fumbling to soften my inquisition, "I mean, when my parents split up, I was about your age, and it was hard." I looked to the rafters for some way to excuse my over-reach. "Nothing was exactly *wrong* anymore—I mean once they *finally* divorced, you know? I was so glad the yelling stopped, right? But nothing was the *same* again. And *that* was weird. Hard."

Lizzie nodded, a little warily. My own daughter was always trying to get me to stop over-sharing and grossing her out. The outrage I had come to expect from Anna clattered around the kitchen. I felt myself tense as if it might pounce. I stood up abruptly and went to the refrigerator.

We all have feelings, I thought defensively. "If we all were just more honest about our feelings, everyone wouldn't get so crazy trying to hide them," I muttered, my back to Lizzie. I pushed a box of leftovers around the top shelf thuggishly. I heard nothing behind me, no uncomfortable shuffling, no impatient waiting. I shoved the array of condiment bottles into a line.

"I think that was the whole problem with my parents."

Wheeling around, I saw only empty chairs.

Of course. Alone. Again. This new Lizzie had simply left in embarrassment. *I would too if I were her.* I set to tidying the countertop. On cue, my parade of lifelong regrets shambled into my mind, both as comforting and as intractable as a rosary prayer. I touched my necklace. *Why do I talk about feelings? Why didn't I say something else? What must she think? Why am I so bad at being normal? When am I ever going to learn?*

Then Lizzie popped back up.

"Oh! Hi." Hand on my heart. "I thought you left."

"No. I just dropped a cracker," and smiled broadly, arm raised in victory. "I have to do all the vacuuming at my house now," as she settled back onto the barstool. "So there's no point in leaving it for someone else to clean up. *I'm* the someone else," she laughed lightly.

I marveled at how different her view was from my daughter's. I was always after Anna to clean up her things. I might have even used that exact phrase with her this week.

"Well! Aren't you helpful? Thank you. Your mom must appreciate your help."

"Sure. Well, I have no idea if she appreciates it. It just needs to be done," she said sensibly. "But, like you were saying, if my parents would just be straight with each other, how they felt, they could have made up." She popped goldfish in her mouth. "Like, if I was that mad at someone, or got my feelings hurt, my mom would make me go talk and make up. Why can't they?"

"That's very reasonable." I took one of her crackers for myself. "It's hard to be honest sometimes, though. It takes a lot more than one argument to justify a divorce."

"Maybe. I don't know. It's not a big deal. It's fine. I mean, what do I care? It's *their* marriage." She slumped her elbows onto the countertop and peered closely at her juice. "I mean, they both said it had nothing to do with me. So, sure. OK. If you say so. I don't care."

My heart gushed for this kid. I remembered this same need to tell people "no, it's fine, I'm fine, it's all fine," as if I was managing my parents' cover-up. Their efforts to comfort me with "it's not about you" just isolated me from them. Lizzie was young enough to *try* to believe the words her parents were saying, but clearly smart enough to see how their words didn't match their actions.

I reached across the counter to touch Lizzie's hand or pat her shoulder or stroke her hair before I remembered she wasn't mine. I had no right to comfort her. My hand changed directions and picked up her glass instead.

"When my mom told me they were divorcing," I offered, "I

felt, um, I remember feeling kind of *relieved*, you know?"

She looked up at me, blue eyes framed in dark lashes.

"I mean, 'relieved' is the wrong word," I said. "But it was like I had been *waiting*, and now it was here and we could finally call it what it was, right? What I'd been dreading had finally happened. It had a name so now we could deal with it." I set down a fresh drink.

"Yeah. I get that. My mom sat me down and made this big deal over 'we're separating' and she wanted me to act surprised and I just... I just wasn't." Lizzie shrugged, eyes focused on the past. "I didn't care anymore. Whatever. Do what you want. I don't care."

"It gets better with time," I offered. "And some days it will be worse. But it'll be OK."

The girl looked at me dubiously and a sigh slipped out. "No, it won't. It won't get better. My dad will have always left us. My mom will always be freaked out and upset about it. I'll always be the weird new kid." She shoved the drink away.

"How did your mom tell you things were going to change? That they were divorcing?"

"Things had already changed by the time she *actually* told me. My dad stopped coming home. It turns out, he was sneaking in while I was at school and, like, packing up his clothes. It wasn't hard to figure out. If none of his stuff was here, he probably wasn't either."

"Oh gosh, I'm sorry." I sighed, and a long-forgotten ache pushed at me. "Your mom probably didn't want to admit what was happening. I'm sure she didn't *mean* to leave you out."

She rolled her eyes impatiently at me. "When she finally *did* tell me, she told me we were moving here. And I was just sort of *nothing* about it," with a shrug. "Then Mom got all mad at me: 'How come you're not more upset?' What was I supposed to say? I already mostly knew. But she wanted some big reaction like I should be outraged or something." Lizzie looked up, still incredulous at her mom's theatrics.

I felt for her mother and opened my mouth to assure Lizzie that moms don't *mean* to be weird, it just comes out that way sometimes.

But she cut me off. "Then my mom kept digging around, asking which friends I would miss most and asked, 'Aren't you going to miss this house?' Eventually, I blew up and yelled at her to stop it. Then she said, 'See, I *knew* you were upset.'"

"Well, *obviously* you were upset. The whole thing, the fighting and then not talking about it, and the move. Your mom was probably saying more about her own emotions than yours." I found myself a little irritated at her mom, too. *But it's not for me to take sides,* I chastised myself and shut down my outrage.

Maybe I could help Lizzie see her mom's point of view. "By the time *my* parents announced," I started, and then hesitated at the edge of my admission. But Lizzie was interested. "I just sort of switched *off*. I could see I wasn't going to make anything better between them. And I couldn't leave. So, I did what I could to *not be there* mentally. I kind of checked out. I guess it worked, you know?"

She nodded, seeing some value in being not there.

I looked up at the rafters, shocked I had allowed that out. "When I think back about middle and high school, it blows me away how few memories I have from then. I remember being mad. And lonely. But I had friends, so I couldn't have been *that* lonely, right? But huge blocks of time are gone," I flicked my hand away. "Then I just sort of *woke up* in college. Like I'd been asleep."

Lizzie nodded, but it was obvious she remembered everything. "Not remembering would be nice. They've been fighting since I was a baby. Sometimes they even tell me stories about the fights they had *before* I was born as if it's part of our family heritage."

I nodded absently, my mind barreling down an ancient track. "All that fighting... You're right. It sticks to you, makes you weird." I could hear my own voice sounding far away. "I realized so much later than most kids—so much later—I didn't know how to just *talk with* someone. I had to learn it the hard way. I didn't know how to disagree without kicking people out of my life. I had to win, or I lost. I still suck at it."

So many missteps. I shook my head slowly, a sad parade of ex-boyfriends, ex-friends, ex-roommates all walking away, never to talk to me again. A single laugh snorted out of me. I touched my necklace absently, my hand flattening over it to protect my throat.

I turned to Lizzie. "And you know what? Even after they ended it, my parents *still* fought. I thought, *What was the point of the stupid divorce? Just stay married and don't have two rent payments.* Their marriage sucked, and then their divorce sucked more!"

Lizzie laughed sharply.

I knew I had stepped across the line between adults and kids. But we seemed to be in this together now.

She pulled her drink back, ran her finger around the rim. "Yeah. My mom was mad before the divorce, like *all* the time. And now she's only sad. I think all the time, too: *Why did she do this?* It's a little better for them because they get to be away from each other. But now I have to listen to BOTH of them complain about the other! When do I get a break?" Her hand went to her heart, eyes wide and indignant. "It's like now she transferred all her anger to me."

I realized her mom may not know where Lizzie was or when she would be home. "Hey, should we tell your mom where you are? Maybe ask if you can stay for dinner?"

"No, she's... she's working." Something pulled her down again. "She's always working."

I didn't push. I knew that look. Only she could navigate through the swamp of needs and expectations she and her mom lived in.

"My mom needs so *much* from me now." Her eyebrows went up. "And then other times she just totally isn't there. She's always working, or when she is home, she's '*tired*.'" Lizzie made air quotes and wobbled her head sarcastically.

"When we moved here," she continued, "I blew it. I missed the bus the first morning. I was waiting at the wrong corner. So, I went back home to get a ride and she got all mad at me because I was going to make her late. I'm just a *kid*! In a new neighborhood! How am I supposed to know where to go if she doesn't show me? She just turned and went into her room. I hate her stupid room! And her stupid door." She slurped at her juice. "I threw things at her door until she came out and took me to school." A mischievous smile crept out, "I made a dent." She looked a little sorry about the dent, but not that sorry.

I wanted to laugh with her about how great it can feel to throw things. Sometimes you just need to throw something.

"And then I'm supposed to just go have stupid Happy Daddy Time. Nobody asked me if I even want to see him. He's a jerk. *He* moved out. But I have to go see him. It is so unfair! If we lived together, I wouldn't have to spend *every* Friday night with my *dad*!"

Lizzie was riled up now. "I can't tell either of them if I had a good time with the other. My mom gets all hurt like, 'you love him more than me.' And I'm not supposed to tell if one took me out for ice cream or who forgot to pay a bill."

I was scandalized by the unfairness of her parents putting

their egos ahead of her needs. She's just a kid. I had pushed my teenage outrages into storage long ago and made peace with my uneven lot. But the vividness of her frustration left me breathless.

Her eyes were wild. "They're keeping *secrets*! I've been told my whole life not to keep secrets! I mean, they're setting a terrible example, right?"

"Right. Well, maybe," I wanted to soothe both of us and laid my palms flat on the cool tile. "There's no tutorial on how to get divorced correctly." Someone had said that to me once. "They're trying."

That idea was flat soda to her. She wasn't ready to be conciliatory yet.

"If I was a better kid, maybe they wouldn't have broken up," and shrugged. "I tried... I tried to be better. I tried to help my mom, I tried to make my dad laugh. I tried to be quiet, I tried to be good at school. It didn't help. Nothing helped. I might as well yell at them and go steal things and break stuff," she said with a pout.

"Look," I took her shoulders and addressed her square on, like a coach before a big game. "You can't see this now because you're so young—but they have their *own* issues they're trying to figure out. But I promise you, you do not want to go back to Before the Divorce. You don't want to go back to when they fought all the time. It wasn't *better*. It was just what you knew."

She looked up, her eyes wide. Her chin wobbled. "But I'm part of them. You know? So, if they're fighting because they don't like each other, then it means they don't like part of *me*."

"No, no." I panicked, desperate to fix this. I had stepped so far over the line of acceptable adult-to-kid conversation that I should be fined. No, imprisoned. "Lizzie. Lizzie, honey, they love you. Believe me, being married is hard. It's really hard. There's so much to negotiate. Some of it is big stuff, and so much is small, and you don't always know which one is which until you've screwed it up. Sometimes you don't get what you want, and you have to do what the other person wants, and then you have to decide if that's an OK trade-off."

"So, it's like being divorced."

My bark of laughter surprised me and startled her. All the walls of decorum between us crumbled. We gave in to the ridiculousness of everyone's drama to giggle at the situations people create for themselves. We were safe for a minute from other people's craziness.

She wiped an eye, then held her juice glass in both hands. An old image must have revealed itself to her. "When my dad left, my mom cried and cried in our rocking chair. She was so sad. I've never seen anyone so sad." Her face pulled down. "I didn't know why she was crying. I didn't know exactly that he'd left yet. I just knew something was wrong. I sat down on the floor and cried just because she was crying." Lizzie let me be there with her, feeling that moment again.

In the face of her honesty and her strength, I was choked by my own shame. I touched my necklace protectively again. I had always, *always* tried to hide the bad days from other people. I wasted so much energy pretending I was okay when I wasn't. Everything I thought I had to do, everything I thought I had to be for everyone else was suddenly of no value. In watching her, I saw that there was another way I'd never considered. I could have just been strong enough to feel it like this girl. I gulped in a deep breath like I'd just surfaced after being underwater too long. *Maybe I could have moved on sooner if I was as honest as she's being,* I thought.

"But I don't think my dad wants to spend Friday nights with me, either." She sagged on her barstool, the fight draining out of her. "He left her. And he left me, too."

I scrambled to protect her. "No, no, you misunderstand, sweetie." My own father admitted years later that he avoided situations with me and was awkward when we were together because he had been embarrassed about the break-up. But, by the time he finally admitted it in my twenties, ten years of corrosive self-doubt had already weakened me and changed my trajectory. An idea I had been struggling for years to see took shape and stepped into the light.

"Lizzie, this is important." I touched my hand to my heart. "This thing happened *near* you, Lizzie." It was vital that she be made to understand this. "*You* didn't make it happen." I nodded. She nodded. "But you do have to survive it."

She looked up, desperate for this to be true. It was taking shape in her mind, too. "Like a terrorist attack?"

"Ha! Sure. Right." I laughed at how a terrorist attack could be comforting, but, fine. "Yes. *You* didn't do this. And, better yet, nobody thinks you did. You have your *own* future to discover. I promise you *will* have a future. It's all yours to make any way you want to."

She shook her head. That was too easy. She pushed it away, unable to see her future.

But I'd spent thirty years thinking about this. Someone was going to hear it. I made a little 'hey' sound, and her chin tilted up. I thought I might drown in her desperate blue eyes.

"You are perfectly loveable, Lizzie. Your path isn't their path, OK? You are going to be just fine, even though this happened."

Her eyes slipped down again, but she nodded dutifully.

I rode the lull swelling between us, as if we were floating just beyond the surf, looking back at the beach and the lives we'd just abandoned.

"You know, these days, my parents mostly get along," I told her. Lizzie made a doubtful sound. "I wish they'd settled down earlier, sure. They could have gotten some peace sooner. They met other people, they did other things. They found some happiness eventually."

"That would be nice."

I wanted Lizzie to have some happiness now, without waiting years for it like I did. Decades. I ached to reach across the chasm that divides people and give her something to hold on to now in her turmoil.

My neck itched, and I reached up to soothe it. By habit, my fingers slid down to the Mobius strip, the shape of a sideways eight, in the necklace's center. Its coolness calmed me. I blindly traced the strip around and around in its infinite roller coaster with my fingertip. Her eyes followed my finger as it looped along the smooth path.

"I want you to have something." I reached both hands back to the clasp. Her eyes met mine, bright and curious. As I took off the necklace, something crackled inside me.

I held out my necklace, and the looping design rocked gently like a swing in the wind. Lizzie touched it with a fingertip, then cupped her other hand under its wide, flat loop. The single strip of gold at the center twisted so the outside became the inside and the inside became the outside.

"I honestly don't recall where I got this, but I've had it since I was about your age." I met her eyes. I was a little breathless, desperate for this to help her. I pushed against a sense that I was losing my grip on something important. But holding on to her right now was more important.

"The Mobius Strip is special." My breath was short. *Is it really hot all of a sudden?* I had to concentrate. "See, it looks like two sides, but it's really only one side. The loop makes it both the inside and the outside."

I nodded to put it on her. She scooped up her hair and I

leaned in. Eyes closed, I swept past the silky soft white hairs behind her neck, breathed in her coconut shampoo, basked in the warmth wafting up from her collar. A darkness crowded into the room, and I heard thunder in the distance.

I opened my eyes to a woman being very close to me, her arms high, fingers behind my neck. I blinked to focus. She said "There. That looks lovely, Lizzie. Wear it and know that things will go up and down, but *you'll* always stay on track." Her bright blue eyes sparkled. I felt safe.

The necklace was a strange, dense weight against my collar bone. *Now I remember!* I got this necklace when I was thirteen. *How could I have forgotten?* I reached up and traced my fingertip around its cool, languid track. I tasted orange juice as I licked my lips.

The cloud shadow shifted, and the room swelled in a burst of yellow afternoon light. I blinked hard against it, lifted my arm to protect my eyes, my equilibrium slipped. I lost track of the lady in my dizziness. Static crashed in my ears. Darkness pushed in at the sides of my eyes, compressing my vision. I held the counter and struggled to hold myself upright.

"Thank you," the girl sitting across from me said. "I think I should go now."

I don't recall her picking up her bag, but she was already retreating down my hall when I looked up. *Did I say good-bye?*

"Mom? Mom! Are you OK?"

Oh, she came back. But it was a different girl. This girl looked familiar. Auburn hair, not blond. Green eyes, not blue. She reminded me of my eldest, but she was older than I recalled my daughter being. She touched my shoulder, concern crumpling her face.

Happiness washed over me. "Oh! Anna! I missed you."

Now abashed at her misplaced concern, she deflected, "Mawm! Jeez! I just went for a walk," and pushed me away playfully.

I touched my forehead and searched for some anchor in time. I leaned around Anna and scrutinized the front door. A stack of towels drooped in a pile in the hall. *Yes, Anna went for a walk. Right, we had a fight. About towels. So stupid.*

"I'm sorry, honey. I got mad... I didn't need to. It was a small thing. Then I made you mad. Look, I don't want to fight anymore. Towels, whatever. They're not important." I nodded toward the pile of years I'd wasted fighting over nothing and being angry and alone.

"We didn't fight." She was light and breezy as she got herself a soda. I examined her closely for deception. Nothing. *Was there really no fight?* That made no sense.

"Oh... and I met your friend. Lizzie? New girl? Your lab partner? Very nice. She came by to study. I guess you just missed her." I pointed at the door limply. "She... she must have just left a minute ago." My head throbbed.

"Mom," she gave me a slow side-eye trying to sort out this latest Mom nonsense. "I don't have a friend named Lizzie. In fact, I've never met anyone with that name except you."

My fingers sought out the comforting loop of my necklace, but only found skin.

"Infinity Necklace" is ©2022 by Lisa Kirkman. It appears here for the first time. "Infinity Necklace" is about that moment we realize we don't have to be the people we used to be. It benefited from support and development at Tahoe Writers Workshop. The author spent her career in advertising and is excited to roll out a new and improved fiction product. She lives on Lake Tahoe's rugged Nevada shore with her husband and daughter.

The ACES Anthology

Sandie La Nae

The Genoa Curses

The community of Genoa, Nevada is very cursed due to three terrible jinxes pronounced over the area by early settlers and residents.

Curse No. 1 - Judge Orson Hyde

To hold control over the land, Mormon elder, Judge Orson Hyde, arrived first in Genoa as directed by church leader, Brigham Young in Salt Lake City. Young dreamed of the area as the western arm of a Mormon super-state called Deseret.

The Mormons organized and built the frontier settlement, then titled Mormon Station, in 1851. They saw the rich farmlands of the valleys as a perfect setting for those traveling to California to rest and replenish supplies. Orson established himself well with a large farm, home and sawmill.

The majority of Americans, however, scorned the followers of the Church of the Latter-Day Saints for their practice of polygamy—which flew in the face of Victorian values, rendering their religion abhorrent.

Eastern politicians crafted measures to prove polygamy was threatening Christian life, leading President James Buchanan to send an army west to control the Mormons. When word of this action came to Salt Lake City, the church leadership panicked. A decree went out to all Latter-Day Saints, in Mormon Station and elsewhere, to sell what they had and swiftly return to the Salt Lake so they could defend their faith from the U.S. Army.

Judge Orson Hyde hurriedly sold out to a non-Mormon who offered a wagon and some livestock as a down-payment, promising to pay the rest of the amount in easy installments. The broken-down wagon and the few beasts of burden were all that the unfortunate Elder Hyde ever saw.

After trying to collect his money to no avail, the judge turned to the power of the Almighty. He cast upon Genoa an awful curse! His anathema was written like this:

"The Lord has signified to me, his unworthy servant that we have been under circumstances that compelled us to submit to your terms, that He will place you under circumstances that will compel you to summit to ours, or do worse. That mill and those land claims were worth $10,000 when we left them; the use of that property, or its increased value since, is $10,000 more, making our present demand $20,000.

"Now if the above sum be sent to me in Great Salt Lake City, in cash, you shall have a clean receipt therefore, in the shape of an honorable quit-claim deed to the property... But if you shall think best to repudiate our demand or any part of it, all right. We shall not take it up again in this world in any shape of any of you: but the said R.D. Sides and Jacob Rose (owners of the land) shall be living and dying advertisements of God's displeasure, in their persons, in their families, and in there substances; and this demand of ours, remaining unconcealed, shall be to the people of the Carson and Washoe Valleys as was the ark of God among the Philistines. You shall be visited of the Lord of Hosts with thunder and with earthquakes and with floods, with pestilence and with famine until your names are not known amongst men, for you have rejected the authority of God, trampled upon his laws and his ordinances, and given yourselves up to serve the god of this world; to rioting in debauchery, in abominations, drunkenness and corruption!"

For seven generations.

The curse came to fruition. A few ordeals include: In 1880, a dam burst in a rainstorm and destroyed the site of the old Mormon mill and town. In 1882, a flood swept away the hamlet of Ophir. Another flood carried away the old Mormon Meeting house—the last structure from the early settlement. Numerous prominent Mormon Station and Carson Valley individuals died from strange causes.

Curse No. 2 - The Hanging Tree

A dreadful consequence happened on Genoa Lane in a copse of cottonwood trees, about a half-mile from the center of town. This was the site of the most horrendous hanging ever in this small community, stemming from a set of equally appalling facts. The story is about an execution from a lynch mob gone mad and the support from the local sheriff's office in the onset of events.

The story:

In the late 1890s, an out-of-town visitor, Adam Uber, went into a small saloon in Millersville (a settlement between Minden and Gardnerville). In the bar he was approached by well-known and mostly feared teamster Hans Anderson, who offered to buy him a drink. Adam refused the request, which was an insulting breach of the old Code of the West. After Hans aggressively pressed him several times, Adam (who was trying to defend himself from Hans' antagonism), shot Anderson dead.

Adam was arrested and held at the Genoa courthouse jail. The valley's teamsters concocted an unspeakable setup. The following morning at 3 a.m., Sheriff Brockless and Constable

Gray lit a candle, setting it in the jail window, which signaled the 20 rowdy union men that the coast was clear. The mob attacked the jail and took a screaming Adam Uber out of his cell, stripped him naked, and forced him to walk barefoot down the then-dirt road in the extreme November cold, all the while beating and cutting him along the way.

At the grove of trees, Adam was shoved to his knees and ordered to say his prayers. The men placed the noose around his neck and, while he was still kneeling, they jerked Adam up into the air. He twisted and turned at the end of the rope, slowly strangling to death. One member of the mob drew his pistol and fired into the man, with others joining in shooting the dying man.

Local law enforcement, to appease Genoa and Carson Valley residents, then tried their absolute minimum to discover the names of the lynch mob. A reward of $500 was offered for any names who took part in the hanging. No one, of course, came forward.

Did Adam actually speak to his heavenly father? Or did he place a curse on the teamsters, the sheriff, and the town? Soon after the lynching, one by one the mob members suffered unexplained injuries and family tragedies. One mob leader had his horses spook as he passed by the hanging tree. His wagon overturned, crushing his leg—which had to be amputated. Another member went mad and ended his days in an asylum. One took poison, and another blew his own head off with a shotgun. Many of the men's family members and farm animals became sick with puzzling illnesses, dying soon after being afflicted. Barns and homes were mysteriously burnt to ashes.

Curse No. 3 – Mrs. Applebee

In the early days of Genoa, there was a little old lady, a widow, who lived alone in a home with a rock wall bordering her house. She had been a seamstress most of her life, and relocated to Genoa for sewing opportunities. She was, however, a very grumpy woman who wasn't much liked.

The mischievous youngsters in town targeted her home for the best place to play tricks. They tromped on her gardens, threw rotten food at her windows and door, called her names, taunted her. She placed broken glass on top of the rock wall, which many children suffered the cuts while climbing over. The back-and-forth hostility went on for a few years.

Mrs. Applebee told the sheriff that, if the trouble didn't stop, she would put a curse on the town. He didn't believe her, and the nuisance continued. Then, many strange occurrences began in the community, but one intriguing phenomenon rapidly came about—and remained.

At one time, the woman planted a special type of flowering shrub in her yard. After she spoke with the sheriff, that plant nearly choked out the entire flora of the town, growing everywhere!

As she was old at the time of the disturbances, Mrs. Applebee eventually passed away. But to this day, that unwanted plant—now considered intrusive—continues to plague Genoa.

The ACES Anthology

Angela Laverghetta
Come Away

Lydia noticed the mushrooms on Tuesday, and by Saturday, she was gone.

Tuesday

L ydia packed Bert's lunch with little effort.

For the last twenty-five years, her husband had wanted the same meal: a half sleeve of saltines, a can of tuna, one sliced apple. An occasional orange or pear was acceptable, but never a peach. And one mint.

As she filled the cooler bag, she gazed out the kitchen window at the unfamiliar backyard. A kingly elm presided over the lawn filled with a village market day attendance of dandelions. Lydia could easily imagine Lilly and Charles playing beneath its boughs in the puzzle pieces of light. But both her children were grown now, and this house, with all its charm, was devoid of the memories made elsewhere.

The sight of smooth, tan lumps peeking out from the tall blades of grass drew her attention. Had the previous owners left

271

toys in the yard?

She paused mid-motion of zipping up the lunch tote and leaned closer to the window.

No, not toys.

"What are you looking at?" Bert questioned, startling Lydia. She spun around. Bert stood in the kitchen archway, adjusting his tie, his thinning hair teased to look fuller.

"There are mushrooms in the yard," she said, unable to hide her smile. Their old house had had either gravel or turf—nothing alive but a few evergreen shrubs.

Bert gave the knot of his tie one more tug before dropping it over his white dress shirt, where it lay like a red-carpet ski ramp over his chest and stomach. "Subtle, Lyds," he said with a hard stare.

She had no idea what she'd said to upset him. Instead of engaging, she turned back to finish closing his lunch. She set it on the island without looking at him and moved to the coffeemaker to fill his thermos. She finally looked up when she turned with the coffee and picked up his lunch.

He reached for both, taking one in each hand. "It's fine. I'll mow this weekend. It's just you know how much it bothers me when you're passive aggressive." He twisted his wrist to see his watch face and lifted his thermos in a farewell salute. "I'm late. We'll talk about it later."

Lydia nodded, certain she'd only meant to show Bert that she was finding positive things about the new house. She stood in the hallway as Bert opened the front door. He paused, glaring at the wreath that the previous owners had left. "I thought we agreed we weren't 'wreath' people?"

Honestly, Lydia had found the circle of ash white wood twigs and bright as blood berries to be a bit unsettling, but she was certain they'd never had any such conversation. "I'll throw it away today," she assured him. Sometimes it was just easier to agree.

Wednesday

With a mug of tea in hand and Bert again off to work, Lydia was ready to tackle the last of the unpacking.

When their youngest had graduated college, Bert decided they should leave the suburbs for the city. He'd assured her she'd love this new house just as much as their old one. "Think of the time you'll save with three fewer bedrooms to clean. You'll have more time for all your little hobbies," he'd reasoned.

"I guess that's true," Lydia agreed.

But even after donating hundreds of items and most of her craft room furniture, she was still finding it hard to fit everything into the considerably smaller house. It didn't help that Bert became overly stressed when surrounded by clutter, so the two bedrooms, one theirs and the other his office, needed to remain clear. Everything left to unpack had therefore landed in the last room to be set up—the living room.

Lydia set her tea on a waist-high tower of boxes. The room smelled overwhelmingly of cardboard and dust. She navigated around the labyrinth of precarious stacks and piles. Placing a knee in Bert's recliner, she reached over the back for the window. The frame squeaked as it inched upwards, breaking away from the old paint. Just like the other windows in the house, there wasn't a screen, but she'd deal with a few flies for a little fresh air.

The first box she opened, she quickly set aside. Going through photo albums would only remind her that the kids no longer lived near and the house they grew up in was gone. How could a 2,500-square-foot home always feel full, but a 1,100-square-foot one feel so empty?

The next box, filled with junk drawer items, felt much more

manageable.

While debating between whether she should place batteries in a drawer in the kitchen or in a basket in the garage, a bird flew in and landed on a stack of boxes near the fireplace. The scrub jay let out a loud cry, flapping its desert sky feathers and puffing out its white chest. The volume startled Lydia and, without thinking, she scolded it, as she would have one of her kids. "Hush. Please use your inside voice."

The bird did a little hop to the edge of the box and canted its head. When it opened its mouth and cried again, the sound was significantly quieter.

There was no way the scrub jay understood her. Still she said, "Thank you."

Should she shoo it back outside? Lydia didn't want it panicking and possibly hurting itself, trying to get free. The scrub jay trilled softly and hopped to another stack closer to her. It didn't appear panicked. Maybe the previous owners of the house had fed it.

"You can stay, but I've got work to do," she told it and grabbed the batteries to take to the kitchen.

The bird was still there when she came back. And for the rest of the afternoon, it hopped from box to box, keeping her company. When the grandfather clock in the hall chimed five, Lydia straightened and turned to her new friend. "Bert will be home soon. He's not the pet type."

She admonished herself for thinking the jay understood her when instead of flying out the window; it flew down onto the bricks and cried, the sound amplified by the fireplace behind it. Lydia weaved closer, hoping to encourage it to fly back the other way and outside, but it just hopped deeper into the soot covered firebox. "No, no, don't go that way," she said, holding her hands like scoops and gesturing at the bird.

With a shush of flapping feathers, the scrub jay flew up the chimney.

"No!" Lydia cried. Rushing over, she dipped beneath the mantel and squeezed into the firebox, trying to see up into the darkness. The shadows were too deep, so she dashed to the newly created "miscellaneous" drawer in the kitchen and grabbed a small flashlight.

Shining the narrow radius of light up the chimney, she couldn't see a bird. Or even hear one. But something glinted, reflecting the beam back at her. Lydia adjusted and squinted upward, moving the flashlight to try to get a better look. *What was that?*

Holding the light in one hand, she reached with the other. Soot rained down on her face and she blinked it away, keeping her mouth firmly closed. Finally, her fingers closed around a wooden handle, jagged at the end. She gave a yank, and the squeal of metal on stone ripped through her ears and made her teeth ache.

With one final yank, whatever it was came free and slipped from her grip to clang to the bricks. Lydia stumbled back, her knees falling off the hearth and hitting the wood floor.

She knew what it was, but she'd never seen one in real life. Of course, the real question was, who would put a scythe in a chimney in the first place?

Thursday

Lydia dragged the green garbage bin to the end of the driveway, the wreath from Tuesday and the scythe with the broken handle from yesterday inside. She'd securely taped up the metal blade between two large pieces of cardboard, like the sanitation website instructed. No point in keeping something sharp that could possibly give them tetanus, and she certainly wasn't going to shove it back up the chimney.

She turned toward the house, but a flutter of wings made her glance over her shoulder.

Her little scrub jay friend from yesterday stared up at her from the concrete, a bit of soot smudged along the dome of its head. "Quite the clever escape artist, aren't you, Houdini?" Lydia teased, and the bird squawked in response. With another cry, it flew up from the driveway and landed in the flower bed that ran behind the front yard fencing.

She watched it peck at the ground, the hard-packed dirt breaking away and scattering. Lydia stepped closer. *Was it digging for insects? What did scrub jays eat?* Where the bird had disturbed the area, something drew Lydia's attention. The bird continued to peck away at the dirt even as she crouched down close.

A stone ring? The bird kept digging.

No. An old iron key. The scrub jay hopped a little distance away, and Lydia reached for it, wiggling it until it broke free. The key sat surprisingly heavy in her palm, rust coating her skin like cinnamon. She looked up at the bird. It seemed expectant. "Ummm, thank you," she said. The scrub jay flapped its wings and hop-flew to another spot in the dirt and pecked at the ground again.

Curiosity had Lydia following and just as before, the bird revealed another key beneath the dirt. *Who buries iron keys in the front yard? Probably the same type of people who shove scythes up the chimney.*

In all, the scrub jay unearthed ten skeleton keys, an old iron tool that may have been a wrench but missing the other part of its jaw, and an iron rail spike. Her friend flew off after she'd pulled out the last buried "treasure." Lydia had a hard enough time finding places for items she needed. There was no room in the house for any more junk. She found a small empty box and wrote FREE on one flap. She set it next to the garbage bin.

The box and all its contents were gone long before the garbage truck arrived.

Friday

"Lyds, no one made you crawl on your hands and knees in the dirt yesterday. I get that you're sore, but it's my job that lets you stay home instead of working," Bert said.

Despite talking on the phone, Lydia could easily imagine the exasperated expression on his face. "It's not just yesterday, moving and unpacking boxes, it's been a lot. I don't think I can host tonight."

There was a long pause on the other end of the line. "Are you honestly saying I'm going to have to tell my boss 'never mind, my wife's too tired to make dinner'?"

Lydia held in a sigh. "No, of course not. I'll rally."

"You're the best, Lyds." Bert hung up the phone without waiting for her response.

All the air left her lungs in an exhausted woosh, and she dropped the cell on the bed. Decades ago, when she'd found out she was pregnant with Lilly, it had seemed the right choice to drop out of college and stay home with the baby. Her degree was only half finished, and Bert was already climbing the corporate ladder. She thought she might go back once Lilly was old enough for preschool, but then Charles had followed two years later. By the time Lydia might have gone back to school or gotten a job, their family dynamic was working, so why change it?

But lately, she'd wondered if the status quo had benefited her at all. Looking back, Bert always seemed to get what he wanted, and her needs were always brushed aside, or worse, argued into nothing. She wasn't complaining. Bert worked hard.

Their kids had wanted for nothing. It's just... sometimes she looked in the mirror and she wasn't quite sure who was looking back.

Lydia retrieved her phone from the bed and placed it in her back pocket, then made her way into the kitchen. With a yank, she opened the freezer. She stared, exhaustion hampering her decision making. Finally, she pulled out some frozen chicken breasts and dropped them in the sink to thaw. She'd figure out what to *do* with them later.

A flutter of wings outside the window grabbed her attention.

Her bird friend was back.

Lydia grabbed a sparkling water from the fridge and stepped into the backyard. If she was going to have to host this evening, she was going to take a moment for herself.

Just outside the door and leaning against the brick siding, Lydia found an old metal folding chair with fraying nylon straps. She lugged it into the shade and popped it open. The scrub jay peered down from the elm's branches, stretching wide and protective.

Now that she was close, she could see the mushrooms she'd noticed earlier in the week formed a nearly perfect ring within the tall grass. Each one unique in size and shape. Wasn't there something about faeries and mushrooms in a ring?

She settled the chair away from them, not wanting to crush any, and gently sat down. The nylon straps let out a crunchy groan beneath her weight, but held. She snapped open her water with a hiss and pulled out her cellphone.

It was the middle of the day, both Lilly and Charles and their children would be too busy with jobs or school to chat on the phone. Not that they answered even when they weren't. Resigned, she scrolled through the latest posted pictures and marked them with a heart. When she reached the ones she'd already seen, she clicked the screen off and set it on her lap.

The scrub jay fluttered down near her and like a majordomo, strutting through the grass and dandelions toward the circle of mushrooms.

A faerie ring! That's what it was called.

A person could just step inside one and end up in the land of faerie. With that thought, Lydia remembered a poem she'd read often as a teenager. She'd loved the melancholy feel of the repeated verse.

Come away, O human child!
To the waters and the wild
With a faery, hand in hand,
For the world's more full of weeping than you can understand.

What would Bert do if she up and disappeared? Certainly not make dinner. She snorted at the thought. Speaking of which, she should figure out what she was going to make. With a heave, Lydia got to her feet.

For a full moment, she stood staring down at the space cradled between the mushrooms. Could there really be a world beyond? The image of faeries hand in hand, leaping to and fro in the moonlight, just as the poem promised, filled her head; infusing her with joy. What would happen if she just took one step and left everything behind?

A low hum filled the air, and Lydia looked down to see bees, dozens of them, buzzing from dandelion to dandelion. How had she missed them until now? She watched as they bounced from golden flower to golden flower. More of them ending up near her as they traveled. It almost seemed like they were flying closer on purpose, herding her toward the mushroom ring. The scrub jay flew back up to the branch, staring down at her expectantly.

A self-deprecating laugh burst from her. There were no such things as faeries or fairytale endings.

Lydia carefully made her way through the bees and went back inside to start dinner. As she worked, she tried to ignore how the fleeting thought of joy had only served to remind her how long she'd lived without it.

Saturday

Divorce.

That's the word Bert had delivered to her last night after their guest had left and the dishes had yet to be washed.

"I thought this move would help," he said, pulling at his tie to loosen it. "That you'd finally be there for me."

Lydia could only stare at him in confusion, a stack of dirty plates in her hand.

"It's like you're just going through the motions." The tie unknotted, and he pulled it free from his collar fast enough to make it sing. "You just sat there. Not a word. You used to try. What happened?"

Too many thoughts ran through her mind at once and, when she didn't respond, he'd huffed away toward their bedroom.

Lydia deliberately took her time washing up from dinner. This wasn't the first time Bert had brought up divorce, but it was the first time the idea hadn't filled her with panic. *What did that mean?*

When she opened the bedroom door, she heard Bert's metronome snore. She quietly undressed and lay down as far from him as she could.

Sleep didn't come for many hours and left her early.

Bert was still asleep when she crawled out of bed. She stared down at him, letting her eyes roam over his thinning gray hair and the deep crevices in his forehead. Marks of the years that had passed. The same years marked on her own body.

Bert's question from last night came back to her. *You used to try. What happened?*

What had happened?

Lydia made her way to the kitchen and got the coffeemaker going. She rested her hip against the sink, the tower of dried dishes from last night in the rack beside her, and stared out the back window. Her scrub jay landed on the windowsill and tapped at the glass. She smiled at it, noticing behind it the folding chair still open on the lawn near the mushrooms—the faerie ring.

With a steaming cup of coffee in hand, Lydia made her way out the back door. She paused on the last step. The morning breeze fluttered the leaves on the elm and made them almost glitter like crown jewels. The dandelions opened their petals to the sun, villagers throwing wide their windows to let in the morning. And the ring, nearly glowed. The poem floated through her memory again.

Come away, O human child

Bert was right. She had changed. All those years she'd given everything to him and the children. All the parts of herself until they'd hollowed her out. Who even was Lydia now? Was she wrung dry and brittle? Empty and of no use? Or was she a carved vessel waiting to be filled again? A child reborn?

Lydia looked over her shoulder at the house that wasn't her own. Bert sleeping inside. Would he back out of his wish for a divorce in the morning light? Did she want him to?

Slowly, she crouched and set the coffee mug down on the step.

Come away, O human child

The bees buzzed in the morning light. The scrub jay cried. And all Lydia could feel was joy.

*The Stolen Child by W. B. Yeats – Public domain

"Come Away" is ©2024 by Angela Laverghetta. It appears here for the first time. A resident of Reno and a graduate of Western Nevada College, the author published her first book, "The Buried Knight," in 2023. The sequel, "The Hidden Druid," is slated for release at the end of 2024. She has a deep love of Northern Nevada and all her stories take place locally. You can join her newsletter for updates at www.angelalaverghettabooks.com.

Richard Moreno

The Old Cowboy

The old man's watery eyes were a tired shade of red, white, and muddy brown. He placed his worn, dark black cowboy hat on the stool next to him, combed his thick sun-bleached fingers through thinning silver hair, and surrendered a deep sigh.

"Barkeep, I would surely appreciate a drink," he said softly. "A man can get a little dry in this heat."

The bartender turned from stacking rows of shot glasses and looked at the old man, who was dressed in a plaid red-and-black western-style shirt buttoned to the neck and neatly-cuffed blue jeans. He'd seen dozens of used-up cowboys pass through his bar trying to trade a colorful story about the old days for a drink or a smoke.

"Got any money, old timer?" he asked.

"I do appear to be a little short at the present time, but I'd be willing to do a few chores in exchange for a glass of cold beer," the old man said.

"Get the hell out of here," the bartender growled.

"Wait a minute," said a voice from down the bar. "I'll buy him a drink."

A tall, thin man in his mid-30s walked over and sat next to the old man. He smiled and thrust out his hand.

"My name is Carl Hayden," he said. "I'm down here visiting from Salt Lake City."

"Nice to meet you friend. My name's Jack, and I'm much obliged for the beer," the man said, the sides of his mouth crinkling up into a warm smile.

The bartender smirked, then poured a mug of cold beer, and placed it in front of the old man.

"You need another one, pal?" he asked Hayden.

"Sure, another ginger ale. It is pretty hot," Hayden said.

The old cowboy sipped the beer and looked at the younger man.

"Are you on vacation down here in Las Vegas?" he asked.

"Sort of. I'm a reporter for the *Salt Lake City Tribune*, and I'm on what you could call a working vacation. I'm looking for human-interest stories that I can write when I get back. In fact, I wanted to talk to you when I saw you walk in."

"What about?"

"Well, it's my impression that cowboying is kind of dying out as a career. I was thinking of writing something about the death of the American West and the end of the cowboy lifestyle. I take it from the way you're dressed that you are, or were, a cowboy?"

The old man chortled, then took another sip of his beer. He slowly shook his head side-to-side.

"Son, you got it all wrong. Being a cowboy ain't a job like working in a bank—or a newspaper. Cowboying is a way of life. For folks that do it, it's as natural as sleeping, breathing, or eating. It gets in your blood, and you can't really imagine doing anything else. Nope, there will always be cowboys."

He stopped, shook his head again and took a long draught from his beer.

"How long were you a working cowboy?" Hayden asked.

"You sure you want to hear all this, son?" the old man responded.

"Sure. I've been fascinated by cowboys since I was a kid."

"Then, I think you've seen too many of them moving pictures," the old man said. "Well, I ain't no Roy Rogers. I don't play a guitar or sing, so don't expect anything special from me.

"I've been cowboying since I was in my teens. I originally worked the old Triple Cross outfit out in southern Idaho, then worked for just about everybody else in that area over the next few years. Had some good times and some not so good."

"Did you ever have to carry a gun?" Hayden asked.

"That's kind of a personal question," the old man said, his shoulders visibly tensing. He finished his beer, and Hayden gestured for the bartender to bring him another.

"Look, I didn't mean to bring up something you'd rather not talk about. I was just curious because it seems life was more violent back then."

"No, it's all right. You just got me thinking about something I ain't wanted to think about in years. You see, I did some time up in Idaho for supposedly murdering two fellas."

Hayden tried not to act surprised. He shifted in his chair and nervously ran his finger up and down the side of his empty glass.

"I can see you're wondering about me now," the old man said, smiling. "Well, let me assure you it wasn't true. Back in those days, they had what we called range detectives or regulators. It was a fancy name for being a hired gun for a cattle boss. I was one of them for a while," the old man said.

The bartender placed a second beer in front of the cowboy, removed the empty, and refreshed Hayden's ginger ale.

"I really wasn't all that good with a gun, but I sure liked to shoot off my mouth," the old man continued. "I was hired by this big cattle man named Mr. John Sparks."

"You mean the former Governor of Nevada?" Hayden interrupted.

"The same. I knew him pretty well. He hired me and some other fellas to keep an eye on the Basco sheep men who were moving into the area. This was back during what they call the great sheep wars. Mr. Sparks told me to do whatever I had to do to keep the Bascos from grazing on his land. The funny thing is, it was range land that he didn't exactly own," the old man said, adding, "Do you mind if I smoke?"

Hayden shook his head and watched the old cowhand pull a partially crushed pack of unfiltered Camels from inside his coat pocket and shake one loose. The old man lit it, inhaled deeply, then barked out a cough.

"I've got to quit one of these days," he said. "They're going to kill me someday."

"Why were you accused of murder?" Hayden asked after the older man had smoked the cigarette nearly down to his finger-tips, tossed it on the floor, and crushed it with the pointed tip of his worn brown cowboy boot.

"I was a bit of a show-off in those days and used to boast considerably about my prowess with a gun. I might even have mentioned to at least a few folks that I'd killed a man or two. 'Course, none of it was true. I never shot anyone, except maybe a few smelly coyotes, but that didn't stop the authorities from arresting me when two Bascos were found dead out near the San Jacinto Ranch."

"What happened next?" Hayden asked, leaning closer to better hear the old man's soft voice. He could tell the buckaroo was enjoying the exchange, pleased that someone was interested in hearing his stories.

"Oh, I had a trial, if you could call it that. It was in all the papers. The judge and the prosecuting attorney decided to make their political careers on my case, and the jury was about as fair as one of these card games around here," the old man said.

"So, you were found guilty of murder and went to jail. How'd you get out?" Hayden asked.

"It took a while. I was sentenced to hang, but the man who really killed the two sheepherders finally came forward. Forgive my language, but those sons of bitches in Idaho kept me there for almost six years. I finally received a pardon, but I never got a dime for spending those years in jail. I guess that's why I've always felt I've been living on borrowed time.

"After that, I drifted around. I did some mining in Tonopah and Goldfield—there's even an old mining camp named after me in Nye County—but that was mostly because I just got too old to sit on a horse and sleep on the ground anymore," the old man continued.

"Do you miss the life?" Hayden asked.

"Every damn day. There's nothing like riding across a big stretch of open valley, feeling the wind at your back and the sun on your face and arms, and knowing you're free. That's what I missed most when I was in jail.

"'Course, things have changed quite a bit since I was earning my keep on the back of a horse. Now, you got automobiles and trucks instead of horses. And people—I ain't never seen as many people as you got in Nevada now. Used to be a man could ride for days, or even weeks, without seeing so much as a ranch or a road. Now, people are all over the place. Can't get away from them. Maybe you're right about the death of the West," he said.

"Do you ever regret anything you've done?" Hayden asked following a long pause.

"Oh, there are certainly a few people I should have treated better, a lady or two I probably should have married, and a couple of lies I probably shouldn't have told," he said. "But I couldn't have asked for a better life. I've been alive during a time when a man could make his living on the back of a horse with only his hands, his heart and his wits. I'm not saying I'm anyone special, just an old cowboy who liked the cowboy life."

"Would you like another beer?" Hayden asked.

"No, thank you," the old man said. "I've been running off at the mouth, talking your ear off. I appreciate the cold beers," the cowboy said as he rose from the stool. He placed his black cowboy hat on his head, tipped it at Hayden, then in the direction of the bartender, and stiffly walked out of the bar.

Hayden sat looking at his folded hands for a moment. He nodded at the bartender and pulled out his wallet to pay the bill.

"That old fart comes in here all the time and tries to talk someone into buying him drinks in return for some tall tale. You just encourage him when you do that," the bartender said.

"It's okay. I kind of liked him and I liked his story," Hayden said. "Do you happen to know his name?"

"I think he goes by Jack, although I've heard some call him Diamondfield," the bartender replied.

Suddenly, there was the high-pitched squeal of rubber tires desperately trying to grip asphalt. Hayden rushed out the door in time to see a small crowd, mostly tourists in bright shirts and shorts, forming around a body in the street. He walked closer, but already knew what he would see.

"Who was he? A movie-star?" someone is the crowd asked.

"No," Hayden said. "Just an old cowboy."

As he turned to leave, he could see the bright neon lights of the surrounding Fremont Street casinos and night clubs began to obliterate the rich, purple early evening sky.

The ACES Anthology

Janice Oberding
Mother, Mae West and I

Mother always lands on her stiletto-shod feet. She never worries when a relationship sours; she simply starts looking for her next mate. And there is always a *next...* and a *next* for mother. She is pretty enough, and temperamental enough and given to histrionics so that she might have been a movie star. She isn't. Mother owns a small Beverly Hills boutique, something she inherited from her parents. Fashion savvy, business smarts and the requisite long hours paid off. She is doing quite well for herself and catering to Hollywood's current crème de la crème.

And wouldn't you know it. One afternoon mother was busy assuring a size 2 film star that her hips were not too wide for a red pencil skirt ensemble when Michael walked in. Michael, as in her future husband (number five, if you're counting).

Like Narcissus, the film star fell in love with what she saw in the mirror and bought the pencil skirt ensemble, and a handbag, and a beret... and out the door she went, leaving mother and Michael alone in the shop. And the laws of attraction kicked in. Spells were cast. Phone numbers were exchanged. Three weeks later, they flew to Las Vegas and sealed the deal with a diamond, a very large diamond.

Mother moved out of her Wilshire Boulevard place and into Michael's swanky Old World mansion on Orange Grove Boulevard in Pasadena. Early California stucco, tile roof, tall palm trees, and an expanse of lawn—the house had the aura of Hollywood circa 1930s. I was visiting for the first time during spring break. The daughter, mother looked much too young to have ever given birth to, I was the inconvenient truth; mother was much older than she appeared. Thanks to good genes, good living and a skilled cosmetic surgeon. Who cares? It's the Southern California way.

But back to Orange Grove Boulevard; I adored mother's new husband, Michael. Mother was happy at last, and her new digs were luxurious in a vintage glamour kind of way. If I closed my eyes, I could almost see old Rolls Royces pulling into the circular driveway, handsome men in tuxes and permed women swaddled in ermine. Over dinner that night, Michael told me that Bette Davis once slept in the very guest house I was staying in.

"The effects of the wine made her nervous about driving," he said, refilling my empty wineglass.

"And darling, tell her about Mae West," mother urged.

Darling did as he was told. Apparently, Mae West had a lover who'd owned the house at one time. The backyard pool parties scandalized the la-di-da upper-crust neighborhood. Swimsuits were options no one bothered donning. Not Mae, not her lover, and certainly not their guests. The hedges were so high neighbors would have needed binoculars to catch the action. They probably did just that. We laughed at the thought of a prim matron watching Mae West *au natural* prancing poolside. If any of the stories were true, Mae really kicked up her heels back in the day.

I returned to the guest house thinking of the old days in Hollywood. Those people really knew how to party, I told myself, flipping on the TV. I laughed out loud when I realized I was watching an old Mae West film: *She Done Him Wrong* with one of my favorite actors, Cary Grant. Now here was suave and debonair. The movie was just starting; I could sleep as late as I wanted, so I slipped into my pajamas during commercials and snuggled into bed.

Mae West had it! She had what Harlow had, and what Marilyn Monroe had, and Jayne Mansfield, to a lesser degree: sex appeal and charisma that reached out from the screen. I wondered what I might look like as a blonde. Hmmm, to think that she swam in the very pool that stood between guest house and mansion. I'm sure there was some remodeling over the years, but all the same... George Washington might have slept there, but Mae West swam here—naked.

Morning brought rain. A real Jane Grey day, anyone who tells you it never rains in Southern California is a liar. Truth is, once it starts, it doesn't stop. And so I spent the morning in the guest house, playing on my laptop, and wondering how to tell mother that I had lost interest in pursuing a business degree. Business was her forte, not mine. I wanted to write. No money, but that's where my heart was. Now, how to explain to mother, who saw me as the CEO of some Fortune 500 company someday. *A nice warm shower might bring forth ideas on how best to approach the subject.*

It didn't.

Regardless, she and I needed to talk. Maybe Michael would intercede on my behalf... I was well into my second cup of cocoa when I saw the shadowy form step from the bedroom.

"Hello!" I demanded.

"Uuuuhello," the form said, slowly taking shape.

That voice... it couldn't be... and yet it was... Mae West was standing in the guest house.

"Don't look so alarmed, dearie." She said, "I've come to help you with your problem."

"I—I have no—"

"Yes you do! Now, tell me, do I look all right in this dress? Is it too matronly for me?"

The dress couldn't have been any tighter. "No matron would be caught dead in a dress like that." I answered.

And then, realizing that Mae West was among the dead, I said, "Sorry."

She tossed back her blond curls and laughed. Just like she had in *She Done Him Wrong.* "Don't be sorry, dearie. I'm a woman of few words and lots of action. Let's get started here."

Started? What was she talking about?

I asked. She answered. "Look dearie, you and your mother are in a world of hurt."

"Please stop calling me dearie! My name is Deborah. My friends call me Deb."

She examined her long magenta nails, and then glared at me. "Personality is the most important thing to an actress' success, and I got plenty of personality, but very little patience, so Deborah dearie here's the deal: Your mother has stepped into it this time. "

"You've already said that."

"If you say so Deborah... dearie."

Our personalities were clashing like plaids, polka dots, and stripes. But I had to know. "About my mother's problem, what is it and how can you help?"

"Your mother's sampled 'em all, smart woman. But this time she's chosen an evil she's never tried before. She's married a vampire."

"You can't be serious! Are you trying to tell me that Michael is a vampire?"

"My, aren't you a quick study." She giggled.

I seriously doubted that. Here I was conversing with a ghost about my mother's vampire husband. Still, I'd watched enough vampire movies to know they melt like cheap lipstick in daylight.

"Mother and Michael golf together. Outdoors under the California sunshine, so tell me, how does a vampire not wither away to dust in the broad daylight?"

"You mean like they do in the movies?" She laughed.

"Take it from me, an old vampire can do just about anything. And Michael is a very old vampire. "

"But he adores mother."

"Oh, I'm sure he does... for the time being. But once the newness wears off, your mother's going to be seriously heartbroken. And so might you be, for that matter."

"I don't believe you!"

"You wouldn't," she scoffed. "Your mother's gonna get old and withered no matter how much money she drops for cosmetic surgery. Michael will remain handsome and virile. Can you see them in twenty years' time? Ghastly, your mother at least—not Michael."

"Stop it!"

"The truth hurts, Deborah! Say, have you ever seen the film *Lustful Heart*?"

I shook my head.

"It's a silent classic! Directed by David Denvers and co-starring your mother's Michael."

I laughed out loud. "That would mean Michael is about a hundred and thirty years old."

"Oh no! He's much older. He was Lawrence LaPere back then." She twirled around and looked at herself in the mirror. Patting her blond curls, she asked. "Not bad for a dead woman, huh?"

"Dead maybe, but your ego is very much alive and well, Ms. West."

"My! Aren't you the catty one! Deborah dearie, a woman must love herself first. But I didn't come all this way to discuss such matters with you. We must get a copy of that film. Do you have the use of a car?"

I did. And after slipping into a pair of old jeans and sweatshirt, I ran down to the garage and started mother's Jaguar, which was at my disposal whenever I was in town. With the ghostly Mae perched queen-like in the passenger seat, I drove toward the Arroyo Seco Parkway.

"It's been a few years, but there used to be this heavenly little shop on Lankershim that sold just about anything you can imagine."

I drove as she directed. A high rise occupied the corner lot where the *heavenly little* shop had once stood.

The rain was not letting up. Neither was Mae. She wanted that movie one way or the other.

"Do you think the library might have a copy?" I asked.

"Keep driving! We're sure to run into a store that sells... Stop!"

I pulled the Jaguar into the parking lot of a large thrift store that sold everything, according to its sign. We foraged through a dusty pile of old VHS tapes and there it was, *Lustful Heart* for 99 cents. But who had a VHS player? Not me!

The store's proprietor turned a gleaming golden-tooth smile my way and assured me he had such a player. And it was only going to cost me seventy-five dollars. A collector's item that worked, instruction manual included. Mae West urged me on. "Buy it and let's get out of this rat hole."

She must have looked at the counter and seen that set of old Mae West collector mugs that didn't do her any justice.

"How much for the Mae West mugs?" I asked.

Old golden-tooth smiled again. "Mae West personally posed for those."

"Liar!" she screeched. "That is the work of one lousy artist."

"How much?" I asked again.

"I couldn't let that set go for less than a hundred dollars." He said.

"Too much, sorry."

"Fifty five is low as I can go."

"Sold!" I said, whipping out my debit card. "That artist truly captured her."

Golden tooth laughed merrily. "My former father-in-law did her makeup. She was not nearly as pretty as you might think. He claimed she had a big nose, pitted skin, and haystack hair." He said wrapping the mugs in newspaper.

Mae was seething. "At least I don't spend my time selling junk and telling lies in some little rat hole!"

"I've always been a fan of Ms. West's." I assured him. "She was such a wonderful actress, and quite beautiful."

"Oh Deb! Thank you." She said happily.

"All true." I told her.

"But of course." He said handing me my purchases. "Beauty is in the eye of the beholder. Would you like me to carry this to your vehicle?"

"Does she look like some little weakling?" Mae asked.

"I can manage." I said, grabbing the VHS player, the tape and mugs.

It was still raining when we returned to the guest house. By the time I got the player hooked up to the television, it was dark and mother was calling about my dinner plans. She and Michael were dining with some of his clients in Beverly Hills, and I could order out or try a frozen dinner. Pizza delivery it was.

The fuzzy credits rolled on screen. *Lustful Heart starring Lawrence LaPere and Geneva Gilberton.* The tinkling piano, led into a woman in distress. Apparently, her house was being foreclosed on. Yes, I read the captions... *Evil bankers all. Destitute little Myra with no one in the world to care for her...* More piano music, and into the scene walked Michael, or rather, Lawrence LaPere.

"I told you so!" Mae shouted.

"That's him! But that's almost a hundred years ago..."

"He's a vampire!"

And then I started thinking about all the things I knew about Mae West.

"Were you and he ever lovers?" I asked. Before she could answer, I shot another question her way, "How do I know you aren't acting out of jealousy to ruin his and mother's marriage?"

"I tried them all. Of course we were lovers. It didn't last. He wanted someone to sit by the hearth. That wasn't me. As far as being jealous of your mother's and his marriage... Puleeze!"

"Then why not leave them alone?"

"I owed St. Peter one more good deed and agreed to intercede if possible—"

"You're an angel?"

"No I am not!"

"You said St. Peter sent you."

"Yes, he did, but it doesn't mean I'm an angel. Can you see me in one of those ill-fitting white robes?"

"No, I can't. But, you've come from heaven, didn't you?"

"We'll discuss that some other time. Now, before you so rudely interrupted me, I was saying that these vampire/mortal marriages just never work out. The mortal always gets hurt. Always!"

We finished watching *Lustful Heart* in silence, save for the piano that was wearing thin on my nerves.

"Tomorrow I'll talk with mother and Michael."

"Then it's ta-ta till then." She said, dissolving into thin air like all ghosts, and angels, are supposed to.

By the time dinner was served the next evening, I'd worked up the courage to talk with Michael and mother. True to her word, Mae was beside me and waiting.

"Tell me about Lawrence LaPere," I said bluntly.

Michael took a sip of his wine and laughed uproariously.

"Hello, Mae. How've you been?"

"Tell him I'm super," Mae said.

"She's super." And to Mae I asked, "How does he know you're here?"

"It's a vampire thing," she answered. "They're very sneaky."

"Right... now what about Lawrence LaPere?"

Mother reached for Michael's hand. "I insist you tell her the truth, Darling."

"As I'm sure you already know, I was Lawrence LaPere in my youth. I fell passionately in love with Mae when she was performing in vaudeville. She dumped me a few years later when she discovered I was a vampire."

I gasped. "You admit it?"

"Certainly, and your mother is aware of my condition." He smiled.

Mother squeezed his hand. "Michael and I are in love. We have no secrets, Deb, none whatsoever."

"The only truth I may have twisted was the identity of Mae's lover who owned this property," Michael said. "It was I, of course. And Mae did swim in the nude here with me on more than one occasion. So tell me, Mae, why are you trying to destroy my marriage?"

"Just so you know Ms. West, Michael's being a vampire doesn't matter to me," Mother said, smiling tenderly at Michael.

I turned toward Mae, who was glaring at mother. "Well?" I asked.

"This isn't at all what I expected," she said. "Your mother is a bigger fool than I realized. There's nothing more I can do here... That's my last good deed, St. Peter. We're even! And as I've told you before, my white robe must be fitted properly."

"Thank you, Mae," I whispered.

"Yeah, okay," she said, before disappearing into a silvery mist.

"Mother, Mae West, and I" is ©2019 by Janice Oberding. It originally appeared in a book by the author titled "Dancing With the Dahlia." The author is a resident of Reno and has published 45 works of fiction and non-fiction, including "The Big Book of Nevada Ghost Stories," "Murders Mysteries and Misdemeanors of Hollywood and Los Angeles," and "Haunted Las Vegas," which are available in the ACES bookshop at <u>acesofnorthernnevada.com</u>. Janice is a true crime buff who enjoys

travel, cooking, history, and the paranormal. You can follow the author at https://www.facebook.com/JaniceOberding.

The ACES Anthology

Sharon Marie Provost

The Road to Joya

Ooooohhhhhh, look at that, Daddy!" Cayden screeched from his toddler seat in the back, instantly breaking Michael out of his highway hypnosis. The scenery had been the same for the last two hundred miles as they drove ever deeper into the desert. Cayden had been sleeping, so there wasn't much to occupy his mind—except the thoughts about their future. Or rather, the future that they did not seem to have.

Michael looked into the rearview mirror to make eye contact with his son as he asked him what had caught his eye.

"There, Daddy! There!" Cayden exclaimed as he excitedly pointed off to the right. Michael was shocked when he looked over to see what appeared to be a lush green valley tucked up into the hills in the distance. They were surrounded by the dry, desert landscape, only broken up by Joshua trees, cactus, and sagebrush. Yet somehow, they saw what seemed to be an unbelievable oasis ahead.

"Home! Let's go. Are we there yet?" Cayden said in a breathless rush.

"No, sweetheart. That is not our home. We won't get to Grandma's house for another hour and a half," Michael said trying to sound less dejected than he felt. If only he could provide such a beautiful place for Cayden to live. His precious son was losing the only home he had ever known just before Christmas, the first one they would be celebrating without Melissa. Instead, they were headed to a small trailer home deep in the desert, miles from any town. There would be no yard to play in, no playground, no other children for miles... not even his own bedroom to hold his cherished race car bed and all his toys. They'd had to sell or give away most of their belongings before they started the trip. There just would not be any room for them.

It was all still a blur in Michael's mind. He could only imagine how hard it was for poor Cayden, but that boy was a trooper, just like his mother had been. Their life had been happy... perfect. Then one day, he got a call from the police that his wife had been in a car accident. They had done everything they could to save her, but after lingering in a coma for a month, she had eventually passed away.

Michael had spent almost every waking moment at her bedside, trying to convince her to wake up and come back to them. When he wasn't with her, he was busy taking Cayden to kindergarten and then daycare afterward before taking him home for the night, hoping to keep his life as normal as possible. His work had been accommodating at first, but then his employers started to question when he would be back. He desperately tried to get them to understand that she was at a critical stage, as was his son, so he needed to be there for them.

His boss called him the day she took a turn for the worse, and he let the call go to voicemail. Then, the day after she passed, he received a letter in the mail letting him know he had been terminated. Now he had no job, no wife, and a mountain of debt staring him in the face. He desperately tried to find new employment, but they lived in an area with a poor job market. There was always someone more qualified, or the hours required did not accommodate a single parent. Eventually, he had to admit defeat and figure out what to do.

Much to his dismay, there seemed to be no option but to call his estranged mother to see if he and Cayden could stay there temporarily while he tried to get on his feet again. His mother had always considered him a failure, so he could just hear the disappointment dripping in her voice as she agreed. This was no home for his son, but he had no choice. He could not afford to live anywhere else, but how could he afford to let his son grow up in the same environment he had?

Michael was once again startled out of his painful memories by his exuberant son.

"It is COMING closer!"

"No, son. WE ARE getting closer," he corrected Cayden gently. He was determined to raise his son to be well-educated and well-spoken, just as his mother had been. However, he was surprised to see how much closer the town was now than it had been just a few short minutes ago. Oddly, it appeared as if they were headed right for the town, but he didn't remember the road veering off to the right at any point. It had been long and straight for hours. He checked the speedometer to make sure he was not exceeding the speed limit. He didn't realize he had been distracted from the road for so long that he had not noticed the distance they had traveled or the change in direction.

Once again, he looked into the mirror as he asked Cayden, "How are you feeling, kiddo? Hungry?" He had intended to buy breakfast as they came into their new hometown, but since they seemed to be headed into this community they hadn't expected, they might as well stop. Michael knew he was feeling hungry himself, and clearly, he needed to get out and move around some to clear his head.

"We should arrive in that town in the next fifteen to twenty minutes I think, so we can stop for breakfast if you like." Michael smiled as his son's face lit up.

"WE ARE HERE! Yay, yay, yay!"

"No, I said...," Michael's voice trailed off as he looked back at the road to see a large yellow sign with bright green writing announcing *Welcome to Joya, your new home sweet home. You will never want to leave.*

Michael stuttered, "I...I... I guess we ARE here." He looked around wildly, trying to understand how they could suddenly be in town when, a mere minute ago, they'd had miles left to go. He tried to calm himself and not make Cayden worry, since he was happily bouncing in his seat.

"Can we go to that park, Daddy, after breakfast?"

Michael turned quickly in the direction Cayden was pointing to see lush green grass in a sprawling park full of playground equipment, a walking trail, tennis court, and plenty of park benches to sit and enjoy. The park was impressively decorated for Christmas with a large throne for Santa to sit upon and have his picture taken with the kids on the deck of the pavilion. The streetlamps ringing the park each had a wreath or large red bow. There were wooden lawn decorations with elves, angels, and snowmen. In the center of the park was a large lighted pine tree with enormous colored baubles, icicles, and reindeer ornaments.

Michael could have sworn that he had not seen that park when they entered town a moment ago. When he turned his back to face the road, he suddenly noticed a small, homey diner off to the right called Cozy Corner. He quickly turned into the lot and switched off the engine.

Michael had not slept well in weeks, and they had gotten an early start. But still, he didn't feel that tired or out of it. Clearly, the stress was getting to him more than he knew. It was obviously time to stretch his legs and wake up while he let Cayden enjoy the playground. First, though, the order of the day was breakfast and a cup of coffee... no, a *pot* of coffee. He didn't see anyone moving around in town, but there was a blinking "OPEN" sign in the window of the café.

"You ready for some food, bud?" Michael asked casually as he tried to shake off his unease.

Michael jumped when the excited affirmation came from the open window beside him. He hadn't even noticed Cayden release himself from his car seat and exit. He climbed out wearily and grabbed his son's hand as they walked up to the door. A bell rang merrily as they opened the door, followed quickly by a warm hello from the waitress helping the couple sitting in the back corner.

"Sit wherever you like," she called out as she walked briskly to the kitchen window and hung the order on the wheel, giving it a quick spin to the waiting cook. Michael led his son to a booth in the front by the window. Clearly, he must have looked as tired as he should have been because Shirley (at least that was what appeared on her nametag) quickly arrived with a large steaming mug of coffee. She handed them menus as she warmly welcomed them to "the happiest small town in America." Then, to his great delight, in front of Cayden, she promptly laid down a small dinosaur coloring book and a box with four crayons.

"Here you go, bug," she said as she ruffled his hair before turning away to give them time to study the menu.

"Did you hear that, Daddy? She called me bug. Just like... just like... just like Mom did," he whispered as he sniffled and fought to hold back the single tear that eventually wound its way down his cheek.

"Yes, honey, I did. Lots of people call kids that. It's a term of endearment."

Cayden smiled softly and started studying the menu. Michael added cream and three packets of sugar to his coffee as he looked at the menu. Shirley returned with a large mug of hot chocolate covered in whipped cream and red and green jimmies for Cayden when they set the menus down, and took their orders for flapjacks, bacon, and scrambled eggs. After turning their ticket in to the short-order cook, she returned to make small talk.

Michael quickly found out that the town had been founded by a group of "dreamers" as Shirley called them. It was originally formed by a band of outsiders, composed of immigrants, physically impaired people, and loners who had met back East as they struggled with bigotry and prejudice. They'd dreamed of founding a new town that they could build themselves, setting their own rules, and working together to support one another. They worked hard to get the supplies and money together to travel by wagon train across the country and had settled here when they found such a lovely, protected green valley amid the harshness of the desert. They had founded their idyllic town and carefully cultivated their citizenship over the years, catering to those in need. It had become a so-called City of Necessity, available to those who needed a loving, supportive home when they had nowhere else to go. So, fittingly, they had named the town Joya, after the old English word meaning "fulfilled dreams."

Michael and Cayden finished their delicious breakfast and thanked Shirley for her wonderful company. Michael noticed he felt more relaxed and comforted than he had in quite some time as they headed over to the park across the street.

Cayden ran ahead and joined the other kids in the park playing on the swings, monkey bars, and the other equipment. Michael decided to sit on the steps of the pavilion in the center of the park. The town seemed to be alive now, as he watched several couples on the walking path, the children playing with his son, another group playing soccer over in the corner, and a group on the tennis court. To his surprise, he realized there was a bustling town center just down the street. A large banner over the quaint, old-fashioned main street announced a New Year's celebration, complete with fireworks and a carnival. Every business downtown was covered in lights, wreaths, and other festive decorations. Wooden stand-up decorations had been set up with holes to put your face through for pictures. Michael just knew Cayden would want a picture taken in each one.

This was just the kind of small town he had dreamed about growing up in when he'd watched shows like *The Waltons* in his youth. The pace of life just seemed slower and more relaxed. People were stopping to greet each other warmly. Cars drove down the street slowly and carefully, watching out for the people crossing the road. Many people were either walking or riding bikes throughout town, rather than driving. There was even a banner billowing in the breeze over the archway into the park advertising Joya Pioneer Days, set for three weeks from now. Cayden ran through the park, playing and laughing with such abandon that Michael's eyes welled up with tears. He had not seen his son this happy since he'd lost his mother. It broke his heart that he couldn't provide his son with this kind of loving environment in which to spend his childhood. Michael knew his own mother was expecting them to have arrived by now and would surely be questioning his delay already. Yet, he just didn't care. He could not tear Cayden away from his happiness or this town just yet. A delay of a few more hours couldn't hurt, and so he let him continue to play.

Before he knew it, twilight was approaching, and Cayden came running up to him with a smile plastered on his face. The other kids seemed to be drifting off toward home, and Michael noticed warm lights in the windows of the many homey little cottages spread throughout town.

"I'm hungry. Is it dinnertime yet?" Cayden asked eagerly.

Michael looked at his watch as his own stomach growled in response. He was shocked to see that it was nearly 6 p.m. He knew he should really call his mother to apologize for their delay, but it couldn't hurt to wait a little longer. After all, feeding his son was the priority. He noticed the café was still open and the most delicious aromas were wafting out through the screen door. They walked back across the street, and they were pleasantly surprised to find Shirley still working.

"Well, hello, you two. I was wondering if I would be seeing you again when I saw your car was still parked out front. Will we be serving you dinner tonight?" Shirley inquired as she led them over to a table with a smile. Cayden snatched the menu from her eagerly as he replied, "Yes, ma'am."

"Now don't you 'ma'am' me, young man. You can call me Aunt Shirley. Everyone around here does. Now let me guess here. Chocolate milk?"

"Yes, please! Thank you, Aunt Shirley." Michael replied as he beamed at her adoringly.

Dinner passed in a whirlwind of the most delightful meatloaf, mashed potatoes and gravy, fresh green beans, apple pie, and conversation that the two had ever experienced. By the end of the evening, Cayden was starting to slump over in his seat as he fought sleep valiantly but to no avail. Michael inquired about a motel or bed and breakfast where they could stay for the night before getting an early start tomorrow. Shirley happily informed him that there was a vacancy at the bed and breakfast she owned just down the road at the very start of Main Street.

While they'd been discussing the arrangements, Cayden had fallen into a deep slumber across the bench seat. Shirley told him that he could just leave his car in the lot and carry him down to the room since it was such a short distance. Michael paid their check, carefully picked Cayden up, and walked slowly down the road to the B&B with Shirley, engaging in pleasant conversation along the way. He placed the boy carefully into the bed that Shirley showed him and then went out to complete the paperwork for checking in and share a cup of coffee with her at the table.

When Shirley asked how they came to be passing through their delightful small town, Michael explained what they had been through the past few months. He was caught off guard by his own candor when he went further and explained where they were going and why he was so unhappy about it. Shirley had tears in her eyes as she listened to his story.

"Michael, I am confident that you would be welcomed with open arms into our humble town. Please consider staying here with us. We could use more people like you. And that boy of yours experienced sheer joy today, which you and I both know he deserves."

Michael shook his head sadly as he explained, "Shirley, I very much appreciate your words. I would stay here in a heartbeat if I could, but we don't have any money to start over. I have a stack of medical bills a mile high waiting for me. We lost our home. I had to sell most of our belongings. Maybe someday..." A tear slowly slid down his cheek as he turned to head to bed. Shirley softly patted him on the back and let him go.

He heard her say one more thing as he headed back to the room. "Joya is not your normal small town. It is special here. Anything is possible, if you just dream."

Michael wearily climbed into bed thinking about what she said. He hugged Cayden close to him and fell quickly into a fitful sleep.

Early the next day, Cayden and Michael rose and prepared to hit the road. Before getting in the car, they stopped at the diner to thank Shirley for her hospitality.

As they left, Michael heard her say, "Remember what I said." Cayden excitedly chattered about his "new friends" and how they would play "next time." Michael didn't have the heart to remind him that there wasn't going to be a next time, especially since he was headed for such a rude awakening to his new life anyhow. Michael placed a call to his mother as they slowly drove out of town to let her know they were OK and would arrive in a little over an hour.

As usual, he could not do anything right. At first, she did not even remember that they had been due yesterday—not that he was surprised. But then she promptly started berating him for being so dreamy and distractible. She told him it was ridiculous and poor parenting to coddle his son in such a way.

Letting the kid experience a little fun and happiness for a day... coddling?

Then the condemnation moved on to him wasting money by eating out and staying the night. It just didn't stop—that is, until she moved on to telling him he wouldn't be in such a situation if he hadn't run off and married that girl because he had "knocked her up so young." At that point, he just hung up. He needed a break, and he would be there soon enough for her to start up again.

The closer he got to his childhood home, the more he knew that it was a mistake to let it be his child's home, even for a short while. His gas tank was getting low: He had enough to get to his destination, but it seemed like a good excuse to stop for a few moments to clear his head and put off the inevitable. They were just hitting the city limits of Delamar, the only city he had expected to see within a relatively short driving distance of his mother's house, so he took the exit and pulled into the service station.

Cayden climbed out and wandered off to the restroom as he headed inside to pre-pay. While he was at the counter, he made a comment regarding their enjoyable day spent in Joya.

The clerk looked at him questioningly.

"Pardon me. I never heard of no place like that. Where did you say you spent last night?" the clerk asked curiously.

"Joya. It's about 30 minutes west of here. In that enchanting green valley tucked up against the mountain."

"Are you OK, sir? You sure it was that close? There is no town in this state named that, that I know of at least. There surely is no town within 60 miles of us, period. The closest settlement of any kind is a couple of trailer homes set a mile or so apart in the middle of nowhere in the desert about 40 miles from here. The only thing green there is one of the trailers," he chuckled.

Michael didn't feel like arguing with this idiot, so he shook his head and thanked him as he paid for his gas. He headed back out to the car and made sure Cayden had returned safely from the restroom.

As he drove out of town, he noticed a small historical society building with an "OPEN" sign out front, so he decided to stop in and ask there. The woman at the desk greeted him kindly and asked how she could help. He repeated his story to her, but he was once again greeted with a confused expression and an assurance that she had no knowledge of any such town. She let him look through records tracing the area's history, but he was unable to find any documentation of Joya's existence. Michael left astonished and frustrated, feeling even more depressed than before.

There was nothing to do but resume their journey, and it wasn't long before they arrived at his mother's home. She wasn't even there to greet them, even though she knew when to expect them. She had left a key and a note on the porch with a curt message: "Get settled. Don't make a mess. See you later."

They removed their shoes as they entered so as not to drag in the desert sand, and Michael led his son to the small room they would share that had been his childhood bedroom. He settled Cayden in the room with some of his toys, as he slowly trudged in and out, bringing in their meager belongings.

Once he finished, he settled Cayden down for his nap, and then went out to the living room to watch some television while he waited for his mother to return. All his stress and anxiety over the coming reunion overcame him, and he fell asleep with his head resting on the arm of the couch.

He awoke with a start when his mother slammed the door.

"Thirty-six years old, and I still have to tell you not to put your feet on the couch. Goddamn it, Michael Evan Goodman. I am too old. Shit! You are too old for me to have to continue to remind you of the rules of my house. Is this what I should expect from your little bastard as well? So help me, you will be out on the street again if you can't get your shit together and grow up. THIRTY-SIX FUCKING YEARS OLD, and you have to come home to live with mommy. You make me thankful all my friends are dead, and I live in the middle of nowhere, so that I do not have to be embarrassed by my irresponsible, deadbeat son."

Michael looked up with horror in his eyes when he heard a noise in the hall and realized his son was hearing this tirade from a grandmother he had never even met before today. Cayden ran away crying as his grandmother started in on him.

"Don't make me box those ears, you little eavesdropper. So help me God, you will learn your manners. Your parents may have been negligent in their duties, but I will not tolerate a rude little bastard in my home. You get back here and listen to me when I talk to you."

Michael's mother stood up angrily and started toward the hall. He jumped up and ran to intercept her. He would not let her touch his son, even if it meant they lost this place to stay. Anything would be better, even a homeless shelter, than allowing his son to be abused. He jumped in front of her and amazed himself when he yelled, "Stop!" He had never dared speak to his mother that way. She stopped dead and looked as if he had slapped her... at first. Then her surprise quickly gave way to blind anger as *she* slapped *him* soundly across the face. When she opened her mouth to unleash another tirade, he simply walked away, shut the door and blocked it with his old desk chair.

He spent the next hour rocking his son in his arms as he promised him that no one would ever hurt him, as his grandmother beat on the door hurling insults. Christmas was going to be a disappointment this year, but he had not intended his son to spend Christmas Eve in tears and fearful. He then quickly repacked their few belongings and listened carefully for the house to get quiet, signaling that his mother had finally given up and retired for the night. When he felt safe, he quietly ushered Cayden out of the house with as much of their luggage as he could carry. He had left the window unlocked in case she woke and locked him out. He locked his son safely in the car, then quickly and silently returned to retrieve the last of their belongings. He drove down the road to a nearby rest stop and reclined the seats so they could get some rest for the night.

Michael did not know what he had planned for their future. He had contemplated returning to Joya—if he could find it again. But he'd never had the luxury of dreaming in his childhood, so he didn't hold out any hope for that option.

Before leaving his mother's house, he had contacted a close friend back where they had lived, who had agreed to put them up for two weeks. He had checked into homeless shelters in that area and had even looked into applying for welfare to see if that might be an option.

Needless to say, it was a mostly sleepless night at the rest stop. He had $2,000 left in his bank account, and he was just going to start driving and see what happened. He was a hard worker, and he had the best motivation in the world to succeed, so he had no doubt it would all work out in the end somehow. He could no longer allow himself the luxury of time and depression. It was time to create his own destiny for his sake and Cayden's.

When Cayden woke shortly after 7 on Christmas morning, they headed back toward Delamar to get a "yummy" gas station burrito for breakfast. The plan was to head back west toward Joya or to his friend's home, whichever worked out. Cayden was excited, but Michael could only feel anxious and desperate. The 30 miles passed quickly with no sign of the approaching town. Michael drove 45 miles before he pulled over to the side of the road, crying and hopeless.

"Don't cry, Daddy. You just missed it. You drove past it. You weren't looking like you should."

"Yes, I did, son. I looked very hard."

"Turn around, Daddy. Look again. Look for our home. You will see it. Please, Daddy."

Michael could see visions in his head of them living happily there. He imagined Cayden joining a soccer league. Leisurely walks down the main street on Sundays. Trick-or-treating at all those cute little cottages. Dinner every Friday night and breakfast every Sunday at the Cozy Corner Café. Evenings spent doing homework and then a brief walk down to the park to play before bed. He could even imagine himself working at the small stone garage in town. He had seen a "help wanted" sign. He was an IT guy by trade, but he had learned to fix cars in high school. He knew he could be happy there. He was sure Cayden would grow to be a well-adjusted, bright young man in that town.

Michael slowly turned the car around and drove back as his son had begged him to do. He felt calmer, even a little hopeful, after his daydreams of the future that could happen; visions of a New Year and new life passing through his head. A few miles later, he began to question whether he could believe what he was sure he was seeing in the distance. But swore he saw a lush green landscape far off to the right tucked up against the mountain.

He looked back at his son to ask him if he saw what he did. The smile on Cayden's face was all the confirmation he needed. But then Cayden squealed with delight, "Here it comes, Daddy."

Michael turned back to the wheel to suddenly see the *Welcome to Joya* sign approaching them. It literally appeared to be *coming at them*. It was appearing much faster than their speed of 45 miles per hour should have allowed. In the moment he recognized this, pieces of the town started appearing rapidly, one by one, literally popping into place. The diner. The park. And then the pavilion in the middle. The tennis court. Then the main street appeared. One by one, little cottages began to dot the landscape. And finally, the townspeople celebrating Christmas came into view, one by one, faster and faster as their joy grew.

Michael skidded into the diner's parking lot and ran up to the door with Cayden in tow. He whisked the door open with a flourish and broke out into raucous laughter as he saw Shirley beaming at them with two menus in hand.

"I just knew you two would be back. You belong here in our little town. I told you this place was special. It is our City of Sometimes. We are here when we are needed. But you see, we need you, too. We can only maintain our little Garden of Eden if it is populated with the right people who want to be happy and support one another. Gordon, the owner of the garage, is waiting for you down the street to discuss your new position. If you don't mind, I will close up the diner for a bit and take Cayden down and get him settled in your new cottage. I need some help decorating your Christmas tree. Santa came last night and left packages underneath, for both of you. It is the pink one just down the way at the corner of Aspiration and Main."

Cayden squealed with delight, and Michael stared at her in astonishment. He could not believe what he had just heard, yet he knew it was all right—even further, that she meant it. Michael haltingly asked her, "But... how? How did you know that I wanted to work at the garage? And the cottage... that was the one we liked. I didn't even know you had seen us look at it. But... but... I told you we have lost everything. I can't afford to rent a cottage like that."

"Shush now, son. It is all taken care of. You want to live here, correct?"

Michael nodded.

"You intend to take care of your son and help support the residents of this village, just as we have helped you, correct? You intend to be a productive citizen of this town?"

Michael nodded enthusiastically again.

"Well then, you better not be late to your quick orientation before your first day at work. Cayden and I will get you all settled at the cottage. After Christmas break, I will enroll him in school for you. You are both invited to Christmas dinner at my B&B at 6. Here is your lunch. Now off you go. We will see you at 1 to open presents and then head down to the park for the festivities."

Michael walked away smiling and chuckling as he shook his head. He had never been a dreamer. That had been discouraged—no, it had not been tolerated in his childhood home. Now, he knew dreams did come true. He was watching his dream skipping down the street next to Shirley chanting, "There is no place like home."

"The Road to Joya" is ©2023 by Sharon Marie Provost. It previously appeared in "Christmas Nightmare's Eve," of which she is the co-author. She is the author of "Shadow's Gate" and co-author of "All Hallows' Nightmare's Eve," both collections of horror-themed short stories. Her debut novel, "Dark Arts," a horror novel revolving around a serial killer, is being released in the fall of 2024. A longtime resident of Carson City, the author is also the co-editor of this volume.

The ACES Anthology

Stephen H. Provost

Messenger Boy

irls? Love?

Who has time for that?

I'm just a teenager, but I'm already way too busy figuring out how to get ahead in this life.

You don't meet girls in a mining town anyway. There aren't many of 'em to begin with, and they just want to put themselves between you and your money. Most of 'em, anyway. They either make a fella pay to spend the night, or they marry him and make him pay to spend *his whole life* with 'em.

The second kind ain't too interested in someone like me. I don't have enough money for them to bother with. Not yet, anyway. And when I do, you can bet your bottom dollar I'll have better ways to spend it than on them.

I've got money of my own to make—which I don't intend to be parting with, unless it's for the greater good.

And let me tell you, this place could use some greater good. It's nothing at all like Seattle, where I came from. It's dusty, sweaty, and full of human bodies hustling and cussing their way to fortunes that don't exist.

That's not quite true. They exist for a select few, not all of them are miners.

I know because I tried it, and it didn't work out for me. But I didn't let that stop me from finding a better way to make money. Look, it's simple: If you can't make money mining, you make money off the miners. You open a saloon or a mercantile and convert other people's dreams into cash.

It's not exactly the safest way to work in a boomtown, where tempers are on a hair-trigger and triggers themselves get pulled if some guy sneezes wrong. The guys who strike it rich are full of themselves, and the guys who don't are full of piss and vinegar, so you've got to know how to navigate things.

And no one likes the middleman.

That's where I come in. I'm the middleman.

At 17, I was a little young to tend bar or deal a hand of faro, but I was already kind of an expert at one thing. My first business didn't exactly set the world on fire, but it was something me and Tommy knew, so we figured, why not make another go of it? Tommy's my buddy and business partner, Tom Sweeney, who came down with me from Seattle looking for gold. But all we found was dust and... well, more dust.

I guess that's what happens in a boomtown, at least in the desert: A lot of hooves and boots come barreling into a place and kick up a ton of dust. They put up tents, then they put up buildings, then the buildings burn down and they put 'em up again—if the mines are still producin'.

I knew this myself. I was born less'n 60 miles northwest of here and spent the first nine years of my life in another dusty mining town. It had pretty much tapped itself out by the time I left in '97. But even when it was booming, it couldn't hold a candle to this place: They say Goldfield's the biggest city in

Nevada now, and I believe it.

Anyone who thinks the Wild West is dead hasn't been to this place. Virgil Earp from Tombstone was a deputy here, if that tells you anything. He died a month before I got here in November of '05. Hadn't lived here very long, from what I understand. Fact is, *no one's* lived here very long because Goldfield *hasn't existed* very long. Four years ago now it was sand and sagebrush, but now there's 20,000 people here—every one of them looking to get rich quick by finding a vein that someone hasn't claimed or an angle someone hasn't played yet.

Being the middleman, I get to meet 'em all. Tommy and me, we run our own messenger service out of the telegraph office here, and the owner guarantees us $50 a month. We earned enough right quick to buy us some proper uniforms, complete with double-breasted, brass-button jackets and striped pillbox hats. We delivered messages all over town on our bikes, from the Northern Saloon to the Esmeralda Hotel to the Montezuma Club, so everyone knew us, and we knew everyone else. Business was so good we took on a third partner, a fellow named John Moritz, who'd come into town from Minnesota.

A lot of times, we carried news about the mines, so of course people would stop us in the street and demand to hear what we knew.

"What's the big news today?" they'd ask, and we'd try—as politely as possible—not to tell them. "You'll just have to wait and see what ol' Tex has up his sleeve," I told an insistent fellow who grabbed me by my coat sleeve and nearly yanked me off my bike in front of the Northern. I'd just picked up a message from Tex Ricard, the owner there, intended for George Nixon over at Consolidated, the biggest mining operation in town.

Truth be told, I didn't need to keep it a secret. News like this was bound to spread faster than the fire that burned down the

Grandview Hotel a few months before I got here.

Mr. Ricard was already one of the wealthiest businessmen in town. He'd come down from Alaska in '04 chasing gold fever from the Klondike down to the Silver State. Wyatt Earp, whom Tex had befriended up in the Great White North, came down with him, and it was Tex who got Wyatt's brother Virgil a job making sure everything was on the up-and-up at the Northern's gambling tables.

High rollers flocked to the place for faro, roulette, craps, and blackjack, and there was never less than $1,500 on the table at one time. The bookkeeper there, a guy named Billy, told me the Northern made $30,000 a night, just from the tables, and $12,000 more serving up booze. It's no wonder ol' Tex had his eye on a bigger prize: that prize being a prize*fight* for the championship of the world.

In one corner would be Joe Gans, the "Old Master," who some people didn't like being champion for the color of his skin. In the other would be Battling Nelson—whose real name was Oscar, which didn't sound nearly so intimidating. Nelson's handlers wanted the fight, but they hadn't heard of Tex before and wanted to be sure they'd get their cut of the purse. They doubted he could pull it off... until he went over to Nixon's John S. Cook bank and laid $30,000 in $20 gold pieces out on the counter.

So the fight was on.

Tex built an arena big enough to seat 20,000 people, and people started streaming into town from all over.

I made a delivery to one of them at the Montezuma the evening before the big fight.

September 2, 1906

I walked up the stairs and rapped sharply on the door of the room where I'd been sent. The delivery was from Tex himself, and he'd told me to be sure I was discrete about it. The gentleman in question did not want his presence known; he wanted to enjoy the fight without being recognized or harassed.

Tex didn't tell me his name; just the room number.

A man with a full white head of hair came to the door. He appeared to be around 70 years old, and he wore a frown that looked like he meant it to be serious... but the twinkle in his eye suggested that nothing was quite as it seemed. The twinkle grew to a sparkle, and a broad grin pushed up against the bushy mustache that adorned his upper lip when he saw the nature of my delivery.

"Come in! Come in!" he said, beckoning me forward with an impatient wave of his hand.

I set down the wire cage in front of a sofa, where the hotel guest ensconced himself, bending down to pull open the little door.

The small calico cat Tex had given me waited for just a moment, unsure of itself, its tail whipping around against the back of the cage. But then, as his eyes met those of the man in front of me, he seemed to calm down... before rushing forward suddenly and leaping into the man's arms.

He was clearly a cat person.

No surprise. Tex knew how to butter a man up when he wanted something. I only wondered what he might want from this gentleman.

I nodded at him and turned to go, but he stopped me before I could reach the door. "Hold your horses, young man," he said. "Where do you think you're goin'? Don't you know it's impolite not to sit a spell and chat when you've made a new acquaintance? Or are you so ambitious that you've got another delivery to attend to?"

It seemed almost like a trick question, and his eyes were still sparkling, which made it seem even more that way. If I answered one way, he'd think me unmannerly, but if I said I had no place important to be, he might judge me a sluggard.

He sensed my hesitation and pointed to a chair across from the sofa.

"Sit," he said, as if it was expected—not in a demanding way, but more matter-of-fact, with an unspoken, "you'll be glad you did" behind it.

I nodded again and took him up on his invitation.

"You're a man of few words," the stranger said. Then he added, "No one's ever accused *me* of that," chuckling at his own inside joke. "And your name is?"

"Jim," I said.

"A pleasure to meet you, Jim." He didn't offer his own name, as though it was either unimportant or he expected me to know it—I couldn't tell which.

"Now, what brings you to town?" he said. He was asking the question of himself on my behalf, I realized, in an attempt to put me at ease. "Well, I'll tell you," he said. "I'm a fight fan from way back. Once I went to a match up north of here, in Washoe, back when they were usin' just their fists. No gloves. It went on a while, before the referee stopped it on a foul. Those who backed the loser took exception to this turn of events, and two men on opposite sides of a wager started shootin'. They even hit a couple of horses." He chuckled again. "I'm not sure anything could top *that* fight, but I'm here to see if this one might. What do you think?"

I didn't know what to say. I'd never seen a prizefight before, and all I knew was what people were saying about this one.

"Isn't the champion supposed to be better?" I offered.

"Damn right!" the man said, slapping the palm of his hand down on the coffee table in front of him as the cat leapt out of his lap. He glanced around for the feline, an apologetic look on his face, and the cat lost no time in returning to its resting place. Before long, she was kneading the man's white trousers, wrinkling them and pricking them with her claws. He didn't seem to mind.

"Of all God's creatures there is only one that cannot be made the slave of the lash," he said. "That one is the cat. We can learn something from our feline friends. They don't suffer slavery, and neither do I. Funny thing about men today is, though, they want to keep having slaves even though the Civil War supposedly settled the matter. Take the champion, Mr. Gans, for instance. Now, as you say, he *is* the champion, but you know something? Our friend Tex is only paying him half as much as his opponent, and for no reason other than the color of his skin."

"That doesn't seem fair," I said.

"That's because it isn't," the man declared, raising one finger into the air for emphasis. The cat didn't jump down this time, but merely followed the finger, seemingly captivated, perhaps hoping for some edible morsel to be released from on high. "Mark my words," he said. "Joseph Gans will emerge the winner tomorrow, or my name isn't... well, whatever it is."

"Mr. Ricard told me you didn't want anyone to know you're here," I said. "You can trust me. I never promise more than I can deliver, and I always deliver what I promise."

The white-haired man nodded sagely. "Impressive," he said.

I was beginning to feel more comfortable with the man—and not just because he'd paid me a compliment. He had a way of joking around without making a person feel inferior. Or a cat, it seemed: the tri-color feline had closed her eyes and was purring in his lap.

"So, you are in town for the fight? Are you up from the Bullfrog District? Or Tonopah? Or up in Reno? Or...?"

He waved a hand in front of his face, as if swatting away a gnat, and shook his head. "It doesn't matter where you're *from*, but where you're *going*," he said. "I lived up in Virginia City a long time ago, during the Comstock boom, but I haven't been back to Nevada in something like 40 years. No one knows I'm here now, except for Tex, and I don't plan on sticking around."

"You're friends with Tex?"

"Not really. Never even met him to shake his hand. But he sent me a cable; wants me to write a book about him or something. One thing I can tell about the man is he's all about talkin' himself up, making himself seem larger than life. Kind of like Barnum. Did you know that man wanted to pay me to be the 'poet laureate' of his circus? Have you ever heard of such a thing? Well, your Mr. Ricard is like Barnum: a source of amusement and exasperation in equal measure."

"So are you going to do it? Write his book?"

The man shook his head and laughed, as though I'd just asked him the most ridiculous question with the most obvious answer. "Of course not. But he tendered the invitation, and being a gentleman of manners—when it suits me, anyway—I accepted."

The cat roused herself from his lap, and climbed up his arm to perch on his shoulder. He reached back to stroke her fur, rubbing her back just above the tail. The animal arched her back, contented.

"Jack London's in town to cover the fight," I offered. "Maybe he could write Mr. Ricard's book."

The man, whose bushy eyebrows gave him the appearance of

a perpetual scowl, produced an actual scowl at this. "The man's only here because he wants to see Gans knocked on his backside," he said. "Calls himself a Socialist in one breath, and in the very next proclaims one race superior to another. The man is a font of hogwash and pious hypocrisies. If a prizefighter of any complexion save his own should ever claim the heavyweight title, London might relinquish control of his faculties."

I found myself listening intently as the man spoke. He had a way with words and a style of oration that naturally drew a person in.

"Do you think that will ever happen?"

"I can guarantee it," he said, leaning forward and raising a finger in the air, "the same way I can guarantee that men of narrow minds will seek to undo it."

He leaned back again, and the calico, who had deftly disembarked his shoulder to find better footing on the back of the sofa, returned to his lap.

"Enough of my chattering," the man said, stroking the cat again. "I deal in stories, and I've heard my own often enough. What brings a young man such as yourself to the middle of nowhere...? Ah, don't tell me. It was all the hoopla over that gold ore in the ground."

I nodded. "I didn't find any."

The man threw back his head and laughed. "Of course you didn't! You should have asked me, boy. I would have told you it was folly. I had the same ambitions myself once upon a time. But feebleness of mind is a natural condition of youth, and wisdom adheres to gained experience.

"I tried my hand at prospecting, but fortune knocks at every man's door once in a life, and in a good many cases the man is in a neighboring saloon and does not hear her. I spent my share of hours in that saloon, but when fortune did knock, it did so more persistently at my door than at most."

I couldn't help but notice that the man, despite his stated intent of hearing my story, had managed to steer the conversation back to himself. He hadn't done so intentionally or from a lack of courtesy, but simply based on his natural inclinations.

"In my circumstance," he continued, "the door happened to belong to a saloon!" He chuckled at the irony of his statement, and the cat responded with a soft meow. It seemed that even she was enthralled by his story.

"Have you ever heard the name Artemus Ward?" he inquired. I shook my head.

"That's the shame of it," he said, looking down at the cat and back up again. "That wasn't his real name. He was born Charles Farrar Browne, but Charlie Browne didn't sound mellifluous enough to his ears, so he invented something else. In years past, everyone knew the name of Artemus Ward. He was a figure of great renown, acclaimed for his exemplary skills as a writer and orator, as well as for his keen wit. Had it not been for old Charlie Browne, I might never have attained the degree of notoriety I have... although I do like to think talent and gumption played no small part in it." He winked.

"I first encountered Charlie in Piper's Saloon, and I plied him with liquor to learn his secrets."

"You got him drunk?"

He raised those bushy eyebrows of his. "You seem taken by surprise," he said. "The truth of the matter is I got myself inebriated as well. It was only fair. Too much of anything is bad, but too much good whiskey is barely enough. Which reminds me..."

He withdrew a flask from the inner pocket of his white coat, undid the cap, and put it to his lips, downing an unknowable amount of whatever was in it with a hearty swig.

He returned to his story without missing a beat. "As I was saying, Charlie and I became fast friends, and sometime later, he wired me with an invitation to submit a story for an anthology he planned to publish."

"Which is how you gained your own fame," I concluded.

But he shook his finger at me. "Not exactly. You see, I spent too much of my time in the saloon after that, and too much time fussing over the story. When the deadline he had given me came and went, I took no notice of it. By the time I finally finished the account to my satisfaction and sent it off, the collection was already off to be published."

My eyes widened. "What did you do?"

He spread out his hands before him. "There was nothing I *could* do. But Charlie kindly forwarded my story to a friend of his at the *New York Saturday Press.* It appeared in print there and in a good many other publications that deemed it worthy of their interest. It proved to be exceptionally popular, much to my delight. It was this experience that introduced me to my new vocation as an author."

I looked at him, perplexed. What was I supposed to take from all of this? Getting drunk and missing deadlines—*that* was the pathway to success? I couldn't accept this, yet it was hard to argue with a man who had achieved the level of fame and prosperity attained by the man before me.

"So that's the secret to your success?" I asked.

"Well, I can't take all the credit for it," he said, stroking his mustache. For the first time, he looked humble, almost sheepish. "If I hadn't had Livy behind me, I mightn't have ever done half of it. She was my muse. Love at first sight it was, and only from seeing her picture. The first time I proposed, she told me no. Can you believe it? A handsome specimen like me?" He chuckled softly. "I knew she was too good for me, but I was persistent.

That young filly broke my heart, which left me with only one option: She had to mend it."

I expected him to laugh at his own joke, but instead he looked down at his lap. I could see he was hiding the tears that were hanging at the edges of his eyes.

I didn't want to embarrass him, so I didn't ask why he was all emotional, but he answered me even so: "She's gone now," he said, looking up at me, his eyes still wet but steely. "Two years ago now. I've written one book since she left me. Got it done this year. But I know it'll be my last."

I should've just said I was sorry or something expected like that, but bein' young at the time, I said something else instead. Something stupid. "I'm never lettin' a woman make me feel like that," I declared. "There's too much to cry about in this world without getting all heartbroken over a woman." I saw the look in his eyes, one part hurt and one part fury, and I clapped my hand over my mouth. "No offense," I added, my voice lowered to half its previous volume.

But then, just when I thought he might try to wallop me for impugning his late wife's honor, he just broke out in a belly-laugh that sent him rocking back and forth and unleashed a different sort of tears.

"How old are you, boy? Seventeen?"

"Eighteen... What's so funny?"

"It's just that I've never seen a boy your age who has no use for the fairer sex—at least not one who means it. If a woman rejects them, they say, 'I never wanted her in the first place.' That type, they're cowards. Scared of their own feelings. But you aren't. They don't mean it, but somehow, lookin' at you, I think *you* do. All I can tell you is you don't know what you're missin'." He laughed even harder at that. "I mean, what would the people of the earth be without women?" He asked, then answered his own question. "They would be scarce, my young friend. Mighty scarce!"

I had to give him that.

But before I could further consider the implications of his words, he stretched his hands upward and shuddered as he yawned. "You must forgive me," he said. "But I fear the day has run its course for me. Please give our friend Tex my thanks for this dear calico's company and my regrets that I am unable to grant his request regarding the project he proposed. Now, if you will excuse me, I shall retire for the evening."

With that, he showed me to the door and bade me goodnight, leaving me to wonder what to make of him.

I was still wondering when the sun rose again the following day.

September 3, 1906

When the sun did rise, it was unforgiving, beating down on the boomtown with blistering ferocity. With the big fight approaching, it seemed cruel to expose spectators to its wrath, let alone the two men poised to square off in the ring.

But nothing was going to stop Tex's spectacle now, as throngs of gamblers, writers, fanatics, and hangers-on streamed into town, joining the rowdy rabble already present.

There wasn't an empty hotel room in all of Goldfield, and the saloons were all humming with activity, their patrons heedless of the hour. Tex was raking in even more money than usual at the Northern, and not just at the faro tables: Action in the fight itself was also heavy, with the majority of the bets being laid down for Nelson.

I was there when the fighters entered the ring, but I only caught glimpses of the fight itself, as my partners and I were running ragged, carrying news from the ring to the telegraph office and back again. From what little I could see, though, Gans was getting the better of it, staying mostly out of reach and ducking in to pummel Nelson with blows to the body and the head.

The fight seemed to go on forever, and it had reached the 31st round when the champion suddenly stopped fighting and began hopping around on one foot. It looked like he was hurt, and he was, but I later found out he'd broken his hand and was feigning the leg injury to throw Nelson off.

It must've worked. Even with the broken hard, the Old Master just kept throwing punches, and Nelson kept on catching them. As the fight wore on, the combination of the heat and Gans' blows took quite a toll on Nelson, who finally decided to end things the only way he could: on a foul.

The fight was halted, and Gans was declared the winner. A lot of people in town lost money on that, and I couldn't help wondering whether Tex's guest over at the Montezuma Hotel had put any money on Gans. I looked for him at the fight, but I didn't see him. In fact, I never saw him again.

One man who was thrilled with the outcome was Tex, who had made a ton of money and was already talking about staging more fights. I had a feeling it was more than just talk.

The other big winner was, of course, Joe Gans.

That evening, I got called to a hotel room in town to pick up a message. When I knocked on the door, who should answer it but the champion himself.

"Here, kid," he told me, handing me a slip of paper, "have this message sent by telegraph: Tell 'em the dog quit in the 42nd round."

He slipped me a couple of gold coins, and I nodded and turned to go, but he stopped me.

"Wait a minute, kid," he said. "I got somethin' else for ya."

He rummaged around in his pocket and produced an envelope with my name in it. "Some writer fella came up and congratulated me after the fight. Gave me this and asked me to give it to Jim the Messenger Boy. That's you, right?"

"Yes, sir," I said. "And congratulations from me too."

He smiled. "Thanks, kid."

September 16, 1906

I was still sleeping after a long night of deliveries. Business was good and had gotten even better since the fight. All three of us had been up late making the rounds, but Tommy and I had turned in around midnight, leaving John to finish up with one last run.

Now Tommy was shaking me awake.

"Wake up, Jimmy!" His voice was frantic.

I pushed him off me and sat up straight. "What's going on?"

When he told me, I must've turned white. Apparently, it was all over town:

John had been riding his bike on his way to that last delivery—to a dance hall in the red light district —when he'd accidentally run into a professional gambler named Jack Thompson.

Thompson had come to Nevada from Arkansas and purchased an interest in the Monte Carlo Casino in town. Whether he'd lost money at the tables or on the fight, had drunk too much, or was just in a foul humor, he was in no mood to be disturbed.

John got off his bike and apologized, but Thompson was having none of it. He started yelling at him and threatening him, so John got back on his bike and went on his way.

A couple of hours later, he was riding back home when he came upon Thompson again in front of the Northern. Without any warning, the man drew a pistol and shot Johnny in the hip, knocking him off his bike. Then he walked over to where he'd fallen, stood over him, and fired a second shot into his chest at point-blank range as he pleaded for his life.

Johnny bled out right there in the street.

I stared at Tommy, struggling to comprehend his words. John had always been considerate and punctual. That's why we had taken him on as a partner.

I knew this was a tough town, but even so, the news that he was dead felt inconceivable. I'd barely had a chance to digest it when I was struck by its ramifications. Tommy and I wore the same uniform Johnny'd been wearing. What if this hothead with an itchy trigger finger came after us?

"What happened to Thompson?" I asked, shaken.

Tommy tried to calm me down. "Everyone who saw it wanted to string him up. He ran into the Monte Carlo, then the law came along and took him out the back door, or the mob would've had their way with him. He's in the lockup now. We don't need to worry about him."

I frowned at him. I wasn't so sure. This Thompson character had money, the kind of money that can buy you lawyers to get you off, the evidence notwithstanding. Even if the charges stuck, how many other tub-thumping ne'er-do-wells were just waiting for an excuse to shoot the messenger? Between gamblers going bust and union agitators in the mines, any number of haranguers and hooligans were strutting around with chips on their shoulders.

"Come on," Tommy said. "We've got work to do."

He was right, but my heart wasn't in it. I couldn't shake the image in my mind of Johnny lying there in his own blood, his murderer standing over him and laughing.

Part of me wanted to be like Joe Gans and keep on fighting: to not be "the dog" who quit the fight. But another part of me wanted to head back to Seattle and make another go of it there.

When I got back to my room that night, I started going through my things, trying to decide whether to pack up my things and head out of town. I picked up a set of trousers, and something fell out of the pocket and onto the floor. It was an envelope with my name on it—the one Gans had given me the night of the fight. I had forgotten all about it.

Curious, I picked it up, opened it, and started reading.

Jim,

It was my pleasure to make your acquaintance this evening. You strike me as the sort of person for whom opportunity might knock more than once.

Me? I was seldom able to see an opportunity until it had ceased to be one. But look at what became of me. Like you, I started off as a messenger, though of a different sort, employed as a newsman.

It was an enjoyable enough vocation until I got on the wrong side of a particularly unpleasant individual who took my words wrongly to heart and challenged me to a duel. In consequence, I took the opportunity to remove myself from the situation and find a different opportunity elsewhere.

If I had one piece of advice to offer, it would be this: Keep away from people who try to belittle your ambitions. If the desire to kill and the opportunity to kill always came together, who would escape hanging? Framed in a more positive light, this tells us also that if we wish to accomplish a particular thing, then we need to increase our level of desire for that thing and to create or seek out the opportunities and right environment for it to happen without fail.

This my counsel to you, for whatever worth you find in it. I am confident that you will convert your next opportunity into a level of success you have not heretofore contemplated. I ask only this: Once you ascend to this far pinnacle, look after the folks who helped get you there and keep you there. If you build up others, you will build up yourself.

Remember, there is no security in life, only opportunity. A man's brief existence consists of highs and lows, of ups and downs. Go out and make your ups.

Yours sincerely,
Samuel Clemens

Postscript:

Oh, and one other thing. Find yourself a good woman. If she doesn't take a shine to you at first, remember this: Persistence pays off. And if you don't listen to your heart when it comes calling, you might not hear it the next time — if there is a next time.

I read the letter, then read it again. The desire to kill and the opportunity to kill might not always come together in Goldfield, but they did far too often for my liking. The city graveyard was full of men who'd met their end by taking a bullet. If Mr. Clemens could find success by absenting himself from a violent predicament, who was to say I couldn't do the same? All I needed to do was to create new opportunities *in the right environment!*

With more experience under my belt, and I knew I could make my business work back in Seattle. So I decided, then and there, to leave Goldfield and return to my roots.

The opportunity was there, and the ups Mr. Clemens had referred to were ripe for the taking.

August 28, 1907

Having returned to Seattle from Goldfield, I borrowed $100 and founded the American Messenger Service with a new partner, promising "the best service at the lowest rates."

Five years later, AMS was running a service with 10 messengers most of the year and more than 70 leading up to Christmas. By that time, the boom was over in Goldfield, and most of the 20,000 people who'd been there in '06 had moved on. The place was on its way to becoming little more than a ghost town, just the latest in a long line of mining boomtowns gone bust.

George Nixon, who'd run the bank there, served in the U.S. Senate until his death in 1912, and George Wingfield, his partner in Consolidated Mining, became the biggest banker in the state.

They had a few more prizefights there, including a bout in May of 1914 that featured a young unknown named Jack Dempsey. He'd come down from Reno to fight a guy named Johnny Sudenberg. The future champ was hauled out of the ring in a wheelbarrow, and the fight was declared a draw. To add insult to injury, his manager skipped town with his share of the purse.

Tex Ricard was one of those who moved on, too. After Jack Johnson won the heavyweight title and beat all comers, Tex coaxed the ex-champ, Jim Jefferies, out of retirement. The fight was staged in Reno on Independence Day, 1910.

Jack London was all for it, of course, touting Jeffries as the "Great White Hope." He'd been retired for five years but was undefeated and had never been knocked down in his pro career. But he was out of shape and showing his age when he entered the ring, and Johnson proceeded to beat him to a pulp—which sparked race riots across the country.

Still, Tex made a killing, and he made even more money years later when that Jack Dempsey fellow became champion. He staged the first million-dollar prizefight between Dempsey and French war hero Georges Carpentier, and the first $2 million fight, matching Dempsey with Gene Tunney.

As for me, my company just kept on growing. My persistence paid off, just as Mr. Clemens had said it would. The horizon, I decided, was as distant as the mind's eye wishes it to be. I changed the name of my company to the United Parcel Service in 1919 and went on to the kind of success I had never contemplated, just as Mr. Clemens had predicted. And, as he'd suggested, I never forgot the workers who helped me get there.

The fact is, I took every piece of advice he gave me except for one: I never married. I'd seen how losing his wife had broken him, at least a part of him, even if he didn't want to entirely admit it. I couldn't subject myself to that, not when I had so much to give to people who could never break me like that. People who needed more than what this world had given them.

Not petticoats and parasols, but a chance to work hard for a good wage so they could make *their* wives secure. And their children.

That was what love meant to me.

Mr. Clemens hadn't meant to teach me that, but he did, and I'll never forget it.

Of course, there's no record of Mr. Clemens ever being in Goldfield. He wanted to remain incognito, after all. And because no one but me and the hotel clerk ever saw him, there are those who'll swear I'm just making it all up.

But as he himself once supposedly said, "Never let the truth get in the way of a good story."

"The destiny of all of us is, to a large extent, in the keeping of each of us."

"One measure of your success will be the degree to which you build up others who work with you. While building up others, you will build up yourself."

— James E. Casey, founder, UPS

"Messenger Boy" is ©2024 by Stephen H. Provost. It appears here for the first time and will appear in the forthcoming collection of short stories titled "Shades of Love," due for release in the winter of 2024-25, of which he is the co-author. A California native, the author is a resident of Carson City and has published more than 50 works of fiction and nonfiction. His books include several fantasy and science fiction novels, along with history books on Mark Twain, Virginia City, America's highways, and 20th century history. All his books are available in the ACES bookshop at acesofnorthernnevada.com. Stephen is a historian, photographer, and former newspaper editor. You can follow him at stephenhprovost.com.

The ACES Anthology

Bruce Rettig

Fallout

B orn and raised in a small southern Texas town few had ever heard of, and one she tried to forget, Virginia Rider once again stared out at a desert highway framed by the inside of a stranger's vehicle. Her father, an oil rig worker who rarely made his way home to his family of five, often proclaimed his work required him to be away for long periods of time. Her mother relied on nightly binges of whiskey and sevens, numbly accepting a life shared with a rambling man who often brought home only half his paycheck.

She remained grateful for having a strong-willed daughter to help take care of the family, and her dependence grew stronger as the days passed. After twenty-one years, Virginia felt as though she had more than fulfilled her duties.

She wondered if she had inherited the same incurable affliction as her father—a longing for something just beyond her grasp. As soon as the opportunity presented itself, she escaped the shackles of family burdens and set out to chase a drifting promise that seemed to hide in the shadowed crevices of each passing arroyo.

Arriving in Las Vegas, she initially had no intention of

staying more than a few days—a quick stopover before heading north, east, or west.

Then she met Conrad at the Last Call, a local dive bar. When he asked her name, she replied, "Gina," thinking it sounded sexier and more alluring than Virginia—what a girl in Vegas should be called. As she attempted to shed her matted past, she felt a potent attraction to the constant glimmer in Conrad's eyes, as if he held an answer to a secret only felt, not told. Like Gina, he too struggled to break free of weighted memories that continued to swarm his thoughts and desires, and believed a respite might be found somewhere down a long stretch of highway. With a shared trajectory and fragile trust in each other, they had set out across the desert.

A red Pegasus. As the flatbed truck pulled into the Mobilgas truck stop, Gina focused on the company's flying horse logo adorning the top of a gas pump. An increasing feeling that their Vegas departure had been bathed in reckless abandon and a lack of concrete planning, set in. Gina thought back to her summer of reading the Greek myths, and imagined herself riding atop Pegasus, defiant and confident, much like Bellerophon in his attempt to defeat the monster, Chimera. Thoughts of Bellerophon falling from Pegasus's back, and his fatal descent, did not soothe her increasing doubts and fears.

"Need to gas 'er up." The driver got out of the truck and adjusted his sweat-stained cowboy hat. "I got it, Tom," he shouted to an attendant wearing coveralls blotched with grease and oil, leaning against a soda machine next to a stack of tires. A clanking of metal against metal reverberated inside the cab as he shoved the nozzle into the vehicle and began pumping gas into the tank.

Gina nudged Conrad, who had slumped against her. With their supply of adrenaline having run out, emotionally empty, they had both fallen into a deep sleep. Conrad awoke with a quick jerk, then opened the passenger door. They slid across the truck's bench seat and stepped outside. The smell of gasoline, oil, and tires wafted in the air.

"All those miles—never caught your name." The man spit, saliva landing on the scorched asphalt with a splat. "Course both of you were quiet as hell and slept most the way."

"Sorry, we had a long night—really need to get some rest. I'm Gina, and he's Conrad."

Conrad squinted at the high desert sun, then looked down and shook his head.

Gina immediately acknowledged her mistake. Why had she told the man their real names after they had fled the Fremont Hotel & Casino Bar with stolen cash less than four hours prior? Conrad had told her to use aliases wherever they went, and whoever they met. They had agreed on "John and Judy." As their fumbling and miscues continued to pile up, she heard her mother's voice: *What goes around comes around. That's how it works. You get what you give. Sooner or later, the universe will serve you the revenge that you deserve.*

"I'm Samuel Hostettler. Call me Sam." The man finished fueling and hung the gas nozzle back on the pump. He tipped his hat to Conrad and Gina.

"Where are we?" Conrad asked.

Sam leaned his elbow on top of the truck bed. One of the man's hands was twisted and misshapen, as if something had once forcibly bent it backward, deforming it into an unnatural position.

"Still in Nevada. This stop's on the outskirts of Alamo—not Alamo, Texas, of course. You haven't been asleep that long." Sam smiled, and Gina noticed a gap where a tooth once resided.

"I didn't know there was an Alamo in Nevada," Conrad said.

"Yep—small farming community. Not much of a town. This is as far as I go. My place is a few clicks down a bumpy-ass road that leads to 'Nowhere.'" Sam turned and opened the driver-side door. "Nowhere's the name of my farm."

"Any place in Alamo to rest up, and maybe spend the night?" Gina asked.

"Coupla' fleabag motels but usually filled up with truckers."

"Stores?"

"Small market's 'bout it. Coupla' greasy spoons for food. I'd stay clear of Joe's Place if you wanna avoid a touch of botulism. Mexican restaurant's good, though."

Sam stared at a cluster of scattershot cracks in the asphalt resembling an intricate spider web. Another truck pulled into the station, the sound of a bell announcing its arrival. The attendant walked away from the soda machine and made his way to the pump islands. Sam looked up at Gina and Conrad, the brim of his hat shadowing his eyes.

"I don't know what your story is and why the hell you'd be hitch'n with one piece of damn luggage in tow." Sam hesitated, then pondered out loud, "Likely on the run from someone or somethin'—maybe yourselves."

Gina bit the bottom of her lip and took a short, quick breath. Conrad shifted his weight from one foot to the other, and gazed at the same asphalt cracks Sam had focused on.

"I guess you're right," Gina said after a moment of nervous hesitation. "Mostly about the latter." She stared into the man's shadowed eyes—nondescript orbs bookended by ragged crow's feet. Once again, she felt as though she revealed too much, and questioned whether she should put her trust in Sam. From the moment they fled the casino bar, everything had seemed like one continuous gamble.

"Like I said, ain't a hell a lotta' of traffic on this stretch of highway. Despite everythin' I just said, I'm a fairly good judge of character—'specially from a person's demeanor. You two look to be 'bout the same age as my son and probably have the same tendency of not lookin' much farther beyond one day at a time."

Sam pushed the cowboy hat lower down his forehead with the crooked hand. "My son's away, so I have an extra room. Nuthin' fancy—"

"We have money," Gina said.

"A coupla' young people hitchin' outta' Vegas with a pocket fulla' money? Congratulations."

"Seriously, we can pay you."

"Won't be necessary. Go ahead and get back into the truck. I'll pay for the petrol, then we'll head out to my place."

Tom began filling the other truck with gas, then met Sam at the cash register at the end of the island. Sam took out his wallet and counted out a few bills, then received change from the attendant. He grinned, slapped the man on the back, then turned to the truck.

"Are we making a mistake?" Gina said as she slid across the truck seat, followed by Conrad.

"What do you think?" Conrad asked.

Gina realized that Conrad relied more on her feelings and intuition the longer that they spent time together. What Conrad had once described as a "brother in arms" relationship had grown and evolved since the first day they met.

"I think he's okay," Gina said. "Besides—we don't have a lot of options."

They turned off the paved highway at a point marked by two silver metal mailboxes, one with black stenciled letters—

"Hostettler." Sam pulled over and opened one of the boxes, grimaced, and shook his head at its emptiness. He gunned the engine, put the truck in low gear, and they lurched forward. The road to Nowhere wound across the high desert like a meandering stream. The truck rattled across washboard ruts and undulating hills surrounded by patchworks of sagebrush, dust trailing the vehicle like a billowing jet stream. Crossing a wide wash, they crested a rocky knoll, and a group of cottonwood trees came into view. A white structure rested in their shade.

A hand-lettered sign at the end of the driveway greeted them: *Welcome to the middle of Nowhere.* A couple of dogs, both beagle mixes, ran alongside the truck as it rolled into the driveway. The sound of barking and howling increased as the vehicle came to a stop.

"Here, here!" Sam shouted out the truck window. "Quiet down, damn ya'."

Conrad opened the truck's door and stepped out, followed by Gina. He leaned over and petted the dogs. Their wet tongues slobbered trails across his arms.

"Pains in the ass," Sam said, "but good dogs in general."

The farmhouse looked as though it had been painted with a fresh coat of white on the southern side some time back, then the project dropped midstream. Two dormer windows projected from a green asphalt-shingled roof. A sun-bleached-grey barn, strong enough to fend off high desert winds, stood a few hundred feet from the house, the smell of manure and earth drifting along a thin breeze. On one side, an American flag, colors sucked dry by the desert sun, hung from several bent nails, thin trails of rust dripping down like sweat and blood across its dusty surface. A John Deere tractor was parked on the other side. Between the barn and the house, underneath a large cottonwood with birds chirping and hopping across its branches, stood a yellow formica table with bowed chrome legs. Wisps of cobwebs hung from its grooved aluminum edges. Three chairs pointed west to an expanse of desert and a rugged ridge stretching north and south.

"My wife's been gone 'bout," Sam paused, squinted an eye, "two years, come next month. Don't seem that long. Helluva strong woman. We thought Louise had a case of the grip, but it was far worse than that."

"Sorry to hear," Gina said. She felt sympathy for Sam living in such a remote area by himself. At the same time, she felt comfort knowing that if anyone were trailing her and Conrad from Vegas, they would have difficulty finding them in the seclusion.

"My son and I managed the farm by ourselves since she passed. He got called to serve over in Korea a few months back, so now I'm on my own. Another goddamn war."

Gina noticed Conrad wince, and she sensed his uneasiness. Memories of his time at war sparked episodes he called "flashes," leading to explosive anxiety and uncontrollable thoughts. The more time spent with Conrad, the greater she experienced similar symptoms. It was as if she could get a glimpse of what he saw and sensed what he felt. She refocused and turned back toward Sam.

"Can we help you unload the truck?" Gina asked.

"Yeah, good idea. I'll pull 'er into the barn."

Inside the barn, a thick wooden plank across two empty fifty-five-gallon drums served as a workbench. Between a vice bolted down on one end, and a power grinder on the other, an array of parts for automobile, tractor, and home projects told a story of repair and making do. An assortment of screwdrivers, wrenches, and hammers hung from hooks and nails on the wall behind the bench. Hanging to the right of the bench, a variety of saws, axes, and a couple of scythes awaited their next task. The barn floor consisted of pebbles, chipped wood, and desert dust stained with oil. Sunlight beamed down from an opening above the hayloft, creating a mosaic of warmly lit textures.

After unloading the fertilizer from the flatbed, they walked to the side of the house. Sam took off his hat and wiped his forehead with a ragged handkerchief.

"There's some venison in the fridge, a can of beans in the pantry. Maybe make some biscuits. That'll be tonight's dinner. For now, a cold beer'll hit the spot." Sam nodded toward the formica table and three chairs. "I'll get us a coupla' cold-uns. Take a seat."

Conrad and Gina sank into the chairs, and Sam returned with three cans of Schlitz and an opener, then sat down. Beads of sweat on his balding head glistened under the desert sun.

"Louise and I inherited this land from her folks. I'd just got discharged from the Army—served in Italy at the close of World War II. I was older than mosta' the other fellas. Our troop was marchin' down a muddy road, and I slipped and fell, flat on my face." Sam held up his crooked hand and shrugged. "Jeep ran over my damn hand."

Sam punctured one of the cans with the opener, then handed it to Gina. He did the same for Conrad and himself. He took a deep gulp of the beer and looked out at a stretch of bright green field next to the farmhouse.

"My first thought when we heard 'bout this place was, *a farm in the Nevada desert?* Christ, probably not worth a hilla' beans."

"How long have you been out here?" Gina asked.

"Seven years come fall."

The two dogs sat at their feet as Sam continued to talk, the sun plodding along its arcing path toward the western mountain range. Gina supposed it felt good for Sam to have visitors at his farm since he spent so much time by himself—probably another reason he was so quick to invite them to stay the night, and why he was so talkative.

"At first, we was strangers in a strange land. All the farmers in Alamo are of Mormon faith, and we were outsiders. But you know, I always felt like I was on the outside, ever since I was a kid. My dad was in the military, so we moved around a lot. When Louise and I moved out here, the neighbors accepted us into their community. Years back, they'd been in search of a place to call their own, too, so I think they knew how we felt. Well, I found a certain peace here. 'Nowhere's' my home."

"Finding something that'll grow out here can't be too easy." Gina leaned back into the chair and glanced at Conrad. He appeared more relaxed and less anxious, drawn into the drone of Sam's throaty voice.

"Ain't that the truth. Some crops take to the climate, others don't. All I grow is alfalfa. Louise used ta have a nice vegetable garden. Other farmers grow other things. Depends on what you like and what'll take root. Some raise animals—goats, sheep, and such. Larger cattle ranches are a ways out. Thank God we're blessed with adequate water. Alamo's in the middle of the Pahranagat Valley, a dent in the high desert that's been capturin' water for thousands of years."

Sam took a sip of beer, then leaned over and picked up a small rock near his foot. He rolled the stone in his crooked hand as he talked.

"People venture out into the desert for all kindsa' reasons. For some it's an escape, a chance to start anew—or maybe they're searchin' for somethin'. Or others might be runnin' away from things—a husband, wife, the law, or somethin' else that's made their life go haywire."

"Seems like the government found a place to operate out here," Conrad said.

"Oh yeah, the A-bomb test. Felt that thing this morning when I was pickin' up fertilizer, before I saw you two on the side of the highway." Sam nodded toward a clothesline near the house. "I finished washin' a loada' laundry yesterday—not my most favorite chore 'round here. Left everythin' hangin' to dry, and it looks like the wind carried a layer of dust directly over Nowhere after the blast. I'll have to pull my shirts off the line and give 'em a good shakin'-off."

Sam looked upward, his eyes following a turkey vulture circling near his alfalfa field.

"I'm not a religious man, but lately I been prone to pick up the Bible. Don't know why that is—curiosity, or maybe old age. Anyways, I'm always drawn to the passage of Jesus in the desert. How he went out into it, only to be challenged and tempted by the devil. Interestin' to read. A man can look at that writin' from a lotta' different angles."

They finished another round of beers as Sam continued to talk about life in the high desert—places to explore in the many canyons, peaks and plateaus; the Milky Way stretching across a starry night sky; drifting snowfall; relentless windstorms—the difference of loneliness as compared to living alone. The sun sank behind the mountain range, casting a soft sheet of pink and gold across the plain.

"You both can stay in my son's room tonight. If it's more comfortable, one can use the couch. I don't mind either way. I imagine that bag you're carryin' doesn't have a lot of room for clothes for both of ya. If needed, there's a coupla' pair of old work jeans in Brett's dresser and you can take 'em, but leave the newer ones. And a denim shirt with splattered paint on it is in the closet. If you intend on carryin' food or more things to wherever you're headed, there's a pile of old seed sacks in the barn. I guess what I'm sayin' is, you're welcome to take whatcha' need."

"We appreciate it. That's very generous of you," Gina said.

"Not ta worry." Sam picked up another small stone from the ground and rubbed it with his thumb. "Maybe someone's watchin' out for my boy over in Korea. Damn, I wish Brett was sittin' here with us now."

Conrad hesitated, then said, "I got back from serving just last year."

Sam let out a sigh, then took a gulp of beer.

"How bad?"

Conrad looked down, slightly shrugging his shoulders.

"That's what I feared."

Sam hurled the stones into the desert. A jackrabbit shot out from a shelter of bitterbrush.

They sat and drank two more beers as stars glittered to life across a darkening sky. Conversation slowed, Sam doing most of the talking, Conrad and Gina doing most of the listening. They eventually went inside the old farmhouse. Sam made a hot supper as the dogs watched attentively, and he shouted at them to go lie down; that they'd have plenty of food in due time. He turned on a radio. Scratchy music drifted from the living room and into the kitchen as he cooked. Hank Williams sang, "Lost Highway."

> I'm a rolling stone, all alone and lost
> For a life of sin, I have paid the cost
> When I pass by, all the people say
> "Just another guy on the lost highway"

Venison steaks sizzled in a pan, beans boiled in a large pot, and biscuits cooked in a cast-iron skillet, all atop a wood burning stove.

"Just another guy on the lost highway
I was just a lad, nearly twenty-two
Neither good nor bad, just a kid like you
And now I'm lost, too late to pray
Lord, I've paid the cost on the lost highway"

As was the case most nights they spent together, Gina noticed that Conrad slept in short increments, often awakening in a cold sweat. They had slept together many times before, but intimacy had faded once they began planning their departure from the Fremont Hotel & Casino Bar. Their plan of simply providing two-week notices at the same time had rapidly spiraled into a scheme to leave the Fremont with a good sum of money to help them in their pursuit of whatever they were looking for. All their energy and emotional exertion had been spent on the precarious endeavor. Sams's farm had been a welcome respite. It served as a time of regeneration before going back on the road. Concerns of being followed had temporarily subsided.

Shortly before daylight, Conrad woke up Gina. She felt foggy headed, a result of one too many beers the night before. They quietly packed and dressed for the road, then walked stealthily out of Sam's son's room. Conrad set a twenty-dollar bill atop the kitchen table. Gina nodded her approval, and they made their way out the front door. Grabbing a couple of seed sacks from the barn, they then walked down the road from Nowhere.

Gina took a final glance back at the farmhouse. Sam peered out his bedroom window, watching them leave.

By the time they got to Highway 93, a cobalt halo had formed on the eastern horizon, a dark mountainscape undercutting it like a jagged knife. The thick smell of sage filled the cool, morning air. They both sat down cross-legged on the side of the road and waited for the next passing car or truck headed north.

Gina looked into Conrad's eyes. With nothing said between them, she heard his voice.

Keep moving.

"Fallout" is ©2024 by Bruce Rettig. It appears here for the first time and is an excerpt from a forthcoming novel. Bruce Rettig is the author of literary short stories, creative non-fiction, fiction, and essays, and works as a travel writer/photographer. His narrative nonfiction/memoir, "Refraction: An Arctic Memoir," won multiple writing awards including a Nautilus Gold Award in the category of travel memoir, a Forward Reviews Silver Award in the category of ecology and environment, and an excerpt from the book was nominated for a Pushcart Prize. Bruce lives in South Lake Tahoe and is a founding member of Tahoe Writers Works. His blog, Changing Tides, along with more information about his writing and outdoor adventures, can be found at www.brucerettig.com or linktr.ee/brucerettig. "Refraction: An Arctic Memoir," can be ordered through all major and independent bookstores, and directly from Wayfarer Books, at wayfarerbooks.org or the publisher's order page at https://bit.ly/3tdZR0R.

The ACES Anthology

Andrea Smutz

Death By Chocolate

John licked the dripping chocolate ice cream from the spoon. Then he dipped it back into the open container of "Death by Chocolate" his most favorite flavor. It was just so heavenly. He closed his eyes imagining being immersed in chocolate. Not that over-the-counter variety, but one with wonderful cocoa butter, smooth dark, rich, sinfully decadent chocolate. At seventy-three, you'd have thought he'd outgrown the chocolate, but as he aged, he wanted it even more. He and Julia had loved each other almost as much as chocolate. Now she wasn't around to share the container. He missed her and the taste of her mouth and chocolate together.

He put the top back on the container and put it back in the freezer. Briefly he reminded himself that he should fill a dish with the ice cream, not eat it from the container. It wasn't very sanitary. He didn't care. He was the only one in the house, and he'd eat ice cream as he liked, thank you very much!

John walked in and turned off the television. Blah-Blah-Blah! Wasn't there any news fit to listen to any more? Killings, riots, fires, earthquakes, hurricanes, yuck. How about reruns of Julia

Child and the Art of French Cooking? Now that had merit. Even if they only showed the desserts she could dazzle with. He walked by the bookcase with all of Julia's and his cookbooks. The fact that she had the same name as the wonderful woman on TV just had made John love her more. In his mind, his Julia could give the TV Julia a run for her money. And John had loved to watch his wife cook.

He had never seen such a superb cook be so neat! She could cook in a fancy black dress, high heels and never have a spot of flour on the fabric. When she was inventing a dish, she might get up in the middle of the night when inspiration hit her. He'd wander downstairs in the morning to some heroic coffee cake, iced and sparkling with sugar and, usually, chocolate. Once he'd come down to such a wonder and cut a huge slice before she came back down. As he bit into it, his mouth flamed! Chocolate and hot peppers lit his tongue and lips and palate. She'd laughed at his discomfort until she cried. But the chocolate milk she gave him soon helped him recover. He never attacked something again without asking what was in it.

He headed to bed. Tomorrow was Friday. That meant he got to go visit the home. He'd play the piano and lead a sing-along for all the seniors. Then he'd head to the Memory Care facility and do the same thing. They sang better, remembered the words better. He liked to do the singing. The staff welcomed him and helped the residents. And, best of all, he got to see Julia.

The next morning he ate breakfast and followed his usual routine. He left right on time at 10:45 in the morning, arrived before lunch at the home. Then he went to the Memory Care at 11:30. He finished by noon so that lunch could be served, and he could see Julia. They ate together. He had to help her now. She didn't remember how to eat. That is, until he brought out the ice cream.

Fridays were fish and chips, and while he didn't care about that, he thought it odd that the Death by Chocolate Ice Cream he brought along always seemed to go with the fish and chips. Maybe he'd just eaten it so many Fridays that he thought they went together.

He finished his set and joined Julia. Together she talked, remembering nothing of her family or husband. The children seldom came to visit because she didn't know them. It was too painful for them. But for John, after 52 years of marriage, he visited each Friday. Julia had started down the dark path four years ago. John had mourned the loss of her intellect, her humor and then her love for him. Only one thing ever seemed to break through to her. He had it with him today, as usual.

"Julia, do you want ice cream?" John asked. He saw the light come into the blue eyes he loved. She nodded. "Is Death by Chocolate okay today?" He asked, knowing the answer. Julia smiled and nodded yes.

He spooned it out of the small carton he always brought. He gave her a bite, then took one himself. She savored it in her mouth. He could see her move the ice cream around in the mouth, smoothing it over all the taste buds. Such devotion to a bite of ice cream baffled him. He watched her swallow, and she opened her mouth like a baby bird. He gave her another spoonful and took one himself again. They repeated it many times. Occasionally, they almost finished the carton. Other times, it was just a couple of bites. Today, they finished the carton.

John sat, hoping for more from his wife. Today was a good day. Julia turned to him and raised her hand. She stroked his cheek and then his hair. Tears flowed from his eyes. He wished she could stay with him and remember him. But he had to take the small times she did and tolerate the rest.

Today, she kept touching him. She raised her hand again and

this time, pulled him to her. John leaned in, following her direction. She pressed her lips to his, and he pressed and opened her mouth with his tongue. There it was. The chocolate kiss he so loved. John came and sat next to her, and they continued to kiss. He smiled. "Julia, I love you so much." He kissed her again, and she continued to respond.

"John, I love you." She whispered in his kiss. As John leaned back, he saw her retreat into the prison of her mind, and he sobbed. He gathered her in his arms and wept. Julia's caretaker came over.

"John, are you all right?" Marjorie asked, placing a hand on his shoulder.

"She spoke to me. She said she loved me." John's tears flowed down his cheeks.

"Now you know she can't speak, John. You must have imagined it. Perhaps she needs to rest. Would you like to also?" Marjorie asked and signaled the male orderly nearby.

"Could I sit with her for a while?" he asked. Marjorie nodded. She helped Julia, and the male orderly helped John. Together they were taken to her room.

Julia was put in bed. John sat in a soft arm chair, next to the bed. His cooler was next to him. Today, for some reason, he had brought two cartons of their ice cream. One remained. The two caretakers looked at the couple and left them together shutting the door, providing a bit of privacy.

Two hours later, Marjorie remembered that she hadn't seen John leave. She walked to Julia's room. As she opened the door, she stopped and leaned against the door frame. She recognized death. She saw it often. But this was unexpected. With tears in her eyes, Marjorie turned, closed the door and went to the administrator's office. He followed her to the room and together they went in.

John was in the armchair. Julia was in his lap. Her head was on his shoulder, and his head leaned on her head. Melted chocolate ice cream lay in his lap. The spoon had dropped to the floor. Both had chocolate smeared on their lips and faces. Sharing the last of the Death by Chocolate, John and Julia had slipped off together, still in love, with each other, and the taste of Death by Chocolate.

"Death By Chocolate" is ©2022 by Amdrea Smutz. It appears here for the first time and will be published in a volume of short stories titled "Love's Cookbook" in 2025. Andrea started writing when COVID hit the world. Isolated, she created a new world of Old West images, stories, and characters. As with Stannis Hopefield, Andrea fell in love with Colorado and the spectacular Rocky Mountains. The series spans the life of Hopefield from his early '20s to his death. The author has traveled throughout the United States and has been to most of the locations where the main character takes us. She encourages you to see our wonderful country, meet the people who still live and love their hard lands, and especially to tell your own story! Hers can also be seen at her website, andreasmutz.com or via email: ASPublishing0522@gmail.com.

Ken Sutherland

Hardship, Nevada

In 1859, astronomers charted an enormous solar flare. A day later, and continuing for several days, the world experienced a series of huge brilliant auroral displays. While normally confined to polar areas, these auroras flashed brightly colored lights over large sections of the planet, including Nevada. Imagine seeing them from the tiny, isolated mining village of Hardship, Nevada (Population 97), with no telegraph, no railroad, no connection to the outside world. Would you be frightened? Sure you would. You might even think the world was about to end. And what if you had an escape route?

July 1969
A small town in rural Nevada

By the time my father was released from prison, he'd been gone half my life. I remembered him as a big, strong man, but I was only eleven when I'd seen him last. Now I was taller than him. His stooped shoulders amplified the effect. His mind wandered when I tried to talk to him. Looking into his eyes, I felt I was peering into a dark cave. His time in prison had wrecked his spirit.

I wanted desperately to help him, but I wasn't sure how. I thought if I stayed close, spent time with him, he would adjust, snap out of his funk and once again become the man I remembered, the man who showed me how to ride a bike, how to catch a baseball.

But it worked the other way. It wouldn't be long before I would follow in my father's footsteps. Richard had a lot to do with it.

Dad had only been a free man for a week when Richard showed up and took control. It was Richard's idea to go to work at the copper mine. They needed guys who could do hard labor, and they didn't mind hiring a couple of ex-cons. Dad and Richard were given sledge hammers and pickaxes and told to crush rocks that might contain ore. They thought it was hilarious at first. Richard liked to make chain-gang jokes about "doing time breaking rocks," and Dad always laughed, even when the jokes weren't funny.

The pay was better than average, but they often had to work underground. It was dangerous, depressing and brutal work. I guess it was a little frightening, too, and the humor soon evaporated.

Richard spent a lot of time at our house. He would turn up after work with a couple of six-packs, and they would watch sports on TV and drink beer and smoke cigarettes. Mostly, they grumbled about their jobs. I noticed it was Richard who did the complaining. Dad just went along. I guess I did, too.

Mom didn't like any of it. "He's not the same since he came home," she told me. "And this Richard character gives me the creeps. Those *eyes*."

She was right, Richard was scary. He was quiet and respectful when Mom was around, always polite. But when he looked at me, I got a sense of impending danger. Trouble never seemed to be far behind Richard. I felt like it was just a matter of time before it caught up with him.

Mom was a checker in the supermarket, and she started taking more overtime, staying away from the house.

I didn't have to be back in college until September, and I ended up spending all my time with these guys. When they weren't criticizing their boss, they talked about their regrets. You'd think they would be remorseful about committing the crimes that sent them to prison, but that wasn't it. Dad regretted that he hadn't planned a better getaway.

"The robbery went fine," he said one evening, full of beer. "But I should have stolen a car. They caught me because I used my own damn car."

Richard told us he wouldn't have gone to prison if he'd had a better partner. "Chump ratted me out, first chance he got," he said. "You can't trust partners."

I was there, but I didn't want to be a part of any conversations about prison. I just kept my mouth shut and drank the offered beer, smoked my cigarettes and tried to blend in with the furniture. Dad must have sensed the growing distance between us. One payday, he showed up in the driveway with a brand new motorcycle. It was for me.

"Peter," he said. "It's a Honda 450. It's good on the road or off. You can go anywhere you want."

And I did. Like my father's parole, I thought that motorcycle was my ticket to freedom.

I remember the date. It was the same day as the moon landing. July 20, 1969. An event that was supposed to change everyone's lives.

Well, my life certainly changed.

July is not the time to be riding a motorcycle across the Nevada desert. The sun was blazing hot, over a hundred degrees and no shelter anywhere. But the bike was brand new, and I wanted to try it out. There was a ghost town about sixty miles away. I remembered going there with Dad when I was a little kid, maybe seven or eight, so I knew there was nothing much to see, it was just someplace to go. I was more interested in the ride. I filled a canteen, checked the gas tank and headed out.

The last twenty miles were on a badly maintained dirt road with nothing to see but sagebrush. I thought about those astronauts, on their long journey through empty space. Hell, if they wanted empty space, they could've just come to Nevada.

A tattered billboard said:

"AUTHENTIC GHOST TOWN FOR SALE."

I'd arrived at Hardship, Nevada. The main street consisted of a rotting wooden boardwalk with several broken-down buildings and a few shanties, all in bad repair. Any paint that may have been on these structures at one time had long since faded away in the harsh desert sun. The raw timbers had aged to a silver-gray hue, the wood grain stretched like swollen tendons. Several roofs had caved in, shutters hung from window frames, and some foundations had failed, leaving a few of the deserted buildings tilting sideways. It wouldn't be long, I thought, before the entire place crumbled into a pile of dusty firewood.

I stopped in the middle of the dirt street, looking around, wondering why I'd come. It occurred to me the attraction might be a psychological one. When I'd come here before, I'd had a pleasant day with my father. The dad I remembered, the man I missed so much.

Now there was no attraction at all, only a bunch of long-abandoned shacks. They were all boarded up, I couldn't even go inside. I was about to start the bike and find something else to explore when I noticed a broken shutter hanging from a window by a single hinge. I put the kickstand down and stepped up onto the creaky boardwalk to investigate.

I craned my neck to see inside the building. When I attempted to slide the dangling shutter aside to get a better view, the whole thing came loose and crashed onto the wooden sidewalk at my feet. There was no glass in the window. Maybe there never had been. I guess glass was hard to come by a hundred years ago in Nevada. I climbed over the windowsill and found myself in a genuine old west saloon.

It was quiet, eerily so. The only residents were spiders, who made no noise but strung cobwebs everywhere. With every step on the ancient floorboards, I stirred up clouds of dust. Coughing, I brushed the spider webs off my face.

As my eyes adjusted to the dark room, the term "ghost town" took on a new meaning for me. Nothing but the insects and the dust had disturbed this place in more than a century.

I was in a large hall with a rough-hewn bar at the far end. It was apparent that no attention had been given to the décor, even when the place was new. The floors and the walls were built with thick wooden planks, now dried-out and cracked. Utilitarian tables were scattered around the room. Straight-backed chairs were pushed out from the tables as if the customers had only just departed.

A blackboard leaned against the bar. It was covered with the grime of time gone by, but I could still read the carefully lettered notice, written in white chalk:

Bar closed for TOWN MEETING about The Lights

15 Sept, 1859, 6 O'clock.
Everyone Invited

Underneath, someone had scrawled

SEE YOU IN 1914!

Thinking I'd seen all the town had to offer, I revved up the Honda and set out to explore something else. More empty space. A couple of miles from the ghost town, a large rocky hill shimmered in the midday sun and I rode over to take a look.

In the middle of the ultra-flat desert, one huge hill stood alone. Too small to be a mountain, it rose from the desert floor, covered in boulders, with nothing growing on it, not even the local sagebrush. It looked somehow unnatural, as if it had been dumped here from outer space.

I wondered if the moon astronauts saw them do it. I drove all the way around it twice. On my second trip, I spotted the cave, its entrance mostly hidden in the shadows of large boulders.

In a mood to explore, I got off the motorcycle and pushed it through the cave opening.

I heard the rattle. A large diamondback rattlesnake was coiled up on the far side of the bike. Some people freeze when they see a snake. For some reason, I did the opposite and pushed forward. When the rattler struck, its head slammed into the moving bike frame as I rushed past.

Inside, the air was much cooler. I lit a smoke and drank deeply from my canteen. Then I looked around, watching for snakes with every step. I was in a large cavern with a high ceiling. So high, it seemed the hill might be completely hollow. Giant rocks, some of them larger than me, were scattered around the cave, breaking up the space. I was surprised that I could see well, although I could find no source of light.

I discovered a natural tunnel that led away from the entrance. I followed it through several twists and turns, expecting it eventually to narrow and disappear. Although it looked natural, the tunnel was of a uniform size, like a wide, well-lighted hallway through the hill.

Eventually I came to another entrance. Even though I must have driven past it twice, I hadn't noticed it. So there were *two* hidden entrances. Odd.

I returned to the main cavern to retrieve my bike and head for home. Approaching the entrance, several large rattlers still basked in a sunbeam, blocking my path. It was an easy decision to leave through the other opening.

Riding back to the ghost town, I was astonished to see painted buildings, cars, and a paved road. A giant sign said:

Welcome to Hardship
Nevada's Favorite Ghost Town.

The falling-down buildings I'd seen only hours earlier had been resurrected. Their foundations repaired, they stood upright, recently painted, glistening in the sun. Shiny new signs said BANK, SALOON & TOWN HALL and SHERIFF, all hand-painted in old-west style lettering.

A couple came out of a building marked GENERAL STORE and drove away in a strange looking station wagon. It said *4-Runner* on the side.

I parked the bike and went inside. When the air conditioning hit me, it was such a relief I wanted to stay forever. A heavyset woman behind the counter in jeans and a T-shirt smiled at me with a big gap in her teeth.

"You're a long way from anywhere, young man."

"Last time I was here, this place was deserted. Looked like it was about to fall down."

"Oh, it was an awful wreck," she said. "Me and my husband bought the whole town six years ago. He's a contractor, and he replaced every stick and nail. Everything is new, from the saloon to the dress shop, but it's all 100 percent authentic. Just the way it looked in 1859, before Nevada became a state. It was a mining town back then."

"I guess the mine played out, huh? And now it's a ghost town." I laughed. "Do you suppose it's haunted?"

She leaned over the counter, telling me a secret. "Worse than that! Everybody in the whole town just disappeared one day." She snapped her fingers.

I shrugged. "Well, yeah. Isn't that what makes it a ghost town?"

"No, I mean *all at once*. On the same day in 1859. They didn't ride off one at a time. Just went '*poof*' and they were gone. Every man, woman and child. Even the donkeys and the chickens."

"What happened to them?"

She shrugged. "They were there one day, gone the next. Nobody knows."

I didn't know what to make of that, so I smiled politely, backed over to the cold case for a Coke. I was surprised the bottle was plastic and not the thick glass I was used to. I put it on the counter and she gave me her gap-toothed grin.

"That'll be two dollars."

My eyes went wide. *Two dollars!* For a ten-cent Coke? Okay, it was bigger, but not twenty times bigger. Obviously, I was in a tourist trap, complete with rip-off prices. But I was thirsty. I fished a couple of one dollar-bills out of my wallet.

"That's a pretty high price for a Coke, but the story was worth two bucks, I guess. 'The Legend of Hardship, Nevada.'"

"We're not sure what it means, or if it even means anything at all, but it happens to be the truth." She took the money and held the Coke over a metal plate that 'beeped,' then slid it across to me.

I noticed they had cigarettes for $8.50 a pack. *A whole carton is only ten bucks!* I decided I had enough smokes to make it home.

Then I saw it. The Reno newspaper, with a headline that read "**55-YEAR ANNIVERSARY OF MOON LANDING.**" She wanted 75 cents for the paper, which was ridiculous, but I was curious enough to put three quarters on the counter. I got the hell out of that clip joint before she had *all* my money.

I pulled the bike around to the shady side of the building, lit a cigarette and opened the paper. The date said July 20, 2024.

2024!

Somehow, I'd gotten hold of a newspaper from fifty-five years in the future! Something must have happened in that strange cave. Either that, or I'd gone completely nuts in the desert sun. I fired up the Honda and headed back to the mysterious hill in the desert.

I entered through the smaller opening I'd used to exit the cave a few minutes earlier. I wouldn't have seen it if I hadn't already known it was there. I hoped it would lead me back to my own time.

Of course, I'd have to deal with the snakes.

Living in the desert all my life, I'd heard stories about methods to drive snakes away. Make noise. Well, I had a motorcycle in a cave. You can't get much noisier than that. There was this woman hiker who was sipping on a Coke when she was threatened by a coiled rattler. She threw the soda on the snake, and it slithered away. The best deterrent, I'd heard, was vinegar, but who carries vinegar around? I revved up the bike. It made a fearsome noise in the cave, the sound echoing off the walls like thunder. Then I put my thumb over the opening of the plastic Coke bottle and shook it up. When I took my thumb away, I sprayed the entrance. The snakes were gone. The noise had already run them off.

I pushed my bike through the opening, and I was surprised to see a man about my own age lying on the ground. He was rolling back and forth, holding his leg, obviously in terrible pain. He called out when he saw me.

"Hey! A snake bit me! Twice."

"These rocks are full of snakes," I said. "Let's get you away from them."

I took him under the arms and dragged him out of the shade into the open. The sun was blazing hot there, but I didn't see any rattlers. He had a bite on his calf and another on his wrist. Both were already discolored and swollen badly. I used my penknife to cut his pants away. His leg looked worse than his arm, with terrible purple swelling.

"Pull your belt off and give it to me," I said.

He was in a lot of pain, but he managed to do it.

I wrapped the belt around his leg above the bite and cinched it tight, then gave him the end to hold with his good hand.

"Keep pulling on this. It should slow the poison from getting into your blood stream."

"Might be too late for that," he said. "I'm already dizzy."

"I have to find something to tie off your arm."

"My pack," he said, breathing hard. "T-shirt."

I scrambled to dump his pack out onto the ground, grabbed a T-shirt and twisted it into a tourniquet just above his left elbow. By the time I finished, the bite on his arm looked as bad as the one on his leg. He seemed ready to pass out. I thought it might help if I kept him talking.

"I came through here a little while ago, and I didn't see you,"

I said. "Where did you come from?"

He shook his head. "You'd never believe me."

"I might," I told him, looking back at the entrance to the strange cave. "What year were you born?"

"2003."

"Yeah, I believe you. I think I just went to 2024."

"What year are we in now?"

"Pretty sure it's 1969," I said, glancing around. "No way to tell from here."

He was having trouble breathing. "I think that's right," he said. "I was headed for 1859. I have to go through the cave three times for that." He winced in pain. "Don't think I'll make it now."

I didn't want to tell him I agreed with his assessment. He was pale and sweating from more than just the hot sun.

"I'm not sure what more I can do for you here. You think you can hold on to me if I put you on the back of the bike?"

He shook his head. Tears ran down his face. "No. It's in my bloodstream. I don't have long. I might be the first man in history to die thirty years before I was born."

It occurred to me the only thing I could do, other than watch this poor man die, was to show him some simple kindness. I offered a drink from my canteen, which he took, eagerly. I had to hold it for him.

"I'm Peter," I said. "Peter Thompson. Born in 1947."

"Brad Smith. Pardon me for not shaking your hand. I'm still putting some hope into this belt." He tugged on it and chuckled, but there was no humor in it.

"Okay, I know *when*, but *where* are you from, Brad?"

"Sacramento. My great-grandfather was from around here. Or maybe he was my great-great-grandfather. There is some confusion around that."

I was starting to catch on. "Because of this cave, you mean?"

He nodded. Pale as a ghost, his voice was raspy. "Are we anywhere near Hardship, Nevada?"

I pointed west. "What's left of it. About two miles that way. Just a bunch of broken-down buildings."

"According to letters the old man sent to his brother, everybody left Hardship when they thought the world was ending. The whole town bailed out. Ninety-seven people. They went through this cave."

Brad was fading fast. I didn't think he had much longer to live. To distract him, and to satisfy my own raging curiosity, I kept up the conversation. "Anything in those letters about how a time-travel cave got here?"

He coughed, held up an index finger on his one good hand. Finally, "Man, this is awful. I think I'm going to..." He leaned away from me and threw up. "Towel in my pack," he said.

I found the towel on the ground where I'd dumped his stuff and wiped his face.

"Nobody knows how the cave came to be. It was always just there. Local people were afraid to go near it until they needed it for their escape route."

"Do you have those letters?"

"At home. I copied a couple of relevant pages to bring with me." His voice was thin and scratchy. I could barely hear him, even in the stillness of the desert. "My mouth tastes like an old tire. Can I have some more... of that water?"

I turned away to reach for the canteen. When I looked back, he was gone. I didn't see any point in trying to revive him.

I went through his pockets and came up with several pieces of proof that he was telling the truth. A quarter from 2001. A California driver's license with a strange-looking hologram on it, expiring in 2027. And $300 in money that hadn't been printed yet.

I had no way to take him with me. I found a plastic ground-cloth in his knapsack and wrapped his body in it. I decided to come back later with Dad's truck to take him into town.

In his pack, I found three folded Xerox copies of pages taken from handwritten letters. I was too curious to go home before reading them. I sat on the Honda in the blazing desert sun and unfolded the first one. It started in the middle of a sentence:

"...because the lights in the sky were making everyone crazy. Huge curtains of green and blue and red. Nobody knew what to make of it. Edwin Miller said it was the Apocalypse, as foretold in the Bible, and there was much discussion about that. It was Mayor O'Malley who convinced us to pack up and leave through the tunnel in the cave, and the sooner the better. He told us the tunnel led to the future. Cries of 'What if it don't?' and 'What if the lights are still there?' were met with shrugs. 'How worse off would we be?' he said.

"We trusted him, or we wouldn't have made him the mayor and we started setting plans to go to the future. We cut the wagons down so they would fit through the tunnel. By the time we were done, they were nothing more than carts, capable of being drawn by a single horse or mule. Ethan Bumbridge had an ox. We took no furniture or other large items. Each cart could accommodate one elder or child and as much food and water as we could carry. The rest of us walked.

"Our destination was Humboldt Wells, to the north, a well-known wagon train stop. If the cave really did lead to the future as O'Malley said, perhaps the promised railroad would be finished and we could board a train there. The

trip through the tunnel was…"

That was all there was of the first letter. Just a single page, including the crudely drawn map of the cave. I noticed the tunnel took them 55 years into the future, just like it did for me. The second one was only a couple of sentences.

"…had confirmed the year to be 1914. We all agreed to keep silent about the lights in the sky and the future-time-tunnel, lest someone lock us away for lunacy.

"Most of our party opted for the eastbound train to Denver and beyond. Half a dozen of us waited another day for the train heading west. I sold the mule and the cart for five dollars, and that was enough to get me to San Francisco."

The third page was fascinating:

"...to see an actual aeroplane. Who would ever have thought that a man could in a machine, leave the ground to fly like a bird, and return alive?

"Living in 1914 provides new astonishments every day. We remain impressed with the number of automobiles and electric streetcars. There is now a canal, right through the middle of Panama, to bring ships from the Atlantic Ocean to the Pacific without going around the horn. Amazing. Many homes and businesses have electric lights. We can even make ice, for heaven's sakes! Somebody figured out how to run a man's voice through a telegraph wire, and people can talk to one another from distant locations. We went to a vaudeville show, and then a week later, paid five cents in the very same theater to see a terrifying moving picture of men fighting the war in Europe. I believe I'll stick with song-and-dance men and French poodles jumping through hoops, thank you.

"Being a carpenter, I was able to find work, and the family is doing fine. San Francisco is still rebuilding from a great earthquake back in 1906. (I continue to have difficulty thinking of 1906 as the past, ha ha.) I am pleased that they still build houses the same way we always did, although they are filled with modern fixtures, like electricity. And indoor privies. That is certainly a blessing on a cold San…"

Riding back through Hardship, I was relieved to see it was a broken-down, ramshackle mess again. I thought about those guys on the moon. Could their day have been any stranger than mine? They went into outer space where anything can happen, but did they meet any time-travelers, like I did? Hell, I even *became* a time-traveler!

Brad Smith was on his way from 2024 to 1859 to meet his own ancestors. I was flabbergasted. I had actually traveled to 2024 myself! I couldn't wait to tell Dad about it.

Dad listened to my story, but he thought it was just something I made up until I showed him the newspaper. Then he got excited and wanted to see for himself.

The next morning he called in sick, and we headed for Hardship. On the road, with only me and Dad in the truck, it was like old times.

"I remember when we went to that ghost town once before," he said. "There was nothing there."

"There's plenty to see now, Dad. It's just not in plain sight."

"Yeah." He took a deep breath and looked out at the sagebrush rolling by, sucking on his teeth. Thinking. When he turned back to me he said, "I'm sorry I wasn't there to help you grow up, Peter. I feel real bad about that."

I wasn't sure what to say. I was sorry, too.

"I thought about you every day in prison. I imagined going to your football games, cheering you on from the stands and such."

"Didn't Mom tell you I was never on the football team? I played baseball and basketball."

He shrugged. "She did. I guess I just *wanted* you to play football."

Then he did something he hadn't done since I was a little boy. He reached across the cab and patted me twice on the knee. This small gesture nearly brought me to tears. I had to look away so he wouldn't see me clouding up.

"I would have been just as happy to watch you play any sport, Peter."

"I—"

"It was all about time. That's what prison does, son. It steals your time. Time I should have spent with you and your mother instead of a thousand other men. I didn't know how important time was until I had to give it over to the state. I wish I could tell you how much I thought about you while I was... while I was gone."

We were silent for a few minutes, until I spotted the faded sign for the turnoff to Hardship, Nevada. "Turn here, Dad."

We bounced along the old dirt road for twenty miles, and when we came to the remnants of the old town, I took him into the saloon to show him the blackboard.

He just nodded. "Let's go see that cave."

We rolled up to the cave entrance, and Brad's body was right where I'd left it. I'd been worried coyotes would find it and tear it apart, but I guess they were nervous about the rattlesnakes, too.

I had a spray bottle of vinegar, and I sprayed all around the body before we touched it, to make sure a rattler hadn't crawled in there with poor old Brad. When I finished, Dad pulled the ground cloth back and took a look. He made an instant decision.

"We can't take this guy into town."

"We can't? Why not?"

"Because you want this cave to be a secret, right? Look at his clothes, Peter. You ever see anybody dressed this way? They don't make boots like this anywhere. If you take him in, you'll get a thousand questions. Like where did he come from in these strange clothes? How did he get into the middle of the desert on foot? Why doesn't he have any ID? And they'll want to see where you found him."

He looked me in the eye. "And there goes your secret cave."

"You're probably right," I said. "So what do we do with him?"

"There's a shovel and a pickaxe in the back of the truck."

We found a spot well away from the entrance to the cave. The dirt was hard as granite, but after a couple of hours of digging in the hot sun, we managed to get a hole about five feet deep. We dragged Brad's body into it and covered him up.

"You want to say something over him, Peter?"

"I'm no preacher," I said.

He scoffed. "And you think I am?"

I nodded and stepped up to the mound of dirt. "Brad, I didn't know you, but you told me you were searching for the secrets of your family's roots. Maybe now you're someplace where they can tell you about it themselves. Good luck, and rest in peace."

I sprayed the entrance to the cave with vinegar again, and we went exploring. The cavern was just as I remembered, and we walked all the way through the tunnel to the other end. We stood in the open air outside the smaller entrance to the cave.

Dad put his hands on his hips and looked over the desert terrain. "This is 2024? Looks just like 1969."

"If we were to go back to Hardship, we'd find a whole new

town, all painted up and air conditioned. Somebody bought the town and turned it into a tourist attraction."

"Well, after all that digging, I'm not up for a two-mile walk in this heat. Probably even farther from this side of the hill."

He smiled and turned back. "I think I'll take your word for it, son."

Before we left, Dad held up Brad's wallet for me to see.

"You kept his ID?"

"Did you notice how much he resembles you?"

"Not really."

"We'll put this in a safe place. You might need it someday." He went to a corner of the cave and slipped the wallet behind a rock.

I didn't know it at the time, but he was already working on a plan. On the way back, he said, "I have to tell Richard about this."

I finally spoke up about Richard. "You know, you're not supposed to hang out with him. You guys are both on parole."

He threw his cigarette out the window. "My parole officer is 300 miles from here. You think he's gonna show up to see if I'm havin' a beer with Richard?"

Two hours later, Richard was at the house, the two of them trying to plan a bank robbery before Mom came home. I was in and out of the room, but I overheard snatches of conversation.

"*...no security guard?*"

"*That place has never been robbed.*"

"*Big surprise for them, I bet.*"

"*We won't even need masks.*"

"*We can get away on motorcycles. They fit through that tunnel.*"

They believed the small-town bank was unsuspecting, overconfident and vulnerable. And twice a month, the large mining payroll came through.

"Hey," I said. "You guys just got out of prison. Do you really want to go back?"

Richard glared at me with those cold eyes. He spoke quietly.

"Shut up, Peter. We're doing this. And it takes three guys, so you're in."

My mouth fell open.

Dad objected, but his voice lacked conviction. "Peter's just a kid. Leave him out of this."

"We're all going to the land of the future together. Then he can do anything he wants, and he'll have the money to do it. We can't leave him here when we go."

"He's only 21—"

I could hear him giving up, even as he spoke.

Richard directed his cold stare at Dad, who quickly backed away. It was clear who was running the show.

"Do you think they have flying cars in the future? Hey, Peter, you see any flying cars?"

It wasn't all that funny, but Dad and I both laughed.

We talked about leaving me out of the actual robbery, but we all knew the truth.

Two more Honda motorcycles were purchased. We made our trial run out to the cave and went through the time tunnel. I showed them the restored tourist village from 2024, then we turned around and went through it all in reverse to return home.

I tried to talk to Dad when I got him alone. It was no use.

"There's no life for me here, Peter. Or for Richard, either. We'll go to the future and start over. We just need the money from the bank."

I don't know why I went along. I will always wish I hadn't.

The day of the robbery, we were ready. Richard had stolen a pickup truck for the first part of the getaway, and we left it running in the parking lot of the bank. We ground out our smokes on the front steps. I didn't want to go in, and I guess it showed on my face. Richard gave me a grim look and a hard shove. I took a deep breath, and in we walked, guns in our hands. There were no customers. We ordered the employees into the vault and made them load the money into three knapsacks.

Of course, they knew who we were. The town was too small for people not to recognize two ex-cons and a kid who grew up in the neighborhood. Mrs. Matthews kept scolding me.

"Peter, you're ruining your life. You'll end up in prison just like your father."

Richard told her to shut up, but she wasn't finished. "I guess the apple doesn't fall far from the—"

Richard slapped her, hard. Her glasses flew off. "Knock it off, lady!"

She screamed in surprise, and tears ran down her face, but she did as she was told. She kept shaking her head, though, giving me that look old ladies always use on you when you're doing something wrong. And she was right. I hated what I was doing. I didn't even know why I was doing it.

Because my dad wanted me to, I guess.

Outside, we stuffed ourselves into the stolen pickup truck, all three on the bench seat. Richard made a show of revving the motor and peeling out of the parking lot, which I thought was foolish, but I didn't say anything. Two blocks down the street, we turned a corner and pulled into the garage of a vacant house where we'd hidden the motorcycles. We changed clothes, and two minutes later we were headed for Hardship.

We made it to the cave without incident. I went in first with my vinegar bottle to keep the snakes away, but the noise from the motorcycles had already done the trick.

Inside the cool cave, we stood the bikes on their kickstands and took a break. We lit smokes, trying to relax and drank deep from our canteens to quell the adrenaline pumping through us. Dad and I stood next to each other, but Richard sat on a large rock against the cave wall, about ten feet from us. He looked up at me. "Peter, you're gonna be glad you did this. In a few hours, we're all gonna be rich."

"In fifty-five years, you mean," my father said, and we all laughed.

Then Dad spotted a rattlesnake slithering out from behind the rock Richard sat on.

"Snake!" Dad reached into his belt for his gun to shoot the diamondback, now coiling up near Richard.

Richard must have thought Dad was about to shoot him.

"What'd you call me?" He dropped his canteen and pulled his own gun. He was faster than Dad.

The gunshot echoed like cannon fire through the cavern, and Dad fell, dropping his gun, clutching his chest.

Acting out of instinct, or maybe horror, I pulled my own gun and shot Richard. I'm not a very good shot, and I missed the mark. I hit him in the shoulder. He fell next to the snake, trapping it between himself and the cave wall. He raised his gun to shoot me, just as the snake bit him in the neck. I'm certain he would have killed me, but between the bullet wound and the snake bite, his aim was off.

I felt the bones shatter when the bullet slammed into my left leg. I went down hard. I scooted behind one of the boulders in the cave for protection, dragging my damaged leg. Richard couldn't see me, but he fired again. I crab-walked around the back of the big rock and discovered I had a clear shot. Taking my time, I aimed carefully, and this time my aim was good.

I passed out from the pain. When I woke up, I was alone with two dead bodies. My leg was severely injured. Both bones in my lower left leg were shattered. I was bleeding badly. I knew if I stayed in the cave, I would soon become the third dead body.

I used my belt to fashion a tourniquet, just as I had done for Brad. Screaming in pain, I got on the motorcycle and started it up. My left leg was useless, and I had a great deal of difficulty holding in the hand clutch while reaching down and putting the bike into gear. I revved the motor loudly to scare off the snakes and headed for the road.

It seemed like I rode that way for a long time, traveling at a low speed because I couldn't shift the gears. Each rut in the road rattled me. It was torture. I'm not sure how far I got before I passed out and crashed the bike. I came to with a middle-aged man bending over me.

"What happened, son?"

"I must have hit something in the road. My leg is broken."

"I have a first aid kit in my car." He took off running toward an idling station wagon.

I must have passed out again. When I looked up, he was wrapping an ace bandage around my leg, pulling it tight. He used a tire iron for a splint, then helped me into the back of his car. The drive to the emergency room was a painful, bumpy ride, even on the paved highway. I wasn't sure I'd make it, and I worried about what would happen if I did.

The hospital took me into surgery, but first they called the police to report a gunshot victim. Everybody knew who I was, and nobody thought I'd been injured in a motorcycle accident. I guess the whole town was talking about the daring bank robbery, only hours earlier.

My rescuer took the police to the place where he'd picked me up, and it wasn't long before they found the cave with all the money, my father and Richard, both dead, and the gun with my fingerprints on it.

Despite the surgery, I never walked right again. My left leg was one inch shorter than my right leg. I ended up with a permanent limp, and a life sentence for armed robbery and felony murder.

That was more than half a century ago. In prison, I became known as The Gimp. Other cons disrespected me, beat me and abused me in ways not fit for discussion.

I kept my mind occupied with that cave. A million scenarios went through my head, but the best one was simple: I would wait for August 21, 2024. I would enter the cave from the back opening. I would hide until the shootout was over, step over the bodies, pick up the money, and leave before the police arrived. Then I would live the rest of my life in luxury. I would be seventy-six years old, but at least I'd have a few years of comfort.

All I had to do was get out of prison.

The time dragged by. I thought about my father's comment many times. Prison steals time. I worked in the laundry, pushed a broom, performed basic maintenance on prison facilities. I had many regrets.

If only I hadn't found that cave.

If only I hadn't told Dad about it.

If only I could have talked them out of the robbery.

If only I hadn't gone with them to rob the bank.

If only I hadn't been so weak.

As she had done with Dad, my mother came to visit once a month, and it was always a sad day for both of us. My father and I had combined our efforts to give her a truly tragic life. Eventually she became too sick to make the trip. She died in 1990.

In 2011, my smoker's cough became severe. I eventually quit smoking, but it was too late. I could barely draw a breath without pain.

I saw a newspaper article in 2018. Some idiot contractor had purchased an entire ghost town in the middle of nowhere, with the intention of making it into a tourist attraction. The state of Nevada chipped in with a big tourism grant to rebuild Hardship, Nevada. I had to smile.

In 2020, the pandemic hit. It was worse in the prisons because we all lived in such close quarters. I was sent to the doctor for my cough, but it wasn't Covid. X-rays confirmed I had terminal lung cancer. I'd already guessed that much.

Prison officials offered to parole me. Maybe they thought I couldn't commit any more crimes in my condition. More likely, they wanted to save the expense of caring for a man who was clearly dying.

Once out, I got a maintenance job at a motel on the highway. They paid less than minimum wage, but made up for it by giving me a room to live in and letting me drive an ancient rattletrap pickup truck. It was an old motel, and the room was basic. Humble, even. But it was far better than the tiny prison cell I'd had to share with another man. And even though I lived alone, I was especially pleased to have a door to close when I used the toilet. It's the little things that make an old man happy.

I was sick, but I kept myself alive by continually focusing my mind on the date: August 21, 2024, the day I would be rich.

Six hours after that fateful 1969 shootout, police recovered just over $350,000 from the cave. That six hours was my window of opportunity. If I could stay alive long enough and manage the timing, I could go back to 1969, get that money before the police found it, and live the remainder of my life in relative comfort in 2024.

Of course, I was kidding myself. All the money in the world couldn't heal my ruined lungs. How much time did I have left to enjoy the money? Money that wasn't even mine. Money that had cost my father his life, crippled me and put me in prison for most of my own sorry existence. Money that had stolen my spirit.

But having nothing else, I continued to wait, to hope, and slowly the clock ticked and the days fell off the calendar and the time went by, as time always does.

On the date I'd chiseled into my brain, I made my way, wheezing and limping, to the old pickup truck and drove into the big empty space of the Nevada desert. Deliberately early, I entered through the 2024 opening, vinegar spray bottle at the ready. My father, his domineering friend Richard, and my younger self would not arrive for another two hours. Remembering the scene from 1969, I ducked behind a boulder, sat down and waited.

The sound of the motorcycles gearing down startled me awake.

I heard Richard's voice first. "Peter, you're gonna be glad you did this. In a few hours, we're all gonna be rich."

"In fifty-five years, you mean," my father said, and all three men laughed.

Then Dad shouted, "Snake!"

Peeking around the big rock, I saw him draw his pistol. I sucked in a ragged breath.

At the moment Richard shot Dad, I lurched out of my hiding place and crashed into my younger self, body-slamming him out of the way. I picked up Dad's gun and fired at Richard.

Somehow the timing wasn't quite the same. As the snake bit Richard, he shot me in the gut before he passed out. I knew he was fatally wounded.

I was, too.

Stunned but uninjured, young Peter stared at me with his mouth agape. He backed away from me and from his dead father, moving toward the snakes at the cave's entrance.

"Who the hell are you?"

Coughing and bleeding, I said, "Come over here, I have to talk to you."

He backed up another step, terrified.

"I have to..." *Wheeze.* "...tell you something. It's important. Hurry, dammit, before I'm dead!"

He cautiously approached and bent over me. I handed him the gun. "Wipe the fingerprints off this. Get all of them, and make sure you don't leave any of your own on it."

He obeyed in a daze, taking the gun and pulling a handkerchief out of his pocket.

"I have to check on my dad," he said.

"He's dead," I told him. Gasping for breath, I pointed to the front of the cave. "If you go out that way, you'll be in 1969. You'll be arrested and spend your life in prison..." *Wheeze.* "...living in misery. Awful food, nasty people. Bad life. Wasted time. If you go the other way," and I managed to point toward the rear entrance, "You'll be in 2024. You can..." *Wheeze.* "...make a new life, be anybody you want to be."

I pointed to the rock where Dad had hidden the wallet. "Get the billfold from behind that rock..." *Wheeze...* "You can be Brad Smith for a while. Nobody has to know you were ever Peter Thompson."

"How did you find out about the wallet? How do you know my name?"

"I have one just like it. And you need to quit smoking. Today. Right now. There, I just saved your life. *Twice.* Now go!"

Obviously in a state of semi-shock, young Peter went to his motorcycle and began to push it toward the rear entrance of the cave.

"Hey!"

Peter turned around and looked at the bleeding old man on the cave floor, lying beside his dead father.

"Take the money, you idiot."

*"Hardship, Nevada" ©2024 by Ken Sutherland, who lives in Reno. It appears here for the first time. The author is a retired advertising executive and broadcaster, and a member of the Nevada Broadcasters Hall of Fame. He lives in Reno, Nevada with his wife, Alene and their dog, Willa. He has written a number of short stories and three novels. **HEARTBREAKER,** the first book in the Chuck Donnegan series, and the thrilling sequel, **THE HOLLYWOOD DIAMOND MURDERS,** are newly released in paperback and eBook. His debut novel, **BALANCE: The 200-Year Journey of Andrew Crawford** is a genre-challenging adventure story, in which a young man tumbles through his own past lives in search of his own true identity. All of the author's novels are available on Amazon. Ken Sutherland is active in the local writing community, belonging to both High Sierra Writers and Northern Nevada Writers.*

Made in the USA
Monee, IL
25 January 2025

10081704R00223